To Allan —
Great to see you
at the reading!
Enjoy!
Kevin

S0-ASH-218

Countdown to Z-Day

By Kevin Kearney

Palisades Press

Countdown to Z-Day
Copyright © 2017 by Kevin Kearney

All rights reserved. No part of this book may be reproduced in any form or by electronic or mechanical means, including information storage and retrieval systems without permission in writing from the author, except by a reviewer who may quote brief passages in a review.

This book is a work of fiction. Names, characters, places and incidents are either products of the author's imagination or used fictitiously. Any resemblance to actual events or locales is entirely coincidental.

Z-Day Minus 6

"Tonight is the night that will change the world!" Andrew typed into the status box of his Facebook page. "Tonight the Shadow Warrior will slip out of his lair, as silent as a . . ."

He paused, his two index fingers poised over the keyboard of the laptop, struggling to come up with an image that would convey stealth, power and sudden viciousness. He scrunched up his face and closed his eyes, like a powerlifter steeling himself to hoist a weight that no man had lifted before. A minute passed before his expression relaxed. He allowed himself a tiny smile, popped a red Skittle into his mouth from the open bag next to the laptop, and started typing again.

". . . as silent as a panther to pounce on criminals and bullies."

Perfect. He banged the Enter key, broadcasting his declaration to a world hungry for a new hero.

The Shadow Warrior was none other than Andrew himself, a pudgy twenty-year-old who was not like most twenty-year-olds. He rode a bike that sported a banana seat and two handlebar mirrors. He'd never been able to get the hang of skateboarding and no one had even thought to ask him if he wanted to learn to drive a car. Too shy to talk to girls, he'd never gone on a date, unless you count the time, as Andrew did, that one of the Special Ed teachers in high school had taken Andrew and four other students to see *Avatar* and Andrew sat next to Jessica Pollard and shared his Skittles with her, their forearms touching. Andrew had clear blue eyes and always seemed to be smiling for no reason. He wore T-shirts that were a shade too tight; his belly would stick out of the gap between the shirt and his waistband, which he didn't seem to notice. When he wore what he called a button shirt, he liked to button the top button. His approach to conversation usually meant blurting out odd facts from a mental storehouse that he stocked through hours of reading, usually submerged up to his chin in the long hot baths he took at least twice a day. He had a part-time job as a costumed character at an amusement park, and made $67.42 per week after taxes, which seemed like a lot. His lair—the Shadow Warrior's lair—was the cramped apartment he shared with his sister Jana and their cat Spunky. Jana, who was really good with computers and the Internet, had set up the Shadow Warrior's Facebook page that he was now updating. It featured a photo of Andrew in a black ski mask that wasn't exactly standard ninja issue, but close enough. In the photo, a selfie, only the bridge of his nose and his eyes were visible. You could almost tell that he was squinting, like a predator sighting his prey.

Carefully hunting the keyboard for the right keys, he continued typing. "Warning to evil-doers: You won't know he's there until it's too late and . . ."

And what? He bit the inside of his cheek and rubbed his head. He could get really frustrated really quickly, but he took a deep breath the way Jana had taught him, waiting for an inspiration, which finally came to him.

". . . and his fists of fury rain down on you."

Satisfied, he hit Enter. Less than a minute later, Ricky Wakefield chimed in, his comment appearing beneath Andrew's post.

"That's totally week! Hahaha!!! Fists of fury? You think your Bruce Lee????"

"That's not how you spell weak," Andrew typed in reply. He was an incessant reader—though these days he rarely strayed beyond the same four dog-eared books about ninjas—and a good speller, which he was proud of.

Ricky Wakefield was one of his two Facebook friends. Like Andrew, he worked at the Bay-View Boardwalk where they were both mascots. Ricky was Toby the Sea Turtle. Andrew was the Smiles Ambassador. Ricky was always showing off and he could be kind of a jerk. He thought he was funny—writing *hahaha* after almost every comment he posted. Jana said that Andrew could unfriend him, but then Andrew would only have one other Facebook friend, Jana, and she was his sister, so he wasn't sure she could really be his friend. But she said she could, and they left it at that.

Another comment from Ricky appeared on the Shadow Warrior's Facebook page. "Bruce Lee would eat you for lunch!!!"

He knew that if he responded the back and forth would never end, and he had more important things to do, namely saving the world from bullies and other evil-doers. But he couldn't push himself away from his laptop before typing one last post: "My actions will tell my story. The world won't know me, but they will know about me." That was pretty good; it didn't sound like he was bragging, just stating the facts. "And with each foe that I vanquish," he added, "my legend will grow."

Ricky Wakefield had to have the last word. "Hahaha!!! Good one!"

As difficult as it was, he shut down the laptop and pushed himself away so he could focus on readying himself to make the world a safer place. Where mothers could walk their children to school without worrying about child molesters following them. Where women didn't have to worry about being grabbed by gropers. And where guys like Andrew who were minding their own business wouldn't be made fun of all the time.

There wasn't much more he had to do to get ready. He was already wearing most of his Shadow Warrior outfit—a pair of black cargo pants, a black turtleneck and black high-top basketball shoes. He strapped on a black web utility belt that held his phone, a flashlight that he could use to shine the light of justice in the dark corners of the savage streets, and his only weapon—a short wooden ninja training sword called a *bokken* that he'd purchased on the Internet after a long negotiation with Jana, who thought it could poke someone's eye out.

He'd pulled on the black balaclava ski mask that he'd bought at Walmart a few weeks back, and then added a final touch to his costume—another Walmart purchase—plastic safety goggles that fitted tightly to his face, held in place by a thick elastic band.

Satisfied that he'd gotten every detail of his uniform just right, he stood in front of the mirror that hung above Jana's dresser. His feet planted widely, he placed his hands on his hips, thrust his shoulders back, and sucked in his belly, marveling at the transformation. He could feel the Shadow Warrior's power all the way to the tips of his fingers. He whirled to the left and then to the right. He crouched in fighting stances, his hands held in front of him like a karate fighter, ready to block a deadly blow or deliver one. He ran to the couch in front of the television, jumped up on the armrest and shadow-kicked an imaginary foe, which caused him to lose his balance and almost fall backwards. Catching himself, he pulled the *bokken* out of its loop on his belt and waved it menacingly. He slashed at an imaginary attacker so enthusiastically that he knocked off a framed photograph of his grandmother, which luckily landed in the clothes hamper next to the dresser, the frame dinged a little, but nothing broken.

Now he was ready. It was time for the Shadow Warrior to venture forth on his first patrol.

Before he left the apartment, he ate a few more Skittles to give himself extra energy, carefully picking out the green Skittles, which he put into a large fishbowl. He hated the green ones; they made him think of Kryptonite. He checked the big digital watch on his wrist. He was fascinated by clocks and watches and timetables. Sometimes he stared at his watch's display for long stretches, trying to anticipate the instant when the digits would change, his favorite being the complete rollover over at the turn of an hour, when every digit would change at once, like a fresh squad of numbers materializing out of nowhere to report for duty. But he couldn't get stuck on his watch and the unstoppable advance of time, not tonight. It was 9:27. Jana didn't get home from her night class until after 10:30. So he had time, but not much time, if he wanted to get in some crime fighting and be home in bed by the time she checked in on him.

When he opened the door to step outside Spunky raced between his legs like a black streak and escaped. She wasn't supposed to go outside after dark, and Jana wasn't going to be happy if the cat was gone when she got home, but he couldn't worry about that now. The crime-ridden streets were waiting for a hero.

Their apartment occupied the back of an old house that had been carved up into four rental units, each with one bedroom, a tiny bathroom, kitchen and living room space. The entry to their unit faced a dark, vacant lot, so once he got past the weak illumination cast by the naked bulb over their apartment door, he was able to slip into the gloomy night undetected by his enemies. Hugging the side of the house, he turned into an alley that connected to a shadowy grid of backstreets that served as a secondary circulation system in the old neighborhood. The alleyways were the best way to get around without being seen. Out on the street you were exposed, but in the alleys you could stay hidden, watchful, ready to spring from hiding to confront the forces of evil.

As he walked, staying on the balls of his feet, ready for action, he scanned his surroundings carefully. Something caught his eye—a movement, a shadow darting along the wall to his left.

"Spunky, go home," he hissed. "You can't follow me." It didn't do any good. She never listened. Sometimes he wondered what the big deal was with cats. Other times, when she curled on his lap and purred as he watched television or read, he got it. But tonight she would just be getting in the way.

The neighborhood they lived in was called River Flats—fifteen blocks of shabby low-rent houses, creaky wooden apartment buildings, corner markets, Laundromats and hole-in-the-wall eateries jammed in between the Milagros River levee and the Bay-View Boardwalk, a slightly rundown vintage amusement park strung along a half mile of beach on the Monterey Bay, where he worked from noon to four. Looming above the Flats was the snaky silhouette of the Giant Anaconda, a rickety wooden roller coaster whose claim to fame was its title as "The West Coast's Oldest Roller Coaster", a boast by the Bay-View management that many people read as a warning label. Up until 9 PM, when the park closed, the screams of riders pierced the night; but it was quiet now, the roller coaster illuminated by a string of lights, a snaky, humpy outline against the dark sky. At the ride's highest point, where the cars paused after their first labored ascent before hurtling downward, a tired American flag flanked by four colorful pennants fluttered in a spotlight.

When they first moved into their apartment two months earlier, Jana had laid down a few hard rules. Always lock the doors; don't leave the apartment after 7 PM, and don't even think about going to the Bay-View after dark. That was a lot to ask. Andrew had decided that as long as Jana didn't find out, he would explore wherever he wanted. He wasn't a kid anymore, after all. But it was true—after darkness fell the Flats got a little scary. He'd seen the dope sellers hanging out on the street corners, the women in their short tight skirts who approached the cars that had slowed down, leaning in to talk to the drivers, sometimes getting into the passenger side. He'd watched as they disappeared into shadowy doorways when police cars cruised by, the way the cockroaches in their kitchen ran for the cracks in the baseboards when he turned on the lights at night. Once he saw three young Mexican guys chase another guy, catch him and beat him, everyone yelling in a scary way. After the attackers fled, spooked by one of the neighbors shouting out a window, Andrew tentatively

7

approached the victim of the assault, who was slowly picking himself up off the sidewalk. Andrew was ashamed that he didn't have the courage to do anything to stop the beating, and confused when the guy who'd gotten beaten up took off running before he had a chance to even ask if he could help.

The experience troubled him. After thinking it over the next few days and consulting the ninja books that served as his reference library, he came up with the inspiration for the Shadow Warrior. The Shadow Warrior would be brave and powerful, a fighter skilled in the ninja arts of combat and stealth. The Shadow Warrior wouldn't have actual super powers, but he would have Truth and Justice on his side, and Truth and Justice were more powerful than any weapon a criminal could wield.

His code, which he had labored over for hours before carefully printing it on a sheet of cardboard that he tacked on the wall, read:

EVIL PEOPLE ARE YOUR ENEMIES, AND THEY MUST BE VANQUISHED, ESPECIALLY BULLIES

COMPLETE YOUR MISSION BY ANY MEANS, FAIR OR FOUL, BUT MOSTLY FAIR

DON'T BE MEAN TO PEOPLE WHO ARE NOT BEING MEAN TO YOU

DON'T BRAG ABOUT YOUR VICTORIES

Over the next week or so he assembled the Shadow Warrior's costume. When he first pulled on the ski mask and strapped on the safety goggles, he felt an almost holy power descend upon him. Looking into the mirror, he didn't see Andrew—he saw a champion for honesty, decency and kindness. And tonight, as he marched forward toward destiny, he walked with strength and confidence. He wasn't exactly sure how he was going to combat evil when he saw it, but he was determined to start his crusade.

He fished a couple of Skittles from his pocket, avoiding the green ones, and popped them into his mouth.

He lingered at the end of the alleyway, where it teed into Barson Street, peering out into the streetscape. Fog had crept in from the bay, dimming the brightness of the few streetlights that hadn't been broken. Cars drove slowly through the grainy yellowish twilight, their drivers indistinct shadows within.

Looking to his left, he saw a young woman standing on the curb about ten yards away. He thought she might be a prostitute. Andrew knew that prostitutes got paid for S-E-X, though he hadn't quite figured out why that was so wrong. It didn't matter, because it was against the Law, and the Shadow Warrior had sworn to defend the Law to his last breath.

She didn't see him at first as he approached. When she did turn to turn to take him in a look of utter confusion came across her face. She was black and skinny. A tight turquoise miniskirt rode high on her hips. She wore bright red lipstick and her bangs were upswept from her forehead in a stiff crest. She clutched a small purse.

"Are you a prostitute?" Andrew asked.

"I'm a meter maid, sugar. What you doin' out here dressed like that, like it's Halloween."

"If you're a prostitute you have to leave. You're breaking the law."

"And just who the hell are you?"

Andrew hesitated. This was his chance to announce the arrival of a new champion and he didn't want to blow it. "The Shadow Warrior."

"The *what*?"

He'd put in hours practicing in front of Jana's mirror, not only his fighting moves, but also the stern warnings he'd make to crooks and villains when he confronted them. He was surprised that his declaration hadn't made more of an impact. His words needed more confidence, he decided, maybe even a little touch of arrogance.

He squared his shoulders, lowered his voice and concentrated on getting every syllable right. "The Shadow Warrior."

She looked around, then back at Andrew, like maybe someone was playing a joke. "You prankin' me? Someone hiding around here somewhere taking a video, gonna put it up on YouTube?"

"I'm cleaning the streets of human scum," Andrew explained, hoping that would clear things up.

"And who would that be?" She paused, but Andrew didn't really think she was waiting for him to answer. "Me? *I'm* the scum?" She looked angry, and maybe a little hurt. Now he felt bad. Maybe he'd made a mistake. He was willing to give her the benefit of the doubt.

"Are you really a meter maid?" He squinted to look at her more closely. His goggles were fogging up.

"I got no time for this bullshit. Look Bug-Eyes, you got thirty bucks, I'll take you down that alley and show you a good a time. Otherwise, get the hell away from me."

Andrew wasn't sure what his next move should be. The prostitute had turned away from him, like she had decided to ignore him. A car slowed as it passed, the driver eyeing them, laughing and shaking his head for some reason. Andrew walked up to the girl again. She had taken her phone out of her purse and was texting rapidly with the clicking tips of her long shiny silver fingernails.

"I don't think you're really a meter maid," Andrew told her. Still trying to be helpful, he said, "You should become a geisha. Geishas are highly trained courtesans," he recited from memory, "who entertain men with arts like singing."

Now she was really upset. "I told you to mind your own damn business!" she flared. "Take your crazy-ass self and bug-eyed goggles and get on down the road." She tapped out another text and stared at her phone.

"Is that an iPhone?" Andrew asked. "My sister has an iPhone."

What she did next, she did so quickly that Andrew didn't have time to react. Shooting out a long, skinny arm, she grabbed his goggles, pulled them roughly off his face, and side-armed them twenty yards down the street. The goggles bounced when they landed, then skidded another five yards before coming to a stop. Andrew's ski mask had gotten pulled down over his eyes. He pulled it up so he could see and located the goggles, then looked back at the prostitute. He felt like he was going to cry, which was the last thing he wanted to do.

"Why did you do that?" he asked, his voice cracking.

"Why you goin' around harrassin' people?" she fired back. "Why you dressed up all crazy like that? Why you want to keep gettin' in my face?"

"Because I'm the Shadow Warrior. It's what I do."

"Yeah, you told me that. Now look here—you better go run after your stupid-ass goggles before a car runs them over and messes them up."

He'd paid $7.95 for the goggles, and didn't want to see his investment get smashed under the wheels of a car, so he ran to pick them up, sprinting with his poorly coordinated, slap-footed gait, which wasn't efficient, but fast enough to allow him to grab the goggles seconds before a jacked-up Chevy Trailblazer could squash them flat.

A close call, he thought, breathing hard as he watched the Trailblazer's red tail lights glide down the street. Scary, but exciting.

Now his goggles were really fogged up. Before he put them back on, he used his shirt to wipe the lenses. He looked back down the street and saw that the prostitute was gone. She must have gotten the message: criminals and lawbreakers were no longer welcome on the streets of River Flats, not while the Shadow Warrior was on patrol.

He felt more confident now. Maybe cleaning up the streets wouldn't be as hard as he thought it would be. But it did make him thirsty.

A block and a half down Barson Street was a corner market, La Tiendita; its junk food selection exerted a powerful magnetic force that pulled Andrew through the store's battered front door. He had gotten into the habit of coming in almost nightly, and always followed the same routine, which required him to stand for several minutes in front of the displays of candies and salty snacks with a thoughtful frown on his face, as though he was pondering the many choices before him. In the end, he always chose the same things—a bag of original Skittles from the candy display, Flaming Hot Cheetos from the rack of salty snacks, and a bottle of Tutifruti Jarritos from the soda case.

The clerk's name was Lupe. He was short, about fifty, with hooded eyes and a gaze that said he didn't have to travel around the world; he'd seen it all from his vantage point behind the cash register at La Tiendita. He'd been busy when Andrew walked in, selling a pack of Virginia Slims and a lottery ticket to a big blond woman whose low-cut blouse held his full attention. He only took Andrew's measure when he stepped up to the counter, looking him up and down, moving only his eyes. Andrew placed his provisions on the counter. He was hoping that Lupe wouldn't recognize him. It seemed important to keep his real identity secret, and yet he was desperate to see if he was making an impression, even creating the tiniest flicker of interest. But Lupe's deadpan expression didn't change as he rang him up.

"$3.85," he said.

Andrew searched three of the six pockets of his cargo pants before he found the crumpled $5 bill he'd squirreled away before setting out on his mission. He straightened it out a little before laying the bill on the counter. He watched Lupe make his change.

"Lupe, it's me," he blurted, unable to contain himself. "It's Andrew." He lifted his goggles and then his ski mask to show more of his face.

Lupe slid a dollar bill, a dime and a nickel across the counter. "You're shittin' me," he said. His weary sarcasm was lost on Andrew. "What you up to? You going to a party or something?"

"I'm cleaning up the streets."

"You need a broom? I think we got brooms over in that corner near the cleaning supplies."

"Ha ha, very funny. It's more like cleaning crime off the streets."

"Oh, OK," Lupe said, playing along a little. "Then you're like a super-hero."

Andrew nodded happily. "Kind of. But not exactly like a super-hero. I'm the Shadow Warrior."

"Shadow Warrior," Lupe repeated, like he was trying out the idea, measuring its possibilities. "What's your super power?"

"Well, I don't really have super powers. It's more like I'm a deadly ninja fighter who can sneak up on you, like if you were committing a crime, and stop you."

"Stop me how?"

"Like with ninjitsu." Andrew had memorized a definition from one of his books, which he thought might be helpful to share with Lupe. "It's a complete fighting system incorporating physical, mental and spiritual aspects developed in ancient Japan."

Lupe was having a little fun with it now. "So you're saying you chase down bad guys and kick the crap out of them when you catch them?"

"Only if they won't cooperate."

"Don't cooperate how? Like if they won't let you walk them down to the cop shop?"

Andrew shrugged. Since he hadn't dealt with any real criminals yet, he wasn't sure how he was going to handle that part. "Or if they don't promise to stop committing crimes."

"So that's how it goes? You ask the bad guys to just go straight, that'll turn them around? They'll cut out all the bullshit?"

Andrew hesitated. He didn't like answering a lot of questions. Jana did that a lot and it made him upset. He grabbed his Tutifruti soda, Skittles and Flaming Hot Cheetos.

"Don't forget your change," Lupe said.

Juggling his purchases, Andrew picked up his change and shoved it into a pocket. He fumbled the nickel, which dropped to the floor and rolled under the counter. As much as he wanted to retrieve it, he decided that it wouldn't look right for the Shadow Warrior to be on his hands and knees, grubbing around for five cents.

"I've got to go," he said.

"That's right. You got some crime to fight," Lupe agreed, nodding. "You be careful out there," he added as Andrew left the store. "Serious. There's some bad dudes out there who don't like super-heroes or ninjas or whatever telling them what to do."

It wasn't Andrew's way to just scarf down junk food. He had to follow a sequence. If he didn't follow the sequence, it wasn't as good. He didn't know why that was, and he didn't ask himself why. The first thing he had to do was find a comfortable spot where he could sit, with enough light to see what he was doing. Not far from La Tiendita, he found a doorway with an overhead light and sat on the doorstep. He set his Skittles and the bottle of Tutifruti soda down next to him, and carefully tore open the bag of Flaming Hot Cheetos. Cheetos first, that's how he did it. The light overhead was essential because he had to examine each Cheeto after he'd pulled it out of the bag, turning it carefully close to his eyes, before popping it into his mouth. He let the

Cheeto rest lightly on his tongue, getting the first taste of salt and heat and cheese dust before moving it back to his grinding molars, where all of the flavors were released in a crunchy explosion. Following this sequence, he consumed the bag of Cheetos slowly, one at a time, every couple of minutes sucking the sticky orange dust off his fingers. It was only after he'd gone through the entire bag and the little Cheeto nuggets at the bottom that he twisted off the cap of the Tutifruti soda and took a long glugging swallow. The sparkly carbonated sweetness of the soda after the salt and heat of the Cheetos was intense, and so wonderful that he had to force himself not to gulp it down at once.

He relaxed, took a deep breath, and then carefully tore open the bag of Skittles. One of the things that he especially liked about Skittles was how you got so many of them, and how when you first got into a bag, it seemed like you could keep eating them one at a time and never run out, especially if you took your time. He liked the red Skittles best, so he ate them first. Then the orange, purple and yellow Skittles, in that order. The green Skittles he saved to add to the fishbowl at home, folding the bag over until it was a smaller package, which he stuffed into a pocket.

He was tempted to call it a night. His first outing had been pretty successful, he thought, and he wanted to get home before Jana returned. He pictured himself in bed, playing *Return of the Ninja* on his Gameboy when she got back. Maybe he could coax Spunky back inside and get her to curl up on his stomach and purr.

Without really deciding to, he started on a different route back home, circling around the block rather than doubling back, walking down Barson toward Linden, which would take him to the front of his apartment house. When he turned down Linden, he saw three guys walking toward him, two wearing dark hoodies, the third in an over-sized plaid flannel shirt with the shirttails hanging out. They walked shoulder to shoulder, taking up the sidewalk. A knot of fear bunched in Andrew's stomach as they drew closer. Were these the guys who had beaten up the kid the other night? The way they were coming at him—cocky, swaggering—made him want to melt away into the shadows, but it was too late to escape their notice. And he didn't want to run, because running would only make him more of a target. Besides, he told himself, the Shadow Warrior wouldn't run. The Shadow Warrior would stand his ground—which is what he did, mainly because when it came down to it, he didn't know what else to do.

He saw them trading glances as they approached, smiling, talking to each other in Spanish, checking him out.

"Who you suppose to be?" one of them asked, the guy in the flannel shirt, who was bigger than the other two, with broad shoulders. He was about eighteen. They were right up on him now. Andrew clenched and unclenched his hands nervously.

He took his time, wanting to say it clearly. "The Shadow Warrior."

"I never heard of you, Chadow Warrior. You new around here?"

One of the hoodies, who was short and fat, said, "You shouldn't be out on the street like that, with that mask and shit. You gonna scare people."

"The only people who should be scared of me are criminals." It was a line Andrew had practiced in front of the mirror and he thought he'd actually made it sound pretty good.

Surprisingly, they all thought that was funny. "*Criminales*? What you gonna to do to *criminales*?"

"I'm going to bring them to justice."

"Chustice? Where's that at?"

"It's not a place," Andrew said, thinking maybe the reason they didn't understand him was because they didn't speak English very well. "It's a—" A what? "Justice is like when you do something bad you get punished for it."

"Something bad? Like taking some *idiota's* money?" Flannel Shirt asked. They were crowding him now.

"Yes. That would be stealing."

"Why you wearing these *gafas*?" the fat guy asked, tapping the lens of his goggles. He was close enough that Andrew could see that one of his front teeth was rimmed in gold.

"For protection," Andrew said.

"For when you're fighting? Fighting *criminales*?"

The fat guy pulled the goggles from his face and let them snap back.

"Hey! That hurt!" Andrew cried.

They were having fun, egging each other on now. A surge of anger welled up in Andrew's chest that he fought to choke back. His hands stiffened, two deadly fighting blades that it might be time to unleash. "I am an expert in martial arts," he warned them.

The other kid wearing a hoodie, who had a narrow, mocking face, was checking out Andrew's utility belt. With a quick movement that Andrew wasn't prepared for, he grabbed the wooden sword, pulled it away from the belt and started waving it over his head.

"This is my machic sword," Skinny Hoodie crowed. "Look like wood but cut like steel!"

"That's a *bokken*. Ninjas practice with it."

Frustration was boiling up inside of Andrew now. He knew when guys were making fun of him. *Bullies.* Bullies were as bad as criminals. They'd be sorry they picked on the Shadow Warrior.

Andrew reached for the *bokken*, but the guy who'd grabbed it easily avoided him. Dancing backwards, he parried Andrew's outstretched arm.

"Why you don't have a real sword, Señor Nincha?" he taunted.

"Because if I had a real blade," he replied, repeating Jana's response when he had asked her the same question, "I could kill someone. Now give it back."

"You gonna have to take it back, Señor Nincha!"

Andrew went into a fighting crouch. The time for talk was over.

"Watch out, he's gonna go all Kung Fu on us," the big guy in the flannel shirt laughed, mimicking Andrew's karate pose. Andrew flailed at him with his arms. With an amused smile, Flannel Shirt grabbed one of Andrew's wrists and held him. His eyes darted to Andrew's utility belt. Andrew tried to pull his wrist free, but the big guy was strong.

"What else you got in that belt?" he asked, snatching Andrew's phone from its holster with his free hand.

"Hey, that's mine!"

The big guy held it up close to his eyes, letting it catch the light from a streetlight so he could examine it. The phone was a basic device, with no Internet connectivity and extra-large raised keys, which Andrew needed if he was to have a chance at successfully dialing a number. Flannel Shirt shook his head. "This piece of shit's not a phone." He tossed it to the fat guy.

"It is too a phone," Andrew told him, almost sobbing now, which made him even angrier. He tried to kick his assailant, but missed widely.

The fat guy said, "It's a *pinche* toy, *pendejo*." He threw it on the ground and stomped it to pieces.

"What else you got? You got money?"

Andrew pulled his flashlight out, but before he could switch it on, the guy who'd taken his sword knocked it out of his hand.

Then he was being pushed to the ground as he lashed out with his free arm and kicked wildly. He heard them laughing, and felt their kicks hit heavily against his back, the side of his head. He tried to shout for help, but his voice sounded strange, almost like a cat screaming, and he wasn't able to form words. Reflexively, he covered his face with his arms and curled up into a fetal position, closing his tearing eyes as tightly as he could, waiting for the attack to be over. They roughly went through his pockets, cursing and laughing, finding only the change left over from his junk food purchase and the green Skittles.

"That's it?" one of them asked, maybe the big guy in the flannel shirt. "Hey nincha, you don't got no wallet"

Another voice said, "Ninchas don't carry no wallets."

"He's a nincha from the barrio, *cabrón*. Barrio ninchas got no money."

"Ain't got shit. And can't fight. You better go back to nincha school, *estúpido*. Else you're gonna get hurt." With that parting advice, and one last kick for emphasis, they left him. Andrew could hear them running away down the street, whooping and laughing.

He lay motionless for a few minutes, his eyes still tightly shut, trying to wish away everything that had just happened. He was sore from the kicks he'd received, but what hurt most was the dishonor of being bested so easily by a trio of punks. A real ninja would have dispatched his three attackers in less than a minute, with blurred punches and whirring roundhouse kicks, the way Andrew had imagined himself prevailing over every one of his foes. For some reason, he thought of Ricky Wakefield laughing at him, which deepened his shame. He had to ask himself if there was truth in what one of the punks had said—that maybe he did need to go to ninja school. He knew he had the heart of a hero, but he'd just learned the hard way that he didn't have the skills. Not yet.

The sound of footsteps approaching snapped him out of his sulk. He raised his head and opened his eyes. A dark shape was approaching, a man coming toward him. He shut his eyes again and curled up tighter, like a pill bug, expecting more rough treatment and resigned to endure it.

He sensed the man crouching over him, felt a hand pushing gently against this shoulder, and heard a voice that was vaguely familiar ask if he was OK.

He opened his eyes, and pulled up his goggles, which had almost completely fogged up. A car came up the street and as the brightness of its headlights swept past he recognized the face of the man hovering

over him by its distinctive craggy features—hawk nose, broad, high
cheekbones and strong jaw.

"Chuy?"

****

Jana had lived in a few low-rent apartments in some sketchy
neighborhoods, but this was the first one she'd rented that had three
deadbolt locks on the door. Probably not a good sign, she thought,
when Mr. Ramakrishnan, the landlord, first showed her the place. But
poverty ain't for sissies and she could almost afford the rent, so she
took it. Solving the mystery of which key fit into which lock was
something she still hadn't gotten the hang of, even after two months.
And it was worse late at night when she got home from class, tired and
maybe a little cranky like she was tonight after a full day at her
marketing internship, followed by three hours of classes and a long
commute back from school.

In the weak light of the naked bulb in the rusting fixture above the
door she fumbled with her key chain as she juggled her purse and a
flimsy to-go container of ramen that she'd picked up from a little
noodle shop on the way home. When she finally managed to fit the
right key into the first lock she found that the deadbolt hadn't been set
in the first place.

In fact, she found after trying the door, none of the three
deadbolts had been set.

Dammit Andrew, she muttered as she opened the door, ready to deliver another lecture to impress upon him—for like the fiftieth time—that River Flats was crawling with thieves and lowlifes who would steal the shine off your shoes if you weren't careful.

The door opened directly on to what they called the living room, but was also—after they spread a sheet and a blanket on the sofa as they did each night—Andrew's bedroom. Andrew was sitting on the sofa with his shirt off, holding a wash cloth to his forehead. It looked like he had bruises on the pale soft skin of his shoulders and his ribs. He wore a strange smile, a little ashamed but maybe a little proud.

"Oh my god, Andrew! What happened to you?"

She was next to him quickly, kneeling and lightly moving aside the washcloth which was pressed against a red knot and a scrape just below his hairline.

"I was in a fight. Three guys. Maybe four. I kicked their asses."

The bump didn't look too bad, so she let herself get angry. "What were you doing out on the street at night?" On the floor next to the sofa, she saw the black ski mask, goggles and the wooden practice sword, the one she had stupidly helped him to buy from a ninja web site.

"I was on patrol."

"*Patrol?*"

A man's voice came from the kitchen. "He's going to make the world a safer place for decent people. He just told me all about it."

She knew who it was before he walked in. Chuy. His face was a little older around the corners of his eyes. His shoulders and chest were maybe a little thicker, but he was still slim in the waist and hips.

23

His black hair was shaggy and uncombed, spilling over his forehead. He still carried himself the same way, not so much like he owned any place he walked into, but could own it if he wanted to.

She didn't know whether to hug him or hit him.

"You don't have any frozen peas?" he asked. "That's what fighters do. They keep a couple bags of frozen peas handy to bring down swelling after taking a shot to the face. All I could find in your freezer was this—" He frowned, reading the print on the front of the bag he was holding, "Gluten-free vegetarian won tons."

Andrew couldn't contain himself. "It's Chuy, Jana."

"I hate frozen peas," Jana said. "And where the hell have you been for the past two years?"

"Away." Chuy was the strong, silent type. Too strong and too silent for Jana, as it turned out. They had a thing, a serious thing, but the thing had ended, and then he disappeared. He handed the bag of frozen won tons to Andrew and instructed him to apply it gently to his forehead. "Mostly in Bakersfield."

"What were you doing in Bakersfield?"

"A little of this, a little of that . . ."

"Did it involve beating people up?"

He shrugged. "A little of that too."

"Why am I not surprised?"

"It's not exactly like you think. I thought I'd get back into MMA. Get in shape, get a few matches lined up. See if I couldn't win some purses."

"How'd that work out?"

"I kept breaking things."

"Like people's noses?"

"Like my foot, my hand. . ."

"Did you ever think about getting a real job?"

"You may be surprised to hear that I actually did. Think about it, I mean."

She looked back at Andrew, who had gotten up to stand in front of the mirror to see if he could get a look at the bruises on his back. "Did you have anything to do with this?" she asked Chuy.

"I found him that way. A couple blocks away."

"It was a real fight, Jana. They were like these gangbangers. I told them to clear out of the neighborhood or else."

"And they chose 'or else', right? Andrew, how many times have we've talked about how you should stay inside at night? You've got the TV, video games, your books . . ." She looked at Chuy. "Should we go to the emergency room?"

"No, I checked him out. He'll be OK. Nothing broken. A few scrapes, but no deep cuts. Ribs will probably be a little sore for a few days."

"Well, should we call the police?"

"What are they going to do? Besides waste your time asking a lot of questions for reports that they'll never follow up on."

Andrew was a little speedy, high on the excitement of having survived a fight with a tale to tell, recounting for them how he'd kicked a knife out of the hand of one of his attackers, and karate chopped another in the arm. "I think I might have broken it. You could hear like a bone crack."

"You and I are going to talk about this, Andrew. We had an agreement. This ninja stuff was just for fun. You can't be running around at night getting into trouble." Andrew was pantomiming a karate kick for Chuy. "Andrew, are you hearing what I'm saying to you now?" She looked at Chuy. "You never told me you were leaving," she said.

Chuy tried to hold her gaze, but it wasn't easy for him. She could tell he was thinking about what he was going to say. "I had to get out of town. And we had broken up, so . . ."

"We didn't break up." Jana wasn't sure why it was important to her to make that point, but she felt she had to.

"We didn't?"

"Not really. We just kind of drifted apart."

"I didn't drift."

"OK. But you left—"

"After you drifted."

"—and no one knew where you went. Not Nico or Tony or even Gallo."

"Gallo knew." Gallo was his father. Like everyone else, Chuy called him by his nickname. "I asked him not to tell anyone."

"And you didn't answer my texts."

"You only sent two texts."

"What was the magic number? Three, four?"

"I don't know. But more than two."

"OK." She decided not to try to argue with his crazy logic. "And now you're back."

Andrew said, "Chuy, did you ever break somebody's arm? Or any other bone, like the femur or the clavicle?"

"What's the clavicle?"

"The collarbone."

"I don't think I ever broke a collarbone."

"But maybe a femur?"

"Maybe." To Jana he said, "Gallo's not doing real good. He's getting a little goofy or something. Can't really manage the taqueria anymore. And he's up to his eyeballs in debt. So I kinda came back to help out."

"Is he sick?"

"Sick? Well, physically, I think he's fine. But, like I said, he's getting goofy. He'll be OK one minute, then he comes up with some crazy shit and you don't even know where it came from. He probably took too many shots to the head all the years he was fighting."

Jana thought about Chuy's dad, Gallo, who wasn't any taller than she was, a bantamweight boxer when he was young, and still wiry when she'd seen him last. And still flirty. "I liked your dad."

"He liked the ladies, that's for sure. And he still thinks he's got it. He comes into the taqueria, gets in everyone's way, hitting on the girls. I guess you don't get by there anymore. . ."

"I was going to a few times, but I just thought it would feel awkward. I dream about his chicken molé all the time, though. I was thinking about it just the other day. Remember how I was almost addicted to it?"

"Yeah. I remember." He was staring at her, and she almost thought she saw emotion in his eyes, which surprised her. This was Chuy after all. "Your hair's different," he said. "Longer, right?"

"A little longer."

"And you used to twist it so it stuck up like in little spikes."

"I'm kinda over that punk thing now."

"But it looks good. Softer." He played with his hands, big and strong with battered knuckles. He saw her looking at them and shoved them in his pockets. "What else is going on?" he asked. "You still working at the fish market for Nico and Tony?"

"No. Not for over a year and a half. I went back to school."

"School? Where?"

"CCSU. I'm getting my degree in marketing. Almost done." She put her purse and the take-out container on a small table in the kitchen, which was only three steps away from the sofa. She couldn't bring herself to ask him if he wanted to sit, have a glass of wine.

"What happened to writing? I thought you wanted to be a writer?"

"I'm tired of being poor, Chuy. It's almost impossible to make a living as a writer."

He wanted to say something else, she could tell, but seemed to be working out how he would say it. What he finally said was, "It's really good to see you, Jana."

She responded carefully. "It's good to see you, Chuy," wondering where this was going.

"You know what's crazy?" he said. "I still don't know exactly why we broke up. It's one of those things where you keep thinking about it and just can't figure it out."

We had this conversation at least ten times, she thought, two years ago. She saw that Andrew had left out a box of cereal—he could eat a big bowl of cereal any time of day—and a carton of milk, which she put back into the refrigerator, just to do something.

Andrew said, "The femur is connected to the tibia. The bone next to the tibia is the fibula." Then he said, "Chuy said he'd teach me some ninja moves."

That's all she needed. "We'll have to discuss that," she said, speaking to Andrew but looking at Chuy. "After tonight we might have to just cool the whole ninja thing."

"He said I have to learn how to protect myself."

"And?" Chuy prompted.

Andrew was confused. "And . . .?" he repeated.

"And you need more instruction in the martial arts before you can fight anyone like a ninja."

"Chuy said he would teach me, Jana."

"Swell," she said.

Andrew looked at her, a look she recognized that meant he needed to shut down for a while. "Jana, can I take a bath?"

"Sure, go ahead." He went into the bathroom. A moment later he opened the taps; the pipes shuddered and the water rushed out loudly.

When Andrew was out of earshot Chuy said, "I was just going to show him what to do if someone comes at him. Defensive stuff. Like it or not, he's getting to the age where he's going to run into trouble out on the streets. You can't keep him locked up. He's an adult."

"I just don't want to worry about him."

"What's he doing when he's not taking a bath or out saving the world?"

"We got him a job at the Bay-View. You know how they have these characters, those mascots wandering around the park, like the sea turtle and Pete the Pelican? Andrew is the Smiles Ambassador."

"The Smiles Ambassador? No kidding? That's pretty wild. What's the Smiles Ambassador do?"

"He gives away free smiles to the kids and spreads good cheer to family members of all ages. That's the job description."

"No shit?"

"They had an old guy doing it and he quit so I brought Andrew in and they hired him."

"*You* brought him in?"

Andrew walked back in from the bathroom, still holding the bag of frozen wontons to his head. "Jana, where's my Gameboy?"

"You can't take the Gameboy into the tub."

"I won't drop it."

"Andrew, we had an agreement. Why do you keep asking? Take one of your ninja books in there if you want something to do."

Chuy said, "Sounds like you and Andrew have a lot of agreements."

"We make at least three new ones every day. Or the same ones. I lose track."

They'd been talking for almost five minutes, and Jana still hadn't invited him to sit. Chuy got it—she had other things to do.

"Look, I'm going to be around for a while," he said. "You want to do something sometime?"

She didn't say anything. Then she said "I'm going to have to think about that. I'm pretty busy with work and school. And I've got this internship I'm doing. It's taking up a lot of my time."

"Internship?"

"I'm a marketing intern at the Bay-View. I'll be graduating in like a month and that's how you get your foot in the door for a job."

Chuy nodded, thinking it through. "That's cool. I mean that you're ambitious and you're going to go places. What do they think about all that ink you've got on your arm?" Tattooed in simple, flowing script on her left arm, between her shoulder and her elbow, was an Emily Dickinson poem, the one that begins, "Hope is the thing with feathers—"

"At the Bay-View? They think I'm edgy. Or my boss does anyway. He thinks the Bay-View has to get hipper."

"Hipper?"

"That's the word he used."

Chuy pulled up his left sleeve. On his hard bicep she saw that her name was still there. She was struck by a memory of his arms, strong around her. She let it flash by.

He smiled. "You still got my name on your ass?"

"On my hip," she corrected him. "On my upper hip. And as soon as I get some money saved, I'm getting it fixed."

"Fixed?"

"Re-worked. You know, where they take a tattoo that you regret getting and cover it up with a new design. But it's kind of expensive and I'm not exactly flush these days."

Avoiding his gaze, she started picking up the things that Andrew had left on the floor, his shirt, black ski mask and goggles. "So. I've got a lot of things to do. Homework, laundry, a huge project for work . . ." In fact, she was getting a little freaked out by a deadline her boss at the Bay-View had given her. She had to create a buzz around a zombie invasion—a promotion for the park he was calling Z-Day—and had less than a week to do it.

"Can I borrow that stuff? The mask and goggles," Chuy said. "Just for tonight?"

She knew better than to ask what he wanted it for. "You're still a little crazy, aren't you?"

"Maybe a little." Jana gave him the mask and goggles. "I could use that wooden sword too," he said.

Of course you could, she thought.

****

On the hottest days in Bakersfield, when the summer sun burned all the freshness out of the morning air by 8:00 and the streets shimmered by 9:00, Chuy dreamed about the cool coastal fog of Santa Carmela, about how sometimes you could see it in the distance, massed out over the bay, a thick bank of gray cloud that lost its clear contours as it drifted onshore and settled over the Flats like a low, lead-colored ceiling; how a strong gust could tear away pieces of the cloud-ceiling, sending shape-shifting specters flying down the streets and through the tree tops like ghosts.

32

As he left Jana and Andrew's apartment, the fog was breaking up in the night sky high above the street lamps, and Chuy could see a star here and there. He knew he looked silly in the mask and goggles, but he didn't feel silly. He walked purposefully, not creeping stealthily, but striding straight ahead like he owned the streets, like he was looking for trouble.

Which he found right away.

Two blocks down Barson he saw a slender young black girl in a tight turquoise dress that rode up her skinny legs, as snug on her tiny butt as cling wrap. Standing the way whores do, like she was waiting for someone, she just didn't know who, checking her phone. Chuy was about ten yards away when she sensed him coming and looked at him, shaking her head. She was irritated; he could see it in her narrow face as he got closer. She looked down at her phone and started tapping at it with her long silver fingernails.

"I told you to leave me alone," she said.

"You never told me anything." Chuy didn't have anything against whores in general, but this one immediately pissed him off.

He angled toward her, and she backed away.

"I told you to get your crazy ass on down the road and now you're pestering me again."

"Pestering?"

"Someone better be comin' to throw a net over you. Put you someplace where you won't be botherin' people."

"I'm just out for a stroll, that's all. Minding my own business."

"Then go on and mind your business and get out of mine."

He was going to move on, because he really didn't want to get into it with this girl who probably had good reason to be pissed off at the world, when a black Escalade pulled up to the curb, the driver's side closest to them. It came up slowly, the driver cutting the headlights before it stopped. Chuy could feel the deep bass vibrations of the car's sound system—some rapper, he couldn't make out who. The Escalade sat for a minute, engine idling, the driver not in any hurry. Chuy could see him in the blue glow of the dashboard lights, a black guy, but really couldn't make out his face. He was lighting a cigarette. Taking his time, he turned down the sound system's volume and leaned toward the window. Chuy heard the soft mechanical whirr of the window coming down. He saw the driver's face, a young guy with a sparse goatee.

"What's this bullshit all about?" the driver asked.

"What bullshit?"

"See, I told you," the girl said. "He crazy."

"Look Atom Ant or whoever the fuck you suppose to be, you're in the way here. You're messing with my business." He was being patient, spelling things out so there wouldn't be any confusion. "You got to move on down the road. Else I'm going to have to move you."

"How's that going to work?"

The pimp looked at Chuy, like there was some huge disconnect that he was going to fix. He said, "Come up here a little closer. I got something to show you."

Chuy took a step toward the car and stood right up next to the driver's door, looking in through the window. He could smell cigarette smoke and weed. And now he recognized the rapper—Jay Z, making it mellow. The driver had his seat angled back, and was slouched comfortably, kicking back. He brought up one of his hands from his lap. He was holding a Glock, a Glock 30 it looked like. The .45 automatic.

"See this? You see I mean business?"

Chuy threw a quick right through the open window, catching the pimp by surprise right in the mouth and rocking his head. With the same hand, he grabbed the pimp's gun hand and yanked the Glock away from him. He pressed the barrel hard under his nose, driving his head back against the headrest.

All of this in less than ten seconds.

For Jay Z, rapping smoothly in the background, it was like nothing had happened.

"Mother*fuck*!" the pimp said, bringing a hand to his mouth. "The fuck did you do? You *hit* me! *Shit*!"

"Get your hand down. Both hands on your lap where I can see them." He pushed even harder with the gun. He turned to check out the girl. She was standing frozen, trying to comprehend what had happened.

"Get in the car," Chuy said to her.

"DeAngelo?" she said to the pimp.

"You talk like a cop. You a cop?" the pimp said, moving his tongue inside his mouth, checking the damage. Chuy kept the Glock in his face. "This is like some kind of setup. Like some crazyass sting. That what this is?"

"Get in the car," Chuy repeated to the girl who was working through a moment of indecision. "*Now.*"

She ran around to the passenger door with choppy little high-heeled steps.

"If I was a cop, DeAngelo, I'd probably do something nice, like arrest you," Chuy said. "But I'm not a cop, and I'm not nice. I want you to drive your pimpmobile on out of here and keep driving. Get out of River Flats and I don't want to see your pimp ass back here." Chuy pulled the gun away from his face. "Put it in Drive and move."

DeAngelo paused, thinking about how he was going to ask something. Then he just asked it. "You gonna give me my piece back?"

Chuy laughed. He couldn't help it. "I can't do that, DeAngelo. But here's a receipt for it." He slapped the gun barrel across the pimp's nose. "Now get on down the road before I shoot you with it."

Clutching his face in pain, DeAngelo cursed, his eyes turned up toward Chuy. The girl moved closer to him, lightly touching her fingers to his face. He pushed her away. Chuy waited. It almost looked like DeAngelo was going to say something, but then thought better of it. The driver's window went up, muting Jay Z as DeAngelo put the car in gear and eased away from the curb. Chuy watched the big Escalade's tail lights move down Barson Street toward the stoplight at the intersection with Ocean, then turn left where the sign pointed the way to Highway One.

Adios, mofo.

Chuy examined the Glock. He could probably use a gun, but he figured it was stolen and he didn't want to be caught carrying it, so he hid it in a scraggly clump of bushes next to a weathered board fence so he could come back for it. He continued down Barson, letting the adrenaline dissipate, thinking about River Flats and how when he was a kid it was like his back yard, every inch of every street and alley familiar to him. There was a different vibe then, not that it was a slice of the American dream, but after dark the homes and business still showed signs of normal life, people hanging out in their front yards and porches, leaning against the doorways of the little markets. But things had changed. People didn't feel safe on the streets at night. They kept their doors tightly locked, their curtains drawn. Chuy guessed that the cops cruised around every now and then, but didn't get out of their cars and actually walk a beat, poking into dark places, putting the dirtballs on notice. Until someone got right up into their faces, they wouldn't give up what they claimed as their turf.

He came up on his dad's place, Taqueria Gallo, closed for the night. He checked the heavy front door just to make sure it was locked. He peered inside through the wrought iron bars protecting the front window. Quiet, the only light within coming from a Cerveza Pacifico clock over the order counter. This was it, he thought, the sum total of all the sweat and punishing hours of Gallo's working life, launched in 1997 with the little money he had been able to set aside busting his ass during the day as a roofer, nights and weekends driving up and down the length of California, boxing for small purses, always wearing a bruise somewhere on his face—this was what it got him, a little hole-in-the-wall taco joint that was on the hairy edge of going under.

He heard the murmur of voices and the noise of metal banging on metal coming from the alley on the back side of the building. He edged toward the corner of the building cautiously. He made out three guys back there, shadows in the darkened alley, crowded around the back door. One of them, the biggest one in a flannel shirt, had something in his hands, maybe a long pry bar, and it looked like he was working it in between the door and the doorframe. The other two, both wearing hoodies, were giving him whispered advice and encouragement.

Chuy crept up to within five feet of the trio. "Place is closed," he said.

They turned toward him all at once, three clowns caught in the act, but not panicking.

"*Chingador!*" the big guy said. "The fuck you doin' back here?"

"Nincha, you want another beating?" the fat one asked, taking a step toward Chuy. Chuy let him come one step closer, then threw a roundhouse kick into his gut, which sat him on his ass, doubled-over. The other two backed up a little, trying to figure out what the hell had just happened. The second guy in a hoodie came at him next, rushing at him, a knife in his hand. Chuy sidestepped him, grabbed his hoodie at the neck, and threw him to the taqueria's dumpster which sat up against the back of the building. He hit it headfirst with a satisfying clang and fell to the ground, maybe knocked out, maybe just dazed, but he wouldn't be a factor for at least a couple minutes, so Chuy could give the big guy, and the pry bar he was swinging, his undivided attention.

"I'm goin' to fuckin' kill you," Flannel Shirt said after Chuy danced away from the first wide swing, trying to figure out how he was going to disarm this guy. He pulled out the wooden practice sword—no match for the heavy steel pry bar, but a distraction, offering an alternative target to Chuy's head. Playing it up, Chuy went into a fighting stance, waving the *bokken* in front of him. Flannel Shirt swung at it, missed; swung at it again, clipping it, but not knocking it out of Chuy's hand. Chuy saw an opening and jabbed him behind the ear with the *bokken*, not much more than a hard tap, but it angered Flannel Shirt, made him come at Chuy again, swinging wildly. He made the mistake of raising the pry bar high over his head, giving Chuy a chance to catch his wrist before he could bring it down. Chuy twisted the straightened arm. Pivoting, he pulled Flannel Shirt down to the ground as he applied pressure to the locked elbow joint. By the time they hit the ground, Flannel Shirt was face down and Chuy was pushing his own elbow into his neck, pinning him. Chuy's knee was on the locked elbow, still gripping the wrist and twisting the arm up.

They were both breathing hard. Flannel Shirt, his face pressed into the gritty asphalt, was cursing, but checking the impulse to resist, realizing it would only increase the pain in his elbow.

"It'd be easy to break your arm right now," Chuy said, real close to the guy's ear. "Dislocate your elbow like a chicken wing. But I'm just going to sprain it a little this time." He yanked back on Flannel Shirt's wrist, pushing his weight on the elbow, but not his full weight, not enough to really mess it up. The kid was a punk, but Chuy had been a punk once. He just needed to be taught a lesson. Flannel Shirt was in pain, but he wasn't going to let himself scream. Instead, he grunted in a hoarse, breathy way. When Chuy got off him, he curled up, clutching his arm, all the fight in him gone.

As Chuy picked up the pry bar, he sensed one of the hoodies coming at him. He whirled around, swinging the bar, and caught his attacker, the skinny guy, on the meat of his right shoulder, not full

39

force, but he whacked it hard. The skinny guy sank to his knees, grabbing at his shoulder, calling Chuy names in a wounded, outraged voice, but he was done for the night too. Chuy saw a gravity knife on the ground, picked it up.

"All right if I keep this?" he said, but the skinny guy didn't answer, and he put in his pocket.

Chuy looked at the fat guy who had been so brave before Chuy had nailed him in the gut. He was still on his ass, catching his breath. "You don't want a piece of this too, do you?" Chuy asked, showing him the pry bar.

The fat guy shook his head.

"You fuckers listen up. If I catch you running around the Flats at night, I'll give you a more serious ass-kicking. Stay home and help your mothers with the dishes, read a book, start an ant farm . . . just stay off the streets. You got that? Nod your heads." The two guys in hoodies nodded silently. Flannel Shirt was too focused on the pain in his elbow to comply, so Chuy went up to him, grabbed him by the hair and lifted his face.

"You going to nod your head or am I going to have to nod it for you?"

Flannel Shirt cursed and spat at him. It pissed Chuy off. He slammed the punk's face into the asphalt.

Chuy stood up. "So we're good, right?" he asked. Brushing the grit off his pants, he slid the *bokken* back under his belt and walked into the shadows.

Z-Day Minus 5

"You coulda covered him up better," Nico Connole said, coming out of the walk-in freezer, eating a Drumstick. He always had a box of the chocolate and peanut coated ice cream cones stuck away on the shelf above the frozen squid. He ate at least two, sometimes three a day. If you made the mistake of commenting on it, you could count on a five-minute lecture on how Drumsticks were the one thing—the only thing he could think of—that hadn't gotten totally screwed up since he was a kid.

Nico's brother Tony, in a blue smock, jeans tucked into rubber Wellingtons, was running a long filet knife down the back of a two-foot lingcod that was laid out on the wet stainless steel table in front of him. A flex hose hung above the table. The tabletop was connected to a sink, and angled so that water could be sluiced down to wash away the blood and guts that smeared the table's surface after a fish had been butchered.

"You only saw him because you were looking for him. I covered him up good in those trash bags, those big ones you got for the outside cans. And those two big halibut they brought in Tuesday are stacked on top of him. You'd have to be looking for him, and who's going to be looking for a body in there?"

"His foot was sticking out of one of the bags. I had to stick it back in."

"His foot?"

"In like some fancy Italian loafer. I covered it up, but you gotta be more careful. What if Ma saw it?"

"Wouldn't be the first time."

They were in one of the prep areas behind their fish market. Tony was thirty-five, big-shouldered and rangy, two years younger than Nico, and still had a full head of hair, which he wore a little long, a little messy, the same way he had since high school. Nico was losing it on top. He was pudgy, and prone to looking vaguely worried, like an accountant who had worked the numbers backwards and forwards and still didn't trust the result.

"Anyone see you bring him in?" Nico asked.

Tony hefted the long filet he had cut away from the lingcod, sprayed it with the hose to clean away the traces of blood, and set it aside, glistening. "It was 3:30 in the morning, Nico. Nobody was around."

"What about Wharf security?"

"Nobody was down at this end of the wharf, Nico. I checked. What do you think, I'm an idiot?" Nico didn't say. Tony flipped the lingcod over to slice off the second filet. He pierced the skin behind the head with a push of the filet knife, probing for the edge of the backbone.

"They say who it was?"

Tony prided himself on having a surgeon's touch with the filet knife. He concentrated on cleanly separating the translucent flesh from the bone with one confident swipe of the knife. He didn't answer his brother until he'd freed the second long filet and all that remained of the lingcod was its ugly, toothy head, long naked spine, and tail.

"They didn't say and I didn't ask. They never say."

"You ever seen him before?"

"I don't know. Maybe. Kind of an older guy with silver hair."

"Silver hair? How was it combed?"

"You're so interested, go in the walk-in and take a look," Tony said. He grabbed what was left of the lingcod by the tail and walked it over to a framed-in hole in the floor. The hole was square, about a foot long on each side. If you looked through it you could see the wharf's pilings and cross framing, and—about twenty feet down—the dark water of the Monterey Bay. He dropped the remains of the butchered fish through the hole and listened to the barking of the sea lions that congregated around the wharf. He watched the alpha male, a bull sea lion they all called Sammy, snatch the carcass as soon as it hit the water and then plunge below the surface. Sammy was like family. He almost always got the good stuff. The other sea lions had to settle for the stinky "Seal Snacks" that the market sold to tourists in little paper cocktail cups. The snacks were made up of bits of fish that had sat in the display case too long. It was Nico's idea, and he was pretty proud of it. They actually made about $75 a day off what they used to just dump—nearly enough to fund a day's pay for one of the Mexican dishwashers. Nico started calling one of them, an older guy with a little pencil mustache, "Freebie".

Nico didn't want to look at the guy's face. He never wanted to look at their faces. But he made himself go back into the walk-in to check him out. He had to move two big halibut that were stacked on top of the plastic-shrouded body. He recognized the guy right away.

"That's Carmine Bosso," he said to Tony after covering the face and returning to the prep area.

"Yeah?"The name wasn't ringing any bells.

"You know, owned the Fior d' Italia, that big restaurant with banquet rooms over in San Jose. Dad brought us over there a few times when we were kids. Mom loved their gnocchi. Every time we went she had to order it. I think Carmine was something in Vincent's organization. Like he ran the San Jose operation. Dad worked with him on a couple things. Nice guy. Friendly."

"Musta gotten on Vincent's bad side somehow."

"Who was it who brought him out?" Nico asked.

"That was the weird part. I got this text around midnight from a number I didn't recognize."

"What'd it say?"

"'Delivery from Vincent in a couple of hours. Meet us at the market.' I was there at 2:00, but they didn't show up for over an hour. Then they drive up in a big Mercedes, and a guy on the passenger side gets out and he's this skinny little shit all jacked up on something. I don't know, maybe about forty or so. He pops the trunk and this other guy, a big dumb looking kid, gets out of back. I go out to talk to them.

"I asked them 'This the delivery from Vincent?' What else could it be, you know? And the skinny guy says 'Get your ass over here and let's get this done.' Pops the trunk and me and the kid haul the stiff out of the trunk, wrapped up in a blanket, and run him into the back here."

"And no one saw you?"

"We had him out of the trunk and into the back here in less than a minute."

"But these were new guys, the guys who brought him out—you never saw them before?" Nico asked, examining the Drumstick for his next point of attack. Tony shook his head. "I wonder what happened to the other guy who used to drive them out. Salvatore, right? That was his name? Sal?"

"Maybe. Who the fuck knows? He didn't have much of a personality, but at least he didn't have an attitude. Not like these new guys. Pissed me off. Especially the little fucker. He was wearing one of those hats."

"What hats?"

"You know, the kind with the little brim. Like you're some cool cat out of the '50's. I hate those hats."

Tony pulled another big lingcod out of a long box on the floor and heaved it up onto the stainless steel table. He turned to look at Nico. "You got a piece of peanut stuck to your chin," he said. "That place where your neck meets your chin."

Nico ran his fingers around the collar of fat beneath his chin, found the peanut bit, which was lodged in a fold of flesh. He examined it and popped it in his mouth.

"And the other guy was like a kid?"

"Maybe twenty, twenty-one. Dumb looking kid. Didn't say a word the whole time. Wore his hat like a skater."

"Skater?"

"Skateboarder," Tony explained, like he shouldn't have to.

"How do skaters wear their hats?" Nico asked.

"Where you been? Baseball caps pulled down low with the whaddyacallit, the bill, totally flat. It looks goofy."

Nico pondered it all for a moment; then he said, "You're gonna take care of it tonight, right?"

"It?"

"Carmine."

"That's the plan." Tony picked up the filet knife, but didn't start cutting right away. "There was someone else in the Mercedes. The driver."

"Yeah?"

"So me and the kid, we brought the dead guy, Carmine, in the back here, and we stuck him in the walk-in freezer. After we come out there's the skinny guy in the hat smoking a cigarette and next to him was this absolute knockout. Musta been driving the Benz. Standing right over there next to the sink."

"A woman?"

"The most beautiful woman you've ever seen. Standing there like she owned the place. Not saying anything, just standing there."

"Who was it?"

"I don't know. She had that look like you don't even think you should ask. She was wearing like a business suit, but fit kinda tight around her tits and her ass, nice shoes with high heels, had a purse, like a Louis Vuitton bag."

"What do you know about Louis Vuitton?"

"You think I live in a cave? I watch TV. Anyway this gal's beautiful. 3:30 in the frickin' morning but she looks perfect. She was just

46

looking around, checking everything out, then she looked at me like she just noticed me and she asked 'How's business?'"

"'How's business?' How did she mean?"

"That's what I asked her. 'How do you mean?' And she just kind of smiled. So I said 'Business is OK. We're getting by.' And she said, 'Getting by,' like it was the stupidest answer I could have given her. 'You been kind of quiet out here in sleepy little Santa Carmela,' she said."

"Sleepy little Santa Carmela? Sleepy? What's that supposed to mean?"

"You tell me. Then she said, 'You know who I am?' I said I didn't, you know, I never saw her before. She said 'I'm Vincent's CFO.'"

"Vincent's CFO?" Nico said.

"That's what she said." Tony had laid the tip of the filet knife's blade on the second lingcod's back, but hadn't started his first cut.

"Like Vincent's Chief Financial Officer?"

"Crap, I don't know."

"You didn't ask?"

"No. It was like I should know, or shouldn't ask. I don't know. She wasn't standing there like she wanted to chat. Then she said, 'We've got to talk. You, me and your brother Nico.'"

"Talk? What about?"

"I don't know."

"You didn't ask?"

"I figured she'd tell me."

"Did she?"

"No. I was waiting for her to tell me, but she just said 'I'll be in touch,' and then walked out."

Nico had popped the last bit of the Drumstick into his mouth, the chocolate-filled pointed end of the cone. He chewed and swallowed it reflectively. His face wore the look it frequently wore, not like he'd been caught at something, but like he was afraid he was going to be caught at something.

"So what do we do, wait till she gets in touch?" he asked.

"You got any other ideas?"

"We could contact Vincent directly," Nico said. "Find out what's going on."

"You want to talk to Vincent?"

"Not really. I mean I really haven't talked to him since when Dad died and he came to the funeral."

"Shit. That's been three years." Tony remembered back to the day their father was buried in Holy Cross cemetery. "Did Vincent look like a classic mob guy or what? The black suit, the black tie, sunglasses, oiled-up hair."

"Old school. He's gotta be in his eighties now. But he had that fine-looking girlfriend. She couldn't have been more than early thirties."

"Someone said she used to be a Raider Girl."

"She coulda been. She had that kind of look." They both took a moment to think back on the girlfriend, who wore a tight fitting black dress with a deep décolletage.

"What'd Ma say?" Nico said. Then he did an imitation of their mother's raspy voice, "*Where she'd get that dress, off Vampirella?*"

"I know she didn't like it. It wasn't respectful."

48

Nico said, "I've been trying to keep a low profile with Vincent. It's when people like that notice you that you've got to watch your ass."

"But you've been paying him, right? Keeping him happy?"

Nico looked down at this shirt and saw that a fleck of the Drumstick's chocolate coating had landed right at the swell of his belly. He walked to the sink, moistened a towel, and dabbed at it, frowning. "I pay him every month. I just sent out a $2,000 check made out to Argiento Linens and Uniforms."

"Is that all? Two grand doesn't sound like much. Maybe he wants more. Didn't we used to pay him a lot more? Like ten grand a month?"

"We can hardly afford what we're paying now. That part of the business was more Dad's thing. We don't have the money coming in, especially since the gooks took over the squid business."

"Did Vincent every say anything about it?"

"We never talk. I just send the money in."

"Don't you think he'd want to know why the checks have been getting smaller?"

Nico was staring unhappily at his shirt, his chin disappearing into his fat neck. He'd only succeeded in making the chocolate smear bigger. "I don't know. You know he had that stroke."

"What stroke?"

"I told you about that, what I heard, that he had a stroke a few months ago, but he was still in charge."

"You didn't tell me that."

"You just don't remember. Strokes change people. Maybe it mellowed him. Anyway, I put a note in with the check last month. In the envelope I send him."

"A *note*? What kind of note?"

"I just explained that receipts were down because of the economy and the gooks and all. How they wouldn't fall in line."

"I can't believe you wrote a note. That's chickenshit."

"You know the way things have been as well as I do. What am I supposed to do?"

They both fell silent. For their father, Nicky Connole, the old ways—loan sharking, shaking down pimps and whores, strong-arming restaurant owners into buying their fish and squid at a premium—had been important, an essential part of his identity as a man. The fish market had been more of a sideline, a front, good for keeping his wife and boys busy, and a convenient way to launder cash. After Nicky passed away, Nico and Tony had kept their hands in the old man's various criminal enterprises, but not their hearts. Nico was a worrier. The older he got, the more he worried. A life of crime didn't suit him. Too many things could go wrong. Tony had more of a violent, reckless streak, but it had been years since he had personally beaten anyone up to show them he meant business, or threatened a pimp with a length of 1" galvanized pipe, or set fire to a restaurant whose owner had decided to buy his seafood from another supplier, and he just wasn't into it any more. They had a guy, Chuy, who used to be their enforcer and that had worked out, freeing up Tony to do other things, but Chuy had gone off somewhere a couple years ago, just disappeared. More recently they'd relied on one of their fish cutters, a kid named TJ, who thought he was pretty tough and liked messing with people, but he was undependable to say the least. And you couldn't trust him to turn over all the money he collected. Always playing his own game. The past couple months he been chilling in the County jail, known locally as the farm, busted for beating up his girlfriend—they called it domestic abuse. Bottom line, the brothers just weren't into the mob stuff. Nico had dreams of turning the fish market and its eight stool counter into a big moneymaker, maybe expand into a real restaurant-type seating area for the tourists, and Tony just wanted to do his own thing, get back to fishing and crabbing in the family tradition.

"So what do we do?" Tony asked.

Before Nico could answer, their mother, Bianca walked in from the food prep area, carrying her chowder paddle. She was sixty-eight, and came down to the market every day to make fifteen gallons of clam chowder in a big stock pot, which she stirred with a sawed-off wooden canoe paddle. She always carried the paddle around. Both Nico and Tony had felt the sharp thwack of the maple blade against their backsides on a regular basis when they were younger. They still feared it and made a quick calculation of its reach whenever Bianca approached with the paddle in her hand. She was still trim, tiny but strong. She wore her dyed hair in a poofy perm, liked loud tops and tight slacks that she covered with a chowder-spattered blue smock when she was cooking at the market. She was trailed by her shadow, Freebie, the older dishwasher, who she'd made her assistant. Shifty-eyed little fuck, Nico thought, working some kind of angle, always buttering up their mom.

"Nicolo, Father Mikey came by to remind me that we're contributing crabs for the Cioppino feed the Woman's Auxiliary is putting on. He wants to pick them up on Friday."

"I know Ma. You told me."

"You're going to have them ready, right?"

Tony said, "Father Mikey is a pain in the ass. A Cioppino feed? What for?"

"They want to renovate the rectory. Fix it up to make it more comfortable. We're doing a big raffle with donated prizes, like a spa treatment and you know, cases of fine wine. Margie Fillipo's son Ken is donating a brand new refrigerator from his store. We've already sold over seven hundred tickets."

Tony made a face and looked at his brother to see if he was thinking what he was thinking—that Father Mikey could jump off the wharf for all he cared. "Christ, he's a priest. How nice does it have to be? I live in a rundown three bedroom craphole that's upside down on the mortgage and he's fixing up that mansion on High Street?"

"Tony, he asked," Bianca said. "What was I supposed to tell him? Besides, I'm the Treasurer of the Women's Auxiliary. I have to do my part."

"You really want my opinion?"

Nico, the big brother and self-appointed peacemaker, shot a look at Tony to shut him up, then looked at his mom. His body language said his devotion to her was like a big weight he was carrying that just got heavier. "How many is he asking for?" he said.

"I told you. Twenty. But you could always throw in a couple more. Cleaned and cracked. We're making flyers and we can mention the market on the list of donors."

Nico looked back at Tony, warning him with his eyes to keep his big mouth shut. "We'll have them ready Friday."

"How much you selling those raffle tickets for, Ma?" Tony asked.

"$15 each. You want to buy some?"

"Maybe you should hit Nico up. I'm tapped out."

"Nico is donating the crabs."

"*Nico* is donating the crabs? I'm the guy who's going out after them."

Nico said, "I'll buy some tickets, Ma." He pulled out a roll of cash from his pocket and peeled off three $20's. "Put me down for four."

Bianca smiled at her first-born. "Thank you, Nicolo. You're going to think about it, right Tony?"

"Sure," he said flatly. "I'll think about it."

****

Shortly after 3:00 the next morning, not quite twenty-four hours after they'd stuck Carmine Bosso in the walk-in freezer, Tony pulled back the black plastic covering one of his legs, pulled up the pants cuff, and touched the ankle. White and cold, like marble. Good. You couldn't cut up a body cleanly if it wasn't frozen pretty solid. You got blood and bits of flesh everywhere, gummed up the band saw that they used to cut steaks from the bigger fish. If you got a body good and frozen it cut clean, like wood. He lifted the two big halibut off the black-bagged corpse, grabbed it around the spot where he thought the waist should be, and hauled it out to the prep area. He laid it down on the tile floor and cut away the trash bags with his filet knife.

Carmine was around seventy, still in pretty good shape for an old guy. Now he was an old dead guy, so what did it matter what kind of shape he kept himself in? His face was composed, eyes closed. He had smooth skin, closely shaved. He was nicely dressed. Around his neck he wore a thin gold chain with a Virgin Mary medal.

"How you doin', Carmine?" Tony asked softly. "What kind of trouble did you get into?" He stared at the corpse for a moment, preparing himself for the task at hand. He pulled on a pair of thick yellow rubber gloves that went halfway up to his elbows, the kind his mother used when she was cleaning up after making the chowder. He never wore gloves when he butchered fish, but this was . . . different.

"So, how'd they do you?" He looked at the body more closely, saw a blood stain on the right shoulder, and rolled him over on his side. The back of his head, next to his right ear, was matted with blood. Gave him a bullet, right up close Tony guessed. Around the entry wound, the Carmine's hair had frozen into blood-tipped spikes. He thought about what his last moments might have been like, and wondered if he knew what was coming when the bullet was fired into the back of his head. He wanted to think maybe he hadn't even realized it was going to happen, that maybe he was sitting in the front seat of a car, talking, laughing, a guy in the back seat just put the gun up there, right up next to the back of his head, and squeezed the trigger. And that was it. Lights out. That wouldn't have been so bad. There are a lot worse ways to go. Some of the dead guys they brought out for disposal were all beat up, their faces a mess. You couldn't even look at them. But Carmine, his face looked calm, even peaceful, his eyes closed like he was asleep.

He hauled the body over to the band saw table, which stood by itself in a corner. He lifted it up and leaned it against the cutting platform, which wasn't nearly big enough to accommodate an entire fifty-pound halibut, let alone a 170-pound corpse. But Tony had learned a few things over the years, and had a system he'd developed. You start at the heavy end, the head and torso, then, tipping the body forward, you slid it down the cutting platform as you progressed. You did the head first, then you did the arms, then the legs. The feet and hands came off last.

As soon as he heard the band saw start up, Sammy start barking beneath the wharf. Like a dog begging for a treat. This isn't halibut, Tony muttered; you're dreaming if you think you're getting any of this. Then he thought, what could it hurt? He sliced off an ear and threw it down the hole in the floor and heard Sammy splash after it. Carmine wouldn't miss it.

It took twenty minutes to cut the guy up, another five minutes to bag the pieces in the same trash bags that had covered him in the freezer. He put the bags into two long plastic bins that they used for transporting ice, and put the bins into the bed of his pickup truck. Dawn was just brightening the eastern sky when he drove off to the harbor.

By 5:00 Tony was pulling out of his slip, seagulls hovering, dipping and rising above his wake. His boat, christened the "Giovanna" after his grandmother, was a 30-foot wooden-hulled classic, originally launched in 1927. It had simple, functional lines, a tiny pilot house and an upcurved bow. A tourist seeing it docked in the harbor might think it was quaint, a good subject for a watercolor, but it was a workhorse, with a 353 Detroit diesel engine that Tony maintained carefully. The Giovanna was his baby. He had it freshly painted every couple of years, white with light blue trim, and was a little obsessive about keeping it clean, the deck scrubbed and tidy, with the lines, nets and tackle all stowed neatly.

His grandfather Carlo, who came over from Genoa in 1922, had commissioned the building of the boat, paying it off in part from the money he made running Canadian whiskey into Santa Carmela during Prohibition. At heart though, Carlo was more a fisherman than a crook, and, after his brief detour into crime, which ended with the repeal of the eighteenth amendment, he spent the rest of his working years pursuing a hard living on the waters of the Monterey Bay, trolling for rock cod, the red cod they called chili peppers, bocaccio, sand dabs, lingcod, salmon and halibut. By the time he died of lung cancer at sixty-three, his face and hands had seen so much weather that they looked like they were carved from wood. His son Nicky— Nico and Tony's father—was raised to be a fisherman, but wanted more out of life, and in the late fifties he found an opportunity to make a little money on the side by running Asian heroin into Santa Carmela from freighters he'd meet thirty miles offshore. He liked the easy money, and he especially liked pushing other people around and playing the big shot. He was a big fan of gangster movies; they gave him ideas about the broader possibilities of his second career. So he expanded his activities into gambling and prostitution, which meant he sniffed out anyone in Santa Carmela who had gotten into those lines and convinced them to bring him on as a silent partner, providing protection mostly, protection from Nicky's gang of thugs, three guys from his high school class who liked loud clothes and hated real work. In 1968 Nicky acquired a bait and tackle shop on the Municipal Wharf, a half-mile long pier supported by crisscrossed pilings, which was pretty rundown in those days, before the city found some state redevelopment money to fix it up. The owner of the shop was a gambler, and not a lucky one. He was into Nicky for over $10,000 and wasn't making any progress paying it off. Nicky convinced him to sign over the business in exchange for forgiving the debt—a proposal he made with a crowbar dangling loosely in his hand and his three guys standing behind him with their arms crossed. Nicky had a plan. He expanded the shop, put in a fish market and a little inside seating area, a counter with eight stools where tourists could get a shrimp cocktail, a cup of chowder or a crab Louis salad. It wasn't about making money as much as giving Nicky a way to launder the cash he was pulling in. He also liked hanging out at the market, smoking his way through a pack and a half of Pall Malls each day, having everyone call him boss.

One thing led to another, and he made connections with mob guys in San Francisco, the Maladago family. They formed a loose alliance. In return for his loyalty and a cut of the profits, the Maladagos threw a few business opportunities Nicky's way, sponsoring his control of the squid distribution out of the harbor south of the wharf, setting him up as the guy who controlled the installation and servicing of pinball machines and later video games in Santa Carmela's bars, bowling alleys and pool halls. Periodically, the Maladagos would call on the Connole's to dispose of a body, no questions asked.

When Nicky died of massive heart attack after helping himself to a third serving of the smothered pork chops at the Elks Lodge lunch buffet, his boys inherited an anemic crime operation which neither one was interested in sustaining, let alone growing. The main source of income had always come from the squid business, but that had dwindled during a cyclical shortfall of the squid population in the bay, and dried up completely after the Vietnamese fishermen, who were the only ones who were still making a living at it, banded together and set up their own distribution company. The Connole's had a few video poker games placed in the dark corners of the last handful of dive bars in Santa Carmela, but the revenue entry that Nico made on his spreadsheet every month for what he labeled "Gaming" got smaller and smaller. It was easier to go online if you wanted that kind of action. What else? The boys still did a little loan sharking, mostly to old customers; they collected a little protection money from the nearby motels where the hookers and pimps plied their trade. But the drug business was a bust, controlled now by Mexican gangs who wouldn't fall in line and threatened to cut off your balls and stuff them in your mouth if you got in their way. Who needed that?

Things were changing for the Maladagos too, at least that's what Nico and Tony concluded, since there hadn't been much contact over the past few years, and none at all since Vincent's stroke. And now they showed up with the Carmine Bosso's corpse and this woman Tony had never seen before, who said they were going to have to talk.

The bay was calm with only a slight swell, and the Giovanna's engine ran smoothly at about fifteen knots. Fast enough. Tony wasn't in any hurry. Unlike his brother Nico, who was afraid of water, uncomfortable around engines and machinery and had a thing about keeping his hands clean, Tony felt at home on the bay, with the boat's engine chugging away below decks, riding the gentle swell out to his crab traps. When he left the harbor the sky just beginning to brighten, but the sun was still hidden. The Giovanna had an old Wood-Freeman auto-pilot that allowed him to point the bow in the direction he wanted and keep it on course, so he didn't have to mind the ship's wheel as long as he kept an eye out for the running lights of any other vessels. He had a Garmin in the pilot house too, just in case, although he would bet anyone that he could find his string of crab traps blindfolded.

This was the best time of the day, a time when Tony could tune everything out but the bay around him, lock onto the mellow vibration of the boat's engine and let his mind wander. His thoughts returned to last night's visit. Vincent's CFO, or whatever she called herself, had made quite an impression. Tony couldn't get her striking face out his mind, especially her full lips, her dark eyebrows and piercing gaze, daring you to check her out. Quite a package from the front, and even better from the back. He'd taken a good look as she walked out, gracefully sidestepping the water puddled on the concrete floor— slender, with a nice ass and ankles and just a trace of definition at the calves. She was wearing expensive looking high heels, nylons with a fine black seam running up the back of her legs.

But what was with all the drama? If the Maladagos had something to say to him and Nico, they could just say it. If they weren't happy with something, just put it out there. Tony's opinion was that they didn't need Vincent Maladago and the crumbs he threw their way anymore. They weren't getting rich, but they were making enough off the fish market, the restaurant and life was OK. They were getting by and not getting hassled.

He set his line of traps in the same place every year, about six miles south of the harbor where the water was fifty fathoms deep, right before the bottom dropped off sharply into the mile-deep canyon beneath the Monterey Bay. It took about twenty minutes to motor out to the string of forty traps that he checked, harvested and re-baited four or five days a week when the weather wasn't too rough during crab season. More ambitious commercial fisherman ran about 400 traps, and went out in teams of three, humping their butts to keep up with the boat, which the skippers, who were almost always the owners, ran without pause. Like being on a freaking treadmill. Tony wasn't lazy, but he moved at his own pace, always had. Because he worked alone and could sell the crabs he caught at retail in the market, he was able to make pretty good money without busting his ass, make a couple thousand a week during the season, putting in about six hours a day.

A pink sunrise stained the tops of the mountains of Big Sur that humped darkly in the distance. The sun would be coming up over the mouth of the Salinas River close to the tall stacks of the power plant at Moss Landing. By the time he reached the first yellow buoy that marked the southern end of his string, it was light enough to get to work.

He idled the boat, and went out to the deck. The first order of business was the burlap bags.

There were three of them, one for the torso, one for the legs, and one that held the severed head, hands and feet. The line from a barely remembered nursery rhyme came back to him, and made him smile. *Yes sir, yes sir, three bags full.* He put four ten-pound trawl weights into each bag. He commemorated the first bag to the deep by muttering "over you go," and the second with nothing more than a breathy grunt. He paused before throwing the third sack over, struck by an inspiration he marveled at for a minute before deciding to go with it.

He left the third sack where it was and instead picked up the long-handled gaff. He used it to snag the next yellow buoy. His hydraulic puller was mounted on a davit, which he swung over the water. The buoy was attached to thick nylon trucker's rope. He looped the rope over the puller, which he started with a foot switch, hauling the first trap up from the bottom.

When the trap came out of the water—holding a jumble of around fifteen crawling crabs—he stopped the winch. He grabbed the trap and pulled it toward him, resting it on the edge of the live well in the back of the boat. The trap was round and deep, with a heavy re-bar frame covered by stainless steel wire mesh. He tipped it over, opening the hinged top door. The crabs spilled out into the well. He usually put fresh bait in the trap next before swinging it back out over the water and dropping it back down into the depths. He used squid for bait, putting it into perforated plastic jars that clipped onto the wire frame of the basket.

But in this trap he thought he'd try something different. Change things up a little bit. Grabbing the last burlap bag, he dumped its grisly contents into the trap. Marveling at what a prick he could be, he flipped the top door down, and swung it back over the water. With

Carmine Bosso's severed head facing him, he lowered the trap slowly, watching it sink below the surface on its way to the bottom of the bay.

That ought to catch you some nice fat crabs for your Cioppino feed, Father Mikey.

****

They *all* have beaver teeth, Jana concluded, looking around the boardroom at the five middle-aged Wakefield siblings who were gathered together for the Bay-View Boardwalk's weekly executive staff meeting. At first glance, it made them look cheerful and ambitious. She was learning that they were neither, with the exception of Teddy, the oldest brother and CEO of the Wakefield empire. Teddy was a bundle of energy and ideas, most of which were wearily rejected by his siblings. This was the first time Jana had been invited to attend the executive staff meeting that they held every Tuesday morning at 11:00. As an unpaid intern, she wouldn't have expected to be asked, but Teddy Wakefield had brought her in to shed some light on the social media blitz that she'd been working on to promote his latest brainstorm, the Zombie Invasion—Z-Day for short—which he wanted to run on Memorial Day, just five days away.

A little apprehensive about making the right first impression at the meeting, Jana had removed the little silver barbell she wore through her left eyebrow, and instead of her usual skinny-fit black T-shirt, she'd put on a long sleeved-blouse—only slightly wrinkly—to cover up the tattoo on her arm.

Teddy sat at the head of the table. Seated down from him on either side were Blaine Wakefield, who was in charge of Finance, Arletta Wakefield, who headed up Human Resources, Stanhope Wakefield who ran Operations, and Glenda Wakefield, who was in charge of Facilities. Besides Jana, the only other non-Wakefield present was the head of security, Conrad Ferl, sitting next to her, a fat ex-cop who slouched in his chair like a good old boy loafing in front of a country gas station. He smelled like comb cleaner and gave off a weird, sleazy vibe, his thinning hair swept back in a banjo string pompadour. He was whittling a stick, shaving off curl after curl of wood onto a neat pile in front of him. It was hard to tell what he was carving, but it kept him busy; the pile kept growing and the stick kept getting smaller.

The first item of business was a discussion of a radical change that Teddy was proposing—replacing the single-ply toilet paper in the Bay-View's public bathrooms with double-ply.

"I don't know, Teddy," Blaine said, peeking around his sister Arletta's ample bosom toward his brother like he was peering around the corner of a building. As Chief Financial Officer, Blaine's considered himself the personal guardian every dollar that came through the Bay-View's gates. "That two-ply paper is pretty expensive."

"You can't get a good wipe with the stuff we're putting in there," Teddy argued forcefully. "Glenda and Arletta, women use more T.P. than men. What's your opinion on this?"

"I wouldn't be caught dead in one of those stink holes," Glenda said. No one thought it wise to point out that the upkeep of those stink holes was her responsibility. Her siblings knew that you challenged Glenda at your peril.

"You just have to make sure you're washing your hands a little more carefully after you finish up," Arletta offered.

"Maybe that's why our water bill's getting so high," Blaine muttered, jotting a note to himself on a legal pad.

"Exactly!" Teddy said, color rising in his cheeks. "It's false economy! And you're kidding yourself to think that folks aren't doubling up that single-ply anyway. It's so thin you can see your fingerprints through it—you pull out big bunches of it and wad it up until you get a fistful."

Blaine had an answer for that. "We worked with our paper supply salesman to get rolls that are just a little tight for the dispenser. Nine times out of ten, all you can pull off is a single sheet. One roll can last a week, even during peak season. I've been tracking it. On a spreadsheet."

Jana tuned the discussion out. She was doodling on a pad she'd brought in with her, trying to come up with an idea for altering the tattoo that read "Chuy", inked high up on her left hip. She could probably get it turned into a butterfly, have the tattoo artist use the capital C as the outline of one of the wings and go from there. But butterflies weren't really her thing. A bat might work though, a black bat with red eyes, wings outspread, showing its little bat fangs.

She started playing with a few cartoony ideas as Teddy Wakefield moved the discussion to the next agenda item: a report from his brother Stanhope on the progress of a new attraction that Teddy had been planning for two years, Creepy Cavern. Creepy Cavern was a repurposing of The Ant Hill, a long winding tunnel that took thrill-seekers in a little train down beneath the Bay-View, deep into the musty interior of what was supposed to be a giant ants' nest. It had first opened was 1962. The Cold War was at its height, and the public was receptive to the phony backstory behind the Ant Hill—that if ordinary ants were bathed in radioactive fallout from a Soviet bomb they could grow into extraordinary ants, bigger than crocodiles, with waving antennae, scissoring mandibles and, it was whispered, an appetite for children. The Ant Hill and its tunnels had been sealed up in 1989, a casualty of waning popularity and the Loma Prieta earthquake, which caved in the queen's chamber.

Prompted by his brother Blaine, who was of the mind that there was no need to let perfectly good giant ants go to waste, especially if you could create a revenue stream from them, Teddy had re-imagined the Ant Hill as Creepy Cavern. They could use the existing tunnels—shoring them up, of course—and the three mechanical ants that hadn't disintegrated in the damp over the past twenty-some years, adding a host of other outsized scary creatures that would suddenly pop out of the darkness as the little train carrying its screaming passengers clattered along the narrow tunnel tracks: a stag beetle as big as a rhino; a nine-foot long neon orange centipede that crawled on the tunnel roof inches overhead; praying mantises ready to grab a meal from the train as it went by; a scuttling scorpion, its stinger poised to strike; a blizzard of screeching bats; and spiders—sleek spindly spiders, thick hairy spiders, spiders that jumped out of trap doors, spiders that raced toward the train, and creepiest of all, a spider that was poised to prey on a struggling fly trapped in its web, a fly with a terrified human face. Teddy had gotten the idea from a movie that had scared the bejeezus out of him when he was twelve.

Teddy had decided to make the grand opening of the Creepy Cavern part of the fun of the annual Memorial Day summer kickoff. It was due to open at 11 AM that day, and a ribbon-cutting ceremony had been planned. The mayor of Santa Carmela had been invited, and the Bay-View's machine shop had been tasked with making a pair of gigantic scissors out of sheet metal for the occasion.

"Creepy Cavern's looking pretty darn good. I'd say we're just about there," Stanhope said, "but we're at the mercy of Mr. Jefferson. And he says he won't wrap things up until we stop charging him rent."

Mr. Albert Einstein Jefferson was the animatronics wizard that Teddy had hired a year earlier to bring his vision to life. His résumé included stints at Disneyland, The Lost World and, more recently, at The Legends of Polka Museum and Gift Emporium in Fergus Falls, where he had breathed life into a twinkly-eyed recreation of accordion maestro Bruno Glanz. A.E. Jefferson had a reputation for being a little quirky, but also, just maybe, a genius. Why else, he'd ask, did his mother name him Albert Einstein?

Teddy was confused. "We're charging him rent?"

Blaine jumped in to explain, "He's been living in his workshop. Sleeping there every night. He's got a little bed in the back and it looks like he's figured out a way to order in Chinese food from the Golden Bhudda across the street. Those little cardboard containers are all over his workbench and the place smells like an egg roll. I called him on it last week and told him we'd have to subtract $400 a month from his pay."

"What did he say?"

"I can't repeat his exact words in front of the ladies in the room."

"Cut the bullshit, Blaine," Glenda said. "Did he tell you to screw yourself? Stick your head where the sun don't shine?"

Teddy said, "I wish you'd discussed this with me first."

"Lodging for employees is a form of compensation," Blaine sniffed. "You can look it up in the tax code."

Teddy turned to Stanhope. "What's left to button up? Didn't you take a dry run last week?"

"I did." Jana could see that Stanhope liked messing with his brother, and was drawing this out for his own enjoyment.

"And . . . was it scary?"

"I nearly pissed my pants when we came around a corner and all of a sudden the bats were flapping their black wings all around me and going 'eek, eek, eek'." Stanhope made a bat face and waved his arms to demonstrate.

Jana decided that she wouldn't go with the bat tattoo after all. The idea suddenly seemed stupid.

"So what's left to be done?"

"Well, the centipede has a little hitch in its git-along that should probably be fixed. And the praying mantises appear to be . . . well, it looks like they're trying to make little praying mantises."

"What do you mean?"

"I mean it looks like the guy praying mantis just had his prayers answered. As you're going by in the little train you see him climb on top of the other one and he starts humping away."

"I'd pay money to see that," Conrad whispered out of the corner of his mouth.

"Entirely inappropriate," Blaine huffed.

"Oh . . . and there's one more problem. You're especially not going to like this, Teddy."

"Not going to like what?"

"Your fly. With the little face."

"He hasn't finished the fly yet?"

"Oh, he's finished it. Sort of. That Mr. Jefferson has a sense of humor, I'll say that. He made the face look just like you, Teddy. Those buck teeth and everything."

"I don't have buck teeth. I have a slight overbite. *You* have buck teeth. Maybe the fly looks like you."

"Maybe. Except here's the other thing—the fly is wearing a silly little bow tie, just like you." Teddy had started wearing a bow tie a couple years back, thinking it would make him look a little zany and fun. He thought of it as his trademark look. The tie he was wearing today was red with yellow dots. The way his face was flaming now as he listened to his brother, it looked like he'd tied it too tight. "So here's this little fly with your face and your bow tie, and it's struggling and thrashing and trying like hell to pull itself free of the web, and this big spooky spider scrambling down the web in that creepy spider way with its fangs dripping, and it's coming after *you*, Teddy."

Teddy fought the urge to say something petty and mean to Stanhope. "If you are trying to get my goat, Stanhope, I'm afraid I'll have to disappoint you. My goat is still firmly under my control." As he always did after he'd made a little joke, Teddy paused to take in the reactions of his audience. The Wakefield siblings and Conrad Ferl stared at him blankly. Jana couldn't quite bring herself to smile, but she winced pleasantly at Teddy, which seemed to satisfy him. "I'll talk to Mr. Jefferson today. I'm sure there's an explanation." He signaled with a purposeful glance at the printed agenda in front of him that it was time to move on to the next topic, the Memorial Day kickoff to the summer season. The summer kickoff was a Bay-View tradition. They gave away free cotton candy to kids under six, and they brought in a famous celebrity, like David Hasselhof, or a novelty act like The Fabulous Break Dancing Chimps to bring in crowds and provide momentum to carry them into their peak season.

"I'm afraid we got some bad news yesterday morning," Teddy said. He hesitated. He was about to drop a bombshell. "The Magnificent Marquardt won't be able to make his appearance." The Magnificent Marquardt was a tightrope-walking daredevil Teddy had hired to traverse a wire stretched high above the Bay-View between the spires of the Moorish turrets at either end of the half-mile boardwalk. "He slipped last week on a high wire up above a Mets game."

Arletta put her hand to her bosom. "He died?"

No, Teddy explained, but it was a close call. He landed smack on the wire with his crotch, which broke his fall. "He was holding one of those heavy balancing pole thingies and the extra weight made him bounce a couple of times, but never actually fell off. So he survived, but his . . . his, uh, testicles are a little worse for the wear. He's going to have to keep them in an ice bath for a week or so."

"I used to get that way after necking with my high school girlfriend," Conrad Ferl muttered, sneaking a glance at Jana, who smiled back at him like someone had ordered her to with a gun to her head. Hadn't these dinosaurs ever heard of sexual harassment? No one seemed to pay attention to him, least of all Teddy, who was eager to share his backup plan.

"The good news is I've come up with a Plan B, and it's a doozy." He paused, waiting for someone to ask him for details. He scanned the table eagerly, but no one bit.

Jana had doodled WTF!!!! on her writing pad and was going over each letter again and again with her pen until she tore through the paper.

The silence was excruciating, finally broken by Arletta. "A doozy?"

Teddy nodded and slapped his hand on the table. "Zombies!" he cried, then rushed headlong into a breathless explanation of his Big New Idea. "In case you haven't noticed, the whole flipping country has been going bonkers over zombies. They're everywhere—zombie books, zombie movies, zombie TV shows. People can't get enough of them. Google 'zombies' and you get 52,000,000 results. Google 'puppies', and you get 28,000,000. What's the math tell us? Zombies are almost twice as popular as puppies."

"Puppies are sure cuter," Arletta said.

"I think zombies are stupid," Glenda said. "I mean they're supposed to be dead, right? So why don't they just go off and leave the rest of us alone? When I die I am not going to drag my putrefying body around chasing after normal people. I plan on going straight to heaven."

Stanhope who had been looking at the ceiling shaking his head, threw in a more practical question. "Teddy, what the hell are you talking about?"

"I'm calling it 'Zombie Invasion at the Bay-View', 'Z-Day' for short. It's kind of a zany, happening kind of thing. You get people to dress up in their best zombie clothes, all ragged and tattered, and make their faces up like they've been dead for a couple of weeks—"

"Sounds like me after my last trip to Vegas," Conrad Ferl murmured. Now he was looking at Jana with one eyebrow raised, like they shared some secret understanding. Her fake smile tightening, she shifted away from him in her chair.

"—and have them all show up at the Bay-View on Memorial Day."

Stanhope studied his brother as though he were a mentally disturbed stranger who had taken Teddy's place at the table. "Maybe you need to take a break from all of the stress you're under, Teddy. I'm no doctor, but you seem a little wound up."

Now Teddy was exasperated. "You've got to think outside the box—all of you! You're getting stodgy. You're out of touch with young people."

"So you're saying that these young people you know so much about are going to get themselves up like they've been moldering in the grave and swarm into the Bay-View?"

"You give them an incentive. Something for free."

Blaine looked like a cat making a convulsive effort to bring up a hairball. Apparently something had gotten stuck in his throat—a single word that he finally dislodged and spat out. *"Free?"* He shook his head violently and pointed out that they're already giving away cotton candy to the kiddies that day. Last year that cost them almost $168.00.

Teddy had no patience for his brother's knee-jerk stinginess. "You make money by giving it away. It's the new viral economy, which you may not have heard about because you're too busy staring at spreadsheets all day. What I'm suggesting is that we give a voucher good for three free rides to everyone who comes to the park dressed as a zombie that night."

No one said anything. Then Arletta ventured a counter-proposal. "Instead of zombies, what if we gave them this voucher thing if they came dressed up as angels? I'm not saying your basic idea's not a good one, but I'd be more in favor of it if we could give it a Christian theme."

Blaine was tapping away at the calculator he always carried. "If we give away ride tickets, we'll lose revenue," he said. "If your average ticket price is $5.00 and you times that by three rides, that's $15.00 and if 1,000 people show up for this thing and are given the zombie voucher that means you've lost $15,000." He lifted up the calculator to show the result to the others at the table.

Teddy wasn't having it. "Small thinking. Those 1,000 people are going to go on other rides, buy 32 ounce sodas, cotton candy, foot longs, play skee ball, have fake tattoos stenciled on their biceps. . . Let's say each of them spends $40.00 on all of that. That's $40,000." Blaine, who didn't trust mental arithmetic, tapped it out on his calculator and grudgingly nodded after achieving the same total as Teddy. "What if 2,000 additional people show up? 3,000?" Blaine was madly tapping away at his calculator to come up with the answers, but

Teddy was moving on. "I've thought this out backwards and forwards, and I'm convinced that it's a winner. Look everybody, we've got to do something. Year after year our receipts are going down. Last year, with the whale and everything, was just about our worst year ever." Everyone thought glumly about the whale for a minute. It was a blue whale, fifty feet long, that had died and washed up on the beach in front of the Bay-View, already in state of advanced decomposition. They tried dragging it back out into the bay, but the tide kept pushing it back in, and the rotting creature kept getting smellier and smellier. The stench was so overpowering that no one wanted to come to the Bay-View for the two weeks it took to get authorization from the proper state agency to bury it. Just when people were starting to come back, the buried carcass—which in its sandy grave had further decayed, distending like a big balloon filled with methane gas—exploded. The Santa Carmela Bugle described the aftermath as "a rancid rain of putrefied blubber." Teddy continued, "The Bay-View Boardwalk has become a relic of a bygone day. This is not just about the money," before Blaine could object to that blasphemy, Teddy intoned, "it's about being *relevant.*"

"With a zombie invasion?" Glenda asked.

"It's like I've been trying to tell you, zombies are a cultural phenomenon. Zombies are hip, right Jana?"

Jana looked up from her doodling. Every beaver-tusked Wakefield face was turned toward her, the stand-in for an entire generation of young consumers. "Totally," she said, thinking that Teddy's embrace of the phenomenon was a sure sign that it was over, gone the way of Beanie Babies and Crocs.

Teddy was on a roll now. "We need something like this to change our image. What do youngsters think of when they think of the Bay-View?"

Conrad Ferl was the only one who offered an answer. "Cheesy rides, barf on the roller coaster, rip-off games, fat girls in tight shorts and skinny dudes with turned around baseball caps . . ."

"We're old school," Teddy continued. "Boring. Your parent's amusement park."

Conrad wasn't finished with his list. "Stinky toilets, brats throwing tantrums, cotton candy stuck to your face, perverts lurking in dark corners . . ."

"This is going to put us back on their map," Teddy declared, talking over Conrad. "I've got Jana here working on a social media campaign." He introduced Jana, and explained how she had won the coveted Wakefield Fellowship at CSUCC, California State University of the Central Coast, awarded to the top Marketing student in the senior class. The honor came with a three-month internship at the Bay-View Boardwalk, unpaid of course, but offering a pre-career experience that was priceless, and a food allowance consisting $12 per day, almost enough for two corn dogs and a small soda.

"Jana, can you tell everyone what you've already done to generate buzz for this thing?"

"Sure." She surveyed the rapt Wakefield faces surrounding her, beaver mouths hanging slightly open, prominent front teeth glinting in the light from the overhead fixture. "I started by creating a new Z-Day Facebook page that I've linked to the main Bay-View Boardwalk page. I've set up an Instagram feed, a Tumblr blog and a Twitter account, @bvzombieinvasion, with tweets going out every couple of hours. If you're on Twitter, you should have started seeing them. We're going to do a YouTube video—"

"I'm going to be in it," Teddy said. "Made up like a zombie."

"I'm hoping to create a comprehensive social media launch platform," Jana continued. "We're already starting to see traffic bouncing back and forth across the different sites, creating some buzz."

Apart from Teddy, who was beaming with satisfaction, the Wakefields seemed mystified by what she was saying.

"How much does all of this publicity cost?" Blaine asked, the fingers of his right hand poised over the keys of his calculator.

Jana deferred to Teddy, who was only too happy to field that question.

"Nothing! All this social media stuff—it's free! And it's already working! SmartWire caught wind of it and posted a blurb which a producer from Good Morning Central Coast saw. I'm going to be interviewed for Friday morning's show. The Twitter thing is really exploding. Jana started sending out tweets the day before yesterday and they're being re-tweeted and everything. I've got some here on my smartphone." He fumbled his phone out of his pocket. "Jana showed me how to get Twitter on it." He squinted at the touch screen of his phone and jabbed it a couple of times with his index finger, frowned and said, "Wait," several times before handing the phone over to Jana, who opened the app and handed the phone back to him. Teddy read from the Twitter feed, "'Being dead has its perks—like three free rides for zombies at the Bay-View on Memorial Day. #Z-Day.' Listen to this one: 'Message to the undead: drag your rotting carcasses down to the BV for the Zombie Invasion. Memorial Day. #Z-Day'. And here's another, 'Who wouldn't be caught dead at the BV when the zombies invade, #Z-Day?'"

Stanhope wasn't happy about something. "You're saying 'BV'. You mean the Bay-View, right?"

"Yes, of course. But Jana thought we should start trying to re-brand. Refer to the park as the BV. It's got a younger edge to it. You know, like 'It's not your parents' Bay-View, it's the BV'."

"B.S." Glenda said.

Arletta had her own question that couldn't wait. "Wait, are zombies dead or undead?"

"They're both," Teddy, who was now an expert, explained. "They die, then they come back to life, but they're not alive, they're undead. But you're all missing the point. You can't get caught up in nitpicking. You've just got to get into the spirit of it." He looked down at his phone as he thumbed up another Tweet.

"Listen, here's one I thought up: 'If you're looking for fun and a social occasion, come down to the Bay-View for the Zombie Invasion.# Z-Day'" Jana fake-chuckled. She still clung to the faint hope that Teddy might pay her a salary someday.

Stanhope frowned. "I think this is one of the stupidest ideas you've come up with, and that's saying something. But it looks like you're not asking us for a decision on this so much as telling us about your decision and advising us to get out of the way."

"I'm tell you this thing is going viral! The train has left the station and it's picking up speed!"

Conrad Ferl had finished his whittling project, and now lifted the finished product, a beautifully turned toothpick, to his mouth. Popping it in and rolling it from one side to the other, he said, "Let me know when we're about to run out of track so I can jump off."

****

Three mascots roamed the spattered pavement of the Bay-View Boardwalk: Pete the Pelican, Toby the Sea Turtle, and the most recent addition to the corps, the Smiles Ambassador. Pete the Pelican was the senior member of the group. The Bay-View website described him as "a wise old bird and seafarer. Pete has roamed the Seven Seas but calls the Bay-View Boardwalk home. If you see him, ask him about the time he took a ride in a waterspout!" Toby the Sea Turtle was "a high energy scamp, who loves eliciting laughter from kids of all ages with his zany antics." The third mascot, the Smiles Ambassador, "has never met a child—or a Mom or Dad—he didn't like. He loves handing out free smiles—just ask!" Teddy Wakefield had gotten the inspiration for the Smiles Ambassador two years earlier after running into a Walmart greeter. Literally. Wouldn't it be great, he thought after helping the old guy up, if the Bay-View had its own doddering oldster wandering around the park dispensing good cheer? His white-haired uncle Niles, who had spent forty years as an insurance agent making his living largely off of his friendly face and family connections, was the logical choice. Uncle Niles had been happily spending his golden years teaching himself to play the Hawaiian lap steel guitar and building birdhouses. He wasn't as enthusiastic as everyone else about the idea, but his wife couldn't bear to hear another strangled note of "Leilehua" while she tried to concentrate on QVC, and Niles was forced to accept the appointment.

Teddy dressed him in a bright pink jacket, white gloves and straw boater. He wore a white paper carnation pinned to his lapel along with what Teddy called "fun buttons"; one that said "Hi!" and another that read, "Free Smiles!"

For two seasons, Niles accepted his daily exile from home with reasonably good humor, smiling, shaking hands and waving at the Bay-View fun seekers. But, as his third season got underway a month earlier, it was clear that he wasn't the same cheerful old codger. The birds had gotten to him, especially the seagulls, which were a constant voracious presence in the park. He had come to the conclusion that they were singling him out, staring at him with their beady red eyes, surrounding him wherever he turned. Spooked, he started chasing after the gulls, shouting and waving his arms. Sometimes his straw boater flew off his head and rolled down the boardwalk like a loose hubcap. His wild charges scared the visitors more than the birds; people started complaining and, after a family conference, Niles was reunited with his steel guitar and the serene home life he'd always dreamed of for his retirement.

When Jana caught wind of the opening, she'd seized the opportunity to get Andrew in as Niles' replacement. She had just started her internship, but had already established a mentor/protégé relationship with Teddy that was based on her ambition and Teddy's flattered response to this cute young woman with stars in her eyes who seemed to hang on his every brilliant word—she even took notes when they talked, which made him feel especially wise.

Andrew had been out of work for a couple of weeks, having lost a job cleaning cages at a pet store, which had something to do with the both the hamster cage and the python cage being left open overnight. So maybe a pet store wasn't the right fit for Andrew; but he'd be perfect, Jana thought, as the Smiles Ambassador. If there was one thing he did well, even at the most inappropriate times, it was smile. Getting him *not* to smile was the hard thing. And while it was only a part-time job, the ambassadorship paid minimum wage, so at least one member of the family could get a paycheck from the stingy Wakefields. Since they'd both be at the Bay-View, Jana could also keep her eye on him, which was no small consideration.

She thought it might be best to broach the subject with her new boss when he was distracted so he wouldn't have to think long and hard about it. She found her opening when Teddy was squinting down the barrel of a rifle.

"How old is he?" Teddy asked. He was on what he called his "quality control rounds". Every day for at least an hour he would walk the park, helping himself to treats at the concessions and stopping at random at one of the booths to play a game. He had wandered over to the shooting gallery and was taking aim at a flotilla of steel ducks, yelping with delight if by some random chance he happened to nail one. When she answered that Andrew was twenty, Teddy frowned, taking aim at line of steel plates that had just popped up.

"We want someone older for this role."

Jana was ready for this objection. "Andrew's an old soul," she said. "He's sweet and people really like him. And I think he'd fit right into the pink jacket."

Teddy squeezed the rifle's trigger, firing a succession of shots. "Did you see that? I hit one! I heard it!" He held his palm up for a high five, and then redirected his keen analytical mind to the question of Andrew's suitability for the appointment as Ambassador of Smiles. "No alterations on the jacket? That's a plus. Why don't you bring him by, take him to Arletta and get him on the payroll."

And it was as simple as that. The next day Andrew filled out his employment paperwork with Jana's help and was given his white gloves, straw boater and pink jacket, which was actually a little tight, especially across his stomach, the site of a dramatic tug of war between the middle button and the button hole.

Arletta asked her son Ricky, aka Toby the Sea Turtle, to show Andrew the ropes.

There weren't many ropes to be shown. Ricky, who Andrew remembered as being a couple years ahead of him in high school—and a terror to the kids in Special Ed—took him through a door that said "Employees Only", then down some stairs that led to the Bay-View's basement level. From what Andrew could see, the subterranean Bay-View was a maze of fluorescent-lighted corridors that stretched underground the length of the park. He was immediately intrigued by the mysteries of this netherworld but Ricky wasn't interested in being his guide. He would only go so far as to say that the basement level housed a machine shop, a space where mechanics worked on the park's vehicles, storage, and what he called "junk like that"—all of which would apparently be too exhausting to detail. Ricky barely took the time to show Andrew the locker where he could change into his Ambassador's get-up.

"Then what do I do?" Andrew asked. "After I put these clothes on?"

"I don't know," Ricky shrugged. "My uncle Niles more or less just walked around looking like an idiot. I guess that's what they want you to do."

He left Andrew to get dressed and find his way back up the stairs and into the sunlight on his own.

Thirty minutes later, Jana, who since their mother died five years earlier had spent much of her life trying to keep Andrew on track, found him staring transfixed at the taffy pulling machine in the Kandy Kitchen. "Come on, Andrew," she said, taking him by the elbow and directing him into the flow of foot traffic. "You've got a job to do."

The first thing Jana did was set his straw boater at a jaunty angle and rotate his fun buttons so the lettering was right-side-up. Then she coached him on how to wave at the visitors—"Pretend you're wiping the fog off the bathroom mirror"—encouraged him to keep circulating, and warned him against staring too long at people.

It worked out pretty well, Andrew thought. The people who noticed him generally seemed puzzled by just what it was he was trying to convey with his spacey smile and mechanical wave. Some thought he was a mime, and took pictures with him. Every so often children would spot him and run up to him, to be quickly rescued by their mothers who imagined some creepy intent beneath Andrew's oddly placid expression. But most people ignored him, and that was OK.

The only problem was that it got boring. Andrew's shift ran from noon to 4:00 PM, and when all you do is smile and pretend to wipe the fog off of the bathroom mirror, it can get a little tedious, even for Andrew, who could easily spend hours staring off into space.

So, especially toward the end of his shift, he tended to gravitate toward the game arcade.

The game arcade at the Bay-View, was a cavernous high-ceilinged room half the size of a football field that was painted in circus colors and echoed with a crackpot symphony of chimes, ringing bells, roaring race cars, the rat-tat-tat of automatic weapons, explosions, and submarine klaxon dive alarms. It was exciting, but pretty overwhelming. Andrew was too timid to play any of the hundreds of games, but he liked watching other people play, especially Ricky Wakefield, who spent almost all of his free time there.

Ricky, with his blond Mohawk, neck twitches and facial tics, was the star of the arcade. He seemed to be surrounded by a force field, an aura of hectic energy. No one else played with as much intensity, straining with every cord of his wiry frame as he worked the game controls or slapped the pinball flippers, muttering, cursing, wincing and coming close to collapsing if the game went the wrong way. He was always easy to spot, and Andrew would edge up to stand at his shoulder, taking in the spastic drama that was Ricky Wakefield singlehandedly battling an army of aliens, or a swarm of zombies, or a flock of razor-clawed pterodactyls.

Ricky was his friend, sort of, but also sort of his nemesis. He thought he knew everything, but he couldn't name all the planets, didn't know what times the 49 bus stopped at the corner of Beach and Barson, and thought he knew more about ninjas than Andrew, which was a joke. He had never even seen half of the ninja movies, not even *Mask of the Ninja* or *Ninja Assassin*, and you could tell he had never read a single book about ninjas. But he let Andrew hang around when he was playing games in the arcade, and that was as close to a friendship as Andrew had.

Besides, they were both members of what Andrew thought of as the brotherhood of mascots, even though Ricky, who ran around the park disguised as a cool, funny creature—a sea turtle in sunglasses who danced and spun and high-fived everyone—never let him forget who sat higher on the pecking order. Maybe that's why Andrew felt compelled to let him know about his own special credentials. Impulsively, less than a week after he'd met Ricky, he had confided his secret identity as the Shadow Warrior, which was probably a mistake.

When he was roaming the arcade, Ricky was locked in a zone, usually so engrossed in whatever game he was playing that he wasn't even aware of Andrew trailing him. Today, standing at the controls of *House of the Dead*, his gaze fixed on the screen, he only took notice of Andrew after his avatar had run out of weapons and was overrun by a vicious pack of mutant devil dogs. The defeat was devastating. He collapsed on top of the game console, burying his head in his arms and diving into a deep personal pit of despair. When he finally emerged, he blinked, took a breath, and looked at Andrew, who had been standing quietly behind him.

Ricky wasn't happy, and Andrew was an easy target. "Why are you always smiling?"

"I don't know."

"Ninjas don't smile."

"Some do."

"Only cartoon ninjas. Not real ninjas. And guess what? Ninjas don't wear headbands that say 'Ninja' on them."

That was probably another mistake, which he'd made a couple days ago, showing Ricky the headband that Jana had helped buy online from a ninja website. But he was so proud of it that he couldn't help it. It was white, with a red blot like a sun above the word NINJA, written in black brush-stroked letters. He wanted to laugh because what Ricky had said just didn't make sense. What else would a ninja's headband say?

Ricky moved off and stationed himself at the claw crane, his eye on a glinting silver watch that sat with tantalizing prominence on top of a jumble of prizes. Andrew followed him.

"I was in a fight last night," Andrew said.

Ricky didn't seem to have heard him. He was concentrating on positioning the claw to drop onto the clear plastic case that contained the watch. His neck was twitching, but he kept his hand steady.

Andrew continued, "Five crooks jumped me when I was on patrol."

Ricky wasn't about to shift his focus away from the watch. "This is the hardest prize to grab because the claw just barely fits around the box."

Andrew found himself drawn into the drama of the claw and the watch, and for a moment forgot the exciting news he wanted to share. With painstaking precision, Ricky put the claw directly above the watch, and then, pressing a button, lowered it squarely on top of it, exactly where he wanted. He paused for effect, rubbed the tips of his fingers together like a safecracker, twirled his index finger and decisively pushed the button that lifted the claw. As the claw ascended, it grabbed the corners of the box so precariously that, as it swung with its cargo toward the prize chute, the outcome was in doubt every inch of the way. It was like witnessing a miracle to see the watch finally drop squarely into the prize receptacle where Ricky quickly retrieved it.

"Pretty awesome, huh?" he asked Andrew after he'd pried open the plastic box, slipped the watch on his bony wrist and held it close to Andrew's face.

Andrew was blown away by the notion that you could insert a couple of quarters into a machine and pull out something as cool as a watch that probably cost hundreds of dollars.

"Could you teach me how to do that?" he asked, eyeing the pile of prizes, particularly interested in what looked like a palm-sized handheld game.

"It's rigged," Ricky said matter-of-factly.

"Rigged?"

"Like fixed. Like you'll almost never win unless you know how it works."

"How *does* it work?"

"I can't tell you. If everyone knew, then they'd win every time and my family would lose money."

"That's not fair," Andrew said. Then he added, "I'd only want to win one time. I've never won anything."

Ricky wasn't interested in the topic and walked on. Andrew caught up with him.

"I was in a fight last night."

"Yeah, you said that. But I think you must have been dreaming. If you were in a fight you'd be in the hospital."

"I'll show you." Andrew unbuttoned the pink jacket and lifted up his shirt to show Ricky the bruises that colored his ribs. These weren't just any bruises, like the small blue marks he'd sometimes get on his knees and shins if he fell or bumped into something. These were mega-bruises, at least ten of them, big purple and green splotches coloring the pale skin of his ribs and upper back.

"Holy crap," Ricky breathed, and Andrew saw something in Ricky's face that he'd never seen before. He couldn't be sure, but it almost looked like admiration. "How did you get those?"

He told Ricky about how he'd gone out as the Shadow Warrior on a mission to clean up the streets, and how a gang had jumped him; how he'd fought hand-to-hand with them, fists flying, trading jump kicks, blocking their punches, springing off a wall to take out two of them at once with a scissor kick. He could picture it himself, like a scene out of *Revenge of the Ninja*, every detail so vivid it was almost like it had really happened.

Ricky didn't know what to make of it. The bruises were obviously real, but. . .

"Maybe you fell off your bike," he said, and started walking again. He was heading for the snack bar. Andrew caught up with him he was leaning on the counter on his elbows, talking to the girl who stood behind it. She was around seventeen or eighteen, Andrew guessed. A little bit fat, but kind of pretty, with dark bangs. She wore an elf's hat as part of her uniform. She had locked eyes with Ricky; she liked him, you could tell. Ricky showed her the watch he'd won, and she looked really impressed. Then he pulled it off his wrist and gave it to her. She smiled excitedly and put it on her own wrist, holding her arm out to look at it. The watch band, which had been too big for Ricky, hung even more loosely on her, sliding down her arm when she raised it.

Andrew hung back, the way he did when he was watching Ricky play the arcade games. The way they were looking at each other made him think that she was Ricky's girlfriend, or that she wanted to be. She gave Ricky a churro from the hot case and didn't ask him to pay for it.

A beeping sound came from his own wrist watch, the digital watch that Jana had purchased for him. She had programmed in alarms to keep him on schedule. He looked down at the big watch face; it read 4:00. Time for him to end his shift, which meant it was also time for Ricky to start his.

He edged up to Ricky and held the beeping watch next to his ear.

"It's 4:00," he said.

Ricky looked irritated. "So?"

"It's when you're supposed to start your shift."

Ricky shrugged like it was no big deal.

Andrew said, "I'm going down to the locker room."

"Good for you."

He glanced at his watch again, nervously. Now it was 4:01. "You're going to be late."

Ricky was completely ignoring him. The girl had given him a raspberry freeze—again without asking for payment—and Ricky was dipping his spoon-straw into it and then sucking the blue slush out of the straw. Andrew turned to leave and Ricky, taking his time, followed him, stabbing his straw into the drink and sucking on it.

Andrew let him catch up. "Is that your girlfriend?" he asked.

"What do you think?"

"I think she is."

"I think you're right."

He wanted to ask Ricky if they went on dates, had kissed, maybe even gone further. It was a subject he was intensely interested in, not so much what you could do with a girl—he'd seen plenty of that on the Internet—but how you would go about getting the opportunity to do it. For starters, how could you get a girl to look at you the way the counter girl looked at Ricky? If Andrew even worked up the courage to say something to a girl, they never took it the right way. He was ashamed of his ignorance, and didn't want to give Ricky another chance to feel superior to him, so he didn't ask him any more about her.

Just past the carrousel, they turned into an alcove on the left, passed a pretty blond security guard and went through a door marked "Authorized Personnel Only". The door opened onto a stairwell that led to the Bay-View's lower level. Once you got to the bottom of the stairs, the men's locker room was the first door you came to on the left. There wasn't much to it. On one side was a wall of lockers with benches in front of them. On the other side were two sinks, two urinals and two toilet stalls.

It took Andrew a long time to do even the simplest things; by the time he had removed his straw hat and was placing it carefully on the little shelf in his locker, Ricky had climbed into the body of his turtle costume, attached the shell—it looked like a turned-over quilted dog bed—to his back with Velcro straps, and was pulling on the turtle head, adjusting it to line up the eyeholes, which were hidden behind a pair of outsized sunglasses. Once he'd got everything the way he wanted, he spun, punched the air, and cried "I'm the Shell from Hell!" Then he said, "See ya—" and walked out, leaving Andrew with a severe case of costume envy as he pulled off his pink jacket.

After he closed the locker door on his ambassadorial get-up, Andrew sat on the bench and asked himself if he had the courage to do what he'd been dying to do since he'd started his job two weeks earlier—explore the subterranean labyrinth of the Bay-View. He could see that the corridor outside the locker room connected to a larger passageway, and imagined that beyond that there were more doors, more passageways, each leading to a new mystery. The Shadow Warrior wouldn't hesitate to check things out, he told himself. The Shadow Warrior would creep stealthily ahead, every muscle tensed, alert for danger.

He fished a bag of Skittles out of the side pocket of his cargo shorts, popped three of them into his mouth, and got up from the bench. Leaving the locker room, he turned left, away from the stairs leading back up to the outside world, and advanced toward the unknown.

****

The main passageway wasn't really scary. It was twice as wide as the corridor he'd just come down, and had a polished concrete floor with an intermittent yellow stripe down the middle and parallel fluorescent light strips above. A motorized maintenance cart driven by a man in a blue jumpsuit came toward him; the man beeped a horn and Andrew jumped out of the way. It looked like the cart was headed toward a wide space twenty yards further down the passageway to his left where boxes were stacked. Andrew chose to turn right. The first door he came had a paper sign taped on it, which read: "Keep Out!! Trespassers will be knocked on the head and suffer horrible consequences, including attack by grotesque monsters!"

The door was open a crack, so of course Andrew had to peek in. The space within was dimly lit. After his eyes adjusted, he saw a room that looked like a disordered workshop: metal shelving racks with bins of parts, a rolling tool cabinet and a couple of cluttered work tables, one mounted with an illuminated desktop magnifier that threw a cone of light on the tabletop. But he could tell by the line of bald, disembodied heads staring from the top of the tallest shelving unit that this was no ordinary workshop. In the shadows he could make out several animatronic figures in various states of completion, one with a face stripped of flesh, revealing eyeballs and teeth set into a metal framework interlaced with springs and wires. He saw what looked like shaggy bear wearing a tight shirt and baggy pants holding a trumpet. Next to the bear stood a short black character with a wild white afro and staring eyes. Tentatively, Andrew took a couple of steps into the room—and the door shut behind him. He started, whirled around and saw Frankenstein staggering toward him. What looked like a toy guitar was strapped around the monster's neck.

He backed up, tripped over his feet and fell down. Frankenstein was looming over him.

From the interior of the workshop he heard a cackling laugh. "Didn't you read the sign?"

Andrew turned and saw that the figure with the black face and teased-up white afro was actually a dwarfish man—a real flesh-and-blood man—who had taken a step toward him and was now appraising him. Andrew scrambled to his feet, keeping an eye on Frankenstein, who seemed to wear the trace of a smile.

"I think he likes you," the black man said. "He doesn't like everyone." Andrew's eyes had gotten more used to the dimness. He saw that the black man, who was not much more than four feet tall, was holding what looked like a game controller. His thumbs moved and Frankenstein reached his hand out.

"He wants to shake your hand. Go ahead."

There was something reassuring about the little man's voice; it was reedy and resonant and slightly amused. And now that he had a closer look, he found Frankenstein's face wore an expression that was almost friendly. The monster's deep-set eyes blinked. His lips moved, and he spoke. "My name is Frankie."

Tentatively, Andrew extended his hand and Frankie gripped it, squeezing it gently. It felt weird, hard and rubbery.

"Is he a robot?" Andrew asked the black man.

"Does he look like a robot to you?"

Andrew shook his head. "Robots usually don't look like monsters."

"And robots don't have personalities, but my boy Frankie does, don't you, Frankie?" He worked the controller and Frankie nodded his head.

"My name is Frankie," the monster repeated. "Pleased to meet you. Do you want to hear a song?"

"He doesn't have a lot to say just yet. And sometimes he can get a little rude."

"Bite me," Frankie said.

The little black man cackled, his fingers dancing on the controller. "Say you're sorry, Frankie."

"You're sorry, Frankie," the monster said. He blinked again, his eyelids rolling down over his big glass eyes and then up again like window shades.

"Let's put you back in your corner, big guy. Let go of the young man's hand." Andrew realized that he couldn't pull his hand free. In fact, the monster's grip was getting tighter. Thumbing the controller, the black man muttered something about a glitch.

"It's starting to hurt," Andrew said. It felt like his hand was caught in vise that was slowly crushing his fingers and knuckles. *"It's starting to really hurt!"*

"That hand is a problem. Gotta do a hard reset," the little black man mumbled. He hit a button on the controller; Frankie's eyes closed and the grip of his handshake loosened slightly. Andrew was able to withdraw his hand and examined it, flexing it to make sure all the moving parts worked.

"Now let's try this again," he black man said, hitting another key on the controller, which brought Frankie back to life.

"My name is Frankie. Pleased to meet you. Do you want to hear a song?"

"You've already met him, Frankie. You just about squeezed the juice out his hand. Now back you go into your corner." He walked Frankie backwards, the monster's legs moving slowly and stiffly, the soles of his boots sliding on the floor, bringing him to a stop in the corner where he'd been standing when Andrew entered the room.

"Getting his grip right is a challenge. The finer motor control stuff isn't trivial. The big guy's grip is strong enough to make a diamond out of a lump of coal. All he's really supposed to do with that hand is grip the neck of his guitar."

"He plays the guitar?"

"He's learning. Wolfman over there is going to play the trumpet." Looking more closely, Andrew saw that the shaggy bear in tight clothing that he'd seen earlier did have a slightly wolfish face. "And the Mummy's going to play the drums."

"Where's the mummy?"

"Chilling in his sarcophagus. Getting a little beauty sleep. He needs it."

"A sarcophagus is a stone coffin," Andrew recited, "typically adorned with a sculpture or inscription and associated with the ancient civilizations of Egypt, Rome, and Greece. I've never seen one except in pictures. Can I see it?"

"You're smarter than you look," the little man said. "Anyway, the fact of the matter is I haven't started on the mummy yet. I was making a little joke. Maybe you don't get jokes."

Walking with a limp that made him pitch from side to side, the little black man placed the controller on the work table, next to a soldering iron and a couple of Chinese food take-out containers. Then he turned his attention again to Andrew. "Now I'm going to ask *you* some questions . . . who the hell are you and what are you doing in here snooping around?"

"I'm Andrew."

"That tells me something, but not very much."

"I work here. I'm the Smiles Ambassador."

"That's you? The one they got to take the old man's place? They pay you for that?"

"Yes. $8.75 an hour."

"Then you should start thinking about doing a better job. When I first saw you on the video feed I thought *you* were a robot. And not a very well-engineered robot. Standing around doing nothing. No interaction with the public. Looks like lately you're hanging around the video arcade more than anything." He paused to think about what he was going to say next. "Are you a little off, is that it? A little slow? Takes you a while to get things?" He asked in a way that was blunt, but not unkind.

Andrew thought about it. No one had ever directly asked him that question, though he asked himself the same thing sometimes. "Some things maybe." He felt OK saying it, comfortable sharing with someone else who was different.

"No shame in that. As long as you're trying hard. And I'm not seeing it. The effort, I mean."

The little man waddled over to stand in front of a laptop that was opened on the work table. He touched the screen and turned the laptop around so that Andrew could see the display. "Look here." He was showing Andrew a thumbnail gallery of paused video streams. He tapped one of the thumbnails, which expanded and came to life. They were looking at the line of people waiting to ride the Giant Anaconda, and there, running back and forth and clapping his flipper-hands enthusiastically, was Toby the Sea Turtle, aka Ricky Wakefield.

"He puts his heart into it. People respond to that wacky turtle." He seemed to assume that Andrew was interested in the video feeds, although for Andrew that was the least remarkable feature of the workshop he'd wandered into. "I can see what's going on anywhere in the park at any time," the man said conspiratorially. "All it took was a simple hack into their network. I can grab all of the feeds that security is getting. Now don't you tell anyone that I can do this. They don't need to know."

"Is it against the law?" Andrew asked.

"What law says you can't have a little innocent entertainment?"

The question stumped Andrew. But he was more interested in the animatronic Frankenstein whose hand he had just shook.

"Did you make that monster?"

"I'm proud to say Frankie is my boy. I've raised him up from the days when he was just a blob of latex and a circuit board, and look

95

how he's grown. He's still a work in progress, very primitive in most respects. When I'm finished with him he'll have motion and distance detecting sensors, a gyroscopic balancer, finer motor control and touch sensors in his hands and someday I'll be able to control him just by thinking about what I want him to do. I'll need to have a chip and a transmitter implanted in my brain, but the technology is out there. You don't believe me, do you?"

"I don't know."

"You're looking at me like I'm crazy, same as everyone else."

Andrew didn't know how to look at someone like they were crazy. "No I'm not. I'm just looking at you."

"I see you smiling. What's up with that smile?"

"I can't help it." Andrew had his own questions. "Is that your job, making monsters?"

"Monsters," he nodded. "Giant scorpions. And spiders." He picked up another controller from the work table and played a sequence on the keys. A spider the diameter of a dinner plate crawled rapidly from under the table, racing toward Andrew, who jumped out of the way. The little man laughed, delighted. "Don't worry. He can't bite. And sometimes one of his legs get stuck and he runs around in circles. That little guy was the prototype for the spiders I've been making for the Creepy Cavern. Big, clumsy, ugly spiders. But that cute little critter I'm keeping for myself."

Unconsciously, Andrew dug into his pants for Skittles. Remembering his manners, he offered the bag to the little man. "Want some?"

"Skittles? Maybe. But I've got a little quirk when it comes to Skittles—I only eat the green ones. That sour green apple flavor just sings in my mouth."

Andrew poured Skittles into the palm of his hand and started picking out the green candies.

"I have lots of green ones. And lots more at home. I keep them in a fish bowl. You can have them all."

"Is that right?" the little man said. "Well now you're making points with me. Serious points. My name is Jefferson. A.E. Jefferson."

After Andrew had handed him the green Skittles he'd separated, he asked, "Can I try that? Making Frankie walk?"

"I'm going to have to think about that." A.E. Jefferson took one of the Skittles from his palm and put it in his mouth, chewing thoughtfully. "Now that is good. A little bit sweet, but mostly sour. Kind of like me. . . Maybe we'll start you with the spider." He handed Andrew the controller. It only took a minute for Andrew to get the spider hopelessly stuck in a corner, just as Teddy and Blaine Wakefield bustled into the workshop, Teddy in the lead and Blaine behind, tripping to catch up.

A.E. Jefferson eyed them suspiciously.

Teddy got right to the point. "Mr. Jefferson, we have a problem."

"*We*, like you and me? Or *we* like you and your cheap-ass brother?"

"We . . ." Teddy sputtered trying to come up with the right answer. "All of the above." He became aware of Andrew, sitting to the side, thumbing a controller, trying to figure out how to get all of the spider's eight legs synchronized so he could back it out of the tight spot where it was wedged. "Who's that?" he asked.

"That's your Smiles Ambassador."

Andrew looked up from the controller. "I'm Andrew."

"Yes, of course."

"Have you punched out?" Blaine asked. Andrew drew a blank. "Your time card?"

"Yes," Andrew answered in his precise way. "At 4:00 PM and twenty-seven seconds."

A.E. Jefferson had picked up another controller and was edging Frankie out of the shadows, walking him toward the Wakefield brothers. "What's our problem?" he asked.

"Blaine and I were informed at our staff meeting that all is not right in the Creepy Cavern. I can take a joke as well as the next person, but your little pranks are not appropriate." Frankie was now standing right behind Blaine, who was trying to ignore him. Apparently he'd been introduced to Mr. Jefferson's monster in the past and the two weren't exactly fast friends. "We're five days away from the ribbon cutting."

Frankie reached out a hand and was mussing Blaine's hair. Blaine ducked and told the monster to cut it out. Catching himself, he turned to A.E. Jefferson and said, "Make it stop!"

A.E. Jefferson asked, "What do you mean 'pranks'?"

"I was told that you had a little fun with the fly."

"The fly? You mean the one with the little face that screams when it's attacked by the ginormous spider? That was a great idea you had. It's going to give the kiddies nightmares."

98

"My brother Stanhope is of the opinion that you made the fly look like me."

"You mean the bow tie and the buck teeth?"

"I don't have buck teeth."

"Then how can it look like you?"

Mr. Jefferson's question stumped Teddy for a moment. "Well, at least remove the bow tie. We wouldn't want anyone getting the impression that I was being made fun of."

"No, we wouldn't."

"And Stanhope says that the centipede is limping. I want to see all of the centipede's legs working in unison, like the Rockettes."

"Simple enough. They just need a little tweaking. What else?"

"The praying mantises . . ." Blaine put in, just in case Teddy had forgotten.

"And the praying mantises—"

"I'm particularly proud of those ugly bugs. They're as creepy as they come."

Teddy fixed a stern look on his animatronic wizard. "Stanhope told me that they appear to be engaged in sexual congress."

"Sexual congress?"

"I think you know what I mean."

"Sure—you mean they're boffing. I thought it wouldn't hurt to add an educational element to the attraction, so long as it was done tastefully. You know, in nature, the females are prone to bite off the heads of their male partners after they've completed their courtship. I felt that might be a little too disturbing for the youngsters."

"We're not interested in educating our younger guests on the subject of mantis courtship. Separate the mantises and have them claw at the passengers in the cars as they go by, with those hook things on their arms." Teddy demonstrated with his curled hands held out in front of him, his elbows bent.

A sly light came into A.E Jefferson's eyes. "You're the boss . . . But I need something changed myself." He brought up Blaine's threat to dock him for rent. "I don't live here. Just so you know, I've got a place across the street. Same building where Pete the Pelican stays, got a room down the hall from him. I just stay here real late most nights, sometimes all night, working on my projects. I'm kind of geeky that way." He paused to let his point sink in. "And here's *my* bottom line. You forget your stupid idea about charging me for rent here, and raise my pay by $100 a week—or I walk. Your Creepy Cavern won't get finished, and you'll never see these musical monsters I'm working on perform live on the Bay-View stage."

With a stubby finger, he jabbed at a button on yet another controller, and the Wolfman raised his trumpet to his lips and blew a blatting note.

"You can't blackmail us like this," Blaine huffed. It looked like he was being held back from charging A.E. Jefferson by an invisible leash that had cinched tight around his neck. A vein was pulsing in the middle of his forehead. "You signed a contract!"

"—which says in the fine print that if I am prevented from completing my deliverables by a work-related injury, I will have no liability. And Gentlemen, it is very easy for a dwarf to get hurt on the job, especially since you haven't invested in any workplace accommodations for me here. For example, I could easily fall off a box reaching for something on one of those high shelves, but if you bought me a hydraulic lifter, it would be a whole lot safer. I saw one on the Internet for around $6,000. I can send Blaine the link to the website so he can see about acquiring one."

Teddy had heard enough. He turned to Blaine.

"Forget about this rent nonsense, and tell Arletta to give Mr. Jefferson his raise—*after* we open the Creepy Cavern. It it's as popular as I think it will be, we can easily afford extra cost. And those musical monsters are going to be a hit!"

At that moment, as Blaine was struggling with his despair at the thought of 400 dollars bills escaping from the Bay-View coffers each month like shimmering minnows from torn net, Andrew stumbled upon the combination of thumb strokes that freed the spider and sent it scurrying toward Blaine's wingtips.

Startled, Blaine jumped straight up. "Oh, my sweet savior Jesus!" he exclaimed as the spider sped beneath him.

Teddy considered his brother sourly. "We're done here, right?"

Blaine laughed uneasily, watching the mechanical spider run in aimless circles around the workshop. "If you say so, Teddy." He was already backing out in the direction of the doorway.

"Mr. Jefferson, I want the Creepy Cavern fixed ASAP. The centipede, the praying mantises, and that fly," Teddy said, as he and Blaine were leaving.

"You're the boss," A.E. Jefferson said, as though it was one of history's great ironies. When they were gone, he turned to Andrew and asked, "Did you ever ask yourself why people like that get to tell people like us what to do?"

"No." He'd gotten the spider stuck again.

"Just as well. Once you start questioning authority, there's no turning back. Before you know it you'll be a sour old man like me."

****

Nico knew who she was as soon as he saw her standing in the doorway of his cubbyhole office in the back of the fish market. A total knockout, like Tony said, standing there with the trace of a smile on her lips, like something amused her, some private joke that he would never get. She wasn't wearing a tailored business suit the way Tony had described her; today she had on casual clothes like you might see on a model in a high-end fashion magazine, posed standing on the sidelines of a polo match. A cream colored linen blouse, beige slacks, expensive belt and open-toed shoes. Her toenail polish was blood red.

She waited in the doorway, not in any rush. She had a cup of chowder in one hand, a spoon in the other.

"Your mom knows how to make good chowder. I prefer the red chowder, what some people call Manhattan chowder, but this is good."

Nico was sitting at his desk facing the door, a yellow legal pad to his right, a plastic paper tray to his left, his computer monitor directly in front of him. "We don't do red chowder," Nico said, pleasant but careful, the way he might talk to a new health inspector who had just showed up unannounced. "We tried it out, but hardly anyone bought it."

She shrugged. Obviously Nico was missing something. "Maybe it was how you were making it. You've got to make it right. Maybe I can show you."

"You work for Vincent?"

"That's right." She tilted her head toward Nico's computer monitor. "You do the books?"

"The books, managing the business." Nico clicked out of the web page he'd been looking at, a how-to article that offered advice for getting rid of gophers, and a link to a patented trap. Gophers were making a mess of his new sod lawn and he had decided to declare war. It wasn't like he was looking at porn or anything, but it would be embarrassing, maybe more embarrassing than porn, if this woman saw what he was looking at. "My name's Nico."

The woman was looking around the office as she spoke to Nico, checking everything out. She picked up a framed photo of Nico's son, little Nicky, in his soccer uniform, and stared at it while she talked.

"I know that. Your brother's Tony, your mom is Bianca. She's a sweetheart by the way. Ladled this cup of chowder for me right out of the pot she was making." She put the photo of little Nicky back on Nico's desk. Something about the way she took one last look at the photo gave Nico the creeps. "And this must be your little boy. Our children are precious, aren't they?"

"Any you're—?" Nico asked.

"Gina. Gina Quattro."

"Four, right? Quattro is Italian for the number four?" Nico said, as soon as the words popped into his head.

She seemed impressed. "You know Italian?"

"I just guessed. I speak a little Spanish. A lot of the words are the same, right? *Uno, dos, tres, quatro.* A few of the people who work for us are from Mexico." He didn't mention that his ex-wife's family was from Guadalajara. He didn't want to get into all that.

"Makes sense. You can probably get away with paying them peanuts. Or maybe sometimes you don't pay them at all. Tell them you'll turn them in to immigration if they squawk."

"How's Vincent doing these days?" Nico asked, trying to move the conversation along.

Gina Quattro took a tiny spoonful of the chowder. She pressed her full lips against the spoon as she withdrew it from her mouth, removing every trace of chowder. "Vincent's getting up there, eighty-five years old his last birthday. He had a little episode a couple months ago." She took a step forward and set the chowder cup on Nico's desk, on top of an invoice from the beer distributor. Nico lifted it off and put it on a spot where there was no paperwork.

"An episode? You mean a stroke? That's what I heard anyway."

"Who told you that?"

"I don't know," Nico back-pedaled. "It was just something I think I heard. Maybe I heard it wrong."

"Anyway, he had this episode. They got him back on his feet and all, but he's slowed down. I've been helping him out with the business."

"Give him my best when you talk to him."

"That's funny you should say that."

"Funny?"

Gina Quattro's busy gaze swept the wall to Nico's right, cluttered with photographs from the old days, of his immigrant grandfather and his cronies in loose shirts with their sleeves rolled up, standing as cocky as young princes in front of the day's catch. She was still examining them when she said to Nico, "Funny because I don't think you've been giving Vincent your best for almost three years."

So this was it, what this visit was all about. It seemed like she was expecting Nico to say something in his defense, but he didn't know what to say. The best he could come up with was, "Business hasn't been so good for a while."

She nodded, a little smile on her lips, like she couldn't quite believe what she'd just heard. "Not so good? That's one way to put it. Not the way I'd put it, but you could say that, I guess."

Then Tony came to the door, looming behind Gina Quattro, who sensed him but didn't turn around, not right away. "It's the compressor, Nico," Tony said, looking over her shoulder.

The ice machine again. All the equipment in the fish market was ancient even when the old man had bought it used years earlier, kept running over the years with spit and duct tape and Tony's tinkering.

"Can you fix it?"

"I've gotta figure out why it's not cycling first."

Gina Quattro decided she could turn to acknowledge Tony now. Tony was crowding her a little. She backed up a step and nodded at him, giving Nico the opportunity to check out her rear end. She works out, he thought.

"We kinda met the other night, but I didn't catch your name," Tony said.

Nico could tell she didn't like the way Tony was pushing into her personal space. "Gina Quattro," she said.

"I'm Tony." He was at least eight inches taller than her, one of those big guys who like to get in close and look down at people. He was wearing his daytime uniform, a stained T-shirt and baggy shorts. He held his big greasy hand out for Gina Quattro to shake, which she did almost reluctantly. Tony held her hand in his strong grasp and stood there, a big sloppy guy who didn't give a shit about what anyone thought about him. Gina Quattro's expression was frozen. Nico couldn't tell what she was thinking, but it couldn't be good.

"You two talking business?"

Nico waited for Gina Quattro to answer.

"Getting acquainted," she said.

Tony let go of her hand, leaving a smudge of grease on it, but didn't back away. "When're we gonna have our talk?" he said.

Gina Quattro looked at him blankly.

"You said the other night you wanted to talk. To me and Nico. Is that what we're doing now?"

"No, that's not what we're doing now. Not yet."

Tony said, "I've got a few minutes. How about you, Nico?"

Gina said, "I had something more structured in mind. I've prepared a presentation I'd like to share with you."

Nico could see that Tony was going to say something smart, so he said, "That would be great. We'd like to see it. Your presentation."

"I've got a suite at the Sunset Inn." The Sunset Inn was a six-story hotel on the beach next to the entrance to the wharf, the tallest building on the shoreline, built before the Santa Carmela city council imposed strict height restrictions. "I came by to see if we could meet there later today. I'd like to bring in Vincent over a conference line."

"Vincent? Over the phone?"

"He wants to participate." Gina Quattro turned back to Nico. "Can we do this around 5:00? That's generally a good time for Vincent."

"I usually pick up my boy from his soccer practice around that time."

"5:00 is the best time for Vincent."

Nico got the message—this wasn't the kind of meeting where everybody checked their calendars and worked something out. "I'm sure I can make it happen. I'll ask my Mom to pick my little guy up. How about you Tony? 5:00 will work for you, right?"

"Yeah, why not? If I don't have the ice machine fixed by then we can just let all the fish in the display case rot."

"I'm in room 612."

Nico wrote it down. "612. 5 PM. We'll be there." Then he thought of something. "Do we have to prepare anything?"

Gina Quattro was edging by Tony. "Just show up." They watched her walk out, dodging the puddles on the concrete floor, both of them staring at her ass.

"What the fuck," Tony said.

"What the fuck is right."

✳✳✳✳

"How long's it been since you were in this place?" Tony asked when they walked into the lobby of the Sunset Inn. Nico had made sure they were right on time. They drove the short distance from the fish market in the van they used for deliveries.

Nico had to think about it. "Jesus, I don't know. Maybe three or four years. Destina had a cousin came into town, and we took him and his wife to the bar here for a drink. Eight-fifty for a beer. I thought maybe I should send one of the dishwashers from our place down here to stand out in front with a sandwich board to let people know we're only charging five bucks for a beer at the market. Same view, pretty much."

"And we got the seals," Tony said.

"That's right. We got the seals."

Never very successful, the Sunset Inn seemed to change hands every four or five years. Most recently, it had been acquired by a Japanese management company. They were of the opinion that the Sunset Inn had an identity problem. They planned to transform it into a themed boutique hotel; Nico remembered reading that in the paper. But he didn't know what that meant until now. Looking around as he and Tony walked toward the elevators he saw that it meant that the interior had a new color scheme—aqua and pink—and that there was a wall sculpture of a flock of shorebirds with long legs and long pointed beaks above the reception area. The staff was wearing aloha shirts.

Maybe they should do something like that at the fish market, Nico thought. Not the new paint, but maybe the staff could wear aloha shirts.

Nico was carrying a leather-look briefcase. He'd taken a wet comb to his thin hair before they left, and you could still see the grooves left by the comb. Tony hadn't bothered to clean up much, hadn't changed out of the sloppy T-shirt hanging outside of his baggy shorts. In the elevator Nico caught a fishy smell. "Did you wash your hands at least?"

"I washed my hands," Tony said. He held them to his nose and sniffed them, then offered them to Nico, who drew back.

They both looked down at Tony's feet, at the old basketball shoes that he wore around the market when he wasn't wearing his rubber Wellingtons. "You could have changed your shoes."

"Look, just 'cause this ballbuster thinks she can whistle and we'll come trotting up like a couple of little dogs, doesn't mean I've got to go home and get another pair of shoes."

"Whatever." Nico said. He could have pointed out that, from what he could tell, Tony didn't have another pair of shoes, but what good would it do? He just hoped he would behave himself, not say anything that would piss off Gina Quattro. Hoping the way you hope for sunshine when all of the forecasts call for rain.

Her suite was on the top floor. After Nico knocked on the door it was opened by a wiry guy, narrow face, big nose, maybe early '40's, with slicked-back hair and rabbitty eyes. He was wearing a pork pie hat and a short-sleeved leisure shirt with a spread color. The shirt had big interlocking diamond pattern on the front. He didn't say anything when he opened the door, just barely nodded and stepped aside. Gina Quattro was standing a few feet further into the suite, almost like she was posing. She was wearing something that looked like a track suit, but fancier.

"Gentlemen," she said. "Thank you for coming. And thanks for being right on time. I appreciate that." Behind her was a large window that took up an entire wall. The draperies were pulled back and the brightness of the late afternoon framed her. Nico saw that the zippered front of the track suit was open all the way to the top of her breasts. He tried not to stare. He knew, without looking at him, that Tony was taking it all in.

"This is my associate, Mr. Hat," she said, nodding toward the wiry guy. Mr. Hat looked at them but didn't offer to shake hands. "And that's Mr. Benjie over there."

Mr. Benjie was a big kid about twenty. Had to go at least 250, 260, Nico guessed. Thick all the way through, arms, legs, shoulders. Not really cut or anything, but he looked pretty solid. He was wearing an immaculate Thrasher skater cap, turned slightly sideways. Either the cap was too big, or his head was too small. The bill of the cap was completely flat, the way kids were wearing them now. Made them look like retards. He wore baggy shorts and a tank top that showed most of an amateurish tattoo inked across his collar bones. With a quick glance Nico could make out the words, "I FEAR ONLY THE LORD." A pair of white headphones hung around his neck. He looked like a kid who didn't want to be stuck hanging around with grownups, like he had better things to do.

They walked into the room, which was a sitting area with a love seat and two arm chairs of the kind that you see in hotels. A flat screen television stood on top of a built-in bar, along with a coffee carafe, bottled water and cookies on a plastic tray.

Gina Quattro didn't offer to shake hands either. Instead, she gestured for them to take in the view. "You live in a beautiful place." Nico and Tony looked out over the bay, the wharf, the surfers carving the break off the point to the north. The view didn't impress Nico and Tony one way or the other. They saw the Monterey Bay every day. To them it was just water, water with fish in it. "You must consider yourselves lucky."

"Lucky?" Tony said. "Maybe. We'll see."

Gina Quattro looked at Tony, assessing him and apparently drawing a conclusion. Nico could feel Tony's bad energy.

He thought it wouldn't hurt to be more agreeable. "You can get a little spoiled if you live here, forget how nice it is. Compared to other places."

Gina invited them to sit down on the couch. In front of the couch was a coffee table with a desk phone on it, the kind with an array of clear plastic buttons. The table was close to the couch, forcing them to draw their knees in tight. Nico balanced his briefcase on his lap, not sure whether it was time to call attention to it.

"I had room service bring up cookies, coffee and soft drinks," Gina said. "Benjie, can you bring the cookie tray over to Nico and Tony?"

The look on Benjie's face said he'd do it, but he didn't like doing it, didn't like Nico, didn't like Tony, and would just as soon take the cookies and grind them into the carpet under his 14 EEE Nikes and dropkick the tray into the wall. But he did as he was told. He brought the tray of cookies over and held them out for Nico and Tony. Nico glanced at the kid's hands; his fingernails were ragged and dirty. He selected a little butter cookie with a gummy blob of red jam in the middle. Tony shook his head, declining.

"You can help yourself to the drinks up here if you'd like."

"I'm good thanks," Nico said. He placed the cookie on top of his briefcase.

"You're not going to eat your cookie?" Gina Quattro asked.

Nico picked it up with his thumb and forefinger, like he was playing tea party, and nibbled at the edge.

"Well," Gina said. And then she didn't say anything else for a moment. She stared at Nico and Tony with a mysterious half-smile on her lips.

Nico wasn't sure how to respond, so he smiled back and bit into the gummy jam center of the cookie. He wished now he had asked for a water.

"Well what?" Tony asked abruptly. "You asked us up here, right? What's the deal?"

"The *deal*?" Gina Quattro looked like she was thinking about how she was going to phrase what she planned to say next. "The *deal* is that I've been reviewing the performance of the Santa Carmela district as part of a complete organizational audit that I'm doing for Vincent, and I'd like to share my conclusions and suggest a remediation plan."

Nico laid his briefcase on the coffee table in front of him, and fumbled at the latches.

"I thought you might want to go over our numbers, so I brought in some ledgers. . ."

Gina held up a hand, palm out, as Nico managed to release one of the brief case's spring-loaded latches. "That won't be necessary," she said. "I've got all the data I think I need." She turned to the laptop that was open on the bar next to the refreshments, slid her fingers over its touch pad and stared at the screen. She tapped a couple of keys and the flat screen monitor to her left lit up. A title slide appeared, bright white letters on a rich blue background. It read "Connole Review".

"I've put a PowerPoint presentation together. Just five slides. I thought it would help everyone focus on the key points."

Nico darted a glance at Tony, who was staring straight at Gina Quattro. He knew him well enough to know that the complete lack of expression didn't mean a lack of reaction. Actually just the opposite. It meant he could go off at any second. The big kid Benjie was looking out the window, probably at the surfers in the distance. Nico sensed that Mr. Hat was standing behind them.

Gina came over to the coffee table, bent over the phone, hit the speaker key and began punching in numbers. "I'd like to bring Vincent in now so he can participate." They heard the phone ringing on the other end, and then a low garbled voice.

"Vincent?" Gina Quattro asked. Another garbled response. "Good afternoon to you. I'm here with Nico and Tony Connole."

"Hey Vincent," Nico said. On the other end of the line it sounded like Vincent was clearing a knot of phlegm from deep in his throat.

Gina said, "We're ready to start now."

Vincent coughed and said something that to Nico sounded like, "Lester Dooley" or "Less to do me", he couldn't make it out, but Gina Quattro nodded and smiled as though she'd heard him perfectly.

"I understand," she said to the phone. "You need your rest. This shouldn't take more than twenty minutes."

She punched a button that started flashing red. "I've put us on mute," she said. "Vincent's episode has made him a little difficult to understand, especially over the phone, but he hates to be asked to repeat anything. Benjie," she said, taking the phone off mute, "please close the drapes."

The room darkened. The title slide on the flat screen burned through the gloom. Gina Quattro held a control device in her hand that she used to advance the slides. The second slide asked the question, *"Who Are We?"* The device that Gina Quattro held was also a laser pointer. She put a red dot of light on the question and then on the three bullet points beneath it as she spoke to each one.

"We're a multi-generational family-run business, founded in New York before the Second World War. We're privately held, with revenues in the high eight figures. We're diversified; our income streams come from a mix of businesses, including trucking, gaming and banking. Our headquarters are in New York, but we have satellite offices in Las Vegas and San Francisco."

Nico asked, "Are we talking about the Galante family?"

"We don't call it that anymore."

"So, what do you call it then?" Tony asked.

"We don't. It's just the organization."

"Makes sense," Nico said, just to be agreeable.

"Not to me," Tony said. "It doesn't make any sense. Every business has a name."

Gina Quattro didn't say anything, so Nico said, hoping to get her approval, "Yeah, but this is a private business. So private that you wouldn't want to have a name. Am I on the right track, Ms. Quattro?"

"Call me Gina."

"Gina" Nico repeated. "OK."

"And yes, you're on the right track. But I didn't bring you two up here for your input on our naming strategy, as insightful as it may be. Let's move on." She advanced the presentation to the next slide, which showed an organization chart. It looked like the diagram of a family tree.

"OK. So this a view of the business from 10,000 feet, the org chart. If I went up to twenty, thirty thousand feet, you'd see other interlocking entities, organizations similar to ours run by different families."

"I don't get it," Tony said. "10,000 feet above what?"

"It's a high-level view, Tony, that's all," Nico said.

Gina Quattro continued with her description. "The CEO and the board are in New York," she said, waving the red dot across the top of the chart, "And each region runs semi-independently with a General Manager at the head. Vincent is the GM of the Western Division." She advanced to the next slide, which showed a similar, though less crowded org chart, titled Western Division. "So here's Vincent at the top, and here's me reporting to him. And here are the five sub-regions. Each sub-region has three to four districts." She drew their attention to the bottom left corner of the chart. "Here's the Monterey Bay district."

Nico and Tony stared at a tiny rectangular text box where she had placed the laser dot. The text within read "MB District, Connoles".

"That's us?" Nico asked. "We don't look like much. In the big picture, I mean." Then his eyes landed on a text box close to theirs, with the designation "SJ District", followed by "TBD." He thought about Carmine Bosso. Had Gina Quattro made the same presentation to Carmine before they offed him? He looked over at Tony, to see if he was connecting the dots the same way. Tony didn't seem to be paying close attention. He was quick-tapping his fingers on his knee, staring up at the ceiling.

The next slide appeared on the screen with a photo of Gina Quattro, a head shot like you might see on the business page of the newspaper, in the section where they put the announcements of corporate promotions. She looked a little younger, and her hair was styled differently. She wore a smile that said, "I'm young, I'm motivated, and I'm going places!"

"Now, a little about me." She did this thing with the pointer where every time she stated a fact about herself, text materialized on the screen, pixels rushing together to form letters.

"I'm a graduate of the MBA program at Rutgers. I was recruited to work for Goldman Sachs out of school, where I was part of the Mergers and Acquisitions team. I spent ten years there, and was promoted to director. Ten months ago, I made a decision to take a position in this organization. It wasn't an easy decision. I was highly compensated at Goldman, and had a fulfilling job. But I have family ties to the organization—my uncle Peter, Loco Pete they called him, took a bullet through his left eye when Jimmy Annuncio was hit in

1992, and my father Carlo is currently hanging tough in the Federal Correction Institution in Fort Dix. It's a family business and family is important to me. But also, I'm the kind of person who is motivated by challenges, and I saw a number of challenges facing the organization. Not to be immodest, but I believe I brought with me the unique skill set required to help the organization not only to survive, but thrive in a new business environment.

"What were the challenges I saw?" She brought up the next slide. "We were a business, and a big, complex business, but we weren't operating like a modern corporation."

Tony got up from the couch and walked over to the credenza where room service had left the cold drinks Gina Quattro had ordered for the meeting—four soft drinks in cans and three water bottles.

"You didn't get any root beer?" he asked.

"Just what's there," she said curtly.

"It's all diet shit," he said, grabbing a can of Coke Zero. "Nico, you want anything?"

"I'm good."

Tony popped open the can, took a long swallow from it, and walked back to the couch, not in any hurry.

Gina Quattro waited for him to sit down. She's pissed, Nico thought. And he's going to belch; that's what he's going to do next.

"As I was saying," she continued, saying each word precisely, "we had challenges. We had a brand; we had a mission and values, but hadn't formalized them. Several of our core businesses were no longer viable. Our accounting processes were a joke. We weren't attracting new talent."

She brought up a slide of a Tyrannosaurus Rex. The caption read, "Evolve or die."

"Look, can I say something?" Tony asked. "All this is good, these slides and everything, but why don't we get to the point of why you brought us up here."

Gina moved closer to the phone. "Vincent, did you hear Tony Connole's question? He wants to know why we're having this meeting."

A low growl came from the speakerphone, three or four garbled words that Nico couldn't make out.

Gina looked up at Nico and Tony. Nico waited a beat, then asked anxiously, "What did he say? I couldn't make it out. Sorry, Vincent," he said to the phone, "there was some static or something . . ."

More growling came from the speaker phone.

Nico looked at Gina Quattro for a translation. Her gaze was cold. "He said you two fucking losers are in trouble. He said since your father Nicky died you haven't contributed shit to the organization. He thinks you've been taking advantage of the fact that he's been sick—"

"I can explain—"

"—he said you two pimples on the ass of humanity owe him big time."

Nico felt sweat pooling in the big crease below his chin. "The business has changed," he said. "These Vietnamese guys got together and cut us out of the squid business. The Mexicans . . . they're selling smack everywhere you turn. They're like cockroaches. You step on one, and three more come out of the cracks. You can't control them. Crackheads from Oakland are running in whores. They don't have any respect for the system we had in place here—" He flipped open the briefcase and pulled out a ledger. "Here. I brought this. I can show you what's been coming in so you'll know why our payments are what they are. It's all in here." He offered the ledger to Gina Quattro. She looked at it like he was trying to hand her a bag of shit. "Here," he said. "We can go over all the numbers together."

Angry barking came from the speakerphone. Gina Quattro stared impassively at the brothers.

Then Tony stood up, grabbed the ledger out of Nico's hand, and was waving it in front of Gina Quattro. "Look, you stuck-up bitch," he said. "You can't come down here and treat us like this. My brother is asking you to go over the numbers with him. Take the fucking ledger—"

The big kid was faster than Nico could have ever imagined. Obeying some subtle signal from Gina Quattro, he flew at Tony like a blitzing linebacker, grabbed him from behind in a bear hug and lifted him off the floor. Tony was thrashing and yelling, but he couldn't get loose. Mr. Hat came up and started punching Tony in the face. He threw a couple of hard shots before Tony started kicking, backing him off.

"Hey!" Nico said. "Hey—" He felt sick, helpless. Blood was pouring from Tony's nose. The ledger was on the floor. He fought an impulse to pick it up.

"Throw that mouthy fucker off the balcony," Gina Quattro said.

"Wait," Nico said, but no one was listening to him.

119

Benjie duck-walked, with Tony struggling in his tight embrace, over to the big glass doors that gave on to a short balcony that overlooked the beach forty feet below. Mr. Hat slid the door open.

"*Wait!*" Nico shouted. Benjie had crossed over onto the balcony and had taken Tony to the railing. Tony put a foot on the railing, trying to push back from the edge. Benjie looked back at Gina Quattro. She shook her head almost imperceptibly. She looked at Nico.

"What do you want?" he pleaded.

"Finally something smart has come out of your stupid mouth," she said. "That's exactly the right question."

****

"$100,000—how are we going to come up with that kind of money?" Nico said as the elevator descended to the lobby. He was holding the briefcase he'd brought to the meeting. The ledger was inside; he'd made sure to retrieve it as they were being shown the door.

Tony had his head tilted back. He was holding a bloody towel to his nose.

"Fuckers," he said into the towel.

The elevator stopped at the second floor. An elderly couple, dressed for an early dinner, bifocals glinting, looked into the elevator when the door opened. They saw Nico and Tony, the towel, the blood. They paused at the threshold.

"We can take the stairs, Beverly," the man said.

Nico hit the button to close the doors. "When we get to the lobby, can you kind of try to hide the towel? People are going to notice."

With his muffled voice Tony said, "I could give a fuck."

"Just while we're walking through. We might see someone we know. Christ, look at the blood on your shirt."

Tony just shook his head. He coughed and spit a knot of bloody phlegm onto a corner of the towel.

"OK," Nico said, "we'll just walk fast and not look around. Look straight ahead like nothing's wrong."

When they got to the parking lot and got into the market van, Nico asked, "Is it broken do you think? Should we go to the emergency room?"

Tony pulled the towel away and gently pressed the sides of his nose just below the bridge. Nico saw that his brother's nose was swollen, as was his left eye.

"I just need to put some ice on it. Let's go back to the market."

They went into the fish market through a door in the back that led directly into the prep area so no one would see Tony. They didn't want to have to explain the blood. Nico got a fresh towel and put ice into it. When he brought it back, Tony was sitting slumped in a chair, like a boxer who has just lost a fight. Not just lost a fight, but had every shred of pride beaten out of him.

"You gonna be all right?" Nico asked.

Tony shook his head, not looking at him. Nico gave him the ice. After fussing with the towel to get it just right, Tony carefully pressed it against his nose.

"OK, well, we gotta think," Nico said.

They both knew that thinking was Nico's department. So he paced back and forth for several minutes, his hands clasped behind in back, a frown of concentration on his face.

The amount that Vincent was asking them to come up with was staggering. $100,000. And they had to come with it by the end of the week—or else, Gina Quattro warned them. Nico didn't ask or else what. You didn't ask that because you didn't want them to say it. But it was easy to imagine. These people didn't mess around. They could burn the market down, or worse, get personal. Hurt people. He remembered Gina Quattro commenting on little Nicky, on how precious children were.

Then there was Carmine Bosso. Nico could picture his face, white as chalk, in the walk-in freezer.

Or else that.

Tony peeked at Nico over the lumpy ice-filled towel, watching him pace. A couple minutes passed. "Whaddya got?" he asked.

"I got nothing. I mean it's like if they said come up with twenty grand in two weeks that would be tough, but we could maybe do it. Or if they gave us more time. Like let us pay it to them in installments."

"You think Vincent's gonna go for that? Like you go to the layaway window at Sears every month? Like Ma used to do for Christmas presents?"

Nico shrugged. "I was just throwing it out there. Thinking out loud." After staring at the ceiling, Nico had another idea. "What about you? Your house? You got any equity in it?"

"Fuck Nico, I did what you did back when it was so easy to get a loan." He had to breathe through his mouth; his voice was thick and nasal. "I sucked all the equity out. Bought the truck. Got the Giovanna all fixed up. Now I'm underwater. What about your house?"

"I used up all my equity on the new roof and the exhaust fan for this place. And that trip to Vegas that Destina wanted to take." That was when Nico finally accepted the fact that his wife Destina was a complete slut. She'd wandered off while he was sleeping the second night they were there, had a little fling with one of the craps dealers at the Bellagio where they were staying.

"That was a good investment," Tony said.

Ignoring Tony's dig, Nico set his briefcase down on one of the stainless steel work tables. He opened it and pulled out the ledger, which was a little dog-eared at the corners. "First thing, we gotta get serious about is calling in some of these outstanding loans." He flipped open the ledger and drew an index finger down the rows of names and numbers, moving his lips. "There's like $30,000 or so here we should be able to collect. That's a start."

"That's it? I thought we were owed more than that."

"Those are the ones that are active."

"Active?"

"That people are actively paying on what they owe."

"What about inactive?"

Nico flipped the page almost reluctantly. Another worksheet, another list of names and numbers. "There's some money there too, but—"

"How much?"

"I more or less wrote off all this."

"Dad wouldn't have done that."

123

"Dad had Chuy to go after the money. Chuy was good. He did what Dad asked and was, you know, conscientious about it. After he disappeared, who did we end up with? TJ."

"Yeah. Fucking TJ."

"He wouldn't exactly have been my first choice, but he was willing to be the guy. Then he ends up in County, and I've got no one to go after the deadbeats. And I didn't hear you offering to go out and break someone's leg to get them to pay up."

"I'll do it if I have to."

"Maybe you're going to have to."

"How much is on that list? The inactive list?"

Nico stared at the columns of names and numbers. "Like maybe $40,000."

"Forty grand! Fuck! How could you let forty grand just sit there?"

"It's just numbers, Tony."

"Just numbers? Numbers with dollar signs in front of them, right? Those kinds of numbers?"

"Most of what's owed is viggerish, you know, interest that's accrued over time. The actual money we loaned was a lot less."

"But the vig—that's why you loan the money in the first place, right? Don't act like it doesn't mean anything. Who's on the list?"

"There's like five guys."

"Like who? Who's the first name?"

"Larry Compton."

"That guy?" Tony pulled the towel away from his face and blinked. He opened the towel, rearranged the ice and brought it back up to his face. "Married Sylvia Croscetti, right? She caught him screwing around and ran him over in their driveway. Big Ford Expedition. Flattened right up against the garage door. It's not like she never played around. Did you ever nail her? Sylvia Croscetti? Remember her from high school?"

Nico nodded. He remembered her, but had never nailed her, not even close. "Larry borrowed like $3,000 two years ago. Never paid anything on it, so it would be like $10,000 now."

"Did he ever come out of that coma?"

"More or less. He died a few months ago. But see, that's what I'm saying. It seems like there's a lot of money owed out there, but it's not as much as it looks."

"Maybe Sylvia got some life insurance."

"Are you serious?"

"It seemed like a reasonable question. Who else you got?"

"Mark Chmiel."

"Chmiel the Schlmiel? We loaned that loser money?"

"He asked me to front him something so he could buy some meth that he was going to turn around in like three days, pay me double what I loaned him."

"Guy was a frickin' crankhead. Where'd he end up? Soledad? For like five years?"

"I don't know. Something like that. We did the same deal a couple times before and it all worked out."

"How much did you front him the time it didn't work out?"

Nico hesitated. "Four grand. With the interest it'd be around, I don't know, twelve, thirteen grand now."

"No wonder we're fucked. You're loaning four grand to a loser like Mark Chmiel who can't find his ass with both hands. The guy he was selling to was a cop, right? An undercover cop?"

Nico didn't answer. He looked down at the ledger.

"Next?"

Nico put his index finger on the next name. "Pete Wakefield."

"The Pelican, right?" That was how they'd referred to him for years. "Is he still walking around the Bay-View in that Pelican suit scaring the fuck out of the kids?"

Nico nodded.

Tony said, "What's he into us for?"

"$11, 478. He's got this little dog, a wiener dog. He's one of these guys who's totally in love with his dog."

"I don't get it," Tony said. "People and their frickin' dogs."

"The dog had some kind of stomach or intestinal problem, something that needed surgery. He borrowed money from me before, a few hundred bucks to cover some gambling debts. Made good on it. Anyway, he needed money for the dog's surgery."

"You loaned him over $11,000?"

"Tony, you're not getting it. *We* loaned him a total of $6,000. The rest is compounded interest over the past eight months."

"Why didn't he just get the money from Teddy Wakefield? The Wakefield's are loaded. He's like a cousin or something, right?"

"That's what I was thinking. First he said he could get it, no problem, he just had to petition the family trust. Now he's saying he can't withdraw money from the trust. It's all locked up or something.

126

He also was telling me that the Bay-View has been sucking money out of that trust for years, till there's hardly any left."

"Well he's going to have to show us some money. I'm going to get into that pelican's face. Anyway, now we're getting somewhere. $11,000. That's a start. Who else is on the list?"

Nico drummed his fingers on the stainless steel table. Then he scratched his left ear. "Louie Galvan," he said.

"Chuy's dad? Gallo?"

Nico shifted his gaze away from Tony and stared at the ledger. The numbers, which he'd scratched in neatly in pencil over the months, adding up the unpaid interest as it accrued, each month filling in a new column to the right, might as well have been chiseled in stone, like they did on grave stones. When he looked up again Tony had pulled the ice away from his face again and was looking at him with open-mouthed disbelief. "You're shittin' me. . ."

Nico got up and went to the walk-in freezer. "I'm getting a Drumstick. You want one?"

"How much is he into us for?"

The frigid air in the walk-in felt good. Nico took his time, glad to escape Tony's inquisition for a few minutes, straightening a few boxes of pollock filets before grabbing a Drumstick. He was carefully unwrapping it as he walked back into the prep area.

"How much?" Tony asked again.

"It started out at $500. About eighteen months ago. He needed if for his taco joint, to tide him over during the winter months when business was slow. He paid me back right away. Then it was a grand. Same kind of deal. Then a couple more. And he wasn't paying me so good. Missing payments, then catching up a little, but never zeroing it out. I told him it was going to get out of control. With the interest and everything. I don't think he got what I was saying. I think he was trying to catch up by betting on Mexican soccer matches, something like that. He kept coming back to me, and at some point I cut him off."

"What's the total? Including the vig?"

"Including the vig? That'd be, I don't know, around fifteen, sixteen thousand dollars."

"Christ," Tony said. "Why didn't you say something to me?"

"Tony, look. For the past three years since Dad died you've been off in your own world. Every decision about the business you said 'You figure it out.' You were either screwing around with your boat, or chasing the waitresses here, or whatever. Dad could keep you focused, but I can't. Besides, most everyone else was paying us. We've been making a little money. Every bank, if you ever read the business section of the paper, every bank has non-performing loans." Nico bit into the top of the Drumstick, sinking his teeth through the hard armor of nuts and chocolate.

"Well, we gotta get it from him."

"How're you going to get that kind of money from Gallo?"

"How'd we always used to do it? Go to his piece of shit taco joint and tell him he's got to come up with it or else. Just like that bitch Gina Quattro just told us we had to do. Shit flows downhill, Nico."

Nico licked a drip of melted vanilla ice cream that was running down the cone. He liked to keep everything just so as he worked his way down from the top. "He's gotten a little funny in the head."

"He was always a little funny in the head."

"OK, well, he's funnier now."

"Like how? Funny how?"

"He doesn't follow a conversation. You say something to him, and he's off on another tangent. Starts shadow boxing. Asks you if you want to go a few rounds with him. Shit like that."

"He's gotta have some money. People are always lined up inside the place. Sometimes out the door."

"They're buying three buck tacos."

"Then maybe he should raise the price. I'll go talk to him tomorrow. Him and Pete Wakefield. We've gotta get something from those two guys. You start calling in the other loans. And one more thing."

"Yeah?"

"How much you think Mom has collected for this raffle?"

"We're not going there, Tony."

"I'm thinking maybe ten, twelve thousand dollars."

"Forget it."

"Look, who needs the money more, that little shiny-shoe priest or you and me? And also Mom, by the way. It would kill her if we lost the market, or something happened to someone in her family. Think about it."

One of the market guys, a kid they called Moochie, wearing a dirty blue smock and rubber wellingtons, came in from the front, walking toward the freezer. "Gotta get more shrimp in the retail case," he said, opening the walk-in door. He came out a few seconds later holding a five-pound bag of bay shrimp. He saw Tony's face.

"Holy fuck," he laughed.

"What?" Tony said, as if he didn't know.

Moochie's whole face had lit up. This was good. "Somebody kick you in the head?"

"A wave came up, surprised me this morning when I was out crabbing. I hit my face against the trap puller."

Moochie knew that was a lie, since there was nothing wrong with Tony's face a couple hours earlier, long after he'd come back with his haul of crabs that morning, but he also knew better than to challenge him. "Sure. Wow. It caught you good. Your face is all beat up like a zombie. You'd fit right in that zombie invasion thing at the Bay-View."

"What zombie invasion thing?"

****

Can a tough guy carry a torch for a lost love? A guy who's made his living beating the snot out of people? A guy who's had his nose broken three times, had a pool cue snapped over his head, lost his right front tooth in an alley fight, busted his knuckles on the hard skulls of deadbeats, even taken a gunshot to the shoulder—can a guy like that nurse a tiny flame in his heart fueled by regret for what might have been?

If that guy was Chuy Galvan, he could.

You wouldn't know it if you hung out with him. With a face that looked like it was sculpted by an axe, you'd guess that he was capable of brute emotions, but you wouldn't peg him for the type who actually had *feelings*. His father, Gallo, who groomed him from an early age to be a boxer, had trained him to suffer in silence, even after taking his worst beatings. Especially after taking his worst beatings. That's when you sucked it up and showed the world that you were made of the tough stuff.

That's how he tried to handle the breakup with Jana two years earlier, by making it look like he'd taken a hard punch, but that he was shaking it off like any hard punch he'd taken. Bouncing back. Moving forward.

He couldn't pull it off. He moped around town, found himself listening to sad songs, staring at the sunset—shit he'd never done before. The worst part of it was that she wouldn't or couldn't tell him why she wanted to end it; all she'd say is that it wasn't about him; it was about her. *About her?* Why couldn't it be about him? He could apologize for whatever he'd done, or hadn't done, or change some bad habit, the way he dressed, the way he blew his nose by pinching one nostril and forcefully clearing the other, whatever . . . The point was he was willing to listen to whatever grievance she might have had about him, and was absolutely open to turning around his whole freaking life if that's what she wanted.

But that's not what she wanted. It wasn't about him. It was about her. Whatever the hell that meant. It drove him crazy.

He decided he had to get out of town. The most dramatic way he could think of to do that was to enlist in the Army and get a ticket—maybe a one-way ticket, he didn't give a damn—to Afghanistan. And he wouldn't tell Jana. He would just disappear and she would come to realize how much she missed him and then months later she'd get the bad news about how he died in combat and finally really understand what a great guy he was and how wrong she had been to break up with him.

Turns out you need a high school diploma in order to enlist, and Chuy had fallen short of that distinction when he dropped out of school halfway through his senior year. Well OK, he decided, if he couldn't banish himself to Afghanistan, he'd go to another hellhole.

Bakersfield.

He had a friend, Berto Dominguez, an MMA fighter he used to train with, who had opened a gym there in one of the tougher sections of a tough town. The plan was that Chuy would work himself into shape, hone his fighting skills, and get back into the cage. He'd start with local bouts, scrap his way up into a few bottom-of-the-card StrikeForce fights in Central Valley towns like Merced and Clovis and Modesto. Position himself for a shot at the StrikeForce middleweight title, get a little buzz generated and try to jump to the bigger stage of the UFC.

After six months of hard training he had his first fight. He won that one, and then a second. He was feeling pretty good, maybe even a little cocky when a week later he broke his foot on the hard head of a sparring partner. Six months after that, fighting for the first time after his foot healed, he broke the trapezium bone in his left hand, a tiny little bone he didn't even know he had. Four months later, almost ring-ready again, he ran into another setback. Since he wasn't making squat as a fighter he'd gotten a job as a bouncer at a strip club. One night a drunken country boy in a pretty straw cowboy hat took exception to being tossed from Sneaky Pete's, grabbed a little .25 automatic out of his pickup truck, stalked back to the entrance and shot Chuy. Just like that. Didn't say a word just lifted the gun and pulled the trigger, and then ran off.

The slug entered just below his left collarbone, clipping a piece of his shoulder blade as it exited. It healed up OK, leaving a small red scar in front and a larger purplish scar in back, but even when he was cleared by the doctor to resume training he couldn't bring himself to get back into it. He needed some time off; he was tired of getting hurt. For a while all he did was hang out with some fools who got high every day and every night. A dealer named Raymond Wilkes liked having him around, started asking him to come along when he was making his rounds. You don't have to do anything, he said. Just stand there with that stare.

What stare? Chuy wondered, but didn't ask it out loud.

Every couple weeks or so he resolved to change his life. Maybe go to a community college to pick up computer skills. Maybe sell cars. Take out a student loan and go to culinary school. He still hadn't gotten over Jana. If he could have figured out what to say, he might have called or texted her. She had texted him a couple times, right after he left, when he was still too hurt to respond. But now he couldn't bring himself to do it. Too proud, or something like that. It drove him a little crazy for a while, so he willed himself to stop thinking about her. Move on. And that's what he did, or thought he did. Other than that he just couldn't get his life pointed in any new direction. So he just did what he was doing. He was Raymond's guy, driving him around, hanging out with him at clubs, making life difficult for the competition. Every now and then he'd have to get rough with someone, which was part of the deal.

133

One year went by, then another.

Then a few weeks back his dad's common-law wife Filomena had tracked him down and told him he better get up there to help out with his old man. *Tu padre,* she called him. He was going goofy, she said, acting like he'd fallen off his burro. *Tumbado del burro* was the Mexican phrase she used.

So he came back—but only to check in on Gallo. He wasn't going to look up Jana. He had no interest in trying to rekindle their romance. He was over it. No more sad songs for him, no more sunsets.

A couple days after he got back he just happened to see her kid brother Andrew with his goofy smile walking in the Flats and followed him at distance to an old apartment house. It was only a few blocks from his dad's taqueria, so you could say it wasn't really surprising that he'd find himself walking by their place a couple times a day after that. And maybe sometimes at night. It wasn't like he was hoping to catch a glimpse of Jana. It was a free country and he could walk where he pleased. But he hadn't seen her until the night he came upon Andrew curled up in a fetal position on the sidewalk, picked him up and took him home.

When he heard her voice, and then walked into the room and saw her, his heart started banging in his chest like an animal trying to get out of a cage. He hadn't expected that. He played it cool because that's how he always played things. He didn't remember much of their conversation; he was more focused on just looking at her and trying to read into the way she looked at him. It was hard to say whether she'd actually missed him. Of course she was probably being careful. And she had moved on, going to school, getting into a career. She wanted him to know that. Meanwhile his heart was like a chimpanzee howling and doing flips in a cage.

The only thing she gave him to work with was what she mentioned in passing about the chicken molé at Gallo's, and how much she loved it.

It wasn't much, but it was all he had, a good reason to drop by her apartment again, he decided—show up after she got home from her evening classes with some molé, a bottle of wine. Invite himself in. If he could just spend a little time with her, maybe she'd remember how it used to be.

And since Filomena always had a big pot of molé simmering on the beat-up Wolf range at the taqueria, he thought it would be a simple deal to spoon out a few servings, throw it into a to-go container along with some tortillas and head out the door.

Filomena thought that was a terrible idea. She was a big woman of around fifty, not tall but wide in the shoulders and across her breasts, which filled the floral aprons she always wore like a couple of sacks of masa. She looked at the world with a watchful, suspicious gaze. Always sizing things up, Chuy thought. Gallo had taken up with her twelve years earlier, not long after Chuy had left the house at sixteen. They hadn't interacted much, mainly because Chuy thought she was bossy and he couldn't understand why Gallo put up with it. But they'd warmed to each other in the weeks since Chuy had come back, finding common ground in their shared affliction, a slightly demented 72-year-old bantamweight known as Gallo.

It was a little after 8:00 PM. The taqueria wouldn't close its doors until 9:00, but business had slowed to a trickle. Chuy and Filomena were in the kitchen, standing in the space between the steam table and the range where Filomena generally stationed herself with the air of the captain of a ship, putting together customers' orders, peering through the pass-through serving window to make sure all was well in the front of the restaurant and barking orders at the kitchen staff, which consisted of a dishwasher named Julio, who was her nephew, and a prep cooked named Clarita, her niece. Or maybe her niece's daughter, Chuy could never figure it out.

Corrida music was playing from a cheap CD player that Julio always kept on a shelf next to the dishwasher.

Gallo was in their tiny apartment in the back, which was a good thing. No one wanted him in the kitchen causing confusion, trying everyone's patience.

After Chuy told her what he was up to, she looked at him like he was crazy.

"You want to take her *my* molé?"

"Hey, I'll pay you for it, if that's a problem."

"You love her?" She said *lub*. You lub her?

"Let's just say I like her."

"You like her a lot?"

She was boring in on him. He couldn't look her in the eye. "Maybe. Kind of."

She studied him, the trace of a smile in the corners of her eyes. "No, you lub her. I can see it in your face."

"What about my face?"

She was enjoying her little inquisition. "You can't hide it."

"Whatever."

"And you want her to lub you."

"OK. Sure. Why not.

"Then *you* have to make the molé. Molé comes from the heart," she explained. "Like lub, you know? Every person has a special way of making it."

"Look, that's good to know. But I don't know how to make molé. I wouldn't even know where to begin."

She gave him a smile, something she didn't bestow very freely. "I'm going to help you."

There wasn't going to be any debate over it. She got things started by taking a whole chicken out of the refrigerator and plopping it down on the work table in front of him. She handed him a knife and told him to cut the chicken in quarters, a task he approached tentatively, hacking and sawing at the bird, the blade getting stuck in the dense backbone. She finally intervened, saying, "Chuy, you don't have to kill it. It's already dead." Taking the knife from him, she deftly quartered the chicken, putting it into a pot of water with onion and garlic, which she set on top of a high flame on the stove. After the chicken started simmering, she gathered ingredients for the sauce from different corners of the kitchen and arrayed them on a work table, describing each: the three kinds of peppers—mulato, ancho and pasilla— the cloves, coriander, anise, cinnamon, sesame seeds, pumpkin seeds, almonds and plantain.

It took a while for Chuy to get into it; he was daunted by the sheer number of ingredients and the complicated steps required to extract their flavor. They started by toasting the chiles, then soaking them. Next, she had him toast the coriander seeds, the anise seeds and sesame seeds, which were then ground together with the cloves, peppercorns, cinnamon. She held the grinder up to his face, and encouraged him to "taste it with your nose". And that's when he started to realize that all the effort might be worth it.

"That is freaking awesome," he said. "That is like . . ." he searched for the right word.

"Like lub," Filomena suggested.

"Sure. Yeah." Chuy breathed in deeply. "Like lub."

Bringing him back to the range, Filomena showed him how to plump the raisins and brown the almonds and the pumpkin seeds in sizzling lard. She added pieces of tortilla, crisping them up. She sautéed the plantain, then half an onion. Everything went into a blender with a little chicken stock to moisten it. Once the ingredients had reached the proper consistency—almost as thick as wet cement— she poured out the contents of the blender into a sauce pan, added a bit more chicken stock, and put the pan on a burner over a medium flame. For her final bit of magic, she broke up a big piece of Mexican chocolate and added it to the sauce, turning it a deep, delicious brown.

She dipped a wooden spoon in the sauce, coating it, and held it out for Chuy to taste.

"What do you think?" she asked. "*Bueno?*"

He looked at her over the spoon. "*Muy bueno,*" he said, two of the handful of Spanish words he knew.

That's when Gallo walked into the kitchen, in a big ornate mariachi sombrero, the cheap kind they sell to tourists in Tijuana. He was wearing a tired wife-beater undershirt and a pair of jockey shorts, a baggy pair whose elastic had long ago lost its snap, although it was clear that their occupant hadn't. A surprisingly robust erection pushed mightily against the weary cotton fabric.

"Filomena," he complained. "You've got to come to bed."

"I'm not getting anywhere near that thing." To Chuy she said, "He got his doctor to prescribe him that Viagra." She shook her head at the craziness of the idea. "I thought we were done with all that. Now it's like he has a new toy that he wants to play with." To Gallo she said, "You go back to the apartment. I'm busy here."

Filomena's niece Clarita came in from the front of the restaurant carrying a bus tub, and Chuy saw her eyes grow wide when she caught sight of Gallo, who was now rotating his hips, like he was doing the Macarena. "Come on, Filomenita," he said, "come back to our love nest."

Filomena raised the wooden spoon threateningly. "You come near me with that thing and I'm gonna smack it like a *piñata*. Go! You're scaring Clarita."

Gallo's face reddened, as though he'd been slapped and suddenly awakened to the fact that he'd crossed an important line. He looked confused, unsure of what to do or say next. Chuy walked over to him and took him by the elbow. "Come on, Dad. Let's go back to the apartment."

Gallo allowed himself to be led out of the kitchen. "What am I going to do with this?" he asked, staring forlornly down at his bulging jockey shorts. "It's like a log."

"Well, I guess you could hang your sombrero on it. Or maybe you should just try to ignore it. Let's go see if we can find something for you to watch on TV until Filomena has closed up the restaurant."

He led him into the small apartment and settled him into his favorite Barcalounger in front of the television. Gallo seemed to cheer up and forget about his erection when Chuy handed him the remote— something else to play with. Chuy left him scrolling through the 1128 channels the cable service offered.

When he got back to the kitchen they finished up the molé by submerging the cooked chicken pieces in the sauce, which was bubbling like volcanic mud. Twenty minutes later, Filomena pronounced the dish finished. She helped Chuy prepare a take-out container with two generous servings, which she put into a plastic bag along with a half dozen warm tortillas that she had wrapped in a clean white towel.

"Now, Tarzan," she pronounced it Tar-sahn, "bring this to your Juana. Go win her heart."

He wanted to bring wine, but the only wine that the taqueria offered came out of a box. Elephant piss—not the kind of wine to accompany his special meal. He decided he'd stop by La Tiendita market on the way. He remembered that he had to return Andrew's ski mask, which he shoved into the back pocket of his Levis, and his wooden practice sword, which he stuck in one of the taqueria's plastic takeout bags so that only the handle was showing, because he thought it would feel goofy sticking it in his belt or just carrying it around in his hand.

It was just after 10:15, around the time that Jana had gotten home the other night. He walked out onto the quiet streets of River Flats with a spring in his step. His heart was singing. He gave a cheery hello to a pair of hookers working the corner, Mexican women, both over forty, short and squat in tiny skirts but wearing shawls like campensinas going to town.

"You wanna date?" one of them asked.

"Got a date, thanks," he said.

It was a little over four blocks from Taqueria Gallo to the apartment of Jana and Andrew. La Tiendita was just about at the halfway point.

When he entered, Lupe seemed pre-occupied and barely noticed him. The small store was about twenty-five feet deep, two aisles separated by a head-high center shelving unit, every square inch crammed with the staples of the barrio, packaged snacks, canned food, tortillas, bags of masa harina, plastic tubs of lard, bottled hot sauce and a sparse selection of household items. Chuy went straight back to the rear wall, most of which was taken up by a glass-doored cold case filled with beer and wine. He positioned himself in front of the wine selection, studying his options. He wasn't a wine drinker, and really had no idea which wine would go best with chicken molé, red or white, so he decided to split the difference and had narrowed his choices to the pink wines when he became aware of a guy coming up to the beer section to his right, opening the cold case door and pulling out two twelve-packs. A guy in a hoodie. He watched as the guy, a twelve-pack under each arm, walked toward the register. Shifting both twelve-packs to one side, the guy paused to grab a big bag of pork rinds then walked right out the front door without paying, like he owned the place.

Lupe said nothing. He barely looked at the guy, his gaze weary, defeated.

Chuy knew the look—he'd seen the same beaten-dog look countless times when he was collecting debts for the Connoles. He grabbed a bottle of the pink wine and walked up to the register.

"Hey Lupe, what just happened? Did he just steal that all that?"

Lupe took the bottle of wine and rang it up. "Some bad kids around here."

"That's not right, punk kids getting away with that. You want it back?"

"Want it back?"

"The beer."

"I don't want trouble."

"It's no trouble. In fact, it'd be my pleasure."

"It's OK," Lupe said. "$9.85 for the wine."

"This shit's expensive. Must be good, eh, Lupe?" It was a joke, but Lupe wasn't laughing.

Chuy threw $10 on the counter, grabbed the wine bottle by the neck and the two plastic bags—one with to-go container of molé, Andrew's sword in the other—and left the market.

He saw three shadows about a half block away, popping their first beers from the stolen twelve packs. It was them—his favorite boy band, Flannel Shirt and the Hoodies. Just to screw with them he took the ski mask out of his back pocket and put it on as he approached them.

When he was around twenty feet away he shouted, "Hey—you going to pay for that beer?"

They turned to see who was trying to spoil their party, and must have seen the mask—probably not a happy association after the beating they'd taken a couple nights earlier—and took off running, splitting up and going off in three directions. Chuy decided to chase after Flannel Shirt, just to scare him because as much fun knocking the crap out of some wannabe gangbanger would have been, the main thing on Chuy's mind was dinner with Jana. Still carrying the bottle of wine in one hand, and the swinging plastic to-go bag in the other, he sprinted after him. He was feeling pretty good, making up ground, when the masked slipped just enough to block his view of the sidewalk in front of him. Going full speed, he tripped on a curb and flew face first onto the pavement, the bottle of wine flying one way, the bag carrying Jana's special dinner the other.

It was a little noisy for a few seconds, with the wine bottle breaking followed by Chuy's breathy cursing. Then it was quiet except for the fading slap of Flannel Shirts footsteps as he disappeared into the night.

Chuy picked himself up. His heart was no longer singing.

****

When he handed Jana the bag, the questioning look she had on her face on when he unexpectedly showed up at her door took a turn toward complete bewilderment.

"I brought you dinner," Chuy said proudly. "Chicken molé. You said how much you liked it. So I made it for you."

She held the bag gingerly, like it might be part of a prank, like a can of nuts that snakes popped out of when you opened it. *"You* made molé?" She was looking a little frazzled from her long day.

Chuy said, "I had a little bit of help from Filomena. But it was mostly me. It's really good." She didn't invite him in, but she backed up from the doorway and he took a step to follow her into her apartment. A laptop was open next to a glass of wine on the dinette table off the kitchen. Music playing. Susan Tedeschi. Blues, that was her thing. The black cat lying on the back of the sofa looked at him, then looked away.

"Should be enough in there for you and Andrew."

Jana smiled, slightly amused, slightly perplexed. Then she looked into the bag and a strange look came over her face.

"What?" Chuy asked.

"So . . . did this get run over by a truck?"

"Is it messed up?"

"More or less."

"Shit, really? I kind of tripped and fell on my way over here. Face first. I was bringing some wine too. But the bottle broke." He leaned toward her and peered into the bag. "Kinda looks like someone threw a grenade in there, doesn't it? But it'll still taste good." He took the bag from her and walked into the kitchen, opening cabinet doors to look for plates.

"Oh, and here's Andrew's wooden sword. Where's he at?" he asked.

"In the tub."

"What are you doing?"

144

"I was working on something. A promotion for the Bay-View. I'm updating our Facebook page and sending out tweets."

"Tweets?" Chuy was aware of social media, but didn't see any reason to mess with it. Jana had picked up her phone and was staring at it.

"Twitter's amazing."

"You're doing it now? Tweeting?"

"Just checking on some metrics. I got over 200 shares on my last post, and we added like 80 followers today."

"You can take a break to eat, right?" He found a plate, spooned a portion of the molé out of the bag and put it on the table. "Here, try it."

She looked away from her phone to the plate, then looked at Chuy. He had rummaged through a couple of kitchen drawers, found a knife and fork for her, and set them on either side of the plate.

Reluctantly putting aside her phone, Jana sat down in front of the food, but hesitated before picking up her fork. Chuy was looking at her expectantly. "What's this all about?" she asked.

"About? It's about how you said you loved the chicken molé at my dad's place, and I wanted to make some for you. Actually, Gallo's old lady helped me, but we made it from scratch. It's a pretty big deal, making molé. You know how many ingredients go into it?"

Jana still hadn't picked up her fork, still looking at him like this might all be the setup for a joke. "I have no idea . . ."

"I don't know exactly either, but it's a lot. All kinds of peppers, all kinds of seeds—like pumpkin seeds and sesame seeds. Then some raisins. Chocolate . . . I couldn't keep track of it all. Filomena was going pretty fast. What are you waiting for? Take a bite. Please."

Jana picked up her knife and fork. She carefully cut a piece of chicken, twirled it in the puddle of sauce on her plate and put it in her mouth.

Chuy watched, waiting for her reaction until he couldn't wait any longer, which took about four seconds.

"Well?"

"It's good," Jana said.

"Just good?"

"Really good." She put another forkful in her mouth.

"Really?"

"Really. You should get a plate and have some. You're kinda creeping me out standing there watching me like that. And get me a little more wine out of the fridge."

"What about Andrew."

"He doesn't usually eat real food. I saw a couple Hot Pockets wrappers next to the microwave when I came home, so he's OK."

Chuy almost fell over himself preparing his own plate and pouring wine for both of them. She moved her laptop and her phone and he sat down across from her at the small table.

As they ate, he told himself to dial it back a little bit. It wouldn't be cool to look like he was trying to vault over the two years they'd been apart in one lunging leap. So he asked about her work at the Bay-View. And she told him about her internship, the cast of characters she worked with, particularly Teddy Wakefield, with his wacky ideas for promoting the old amusement park, especially his latest

146

brainstorm, the zombie invasion, Z-Day. She explained the social media campaign she was running to promote it, setting up the Facebook page, a Twitter stream, stuff like that. To see Chuy sitting at the table listening to her, you'd have thought he was fascinated by every detail of her explanation, but it was all gobbledygook to him. Mostly he was listening to the music of her voice, nodding sympathetically when she sighed in frustration, laughing when she laughed, even if he wasn't sure why.

Twenty minutes into the meal, she cleaned the last bit of molé sauce from her plate with a tortilla and she lifted her eyes to him. The wariness was gone from her gaze.

"That was really, really good, Chuy."

"You don't think it could have used maybe just a bit more chocolate?"

"It was perfect. Maybe you've got a future as a chef. Maybe you could take over the restaurant from your dad."

Gallo's future, and the future of the taqueria, had been on his mind. The day after he'd come back, he'd found Filomena fighting back tears in the restaurant's cramped office, overwhelmed by past-due bills from their suppliers. "We're gonna have to figure that out. He's not any help any more . . . gets in the way mostly. Filomena's been holding it together. But it's a juggling act. They're on COD with just about everyone, and she had to run down to PG&E last week to work out a deal on the electric bill so they wouldn't turn it off. I'd say sell the place, if he could get anything for it. He needs the money, because the only other thing he has is a little Social Security. The thing is, the place could support him and Filomena if he didn't have to pay off the debt he took on over the past few years. The health department made him replace all of the kitchen venting, then they found dry rot in the framing supporting the roof, so he had to have major work done on that. It was a nightmare. Maxed out credit cards, the bank, and who knows where else he borrowed from. Meanwhile, he's kinda losing his marbles. He's lucky he's got Filomena."

But he hadn't come to tell Jana about his dad and the taqueria. He grabbed the wine bottle and topped their glasses. "Look," he said, "I've got to ask you something."

She waited, the wariness back in her eyes.

"Did you ever think about me over the past couple years? Did you miss me?"

She sipped her wine, thinking through her response, trying to be careful. "Of course. Sometimes."

"Because I missed you. It was crazy. For a while I thought about you all the time."

"But you didn't text me or anything."

"That's because I forced myself not to. I thought I had to get over you." She waited while he formed his next thought. "The way you broke it off almost drove me nuts. It wasn't fair."

She tensed up a little. "I don't know what you mean."

"OK, well, we had that little talk, remember? We were walking along the cliffs and you got all serious. You said you thought we should take a break, you know, from seeing each other. Remember that?" She nodded. "And you said it wasn't about me, it was about you. That drove me freaking crazy."

"I said that? Why would I say that?"

"Why are you asking me?"

"Because the way I remember it, it was about you."

"That's not what you said."

"OK, I don't remember exactly what I said. Maybe I didn't want to get into all that then, you know, and start some long painful discussion."

"What was it about me?"

"Chuy, I just didn't see a future in it."

"In *it?*"

"OK, in us. So maybe it was about me. I was starting to see my life differently, starting to get more serious, applying for school, thinking about a career. You were making your living basically as a thug. Nicky Connole's muscle."

She'd hit a nerve. "I was also making deliveries," he protested. "Driving a truck, making the rounds to restaurants in the morning. The other stuff was just something I got into, you know, being around the market and all. Big Nicky knew my dad had trained me to fight, that I'd gotten into Brazilian jiu jitsu and all that. You know, that I knew how to hit someone if I had to. Which I almost never did, unless they had it coming," he insisted. "They knew the score when they borrowed the money. And don't make it out like we were these vicious mob guys. We were mostly like a bank, just collecting on money that was owed by deadbeats. Most of the time you just looked at them cross-eyed and they figured out how to pay you. But listen, I would have changed if you'd just come out and asked me to."

"I guess I didn't think you could change. Then you got that tooth knocked out in a fight, remember? One of your front teeth? And you got that disgusting partial denture thing you used to pop out?"

Chuy moved his tongue around in his mouth and popped out the plate with the fake front tooth.

"You mean thith?" he smiled. With another twist of his tongue he deftly nudged it back into place.

"Every time you did that it reminded me that you were a goon."

"A *goon*?"

"That's what they call guys who are paid to beat other people up."

Chuy was offended. "No one ever called me a goon."

"Because if they did you would have beaten them up."

He felt himself getting a little hot. "Did I ever lay a hand on you? I mean in anger." She didn't answer; they both knew he'd never been rough with her, never even entertained the idea. He softened his tone. "I don't even know what we're talking about. Listen, Jana. I want another chance with you."

"Chuy, I . . ."

"You're not seeing anyone, are you?"

"I don't have time to see anyone."

"I'll work around your schedule. We don't have to get hot and heavy right away. Maybe we could just hang out a little bit. We could even go on a date or something."

"A date? That'd be a first."

"We went on lots of dates."

"Shooting pool at the 2001 Club is not a date. Watching HBO on the couch is not a date."

"What about that time I took you to the Hampton Grille for Valentine's Day, remember? And I brought you those roses?"

He could tell she was remembering it. "Yeah. OK. That was nice."

"And besides, you liked playing pool. You were a shark. And as I recall you didn't have any complaints when we were on the couch. Or later on. Come on, let's give it another shot."

"I don't think it's a good idea, Chuy. I've got a lot on my plate with school and this internship . . ."

"But you'll think about it, right? You know I'm not going to give up on you."

Andrew saved her from having to respond. They heard the bathroom door open and he emerged with a towel wrapped around his waist. The skin of his chest was moist and splotchy. His face was red; his damp hair was flattened against his forehead.

"Chuy!" he said, surprised. "You're here?"

"Hey Andrew. I brought a little dinner over for Jana."

"I can hold my breath underwater for forty-nine seconds."

"That's pretty impressive."

"Ninjas train to swim long distances underwater by holding their breath. It's called *Siu-Ren*."

"I didn't know that."

"If they were going to attack an island stronghold of an evil lord they would slip over the side of their ship and swim to shore, but underwater, so the guards patrolling the island wouldn't know they were attacking until they disabled them with a *hiji uchi*. That's an elbow strike." He demonstrated with a sideways thrust of his bent elbow. "Or *kocho giri. Kocho giri* is the butterfly kick. My towel might fall off if I tried to show you that."

"Maybe some other time then."

"Tomorrow?"

"Tomorrow what?"

"Tomorrow can I show you? And you can start training me."

Me and my big mouth, Chuy thought. "Don't you have to go to work at the Bay-View?"

"Not till noon."

He looked at Jana, who wasn't going to help him get off the hook. "OK. Meet me at the beach in front of the Bay-View. At 10:30."

"Have you ever heard of *mae giri*? That's a front kick." Andrew demonstrated another move that wouldn't compromise his towel, slashing the air with his outspread fingers. "*Shako uchi.* The claw hand strike."

"You can show me all that stuff tomorrow. And I'll show you a few things."

Jana used Andrew's interruption in their little talk to cut it off. "Andrew, why don't you get ready for bed?" she said. "Chuy," she angled her head toward her open laptop, "I've got work to do . . ."

"I'll see you tomorrow, Chuy. Do you wear a watch? How will you know when 10:30 is?"

"I'll figure it out. I'll see you then."

"Later, gator," Andrew said. Jana had taught him to say it years ago. It was something he always said to Chuy.

"Later, gator."

Jana looked at Chuy. "I've got to make up Andrew's bed for him. He sleeps in here. The sofa pulls out."

"Sure." Chuy edged toward the door. "So how'd we leave it?" he asked her.

She met his eyes with a neutral gaze. "We'll see. Like I said, I've got a lot on my plate right now."

"I can change," he said.

"Good night, Chuy." She was waiting for him to back out the door.

"Yeah, OK . . . good night."

He paused on the stoop before closing the door.

"Jana, come out here for a sec. There's one more thing."

She hesitated, then stepped outside with him. Her phone was in her hand.

"Chuy . . ." she said warily.

He gently put his arms around her waist and looked closely at her face. Her eyes were wide, not afraid, but uncertain.

"Can I kiss you?" he asked.

"I'm not sure that's a good idea."

"I think it's a great idea. The best idea I've ever had."

He moved his face slowly toward hers. She didn't draw back, but waited, like she was trying to make up her mind about something. He carefully pressed his lips on hers. At first, there was no return response; then he thought he felt her relax into it a little bit. He thought he could taste a hint of the molé on her lips.

She pulled away and pulled his hands off her waist.

"How was it?" Chuy asked.

"It was nice, Chuy. But . . ."

"I'm not in any rush. I just want you to think about it."

"I've really got to get back to what I was doing."

"Sure." He came closer, thinking he'd try for another kiss, but she slipped back through the door and started closing it.

"So I'll see you later," Chuy said.

"Sure," she nodded, still with that wary look in her eyes, "Later." And she closed the door.

But she didn't slam it, Chuy noted happily, and his heart started singing again.

Z-Day Minus 4

It was easy to spot Andrew on the wide beach in front of the Bay-View. It was still too early for the beach to be crowded; there were a few dog walkers, a couple of girls bumping a volleyball back and forth, and an old guy—was it always the same old guy?—waving a metal detector over the sand; but even if the beach had been busier Andrew would have stood out. He was wearing baggy Hawaiian print board shorts and an unbelted karate jacket. A headband was tied ninja-style around his forehead. But it wasn't just what he was wearing that made him stand out; it was the jumping, twirling, kicking and punching the air that really made him conspicuous.

He was so absorbed in fighting an army of imaginary enemies that he didn't see Chuy trudging toward him.

Chuy got within about ten feet of him, stopped, folded his arms and watched for a few minutes. It was only when he asked, "Who's winning?" that Andrew realized he was being watched.

"Chuy—you're late." He was breathing hard. A sheen of sweat glistened on his cheeks and upper lip.

Chuy shrugged it off. "Maybe a little."

Andrew checked his big digital watch. "Eleven minutes and thirty-eight seconds late."

"Don't let it ruin your day. I got busy with a few things and didn't see the time. But, hey, I was watching you as I came up. You've got some pretty impressive moves there. Where'd you learn them?"

"Books. And videos. And ninja movies."

"Cool headband," Chuy said. It was the one with Ninja spelled over a big red dot.

"This one is for training. Fighting headbands have like a metal plate in front."

That seemed a little silly to Chuy. "Like to protect you from a sword?"

Andrew didn't get the sarcasm. "Or maybe an arrow," he said. "Do you know ninjitsu?"

"Ninjitsu? I never got into that. But I know karate. I was really into that for about four years. And tae kwan do, Brazilian jujitsu—I messed around with those too. And boxing." Gallo started training him when he was eight; each glove was as big as his head.

"Ninjitsu," Andrew explained, as though he was sharing information that was very solemn and important, "is the ancient art of the shadow warrior. It has eighteen disciplines, like unarmed fighting, sword techniques, throwing weapons, escape, concealment, and espionage. And other stuff."

"You know a lot about this stuff."

Andrew nodded. "I want to fight evil, and evil people like criminals and bullies."

Chuy couldn't help but laugh a gentle laugh. "You're taking on a lot there, Andrew. You might want to just stay out of their way." Andrew wasn't laughing; this was serious. "OK," Chuy conceded, "I don't know much about ninjitsu, but I can show you a few things that might save your ass." Chuy was wearing black jeans, a black t-shirt and black training shoes. He slipped off his shoes, along with his socks. He stood barefoot in the sand, feet planted the width of his hips, knees slightly bent. "What if I was your enemy?"

"If you were my enemy? I'd fight you."

"But you just let me walk right up on you a few minutes ago. If you let your enemy get that close to you without even noticing him, you might not get a chance to fight. First rule," said, making it up as he went along, hoping to make it sound like something a ninja master would say, "is you have to blend into your surroundings. Concealment—that's one of the ninjitsu disciplines you just mentioned, right? Otherwise, how are you going to surprise your enemy?"

"I don't know."

"OK . . . so be sneaky. And you've got to be super-aware of everything going on around you."

"Be aware . . ." Andrew repeated.

"Every one of your senses should be on high alert."

"High alert . . ."

"Pay attention to every movement, every sound."

Andrew narrowed his eyes and scanned the beach with a fierce look on his face.

"That's good," Chuy said.

Andrew could only remain vigilant for a couple of minutes before he lost interest. What he really wanted to do was show Chuy his fighting moves. Tightening his face like a ninja who meant business, he dropped into a combat posture, his left hand extended in front, right hand cocked over his shoulder. "This is the Angry Tiger stance."

"All right, Tiger, what if I was coming toward you on the attack?" Chuy took a step toward Andrew; Andrew jumped out of his pose and kicked wildly. Without flinching, Chuy grabbed him by the ankle and tipped him over onto the sand. Andrew looked up at him, mystified by how quickly he'd been taken down.

Chuy extended a hand and helped him up.

"So, what just happened?" Chuy asked.

"I don't know."

"You got ahead of yourself. Trying moves that you're not ready for. You need to start with some basic moves, get them down, imprint them in your muscle memory so you don't have to think about them. And before you work on fancy attack moves, you should really master a few reliable defensive techniques." Chuy got back into his relaxed ready stance. "OK, pick up that stick there and pretend it's a knife and you're coming at me."

Andrew picked up the six-inch piece of driftwood that Chuy had pointed out. "Now come on," Chuy coached, "rush me with it."

Andrew cocked the arm holding the stick like a crazy man and ran at Chuy. Chuy smoothly sidestepped him, grabbing the arm that held the pretend weapon. He drove Andrew toward the sand with his shoulder, careful to catch him before he hit the ground.

Andrew's face was almost as red as the Japanese sun on his ninja headband. "How'd you do that?"

Chuy helped him get back on his feet. "I'm going to show you. First we're going to break down the move into four parts. Grab. Lock. Pivot.

Pull. Grab the wrist; lock the arm at the elbow; pivot into the guy with your shoulder; and pull him down." He demonstrated each step in slow motion. "Grab, lock, pivot, pull. Can you remember that?"

"Grab, lock, pivot, pull." Andrew repeated.

"OK. Good. Now we're going to practice it. Over and over again."

For the next ten minutes, Chuy alternated between playing the role of the attacker and the victim, instructing Andrew on how to use his opponent's momentum to his advantage, grabbing his attacker's arm by the wrist, locking the arm straight at the elbow, then pivoting into him with his shoulder as he pulled him to the ground. Andrew tried his hardest, but never quite got it. He could remember the words, but couldn't sequence the actions.

They stopped when two security guards from the Bay-View came across the sand to investigate. One, a guy, was slender and tall, with a narrow face. His hair was cut short and he wore wraparound sunglasses. The nameplate above his breast pocket read "LT Martin". The other guard, who was hanging back a little, was a young woman, a blond with a sweet face. Her nameplate read "CPL Cartwright".

"What's the problem here?" Lieutenant Martin asked.

Chuy didn't have much use for cops, much less wannabe cops. "No problem here, Chief."

"It looked like you're fighting. There's no fighting on the beach."

"We're training," Andrew said.

Even though Chuy couldn't read the eyes behind the sunglasses, he got the vibe—the guard was going to let him know who was in charge.

"You're going to have to stop it and move on."

"Because . . .?"

"Because you're causing a disruption."

Chuy scanned the beach around them. A few more people had wandered onto the sand, a volleyball game had started, and the old guy with the metal detector was combing an area about a hundred yards away. But it was still pretty empty. And no one was paying them any attention. Except the guard.

Chuy folded his arms across his chest and looked at the guard, not really angry yet, but not quite ready to let it go. "Bullshit. And besides, this is a public beach. What are you coming down here hassling us for? You're what? One of those $10 an hour dinks the Bay-View hires to yell at the little kids when the start running around after they get all jacked-up on cotton candy?"

"It's a city beach, and the city has an arrangement with the Bay-View to patrol the beach in front of the park. I can use my radio to call one of the local cops so you can talk to them directly if you'd like."

"It's OK, Chuy," Andrew said. "We can stop for today. I'm pretty thirsty."

Chuy didn't say anything for a minute, and the guard didn't say anything. Then Chuy said, "OK. I'll buy you a lemonade."

"Mountain Dew," Andrew said, "A Mountain Dew slushee."

They walked across the beach, took the steps up to the Boardwalk and Chuy bought them slushees at the Heroes and Gyros stand. They sat on one of the benches overlooking the beach, watching families spread towels and stick umbrellas into the sand.

"Are you going to start taking out Jana again?" Andrew asked.

"I don't know. It sounds like she's pretty busy."

160

"You should take her out. Remember when we used to go bowling? I liked that."

"I remember that you rolled a strike once and you went ape-shit."

"And when we watched Bruce Lee movies and monster movies together." All three of them sitting on the little couch in Jana's previous apartment, eating popcorn. Chuy thought back to those times.

"It's up to Jana really," he said; then he thought to ask, "Has she had any boyfriends . . . you know, since I left?"

"Boyfriends?"

"You know, anybody staying over the way I used to stay over?"

Andrew sucked thoughtfully on his straw. "I don't think so."

"It would be OK if she did. I'm just curious, that's all," Chuy said, giving Andrew a chance to think about it a bit more.

But Andrew had something else on his mind. "Why did you run away?" he asked.

"Who said I ran away?"

"I don't know. I just think that." Andrew looked up from his slushee, squinting at Chuy. "Because you didn't tell anyone. You just left."

"I was trying to sort things out."

Andrew made a loud slurping sound with his straw. "You should never run away. You bring dishonor on yourself. You should always stay and fight."

"That's not what a ninja would do, I guess. Anyway, it's not so . . . straightforward."

They both pondered that thought for a moment.

"I've never had a girlfriend," Andrew said.

"How old are you now?"

"Twenty."

"You've got time."

"I know." He stuck the bottom end of the straw and sucked out a slushee clog. "I think I'll probably save some girl's life, and she'll become my girlfriend."

"Sounds like you've got it figured out."

Chuy stared out at the beach. Andrew scraped the last bit of slushee from his cup.

"What time you got?" Chuy asked.

"11:23."

"I've got to get going. What time do you start doing your thing here? What exactly is it that you do, anyway?"

"I'm the Smiles Ambassador. I pass out free smiles to kids and families. My shift starts at 12:00 noon. I have to get changed first. I start to get changed at 11:45, because it takes me fifteen minutes. We have a locker room down a stairs over there. Next to the merry-go-round. There's like a whole secret world under the Bay-View."

"Very cool," Chuy said. He sensed that Andrew wanted him to ask about the secret world, but he had to get back to Gallo's. He tossed his empty cup into a nearby trash can and stood up. "We'll do this again. In the meantime, you've got to keep practicing."

"Grab-lock-pivot-pull."

"That's it."

"And what else? The most important thing."

Andrew couldn't think of anything else. Chuy had to remind him. "Be aware."

"Be aware," Andrew repeated. He stood up, brushing sand off his pants. "When can we train again?" he asked.

"In a couple days maybe. We'll figure it out. But I gotta get going now. I gotta meet a guy around noon."

"What guy?"

"Just some guy. He wants to look at a car I'm selling."

"What car?" Sometimes Andrew did that, just kept asking questions so you'd talk to him a little longer. Chuy didn't have time for that today.

"I gotta run. Later," he said and started heading back to the taqueria.

"Later, gator."

The fastest way back to Gallo's was to cut through the Bay-View. Chuy headed down the midway toward the Barson St. gate and ran into a strange clutch of creatures coming his way. Leading the parade was a cameraman walking backwards, a Channel 7 News video camera on his shoulder. Following him was a group of four people, zombie-staggering with their arms outstretched. Their clothes were ragged, their hair was in disarray and their faces were made-up—ashen skin, dark pools of shadow under their eyes. And as they got closer he heard them moaning lowly. Was one of them Jana? As they came past, he called out to her. She shot him a look that said, "Please shut up," and fell back into character as one of the walking dead.

Chuy pushed back his hair, smiling to himself. Jana had told him about the zombie invasion, a silly-ass idea that he hadn't taken seriously, but apparently the zombies really were coming, and Jana was at the head of the pack.

****

The Pelican spotted Tony from about thirty yards away, and started running, or started moving in a way that would have resembled running if his progress hadn't been seriously impeded by his costume's big floppy webbed feet and the padded belly bouncing up and down front of him like a swallowed medicine ball. He dodged through the Bay-View's sparse late morning crowd, somehow managing to bump smack into a chunky kid eating an ice cream cone, knocking his double scoop of Peppermint Swirl onto the pavement. The kid looked at the misshapen, melting mound of ice cream at his feet in disbelief and started crying; his mother yelled at the fleeing Pelican, who was quickly running out of gas. Tony Connole, his battered face set grimly, barely had to jog to catch up to him. Tony was carrying a Mike Schmidt signature Little League baseball bat at his side.

The Pelican was bent over, panting. The sea captain's hat that crowned his costume had fallen off. Tony picked it up and handed it to him.

"What's the rush, Pete?"

The Pelican slowly lifted his head. The sound of labored breathing came from somewhere behind the fixed happy eyes and open beak, whose corners were curved up as though he were smiling. As if, Tony thought, a freakin' pelican could smile—especially this one.

"Shit, Tony," the Pelican said. "Don't come here while I'm working."

"How else am I supposed to find you? You weren't at your apartment."

The pouch hanging beneath Pete the Pelican's beak trembled. Clumsily—his arms and hands deep inside the loose swinging sleeves that were supposed to evoke wings—the Pelican placed the captain's hat on top of his head.

"Is it on straight?" he asked through his beak.

"Straight enough," Tony said. Truth be told, it sat a little cockeyed on the big white head, but the hat was beside the point.

"You went to my apartment?" the Pelican asked.

Tony ignored the question. "Pete, you know why I want to talk to you, right?" Tony looked directly at the Pelican with his "This shit is serious" stare. The Pelican, with his happy plastic eyes and smiling beak, nodded tentatively.

They were interrupted by the mother of the kid that Pete the Pelican had bumped into as he was trying to flee. She bustled up to them holding the kid's hand, dragging him behind her. "You'd better stop, mister," she said to the Pelican, out of breath herself. She was wearing big sunglasses with red frames. "Do you realize what you just did? You nearly knocked my son over! He's been beside himself all week waiting to come to the Bay-View—he actually had us waiting outside the gate twenty minutes before the park opened—and we're not here more than five minutes when you come barreling into him like a truck, you knock his ice cream out of his hand. . . and then you just keep going? His day is ruined. Look at him. He's traumatized."

Pete the Pelican and Tony both looked at the kid. Tony couldn't tell if he was actually traumatized, but he didn't look happy. The kid was still holding his empty cone. Tears were streaming down his cheeks. It amused Tony to see little fat kids cry. A character flaw, he knew, but he couldn't help it.

Now that she'd come closer to Tony, the woman saw his face and was a little taken aback by the bruising and swelling. She paused, maybe rethinking the wisdom of the confrontation. Tony could see his reflection and the Pelican's in the lenses of her sunglasses as she made the decision to shorten her harangue and get to the point. "What are you going to do about it?" she asked.

Tony roughly grabbed the empty cone from the kid's hand and heaved it toward the beach. While it was still in flight, a screeching storm of seagulls surrounded it and followed it to the sand, where they noisily fought over it.

"That's what we're going to do about it," Tony said. "Now move along. This is a private conversation."

The woman was speechless for a minute. The kid had stopped crying, fascinated by the seagulls. "I'm reporting this to Security," she said. As she was waiting for a response, Tony threw a wadded $5 bill at them and told the mother to get the kid another freakin' ice cream cone. He took the Pelican by elbow and walked him toward the railing that separated the midway from the beach, where they stopped.

A group of moaning zombies being filmed by a cameraman trudged by. Tony was mildly curious about the little parade, but had more pressing business to attend to.

"Pete, Nico tells me you owe us over $11,000. Tells me that he's been asking you for it again and again but you've stopped making payments. Maybe you think you can shine Nico, Pete, but you can't shine me."

"I'd pay you guys if I could, Tony. I would. I told Nico that. I just don't have the money now."

"Yeah, that's what Nico says you've been telling him. For six months now. I don't have that kind of patience, Pete. You gotta get us that money by tomorrow." It was time to show him how serious he was. He pulled out a little dog collar, studded with rhinestones, from his pocket. "You recognize this?"

The Pelican's blank happy stare didn't change, but Tony could see his shoulders slump. He grabbed for the collar with the tips of one of his wings. "Schnitzel!" he cried.

Tony yanked the collar back out of the reach of the lunging six-and-a-half-foot tall pelican.

"Where'd you get Schnitzel's collar?"

"Same place I got Schnitzel. Out of that junky little apartment of yours. The dog was happy to see someone. She looked lonely."

"You took Schnitzel? You broke into my apartment?"

"You need to understand how serious we are about getting paid what we're owed."

"Where is she?"

"Don't worry about where she is. You worry about getting her back. If we don't get the money from you by tomorrow, I'm going to use her to bait one of my crab traps."

"She's on a special diet."

"She's going to *be* a special diet if you don't come up with the money."

The Pelican grew animated, flapping his wings. "I don't have it, Tony. I spent it all on vet's bills and there's more I've got to pay off."

"Get it from your family."

"I told Nico this a hundred times. The Wakefield trust isn't like a bank account where you just withdraw money. Teddy and Blaine control it, and that Blaine is a tight-ass. Besides, I'm just a cousin. They think they're doing me a huge favor just by giving me this crappy little job. Do you know how humiliating it is to put on this stupid costume and pretend to be friendly? How degrading? How many times I've wanted to grab one of the spoiled little brats who pull my tail feathers, or the pimply punks who grab at my cap, and plant one of these big webbed feet on their ass?"

"I don't want to hear your sad story, Pete. Maybe you need to see a shrink to go over all that with. I just want what you owe us. And I want it by tomorrow. Before noon."

He turned and started walking away.

"She can't eat just anything," the Pelican said. "Only this all-natural kibble. The brand is 'Doggone Good'. It's got avocadoes, chia seeds in it, brown rice, stuff like that. It's for dogs with stomach problems. They sell it at Whole Foods."

Tony kept walking.

168

"Wait." The Pelican ran up behind him. "Wait. I got something else. Maybe we can make a deal."

Tony kept walking, but slowed a little.

"We're talking hundreds of thousands of dollars."

Tony slowed a lot, letting the Pelican catch up and circle around to face him. He waited. The Pelican looked both ways and said, "You guys are criminals, right?"

"What guys?"

"You and Tony and like your dad and all that."

"Criminals? I don't know what you're talking about. We've never been convicted of anything," Tony said emphatically. "Nothing major anyway. We're business people. Dad got a plaque from the Chamber of Commerce once."

"OK. But if you were criminals and got some inside information on how the receipts from all the games and rides are transferred to the counting room and how all the cash just piles up over the weekend, and if you knew when the armed guard who's usually standing out in front of the counting room door takes off for fifteen, twenty minutes each night . . . that'd be worth something, wouldn't it? There's a lot of cash that goes into that room."

"Like how much?" Tony asked.

"If you're talking after a weekend, it's got to be over a hundred grand."

"A hundred grand?"

"Sure. Even more after a big three-day weekend like Memorial Day weekend. Think about it. Three busy days like that, each day you get three to four thousand people coming into the park, all carrying cash and each one spends $25, $30 . . . it could maybe add up to two hundred grand easy."

"And it's all sitting there in this vault?"

"There isn't any vault."

A weird moon-faced character in a pink jacket and straw hat wandered up to them and just stood there, smiling. The smile was a little creepy, Tony thought, like the weirdo had been sucking happy gas.

The Pelican turned to talk to him, saying "Andrew, there's a little boy crying over near the Teacups—can you go over and cheer him up?"

"Sunrise was at 5:14 this morning. And sunset will be at 7:59."

"Good to know, Andrew. Now go find that little boy. He needs a few smiles."

Tony waited for the smiley guy to walk away. "The counting room. You were saying all this cash goes into the counting room. They can't just let it sit there. . ."

"Cost saving. My cousin Blaine said that the armored car company charges double to come out on weekends, so they just stash it till Monday, or Tuesday if it's a three-day weekend."

"But they gotta have pretty heavy security. . ."

The Pelican got cagey. "That's all I'm going to give you for now. I'll give you more details once you and Nico and me come to an agreement about what I owe you."

"I think you're bullshitting me."

The Pelican stared at him blankly, which he'd been doing the entire conversation, since his eyes were painted on his pelican mask.

"Where do you have Schnitzel?" the Pelican asked.

"Don't worry about where I've got her. She's OK—for now."

"So, can we work out a deal?"

"You're not giving me very much."

"And I'm not going to until we have a deal."

Tony hated negotiating. It wasn't his thing. He liked the more direct approach—beat the other guy with your fists until you can come to an agreement. It was a long shot, but maybe the Pelican had something that could save their bacon. He pushed his hair back, thinking.

"I gotta run this by Nico. Maybe we can work something out, I don't know. If you're not B.S.ing me. You gonna be around later?"

"I get off at 8:30."

Tony asked for the Pelican's cell number, which he tapped into his own phone. "Maybe I'll call you. After I run this by Nico." He started walking away.

"What about Schnitzel? She needs her special kibble or else she gets horrible diarrhea."

Tony had left the agitated dachshund in the cab of his truck, which seemed like a good idea at the time, but now maybe not so much. When he got back to his truck and opened the driver's door the stink hit him right between the sinuses like a ballpeen hammer.

"Jesus H. Christ!"

Schnitzel cowered on the seat, whimpering quietly. Her glistening dark eyes bulged out of her tiny head. They were the size and shape of grapes.

Tony wasn't as tough as he looked, not with animals anyway.

171

"You should be ashamed," Tony said. "You pull this kind of thing again and I'm going to introduce you to a big sea lion named Sammy who will eat anything, even wiener dogs."

It wasn't as bad as it could have been. The dachshund had messed in the front seat, but it had puddled on an old blanket that he'd taken from the Pelican's apartment when he grabbed her. After throwing the blanket into a trash can, Tony got into the driver's seat, turned the ignition and lowered the windows, hoping to air the cab out.

On to the next deadbeat on his list.

Gallo's taqueria wasn't far from the Bay-View, just two blocks down a side street in the River Flats barrio. Customers would be lining up for lunch soon, but it was still quiet now. Pigeons pecked at bits of food among the discarded wrappers at the edges of the sidewalk.

Before he got out of the truck, Tony checked out his face in the rearview mirror. He couldn't help himself. Both eyes were swollen, his right eye almost completely shut. A mask of darkened blood had pooled beneath them. His nose had ballooned, especially at the bridge and the swelling filled in the space between his eyes and the ridge of his forehead. If the baseball bat doesn't scare him, he thought, this face will. He grabbed the bat from the passenger seat and got out.

Before closing the truck door, he decided to grab the dachshund and bring her along, tucked under his arm. He didn't trust her in the truck.

It smelled good, of roasting pork and onions, when he opened the door to the taqueria. Inside there was a small dining area, four tables covered in plastic table cloths with cheap stacking chairs pushed in around them. A cold case with bottles of soda and beer stood against one wall. On the walls were black and white photos of a skinny kid in oversized silk boxing shorts crouching behind his upraised boxing gloves. El Gallo—The Rooster. The décor also included a velvet painting of a handsome guy in a sombrero and tight pants twirling a senorita with a rose in her hair, and a map of Mexico. Then there was the counter where you ordered, and behind the counter you could see the kitchen area. Two women in floral aprons and hairnets were prepping for the lunch rush. One of them was barely twenty and had the guarded look of someone who had only recently crossed illegally from Mexico and above all didn't want to be noticed. The other woman was in her fifties, a, short, broad woman who carried most of her weight in her shoulders and breasts. She looked up when Tony walked in, saw this big guy with a scary face holding a baseball bat and a dog. She paused the circular stirring of the pork *carnitas* that she was crisping in a heavy cast iron roasting pan that sat on top of the high flames of two burners. Her eyes showed curiosity, but not fear. Filomena Carrasco didn't scare easily. After growing up dirt poor on a little rancho in Michoacán, having made the long trip North up the spine of Mexico to cross the border (and raped twice during the journey); after raising two boys (one now in the Marines, the other shot dead by gangbangers because he was wearing a red ball cap); after enduring the last seven years as the common-law wife of a philandering ex-boxer who was slowly losing his mind; and after trying to keep a rundown taco joint afloat when purveyors, employees, and the tax man were trying to take every spare nickel they made, Filomena Carrasco could train her flat, seen-it-all gaze on Tony without flinching.

"We're not open now," she said. "Come back in twenty minutes."

"Where's Gallo?" Tony asked.

She continued stirring the *carnitas*, scraping the bottom of the pot to make sure all sides of the meat browned nicely. "What you want with Gallo?"

Now he saw it, her attitude, the challenge in her eyes, and it pissed him off. Tony didn't like it when people didn't take him seriously, especially women.

"That's my business. Where is he? He in the back?"

"He's not here. He's still sleeping. He sleeps late."

Was she lying? He lumbered around the counter, the baseball bat dangling by his side.

She didn't stop stirring. "You can't come back here. You want some food, you have to wait for 11:30. And you gotta stay on the other side of the counter. And no dogs."

"*Gallo!*" Tony called.

Swinging the bat, he swept away a line of empty stainless steel inserts that were lined up on the counter of the steam table and sent them clattering on to the tile floor. Cradled in the crook of his other arm, Schnitzel started whimpering.

Filomena responded with a volley of Mexican curse words, impugning Tony's mother, his manhood and the length of his penis.

"What did you call me?" he said.

She repeated the epithets, adding a bit more detail. Tony didn't understand the words, but he got their meaning. He started pounding on a work table, scattering the lineup of tomatoes, onions and jalapenos that had been set out to make *pico de gallo*, the next task on Filomena's prep list.

"*Hey!*" A shout came from the back of the kitchen, a cracking screech that belonged to Raul "El Gallo" Galvan, who burst into the kitchen from the back apartment. He hadn't donned his sombrero yet. His hair was oiled and combed back flat against his head. Like the neat little mustache that rode atop his upper lip, it was dyed jet black.

Someone had some explaining to do.

"What's going on in here?" he yelled in the high scratchy voice that over fifty years earlier had inspired his nickname. "Filomena, what's all the goddam noise about?" Unlike Filomena, El Gallo had been born in California, and only knew how to swear in English, which he did with high-pitched vigor, firing F-bombs in every direction until his gaze found Tony. "Who's he? Who the hell are you?" He noticed Schnitzel. "And we don't allow no dogs in here."

Tony stared at him, wondering, does he seriously not recognize me? Growing up, his brother Nico had been best friends with Gallo's son Chuy, and they'd all hung out, gotten boxing lessons from the old man. But it had been at least ten years since he'd been in the taqueria. He stopped coming in after he nearly choked on a chicken neck bone that had found its way into a super burrito he'd been wolfing down after a night of drinking.

"It's Tony Connole, Gallo. You know me. Nico's my brother."

"Nico? Who the hell is Nico? Why are you making this mess in here?" He bent down to pick up the stainless steel inserts that Tony had scattered on the floor.

"Nico Connole. You know Nico," Tony said, wondering why he should have to explain anything. After all, he was the guy with the bat. "You borrowed money from us and we want to get paid."

"You gave him money?" Filomena asked Tony, like it was one of the saddest and craziest things she'd ever heard. "You gave *Gallo* money?"

Gallo was picking up the inserts and carefully placing them, one by one, on the counter, muttering unhappily. He looked at Tony. He seemed confused. "Who did this? You did this?"

"Did you borrow money from them, Gallo?" Filomena asked.

Gallo was on his hands and knees now, crawling on the floor to pick up the tomatoes and onions.

"Look at all this on the floor," he said. "It's gotta be picked up. You can't have food on the floor."

Tony decided it was time to cut the bullshit. He slammed the baseball bat on the counter, rattling the stacks of plates. The loud noise startled Schnitzel, who squirmed under his arm. "You—" he started to say to Gallo, who was now halfway under a table reaching for a tomato that had rolled under it and not paying attention to him. Tony turned to Filomena. "—he owes me and my brother $15,168. My brother Nico's got it all in a book."

"He can't pay you," Filomena said. "He's got no money like that."

They still weren't getting it, that Tony hadn't dropped by to *ask* for money—he was *demanding* the money. He started smashing plates with the bat.

"$15,168," he repeated each time he created another pile of crockery shards out of a stack of plates. "$15,168!"

"*He don't have it!*" Filomena shouted.

Gallo emerged from under the work table with a tomato in his fist. "I got one tomato!" he announced happily.

Tony was looking for his next target when Filomena heaved the entire contents of roasting pan that she'd been tending at him. Chunks of meat, onions and sizzling lard hit him like a cluster bomb, burning his face and arms and spattering his clothes.

"*Fuck!*" he bellowed. He lunged at her, but slipped on the greasy floor and went down hard, landing on an onion at the point of his hip. By the time he regained his feet, Filomena was throwing pots at him, which he batted away, cursing and panting. Schnitzel had gotten free and was sniffing at the *carnitas* scattered on the floor, which were too hot for her to eat just yet.

Tony came after Filomena, stepping over Gallo, who was still on his hands and knees, pushing away the dachshund, carefully picking the *carnitas* off the floor and returning them to the roasting pan.

"What a mess," Gallo muttered, oblivious to the battle royal going on around him.

As Tony plodded toward her, Filomena retreated behind a standup Hobart mixer, grabbing cooking utensils from a nearby work table to throw at him. She whanged him with a ladle, a cheese grater and the ice cream scoop they used for portioning out guacamole. And now she had picked up a cleaver and cocked her throwing arm.

The cleaver gave Tony something to think about. He'd already learned that Filomena didn't throw like a girl. And a meat cleaver crashing against his skull would be a little harder to shake off than a cheese grater. Breathing hard, he took a moment to rethink his strategy. Why was he even chasing her? The person he really wanted to make an impression on was crawling on the floor at his feet.

He pulled Gallo up by the back of his shirt. Gallo responded with a punch, a surprisingly good punch straight to the solar plexus that knocked the wind out of Tony. Releasing his grip on Gallo, he fell to his knees, trying to draw in a breath. Gallo gave him a shot to the chin. Tony struggled to his feet, and swung the bat wildly at the old boxer, who backed away, slipping the blow the way he'd slipped so many hundreds of punches during his ring career. Tony staggered after him, knowing he'd corner the old man eventually.

Except the old guy, who was surprisingly light on his feet, scampered out of the kitchen and into the back apartment, slamming the door behind him.

It got worse. The cleaver was flying at him. He jerked his head his head to the side, but it hit his shoulder, stopping him in his tracks for a beat because it hurt like a sonofabitch. "OK," he said to Filomena, steadying himself, "OK," he repeated with grim determination. "I'll deal with Gallo later. First I'm gonna take care of you."

"*Hijo de puta!*" Filomena answered, looking for something else to throw.

Tony chose his line of attack, tightened his grip on the baseball bat, took two more steps and then collapsed. A searing pain burned behind his right knee, like he'd been shot. He tried to get up, but his leg seemed to be paralyzed and gave out on him when he tried to put weight on it. He tried to balance on his good leg, then slipped on a puddle of grease and fell to the floor again. Hard. A slotted serving spoon hit him on the nose.

Most of the fight had left him. He took cover behind his bent elbow, fending off a vegetable peeler, the last utensil that Filomena could easily grab. Not that she'd run completely out of ammo--she started firing the tomatoes and onions that Gallo had picked up off the floor. The onions were as hard as baseballs.

He heard a vaguely familiar voice from behind him. "Man, you're crazy to pick a fight with Filomena."

Tony did a modified combat roll to check out the source of the voice. A tomato hit him behind the ear.

"*Chuy?*"

"That woman is like a she-bear. You must've come in here and dissed her salsa for her to get mad like that."

An onion hit Tony's neck with the sting of a big league fastball. "Tell her to stop throwing shit."

"She doesn't take orders from me. But it looks like she's almost run out of stuff to throw." It was true; the last thing to hit him was a bunch of cilantro. "What the hell happened to your face? It looks like a mule kicked you."

"What are you doing here?" Tony asked. He tried to pick himself up, but wasn't having much luck. The pain behind his knee was excruciating.

"Me? This is my dad's restaurant. What are *you* doing here?"

Tony couldn't do it; he just couldn't stand up. His knee was completely buckled. He shot Chuy a defeated look. "You kicked me, didn't you? You snuck up behind me and kicked my leg with one of those karate kicks. You fucker. You broke it or something."

"Just trying to keep the peace, Tony. It looked like you were on a rampage or something, chasing after Filomena with that Louisville slugger." The bat was on the floor next to Tony. Chuy picked it up and examined it. "Mike Schmidt model. You've had this since we were in Little League, haven't you?"

"Your dad owes us money. Over fifteen thousand dollars."

"You loaned Gallo money?"

That seemed to be the punchline of the day. Tony, stuck on his hands and knees, said, "Nico loaned him the money."

"Nico's an idiot."

"That's not the point. You owe us money, you gotta pay it. You know how it works. You were the guy who used to give that message to the deadbeats who came up short on us. You were the guy with the baseball bat."

Chuy smiled. "Those were good times. Threatening people. Beating them up. Too bad they had to end. You can't get up, can you?"

"My leg is messed up."

"Can you crawl?"

Tony couldn't stand, but he didn't want to crawl. Not until Chuy booted him in the ass. "Get the hell out of here, Tony. Go on, move." He kicked him again, a good solid kick that pitched Tony forward.

"You're making a mistake messing with me like this, Chuy."

"I'm waiting."

Reluctantly, Tony started crawling out of the kitchen.

"Is this your little dog?"

"He carried it in here," Filomena said.

Chuy gathered Schnitzel up in his arms and followed Tony, who was muttering, "You were always too cocky, thought you were such a badass. . ." Chuy gave him a move-along kick, just to keep him heading in the right direction.

"You do that again I'm going to kill you." They were in the front of the restaurant now, Tony on his hands and knees, Chuy right behind him.

"I'll get the door for you," Chuy said, circling in front of Tony to grab the door.

Tony looked up at him as he crawled across the threshold and out onto the sidewalk. "$15,168, Chuy. We're serious. We'll burn this place down if he doesn't pay us."

Chuy set Schnitzel down on the pavement next to Tony. "Come back when we're open sometime," he said. "I'll buy you a taco."

****

Nico was putting cash into the register behind the fish market's open-air counter when the Mercedes pulled up, parking in one of the diagonal spaces in front. He didn't notice it right away; he was too absorbed with getting the register set up just right for the day. Nico loved handling money, loved to sort it and count it and put it into neat stacks of fives, tens, twenties and fifties, making sure each stack was tight and orderly, each president facing the same way. He liked the heft of the fresh rolls of coins, and had a way of rapping them against the edge of the cash drawer to split them open so he could spill out the

181

coins into their individual compartments. Around him, Moochie and the other market guys were getting the display cases ready with fresh crushed ice and arranging the fish and shellfish for the day's trade, bullshitting and giving each other a hard time. Fifty Cent was on the sound system.

Nico didn't hear Gina Quattro the first time, maybe the first couple times, she called his name.

Then he looked up and saw her. She was behind the wheel of the Mercedes, and she'd stuck her head out the window. She was wearing designer sunglasses with a gold monogram on the wide stems.

"Nico, c'mere," she called impatiently.

It was like the whole day had darkened. "Give me a minute."

"No, I mean come here now," she insisted.

He carefully closed the register drawer and slowly walked the length of the counter, around into the restaurant and out the door. Gina was watching him from the window of the Mercedes. It was a beautiful car, a Lunar Blue E250 Sedan. Nico had owned a Mercedes once, before he got married. Not as nice as this, a silver 2005 E350, pre-owned, but clean. That was before he got divorced and filed for bankruptcy, all of that. He saw that the guy she called Mr. Hat was in the passenger seat, and through the privacy tinting of the back window he saw a big hulking shadow that he guessed was the kid, Benjie.

"I'm kinda busy," Nico said. "Trying to get the market ready for lunch."

She pulled off her sunglasses and squinted at him. "I want you to take a ride with us."

"I just can't leave when we're about to open. . ."

She turned away from him and spoke to Mr. Hat. "Hat, get out and give your seat to Nico."

Mr. Hat got out and held the passenger door open for him. He was wearing his little short brimmed hat with a striped band, wraparound sunglasses. "You need to get in the car," he said to Nico.

Nico looked back toward the market. He saw his mom putting a container of chowder into the soup warmer. He called to her. "Ma, I gotta run out for a while."

She looked confused when she saw him standing next to the car. "Run where?"

Nico looked questioningly at Gina who shrugged. "Tell her you're going to a meeting."

"To a meeting."

"What meeting?"

Gina craned her neck out of the Mercedes so Nico's mom could see her. "It's OK, Mrs. Connole," she called. "He's with us. We've got a business meeting. Can you take care of things till we bring him back?"

"What meeting, Nico?" his mother asked again as he eased himself into the passenger seat. Mr. Hat shut the door—it made that nice soft sound that only a Mercedes door can make when it's closed—and got into the back next to Benjie.

Nico buckled his seatbelt as Gina backed the car out. He wanted to ask her if she was going to take him some place and shoot him, make a joke about it. But he didn't. Why give them any ideas? Instead he said, "I can't just leave work like this. If you wanted to meet, you should have called me."

The truth of it was that Nico's nerves were frayed. He'd tossed and turned most of the night, worrying. Sweat was beading up on his forehead and upper lip.

"You're right. I'm sorry, Nico. I get these ideas and I just act on them. But I kind of thought you could accommodate me on this."

"On what?"

"You're a little upset, aren't you?"

"I'm not upset. I just want to know what's going on."

She was looking at him as she drove down the Wharf. "No, you're upset. You don't have a very good poker face. And you know it. That's why you don't want to look at me."

He turned toward her. She had a little encouraging smile on her full lips, like she had just seen a baby take his first step and wanted it to take another. "OK," he said. "Now can you please tell me where we're going?"

"We're going to the harbor and the office of Mr. Van Phuc." She pronounced it Fuck, not the way the Vietnamese pronounced it, which was Pook, something like that. He didn't correct her.

"We're going to fuck with Phuc," Mr. Hat said. It sounded like a joke they'd already worn out.

"You've got a meeting set up with him?"

"Let's say we're going to drop in," Gina said.

"This isn't a good idea."

She turned down Beach St., then cut through the River Flats neighborhood, heading south toward the harbor.

"I think it's a great idea. Hat thinks it's a great idea. Benjie thinks it's a great idea, don't you Benjie?" Benjie didn't say anything. Nico peeked over his left shoulder and saw the kid staring sullenly out his window.

"You're not going to get anywhere with those people," Nico said. "Me and Tony tried."

Gina said, "I think that's the problem. You and Tony tried. Tweedle Dee and Tweedle Dum."

"Tweedle Dum and Tweedle Dummer," Hat said.

"Whatever. But it's not like he's some pushover. And he's got his own guys."

"OK. I get it." She drove in silence for a few minutes, across the bridge that spanned the mouth of Watson's Lagoon and up the hill. The silence made Nico even more uneasy. When Gina finally spoke, she said, "You and Tony don't carry any wood. That's a metaphor. You know what it means?"

Nico was picking at cuticle on this thumb. He noticed it was bleeding. "A metaphor?" he said.

"Yeah, like a metaphor. It means you've got little dicks. And everyone you talk to gets that about you right away. That your dicks are like an inch long."

Nico put his thumb in his mouth to suck at the blood. In the back seat, Hat snickered.

"Like right now," Gina continued. "I say that to you, insult your manhood, and what do you do? You're sucking your thumb."

"It's bleeding." Nico returned his hand to his lap.

"If you carried wood you'd feel dishonored and you'd show it. You'd go off or something."

"I've got my own way of showing things," he said.

185

"I can see that," Gina said. "That's becoming abundantly clear. So tell me about these people. These Fucks."

In the five minutes that remained of the drive to the harbor, Nico told her how the Vietnamese came in about thirty years ago, pooled their money to purchase some sorry-looking boats, and started fishing squid, which wasn't as popular in California restaurants then the way it is now, but the Vietnamese and other Asians couldn't get enough of it. The Italians tried to push them out, messed up their nets and boats, but they wouldn't leave. Fishing is a tough business. First generation immigrants could put up with the danger, the long hours and unpredictable return. But the Italian families had been at it for over seventy years—long, hard years. Their sons and now their grandsons drifted away from it, getting into things like construction, selling insurance, restaurants. Every year, more of the boats that went out of the harbor were crewed by Vietnamese, but up until a few years ago, they still brought their catch into the processing distribution operation that Nicky Connole had set up with a cousin, Angelo Bruno. Then Angelo got busted for pocketing the workers' comp premiums he was collecting and the business got shut down. Not long after, Big Nicky had died at the Elks Club; Nico and Tony had their hands full with other stuff and weren't interested in the cleaning and packaging of squid. The Vietnamese put their money together, purchased the building and the processing equipment and set up their own business.

"What'd he say when you asked for your cut?"

Nico thought about how he should answer. "Nothing."

"*Nothing?* I don't get it."

"We kind of put it out there, but we didn't press it. And nothing ever happened. Tony didn't want to deal with it. I guess I didn't either. These people, these people from Viet Nam, they're tough. You think because they're small that maybe you can push them around, but you just can't threaten them and expect them to roll over."

"You can't?" Gina said. "We'll see." She pulled into the harbor. Nico directed her to what they called the lower harbor, which was the scruffier end, where the fishing boats were moored.

"It's that corrugated metal building over there," he said. "See the sign?"

It was a beige building, twenty feet tall, about 5,000 square feet, spattered with seagull droppings.

Gina read the sign over the front door. "Yummy Squid? That's what they call it?"

"What kind of fucked-up name is that?" Hat said.

Gina parked the Mercedes.

"So what are we going to do?" Nico asked.

"We're going to go in and talk to Mr. Fuck."

Gina, Hat and Benjie were getting out of the car, Gina carrying her big purse.

"But I mean," Nico said, catching up as they walked toward the door, "about what?"

They were already through the door, Gina leading the way, her high heels tapping the floor. Nico fell in behind Benjie, whose wide shoulders blocked his view as he entered the building. Nico knew the building from when Angelo Bruno ran the operation, but it looked different now. It was a little more crowded with work stations, and the corner office where Angelo hung out, usually with a phone cradled under his chin, had been removed, opening space for another work station. Hair-netted women in smocks sorted big plastic tubs of squid, others were cleaning them, pulling the head and tentacles away from the body, discarding the inky innards, throwing the good stuff into rinsing basins on carts. Other women were scooping the squid out of the rinsing baths, weighing it and arranging it neatly in boxes—tubes on one side, tentacles on the other—which were then closed up and carted to a refrigeration unit attached to the rear of the building. Several of the women looked up from their work to see who'd come into the building, but kept their hands moving.

A couple of Vietnamese guys were talking to each other near the entrance to the refrigeration unit. One of them was Van Phuc. He was around fifty-five and fit, wearing a blue and white trucker's cap with the word "Stor-Cold" on the front. He walked toward them, looking at the strangers and then at Nico.

"What's going on, Nico?" he asked. He only had a trace of an accent.

"We—" Nico started to say, but Gina cut him off.

"We're from the insurance company, Mr. Fuck," she said. "Nico referred us to you. Can we talk?"

Van Phuc didn't get what was going on, and looked at Nico for a clue. "Thanks," he said carefully. "But I think I've got enough insurance."

"We don't think so," Gina said. "That's what we want to talk to you about. Explain a few things. Do you have an office?"

"Just a desk. Over there." He tilted his head toward a corner of the work space. "But we're pretty busy. Maybe you could leave a brochure and come back."

Gina wore a cold half-smile. "We're pretty busy too. But this is important. Let's go over to your desk so I can explain our program."

Van Phuc was still looking at Nico.

Nico said, "We just need a few minutes of your time." Trying to let him know that this wasn't his deal, but it would be a good idea to go along with it.

"OK. But I don't think I need any more insurance." Van Phuc turned and led them to a battered desk with a laptop and loose papers, reading glasses. He sat down in a cheap office chair behind the desk. Gina took the single chair in front of the desk, resting her big purse on her knees. Nico, Benjie and Hat stood behind Gina, Nico separating himself a little to stand behind the other two. He didn't want to look at Van Phuc, didn't want to meet his questioning gaze, so he pretended to be interested in the work going on around them. He noticed Hat walking off onto the production floor, nosing into things.

Unlike most insurance salesman, Gina Quattro didn't see the need to engage in any small talk. She got right to the point. "See, the thing is Mr. Fuck," she said, "that all businesses are exposed to risk, but especially a business like yours. Bad things can happen that could be prevented with the proper insurance."

"Do you have a card?" Van Phuc asked.

"A card? Like a business card?"

"With the name of your insurance company."

"We're not that kind of insurance company."

"Not what kind?"

"The kind with a name and business cards."

Nico couldn't help looking now. He saw that Gina had taken her iPad from her big purse, had brought the screen to life and was tapping an icon.

"Everything's digital these days, right?" Gina said, smiling, but not warmly. "It almost makes brochures obsolete. But I've got some information on my iPad that I can share with you. Kind of let you know why we thought it would be a good idea to come meet with you today."

Van Phuc caught Nico's eyes now. He knew what was going on, that this was a shakedown, but he didn't look scared. He looked pissed, his jaw set, his mouth turned down.

Gina had set the iPad down in front of Van Phuc, turned so he could get the right perspective on the screen. Nico could see that she had brought up a slide show. She loved her slides. The first slide, it looked like a newspaper photo, showed a building consumed in flames. "These are the kinds of unfortunate things that can happen to a business like yours. A fire like this . . ." She swiped at the screen and pulled another photo into view, this one of a liquor store with broken bottles strewn everywhere. "Or an intruder could break into your business and smash things up like this." She swiped at the screen again. It took Nico a second or two to make out what was happening in the grainy black and white photo as he looked over Gina's shoulder. He saw a delivery truck, and what looked like a pile of laundry on the ground beneath the open driver's side door. "Then the most unfortunate tragedy of all . . ." Gina said. Nico now saw that it was a body on the ground, in a collapsed heap, face down.

No one said anything. Then Van Phuc said, "You're messing with the wrong guy."

The little half-smile had never left Gina's face. "No. I'm pretty sure you're the guy," she said. She sounded calm, maybe a little cocky. "You've got to think this through a bit more. For example, my organization isn't scared by the police. We wouldn't have been in the insurance business for all these decades if we were. See, if the police get involved, even worse things can happen. Like to family members. Parents, wives, even kids. Nico can tell you."

Nico had shift his attention to his shredded cuticles. He looked up, wondering if he was being called on to say something, but no one was looking at him.

"That's why," Gina said, "people always decide to buy the insurance. Peace of mind, right? For you the premium is going to run you $10,000 a month. Small price to pay not to have to worry about all the bad things that can happen."

Van Phuc was thinking, staring at Gina, the muscles in his jaw and temples bunched. Then his eyes wandered to his left. "What's he doing over there?" he asked.

They all turned and saw Hat about twenty feet away, standing over a big plastic tub of squid. His back was toward them, but it was obvious what he was doing. They could see the arc of his piss splashing into the heaped squid.

"That's the kind of thing that can happen," Gina said. "You can't anticipate stuff like that."

191

Van Phuc stood up from his chair. "Get out. Now." He called to one of the guys he'd been talking to when they'd walked in, saying something in Vietnamese. The guy was already trotting toward Hat, and now quickened his pace. Benjie, who had suddenly come out of his sullen trance, intercepted him, blocking him like a human wall as Hat turned, calmly zipping his fly.

Another guy had come out of the back and was also approaching. Nico recognized him; he'd seen him around the harbor. He had a deep scar running from the corner of his mouth to his ear. He always looked pissed off. Letting you know he was a badass. He was holding a boat hook with a four-foot handle.

Gina calmly put the iPad back into her bag and rose from her chair. "Think about it, Mr. Fuck. Talk to your associates. Try not to get emotional about this. It's just business. Nico will get back in touch with you Friday."

"Friday?" Nico said. "This Friday?"

"To collect the first premium," Gina explained, as though this was something they'd discussed already.

"You're not getting $10,000 from me," Van Phuc said. "This is some kind of joke, right Nico?"

Gina headed toward the door, her quick, purposeful strides shortened by her tight skirt and heels, with Hat, Benjie and Nico trailing behind her. Nico snuck a glance over his shoulder. Van Phuc and the other guys were following them. "Nico, hold up," Van Phuc said.

Nico stopped and reluctantly faced them. They were less than ten feet away. He started to tell them that he really had to get back to the market to make sure everything was ready for when they opened, but Van Phuc cut him off.

"You or your friends come around here again, Bui's going to rip off your balls with his boat hook."

When Hat heard that, he peeled away from Gina and Benjie came back in a rush to stand at Nico's shoulder, all wound up and ready to go off. "Boat hook? You got a fucking boat hook, I've got a Desert Eagle. You ever see one of these?" Nico saw that he was holding the biggest handgun he'd ever seen; he guessed that Hat must have had it hidden somehow under his jacket. ".50 caliber. You could shoot a hole through an engine block. Like looking down the mouth of a cannon, isn't it?" Van Phuc and his guys didn't answer. They were trying not to look at the handgun. "Come on," Hat taunted. "Come at me with that thing, your little boat hook."

"We're just talking here," Nico said, because he had to say something. "Right? Just talking?"

"Hat, let's go," Gina said. "They've got some thinking to do."

Hat said, "Let me shoot something. Like that forklift over there."

"Not now. Come on." Gina was walking toward the door. Hat was disappointed, but followed, walking backwards the first few steps, waving the Desert Eagle. Nico couldn't leave fast enough.

Van Phuc said loudly as they left, "We'll be ready for you if you come back here. Nico, tell them we can't be pushed around."

After they'd settled into Gina's Mercedes, Nico said, "I really don't think he has that kind of money".

Van Phuc and two other men were standing in the doorway of the corrugated metal building, glaring at them.

"I heard him," Gina said as she backed the car out. "And I don't give a fuck."

Hat laughed his hyena laugh. "A *fuck!*"

"Hat, just shut up. That joke is old. The point is," she said to Nico, "whether he has it or not, he's got to find it. And you've got to get it. Because if I don't get it, there's going to be a problem."

Nico said, "I'm just trying to be realistic. You don't make a lot of money in that business."

Hat said, "You see how they stopped in their tracks when I pointed my Deagle at 'em? Gave 'em a little something to think about."

"I'm hungry" Gina announced. "You guys hungry?"

"I could eat something," Hat said. "And Benjie is always up for some chow."

"Let's go to Nico's place. Get some oysters, fish and chips. Maybe some calamari."

"No squid for me," Hat said, laughing.

****

The decision to sell Gallo's ride, a Riverside Red '64 Chevy Impala Super Sport, hadn't been an easy one. Chuy had put it out there to Filomena because he thought they didn't have a choice. They needed the cash to keep the restaurant open. All of their suppliers had them on COD, even La Michoacána, the tortilla factory. Filomena wouldn't think of it at first, even though she'd hidden the keys from Gallo months earlier because he was a danger behind the wheel. It would kill him if we sold it, she said. This place is sinking and we need the money to keep it afloat, Chuy insisted. They also had to raise prices, he said—Christ, they were only charging $2.75 for a taco—but that was a different discussion. Right now they needed around $10,000 just to get square with everyone, not including Nico and Tony, who could piss up a rope. What would be worse, he asked her, losing the taqueria or losing the car?

He looked Filomena in the eyes and he could see she knew they had to do it. "I'll put up an ad on Craigslist, you know, with a picture and everything," he said. "You've got the pink slip somewhere, right?"

"Doesn't Gallo have to sign it?"

"Don't worry about that. I started forging his signature in the second grade," Chuy said.

This discussion had taken place a couple days ago. Chuy wasn't a computer guy, so he had to enlist the bus girl Clarita's help for the Craigslist ad. She wasn't a computer whiz herself, but she knew enough to take a photo of the Impala with her phone and transfer it to the old Dell that Filomena used to do the taqueria's books. It took Chuy a couple hours to figure out the rest. Using ads for similar cars that he found on the Internet for reference, he wrote the ad copy and decided on a price, $12,999, which seemed to be right in the ballpark based on what similar '64 Impalas were going for. He always thought it was a little sleazy when car dealers priced their cars always just under the next highest round thousand-dollar number, but when he typed in $13,000, it just seemed a lot more expensive. He uploaded the photo that Clarita had taken. He'd pulled the Impala out of the garage behind the taqueria, and it looked good, with sunlight glinting off the hood.

He described the car this way: 1964 Chevy Impala SS. 2 door coupe. Cherry condition inside and out. 327ci Chevrolet V8, 4-barrel carb. Muncie 4 speed transmission. 89K miles. $12,999. No bullshit calls.

In spite of that stipulation, four of the five people who called after the ad went live wanted to get him to slash the price before they even came out to look at the car. One guy wanted to trade him even for a dump truck that needed brakes. His exact words were, "It kinda needs brakes". Chuy blew all of them off.

The fifth caller was a guy named Jason. Jason said he could come out to look at the Impala around noon. He sounded a little young, but he didn't try to beat Chuy down about the price over the phone, which was a good sign.

When Chuy got back from his session with Andrew he went back to the little locked garage, which also served as a storage space for the taqueria. Before he could back out the Impala, he first had to walk out his Harley, which was parked right next to the Chevy's rear bumper, and a big box of paper napkins that blocked access to the driver side door.

The Impala hadn't been driven much in the past year or two, but it fired up nicely. He brought it out onto the gritty asphalt parking lot behind the taqueria, and gunned the engine a few times. He'd almost forgotten how sweet the small-block 327 sounded, like it was growling when it was idling, and roaring when you hit the gas. He took a soft cloth and went over the bright red exterior, wiping off the dust that had settled on it in the garage.

He was hoping Gallo wouldn't hear it and rush out to see what was going on. Then he'd really have a fight on his hands. Gallo bought the Impala in 1984. It was in pretty good shape then for a twenty-year-old car; he had it repainted and replaced the driver side bucket seat, which was coming apart at the seams. But he never got into the whole low-rider thing—modifying the suspension, customizing the paint job with metal flake or pin striping or anything like that. No, Gallo was determined to keep the Impala stock, or as close to stock as possible. All that other stuff he said, was like putting a bunch of makeup on a beautiful woman. He'd always been extremely careful with it, letting Chuy drive it only once. Chuy was sixteen, had just gotten his license and he kept bugging Gallo to let him take the Impala for a spin around the 'hood. Gallo finally relented, giving in as a way to reward Chuy for working three double shifts at the restaurant over the July Fourth weekend. But he insisted on sitting in the passenger side and made the whole experience miserable. Everything Chuy did was wrong. Gallo kept yelling at him, screeching like a rooster. He was going to burn out the clutch, or hit a curb. He braked too late coming up to a stop sign. Chuy got nervous and stalled the car five blocks away from the restaurant. He said Fuck it, got out, and let Gallo drive the car back. And never asked to drive the Impala again.

Jason, the guy who called about the Craigslist ad, showed up a little after noon. He was about thirty, carried a Starbucks cup, and was accompanied by a girl who looked slightly younger. Her name was Clarisse. Jason was tall and gawky. He wore skinny jeans and a black

T-shirt with lime green lettering that said "Keep Calm and Code On!" He wore the kind of geeky black rimmed glasses that had become cool. Clarisse was wearing skinny jeans too, a loose tank top and black Converse All-Stars. Her tangled hair was stuffed into a stocking cap and her eyes were hidden behind oversized aviators. Nerds, Chuy thought. But hopefully nerds with money. He guessed that they'd driven up in the new white BMW 320i that Chuy saw parked on the street.

When they introduced themselves Jason said, "Chewy—that's a cool name. Like a candy bar."

"Not exactly."

"This is it, huh? The Impala?" Jason asked. No, Chuy wanted to say, this is an ice cream truck. But he kept his mouth shut. Jason circled the car, taking it in. "Check this out, Clarisse," he said crouching down at the rear of the car. "See these crossed flags Super Sport emblems? How cool are they?"

Clarisse was looking at her phone. She might have raised her eyes to see what Jason was so excited about, but Chuy couldn't make out what was going on behind the aviators. Jason opened the driver's door and checked out the interior, nodding and smiling.

"You want to check out the engine?" Chuy asked. "I can pop the hood."

Jason said, "Sure, why not?" When Chuy lifted the hood, Jason looked blankly at the clean 327 cubic inch V8, with the heavy duty single snorkel air cleaner atop the four-barrel carburetor, giving no indication that he was knew how special, maybe even legendary in some circles, the Chevy engine was. A true gearhead would have gotten a boner.

"Nice," he said, just to say something.

"My dad kept it up pretty well. It was kind of his pride and joy." Chuy dropped the hood.

"This was your dad's car, huh? Why are you selling it?"

"He can't really drive it anymore."

"That sucks. For him anyway."

Chuy didn't want to talk about his dad with Jason.

"Hey Clarisse, what do you think?" Jason asked.

"It's OK I guess."

"*OK*? This car is super cool. It's a total classic." He turned to Chuy. "I'd like to drive this bad boy. That OK?"

Chuy said, "Sure, we can do that. But I've got to ask you first how serious you are. About this bad boy." He just had to throw that in. "I don't want to waste my time if you just want to joy ride a little."

"I'm super serious."

"And you're OK with the price?"

"I can totally handle the price. No problem."

Chuy nodded, pulled the car keys out of his pocket and handed them to Jason. The fob on the keychain was a little brass boxing glove, something Gallo had come across years ago. "OK. Let's take it out."

"Come on, Clarisse, get in," Jason said. Clarisse made them wait while she took a selfie next to the Impala, and sent it off to her eager public. As Jason got in behind the wheel, Chuy opened the passenger side door, and waited for Clarisse to slide into the back seat. Chuy got

199

in and closed his door. He saw that Jason, still holding his Starbucks cup, was looking around the Impala's interior.

"No cup holders I guess."

Chuy just looked at him and held out his hand to take the cup. Jason gave it to him. Chuy got out and threw it in the dumpster behind the taqueria.

When he got back in, Clarisse was looking at her phone and reported to Jason that someone named Morgan said her granddad had a car like this. Then she said, "She wants to know if big dice are hanging from the mirror. Why aren't there any dice?" she asked Chuy.

"My dad wasn't into dice or bullshit like that."

Jason started the car and pumped the accelerator, revving the engine. "You want to ease up on the gas before you let out the clutch," Chuy warned him, about a half-second too late. They jumped forward and Jason slammed the brakes just short of crashing into the garage. They rocked in their seats.

"Whoa," Jason said.

"And you're going to want to put it in reverse," Chuy said, trying to keep cool. "You know, to back out onto the street." Jason was looking at the shifter, trying to figure it out. "To the left and up," Chuy said. "Easy on the gas and let up slowly on the clutch."

Jason seemed to have it, but when he let up on the clutch they rocketed backwards out onto the street, clipping the front of the BMW. Jason said, "Whoa," again.

"Yeah, whoa," Chuy said, shaking his head. He was pissed off now, but trying not to go off. "You ever drive a stick before?"

"A couple times."

"That's your car, the BMW?"

Jason nodded.

Clarisse had snapped a photo of Jason behind the wheel and wanted to show it to him on her phone. "You look so flustered," she laughed.

They all got out of the car and checked out the damage. Fortunately, it was minor. The Impala's heavy rear bumper had glanced off the BMW's front bumper. Apart from some white paint that Chuy could scratch off the bumper's chrome with his fingernail, the Impala was OK. The BMW had fared worse. There was a big scratch on the white polypropylene front bumper.

Jason examined the scratch while Clarisse snapped photos with her phone and then examined them, squinting.

"Wow, I'm sorry, Chewy," Jason said. "I mean shit, I just touched the gas. . . Anyway, I've got insurance. You want to see my insurance card? I'm pretty sure I'm covered for anything. Or I could just buy it," he said hopefully, like a guy who was used to solving problems by spending money, "and you won't have to worry about it."

Chuy had had enough. He wasn't going to sell them the car, and right now wasn't sure he was going to sell it to anyone. The whole thing made him feel like he'd been punched in the stomach.

"I'm going to pull it back in."

"But we were going to go for a test drive." He sounded like a kid whose Mommy had just told him that it was time for his nap.

Clarisse read a new text on her phone. "Morgan sent me a link to this really cool site where you can buy the fuzzy dice. You can also get one of those little hula girls to put in the back window."

Chuy was getting more pissed off by the second, and not just at this idiot Jason and his idiot girlfriend. He was pissed at Gallo, for getting old and senile. He was pissed at himself for getting sucked in to trying to save Gallo's two-bit taqueria. And for having to sell his Chevy, which was like kicking the old guy in the balls.

"I don't think you're the right guy for the car."

"I have the money, I swear. I just sold a boatload of stock options." Jason blinked behind his glasses.

"Thanks for coming by."

"What, now he's not going to sell you the car?" Clarisse asked.

Chuy got into the Impala to make the short drive back into the garage.

****

Across town, in a quiet, middle class neighborhood, Nico was wrestling with his own act of betrayal. He knew he had to steal the raffle receipts—Tony was right—but it made him sick to think about it as he stood outside the patio door at the back of his house, looking at the fence that separated his back yard from his mom's.

As if he didn't have enough to get twisted up about, Nico counted three new gopher holes in the lush green sod he had laid down in April and had been carefully tending ever since. Fed up with the way they were wrecking his lawn, he had declared war on them a week ago. His life was simpler then. Not that gophers weren't challenging adversaries, voracious and cunning. But the rodents he was pitted against now—Gina Quattro, Hat and Benjie—were bigger, rougher and dangerous. Maybe a little crazy. And they killed people. He hadn't slept more than four hours in the past two nights, thrashing around on his sweat-dampened sheets, worrying about what they might do to him and his family—especially little Nicky—if he and Tony didn't come up with the money Gina Quattro had demanded.

But still . . . he couldn't stop thinking about the gophers and how they were destroying the sod—*his* sod, the sod he'd chosen carefully out of the five different options at the landscaping supply store, the sod he'd paid to have installed, the sod he'd been babying with water, fertilizer and weed killer. Pausing on his way to the gate between his back yard and Bianca's, he studied the fresh mounds of dirt the gophers had piled around their new holes. "You sonsofbitches are in for a little surprise," he muttered, thinking about the traps he'd purchased on the recommendation of a legendary gopher exterminator in a YouTube video. He—the legend—called himself the Gopher Slayer, and the traps were his own special design. Nico purchased two of them through Amazon; according to the last tracking update, they were due to be delivered that afternoon.

Nico's parents had helped him buy his house a few years after he got married. The elderly couple in the house behind big Nicky and Bianca were moving into an assisted living facility, so Bianca made sure Nico got the first offer in and talked big Nicky into contributing to the down payment. Bianca paid to have a gate put into the fence between the two yards. She liked being able to drop in to check in on her son and grandson when the mood struck her. Destina wasn't thrilled at all, but what was Nico supposed to do, tell his mother she wasn't welcome?

The gate made it easy enough for Nico to slip unseen into Bianca's back yard when he knew she would be getting her hair done at Mr. Larry's Salon D'Elegance, a standing appointment she'd had every Tuesday afternoon for nearly thirty years.

Nico's heart was heavy with guilt as crossed Bianca's patio and pushed open the sliding glass door that brought him into his mother's living room with its heavy furniture that included a big walnut credenza-style Magnavox hi-fi that had been his dad's pride and joy and now served as an altar, supporting Bianca's memorial to her husband, big Nicky Connole, the man and the legend. A collection of framed photographs was arrayed on the polished walnut surface: Nicky, the pulling guard, in his high school football uniform; Nicky behind the wheel of a '58 Ford delivery van, his T-shirt sleeve rolled up around a pack of smokes; Nicky with three of his buddies at the golf course; Nicky playfully holding his grandson, little Nicky, then two years old, over the backyard barbecue grill like he was going to cook him; Nicky and Bianca, just kids, on the day of their wedding; Nicky behind the counter at the fish market, flanked by Nico and Tony. Most prominent was a studio portrait taken prior to his induction as Leading Knight of the Elks Lodge, a heavy ceremonial necklace draped over the front of his tuxedo. In three quarter profile, dignified, no hint of the wide grin that so often spread across his face, splaying his big nose, or the larcenous glint that played in his eyes. His graying hair was neatly barbered and combed back, like a banker's.

Nico paused to explain himself to the Elks portrait, letting his dad know that he didn't want to do what he was going to do, but that he had no choice. "Like you always said, Dad—sometimes you gotta be a shit."

Like most emotions, guilt made Nico a little hungry, so he took a detour into the kitchen and opened the refrigerator to see what kind of leftovers his mom had put away. He hit the jackpot right away when he lifted the aluminum foil off the top of a casserole dish he found on the second shelf—four spiedini, seasoned meatball skewers, one of Bianca's signature dishes. She won't miss one, he thought, nibbling at it carefully as he walked through the living room and down the hall to his mother's bedroom.

After his dad Nicky's death, his mother had become more ardent in her faith, and the bedroom reflected her devotion. A crucifix had been hung above the king-sized bed, crisscrossed with dried palm fronds, a remembrance of Palm Sunday. A portrait of Jesus pointing at his sacred heart—wrapped in thorns and surrounded by an aura of flame—hung on the wall over what had been his dad's dresser. Jesus seemed to be showing his tortured heart to Nico, as much as saying to him, "I died for your sins, and look how you're repaying me." On Bianca's dresser, amid the ointments, perfume bottles, photos of little Nicky, costume jewelry boxes, baby powder and nail polish remover, was another statue of the Virgin Mary, a third of the size of the one in the living room. The Virgin's face was sweet, serene. She had held her arms out gracefully, palms up, offering her love to the world, even to Nico, and that made it even harder to do what he was going to do— what he had to do—which was to root around his mother's underwear drawer. That's where she stashed things she considered special or precious in a battered Christmas cookie tin: old documents like her marriage license, her $5,000 whole life policy, a lock of Nico's baby hair, the first baby tooth that Tony lost, a creased photo of her parents, those kinds of things, and that was where he knew she would have stashed the receipts from Father Mikey's raffle.

What he saw when he pulled opened the drawer almost made him choke on his last meatball. There, on top of a tangle of granny panties and industrial-strength brassieres, was a pair of black, see-through panties.

"Holy fuck," he breathed. Then, shamefully, he remembered that he was inches away from the Virgin Mary and reflexively asked for her forgiveness for his bad language. He lifted up the panties which were cut so high in the front that they would barely cover anything down there, and narrowed to a T in the back. They had almost no substance to them, like they would melt in your mouth like cotton candy. Digging into the drawer a bit further, he found a matching bra. He held both items, the panties in one hand, the bra in the other, and sought an explanation from the Virgin Mary, whose sweet accepting smile didn't change.

He heard voices—voices in the living room, then coming down the hallway.

Panicked, knowing there was no way to escape, he darted his eyes around the room looking for a place to hide. He'd never fit under the bed; his mother's closet was the only option. He quickly threw the risqué underwear back into the drawer and shut it, then made for the closet, just managing to close its louvered folding doors behind him as the voices came into the room.

If the see-through panties hadn't been shock enough, what he saw now through the slats of the door turned his world upside down and shook the few eternal verities still attached to it loose like bar dice in leather cup. His mother, the one-time blushing bride of Nicky Connole, the grandmother of his boy, Nicky, the Treasurer of the St. Joseph's Women's Auxiliary—*his mama!*—had come into the bedroom with a man, and was matter-of-factly taking off her clothes on one side of the bed, and the man was peeling off his clothes, and they were embracing on the bed and the man rolled over on his back, and she was taking him into her mouth and . . .

. . . *and the man was Freebie!*

Nico shut his eyes tight, trying to will the image away, but he could hear the low murmurs of pleasure and then the panting, the flesh slapping. And what was that strange noise? Yelping? Was his mother yelping? And then she cried out. And then it was quiet.

A minute or so passed. "You're a good boy," Bianca said dreamily. Some boy, Nico thought, the little shit Freebie was easily fifty years old. He opened his eyes and saw that they had flopped over on their backs and his mother's hand was idly toying with what just a few minutes before had been the pillar of Freebie's manhood, but was now a weird little pupa-like thing, like something you'd find curled up under a rock.

"*Finito,*" Freebie said.

"*No más?*" Bianca asked. When did she start speaking Spanish?

Freebie sighed, "I gotta go. I gotta pick up my little granddaughter from school."

"Are you going to shower?" Bianca asked. Her voice was weird; it was his mom's voice, but not as raspy and impatient. Softer, sweeter. It made him want to puke. "A shower would be nice. You could wash my back."

"OK. Maybe a quick one." Freebie had risen from the bed. Nico saw his mom getting up and shut his eyes to block out her nakedness as she crossed the room to join Freebie in the master bath.

In a minute Nico heard the muffled stream of the shower. Seizing the chance to make his getaway, he slipped out of the closet. He couldn't get out of the bedroom fast enough. But first he had to get the raffle money out of the cookie tin. The damn lid was stuck—he had to work it off slowly, fearing any minute that he'd be found out. Finally, it popped off. Nico grabbed the cash and made his getaway just as the noisy shower went quiet.

Before he slipped through the sliding patio door, he paused before his mom's memorial to Big Nicky, locking his gaze on the Elks Lodge portrait. He shook his head in despair and prayed that the old man's spirit wasn't looking down on anything that had just happened. Or looking up—the more likely direction. Hopefully, he was too busy playing bar dice with the devil.

He toyed with the idea of snagging one more spiedini before he left, but he was too sick to his stomach to even approach the fridge.

****

He didn't feel like going back to the market. He wasn't ready to see his mom, who was probably going back there now. The feeling that someone had socked him the gut was too strong. He had to lay down. He was flat on his back on the couch in his living room, staring at the ceiling when he heard the UPS truck come up, and then the thud of a package being dropped on his front step.

Ten minutes later, thankful for the distraction, he was kneeling next to a hole he'd dug in his lawn, consulting a set of instructions for the two gopher traps he'd purchased from the Gopher Slayer's web site. Behind him, leaning on a pair of crutches, stood Tony, who had just shown up. A brown dachshund sat at Tony's feet, a wary look in its bulging brown eyes.

"Chuy did that?" Nico asked, nodding at the leg Tony had lifted off the ground and the crutches.

"Sonofabitch snuck up on me and threw one of those kicks. It was like getting shot or something. I just went down. The doc said it looks like some ligaments are either sprained or maybe torn. Thinks I could be on these things for three, four days."

"Chuy, huh? When did he get back?"

"I don't know. We didn't exactly chit-chat after he pulled that Kung Fu shit on me."

"Is he gonna be around for a while?'

"You're so interested, maybe you could go ask him. And you could tell him we're serious about the money Gallo owes us. I for one am not going to let it go. Especially not now. Sonofabitch coulda crippled me."

"I just wonder what he's doing back in Santa Carmela. We could use him."

"To hell with that," Tony said. All this interest in Chuy was exasperating. "Weren't you listening to what I was just telling you? The fucker attacked me."

"You were swinging a baseball bat. What did you think he'd do?"

"Fucker snuck up on me," Tony sniffed.

"Chuy did good work for us. People didn't want to mess with him. You and me didn't have to screw around with collecting money."

"Payback's gonna be a bitch."

"Let me talk to him first. Maybe we can work something out."

"Sure, you talk to him. Tell him I got something for him. I'm gonna stick one of these crutches so far up his ass the rubber tip's gonna come out of his mouth."

Next, Tony recounted his conversation with the Pelican. Nico listened as he fiddled with the traps. With all the bad stuff that was happening, the challenge of killing a couple of gophers was a welcome diversion.

"You think there's something to it? The Pelican's deal?" Nico asked. He held one of the traps, a complicated little death machine fashioned out of a cat's cradle of heavy-gauge wire whose main features were two sharp prongs and a central spring. The trick was to figure out how to pry the prongs apart and set them against the force of the spring. Once the unsuspecting gopher tripped the trigger, the prongs would fly together, impaling it from both sides.

"Do I think they could pile up a lot of cash over a three-day weekend?" Tony said. "Sure. Makes sense. Do I think we could steal it? I'd have to hear what else the Pelican had to say, you know, about the layout, the guards' schedule, what we'd find if we got into the counting room. I mean, the money can't be just sitting there. Then we'd have to figure out how to get away. We gotta lotta blanks to fill in, know what I mean?"

Half-listening, Nico prized the prongs apart and pushed them down against the resistance of the spring. Like a mouse trap, it had a trigger that you set, but Nico couldn't figure out how you did it. Holding the prongs apart, he screwed around with the trigger wire, trying to insert it up to a carefully calibrated point through a hole in the little trigger plate where it would hold back the force of the killing jaws, but just barely—just to where, if even a gopher's whiskers brushed against it, it would snap shut. He squinted again at the instructions, trying to decipher the meaning of the numbers and little arrows superimposed on a diagram of the trap.

Just when he thought he had it worked out, the trap snapped shut on his hand.

He threw a few F-bombs, waving his hand violently, as though he could shake out the pain.

"You should try flooding them out," Tony offered. "Stick a hose down that hole, wait next to the other hole with a shovel, and whang the little fucker when he sticks his head up for air."

Nico checked out his hand; blood trickled out of two ugly puncture wounds just below his knuckles.

"That hose thing doesn't work," he told Tony, a little testily. "I researched all this on the Internet. These traps are what the experts recommend." He brought his hand to his mouth and sucked on the wounds, trying to remember when he had his last tetanus shot.

Tony had another suggestion. "What about connecting a hose to the exhaust pipe of the van, and running it down into the hole. Gas 'em."

The dachshund had mustered the courage to venture away from Tony's legs, exploring the lawn. It had that look, that look that dogs get when they've got to go.

Nico forgot about his hand for the moment. "That dog is going to take a crap, Tony."

"So? That's what dogs do. You think I could stop it?"

They both watched as Schnitzel squatted and let loose.

"Jesus," Nico said. "You're gonna clean it up, right?"

"It's just dog doo," Tony said.

"Just dog doo? It's a mess. He was squirting it out."

"It's a she. Her name's Schnitzel. She's got intestinal problems. That's why it's so runny. What are you worried about? It's good for the grass, like fertilizer."

"No it's not. It's going to burn it."

"You're getting worked up about the wrong stuff right now, Nico." Clenching and unclenching his punctured hand, Nico had gotten up to get the hose from the side of the house. He pulled it toward the mess that Schnitzel had just made. "The gophers, your freakin' grass . . ." Tony continued. "We've got more important thing to focus on, Nico." Meaning of course the money. Nico aimed a high pressure stream of water from the hose nozzle at the mess Schnitzel had left on his lawn. "How did it go at Mom's? Did you get the raffle money?"

"Yeah, and I felt like a shit doing it." The last thing Nico wanted to do was tell his brother about what he'd witnessed. He was trying not to think about it.

"How much was it?"

"Not that much. Like $7,000, maybe a little over $7,000. Something like that."

Tony was quiet for a moment. Then he said, "What are we going to do? With the raffle money we've got like $30,000, but that's not going to cut it."

Nico shook his head. He twisted the hose nozzle to shut off the stream of water.

"Wait," Tony said. "Try that thing with the hose. Go on. Stick the hose down that hole and shoot the water down there."

"It won't work."

"Just try it."

Just to shut his brother up, Nico stuck the hose down the hole with the nozzle wide open. He held it there for a couple minutes. The water gurgled deep in the hole.

"See. Nothing."

"Just a little longer."

Then a weird thing happened. Out of the corner of his eye Nico saw the little dachshund flash toward one of the other gopher holes, shove his muzzle down into it and come up with a struggling gopher in its jaws. Schnitzel shook the gopher violently and then dropped it. She stared at the lifeless body for moment before looking up at Tony, wagging her tail.

"Ha!" Tony shouted triumphantly. "See! That's how you kill the little sonsofbitches!"

Nico shrugged, turned off the water and walked the hose back to the side of the house.

"What about the Bay-View?" Tony asked. "If it's for real, we could take care of all this bullshit, get that bitch Gina off our backs and maybe have a little extra."

Nico was carefully winding the hose around a hook, getting each loop to hang just right. "We've never done anything like that. Like pulling off a robbery."

"We stole that truck," Tony reminded him, "the one with all those vitamin supplements."

"We didn't plan that. It was just sitting there with the engine running while the driver ran into the 7-11 for something. And it was Chuy who actually jumped in and drove it away. You and me, we just helped him unload it."

"I still got some of that brewer's yeast. You think it's still good?"

"My point is," Nico said, ignoring the question, "that you need the right kind of guys to do something like that. Strong-arm type guys. Pros. Who do we got? You're on crutches. Moochie can't count up to eleven. And I wouldn't be any good at something like that. I could maybe plan it, but I know who I am and I'm not the guy who sticks a gun in someone's face."

"So what do we tell Dragon Lady?"

"I think we're just going to have to lay our cards on the table when she comes back. She's a businesswoman; she understands that things happen, delays, and that sometime you've got to adjust your expectations. I'll put together a payment plan, put it on a spreadsheet, show her how we can pay her off over time."

"You really think she's going to buy that?"

"I don't know what else to tell her."

The dachshund was digging furiously at another hole. Nico yelled and ran at it. The dog scampered away.

"Can you get the freakin' dog out of here?" he said to Tony.

Tony got the crutches positioned just right under his arms, getting ready to take off. "I was thinking maybe you could keep it here till we get things sorted out with the Pelican," he said. "I don't have a fence around my yard like you do."

✳✳✳✳

So now Nico had one more problem—the dog. And it only got more complicated after little Nicky got home from school and saw it in the back yard. He was thrilled, thinking at first that his dad had got the cute little dog for him. Nico explained that they were only watching it for a friend who was out of town, but that didn't stop Nicky from falling in love. He immediately gathered up the dachshund in his arms, and wouldn't put her down. Schnitzel kept her pointy snout stuck in his face, licking him. Nicky was finally persuaded to put the dog down when they ate dinner, but at bedtime he insisted on bringing her into his bed. Against his better judgement, Nico let it go. He didn't like saying No to Little Nicky.

Z-Day Minus 3

It was 2:43 in the morning when Nico heard the banging on his front door. Once again, he hadn't been sleeping worth a crap. He was in his pajamas, the ones with the sailboats, making warm milk in the kitchen—he'd read somewhere that warm milk was calming. The banging on the door boomed through the quiet house. Nico turned off the stove and rushed to the door.

It was Tony, dressed in a ratty sweatshirt and jeans, leaning on his crutches.

"Jesus Christ, Tony, you trying to knock the door down? You could wake up Nicky."

"We gotta get down to the Wharf."

"What are you talking about?"

"She called me. Gina. Said for us to meet her at the market. She's down there now. It doesn't sound good."

"Called you? In the middle of the night like this?"

Tony said, "Come on. We gotta go. I don't want to deal with these psychos by myself."

Nico was trying to sort it all out. "It's the middle of the night," he repeated. "I can't just leave Nicky here by himself."

"Bring him with us. Nico. They're batshit crazy. Middle of the night doesn't mean anything to them. Come on, let's go." Tony turned and crutch-walked toward his truck, which was parked on the street, still running.

Nico hesitated, then went to get little Nicky, who was fast asleep with Schnitzel's head on the pillow next to him. Explaining gently that there was an emergency at the market, he picked up Nicky, his blanket and pillow, and carried him, still half-asleep, to Tony's truck. The dachshund followed and jumped in when Nico opened the passenger's side door.

Tony said, "We're not bringing the dog, Nico."

"He'll be OK. I think his stomach has calmed down." Nico settled into the truck with Nicky on his lap.

"He makes a mess, you're cleaning it up." Tony looked at him more closely. "You coulda put on your big boy clothes," he said.

"You made it sound like an emergency. Should I go back and change?"

Tony pulled the shifter into Drive and pulled away from the curb.

"Christ," he said, "in their minds we're already a pair of numbnuts, and you got on those pajamas."

"I could go back in and change."

Tony was already driving away. "Let's just go."

"Why did you say it didn't sound good?"

"I don't know. Just the way she sounded. And it's 2:30 in the freakin' morning. What could be good?"

It took them five minutes to get to the fish market. When they pulled up out front it was dark. Gina Quattro's Mercedes was there. Parked in front of it, a bulky shadow, was a delivery truck, the kind with a roll-up rear door. The Mercedes' interior lights came on and the driver's door opened. Gina got out. Nico saw that Hat and Benjie were standing at the rear of the delivery truck.

"What took you so long?" Gina asked Nico, who got out of the pickup first. Little Nicky was now sound asleep again and he arranged his blanket over him carefully. He was going to leave him in the cab with the dog, who was also sleeping.

"I can't stay long. I had to bring my kid."

Gina raised her eyebrows disapprovingly. "This shouldn't take long," she said. She saw Tony clumsily standing up his crutches as he got out, getting them set under his armpits.

She did a smirking double-take. "What happened to you?"

"I musta slipped or something."

Gina Quattro wasn't interested enough to ask for more detail. "Let's get this done fast." She looked at Hat, who jumped onto the rear bumper of the delivery truck and lifted the rollup door. "You guys serve calamari, right? Big seller on your menu? We got about a thousand pounds of squid here looking for a home. How much can you put in your freezer?"

Nico didn't have to ask where they got it. "We can't take that," he said.

Tony said, "We could always use squid."

"Not this squid," Nico said.

"What do you mean?" Gina asked. "Squid is squid. Come on, get a dolly or something so we can move it."

Tony hadn't caught on. "Where's it from?"

No one answered him.

"We just can't," Nico said to Gina.

"Of course you can. Those gooks owe it to you. They impacted your livelihood and now they've got to pay you one way or the other."

"We've got a legitimate business here," Nico said. "We can't jeopardize it like this. Driving a truckload of stolen goods right to the front of the market, that's crazy."

"We could take some of it," Tony said. "Go get the hand truck, Nico."

Nico looked at Tony. "What, are you crazy too?"

"Come on, chop-chop," Gina said. "The sooner we offload this, the sooner we can get this truck out of here."

"Go get the hand truck," Tony said again.

There was no way to argue with them. Nico went around the back of the market and came back with the hand truck that they used to move around stuff like cases of beer and buckets of ice.

But he had to draw the line somewhere. "We only have room for about twenty boxes," he said.

Hat was peering into the delivery truck. "We got at least 500 boxes here."

"We don't have room in the freezer."

"What are you going to do, let it go to waste?" Hat asked.

"OK, your call," Gina said to Nico. "But this in a nutshell is why you're not a success. You're too chickenshit. I offer you over 500 boxes of free squid and you only find room for twenty."

"They got this from Yummy Squid?" Tony asked.

"If you don't have much room in your freezer, maybe we should get this other thing in there first," Gina said. "Hat, drag him out and give him to Benjie."

"*Him?*" Tony asked. Nico closed his eyes and shook his head. How could this be happening?

Hat dragged what looked like a hastily rolled up sheet of six mil plastic to the edge of the truck bed. The plastic was wrapped around something, something with weight. Benjie grabbed it and threw it over his shoulder. An arm flopped out of the plastic.

"Open the back door, Nico," Gina said.

It was one of Van Phuc's guys, they saw after they'd brought they body around back and into the prep area. The guy with the scar who'd threatened them with the boat hook. Apparently, on his own initiative, Hat had returned to Yummy Squid after midnight, intent on some kind of payback. He'd seen the truck being loaded, then saw the driver, the guy with the scar, go back inside the warehouse, leaving the idling truck unattended for a minute. It was like a gift, just sitting there, waiting to be taken. Hat told Benjie to follow him in the Mercedes, then jumped in behind the wheel. As he was pulling away, the Vietnamese guy came out and started chasing him with a gun. Hat didn't have any other option. He had to defend himself.

The plastic was smeared with gore.

"That's a lot of blood," Tony said. They were all standing around the body, which Benjie had deposited on the floor of the prep area. "Good thing we got a drain in the floor."

"I got some on my shoes," Benjie said unhappily, looking at Hat.

"You get smacked with a .50 caliber round, it ain't pretty," Hat said. "Get a towel or something," he said to Benjie. "Dab it with cold water before it dries."

Nico rubbed his eyes. "I can't deal with this." He thought he might get sick and sidled over to the sink. Good thing they'd left little Nicky in the truck. Benjie pushed him aside. He found one of the white kitchen towels they used in the prep area and was saturating it with cold water.

Gina told Benjie to unload twenty boxes of squid from the truck and bring it back with the hand truck.

"After I clean my shoes," Benjie said.

"Forget your stupid shoes. Go get the squid like I said," Gina said.

"Kids and their fucking shoes," Hat said.

Tony, leaning on his crutches, was thinking things through. "We've gotta make some room in the freezer. Re-arrange things. I wish you would've given me a little more advance notice that you were going to doing this. I could've been ready."

Nico was looking at the body, wrapped in bloody plastic with the lifeless arm extended. He looked at Hat, he looked at Tony, finally letting his gaze land on Gina. "This is completely insane."

"Look, it happened. Maybe it was a stupid thing to do, but we've got to deal with it," Gina said. "What are those, sailboats?" she asked him.

"These are my pajamas. I wear them to bed, you know, like a normal person. Normal people are in bed at 2:30 in the morning, not standing around a dead body."

Hat couldn't resist making a crack. "Does your mommy tuck you in?"

"OK, so you're normal," Gina said. "We get that."

"We gotta move stuff around in here," Tony said, pulling open the door to the walk-in freezer while propped on his crutches. Benjie wheeled in the boxes of squid stacked on the hand truck, stopping to wait for directions.

"Hat and Benjie, you help out in the freezer," Gina said. They all crowded in. Then Nico was alone with the body and Gina. Gina was looking at him. "Well?" she said.

"This has got to stop. We can't take in any more dead bodies like this. We're a respectable business."

"Look at you, in your pajamas with the sailboats, laying down the law."

"My pajamas have nothing to do with it."

Tony popped his head out of the walk-in. "Nico, we got about ten gallons of frozen chowder that Ma put away about four months ago. Can we get rid of it? We need the space."

"Yeah, sure."

Gina said, "Can we move on to a more important subject?"

"What?"

Gina acted incredulous. "*What?*"

"The more important subject . . .?"

"You've got a dry sense of humor." A fixed smile hung on her face, showing her impossibly white teeth. "Droll. That's the word. You're a droll sonofabitch."

"If you say so—"

"You remember," she said with mock patience, "the discussion we had two days ago? Our agreement?"

Tony poked his head out of the freezer again. "What about all this frozen scalone you bought last year on special that no one would eat? Looks like it got freezer-burned."

"We can dump it," Nico told him. To Gina he said, "You mean the money?"

"Bingo. That's it, the money. $100,000."

"I thought we had until tomorrow."

"It is tomorrow."

"I mean like later in the day."

Benjie had taken the frozen chowder and a case of scalone steaks out of the freezer and put them on the floor next to the plastic-wrapped corpse. Tony and Hat came out too. Benjie and Hat picked up the body and went back into the freezer. A pool of dark blood was on the floor where the body had been.

Gina was waiting for Nico to give her a better answer. Tony was looking at Nico too.

"We're getting it together. Making progress."

"So you're going to have the 100 grand for me later today?"

"Actually, it's looking more like fifty grand."

"Fifty grand?"

Hat and Benjie had finished in the walk-in freezer. They both emerged, peeling the wrappers off Drumsticks. Now everyone was crowded in the prep area.

"The deal was for $100,000," she said.

"I know. But the thing is, we need a few more days. Till after Memorial Day."

"What's going to happen after Memorial Day?"

Then he just blurted it out. He didn't know why he was saying it other than he felt cornered, desperate.

"We've got a score we're working on. A heist."

"A heist? No one uses that word anymore."

"OK, like a robbery." Gina waited. He felt like he had to give her something good, so he embellished a little. "It might be worth a couple hundred grand." Then he laid it out, what the Pelican had told Tony about the Bay-View Boardwalk, and all of the cash receipts they collected over the weekend, how it piled up, especially during a busy three-day holiday weekend. He told her they had an inside guy who had tipped them off as to when the armed guard stepped away from the counting room. "There's this window of opportunity when we could get in and more or less help ourselves."

Tony was looking at him, like "What the fuck?"

"This is a new twist," Gina said. "A whole new twist. Who's we?" she asked. "Who is it who's going to pull off this heist of yours? Not you two pencil dicks by yourselves, I assume."

"We got some guys," Nico said. "Guys we trust." Tony was still looking at him like he was nuts.

"Guys? What kind of guys?"

"OK, so one guy actually. We used to work with him. Standup guy. He's tough too. He was one of those cage fighters. He could kill you with his hands."

"Hat, what do you think? You think these two clowns could rob that crappy little amusement park on the beach."

Hat had gotten the wrapper off his Drumstick and was making quick work of it. "These guys?"

"We've got this other guy too," Nico said.

Hat said, "I wouldn't trust these guys to take milk money off a kiddiegartner." He clearly didn't know how to eat a Drumstick, Nico thought, the way he was just chomping away at it like a horse eating an apple, peanut bits falling to the floor.

Gina had her doubts too. "I'm going to need to know a little more about this heist of yours."

"We're still working out some of the details. Still got a few things to iron out."

"Like?"

"Like logistics."

"Logistics? Do you know what that word even means?"

"It means . . ." What did it mean? Nico was stuck for a moment.

Tony had had enough. "Look, I'm tired of your fucking arrogant attitude. Like Nico said we're working out the details, however you want to say it."

Gina decided to come at it from another angle. "Maybe we can help with that. Hat here has participated in a few heists, right Hat?"

"One or two," Hat said.

"You wouldn't mind if we consulted on this would you?" Gina asked Nico. "I mean as a condition of giving you an extension on your deadline. After all, we're what you'd call stakeholders in this thing. So first, we want to make sure that the opportunity is real. Then we want to know if the plan is realistic. Then there's the whole question of executing the plan to ensure success. It's common practice for businesses, corporations. Bring in a consultant with expertise."

Everyone was staring at Nico, waiting. He looked at the blood on the floor.

"We're going to meet tonight," he said. "A planning meeting."

"When and where?"

"At the Bay-View. Kinda case the place out. I haven't set the time yet, but after we close the market."

"Call me," Gina said. "Put my number in your phone."

Nico said, "I don't have my cell phone on me." He looked down at his pajamas. "No pockets."

She'd seen the grease board on the wall where they wrote down supplies that had to be ordered. She picked up a grease pen and wrote down her number.

"This heist better be real," she said.

Tony said, "What are you going to with the rest of that squid?" like maybe he was having second thoughts about letting them just drive away with it.

"What do you care? Your brother says a respectable business like this won't take any more than a few boxes."

"Just wondering, that's all."

"I'll make a few calls. We'll find someone who's got room to take it up in San Francisco. We've got business partners up there who'd be happy to have it. You guys just worry about getting rid of that stiff."

Benjie hovered over the hole in the floor where they dumped the fish scraps, barking like a seal. Sammy answered back.

"He sounds lovesick down there, Benjie," Hat said, making kissing sounds with his puckered lips.

Gina Quattro had had enough of all of them. "All right you two, let's go." She turned to walk back to her Mercedes. Hat and Benjie followed. "Make sure you call me," she said to Nico.

After they left, Nico filled a bucket of water from the prep sink to wash the blood down the floor drain.

Tony said, "Are you fucking nuts? Why did you say that? About the heist?"

Nico emptied the bucket on the floor, then got a long-handled squeegee to push it all down the drain. Sammy was still barking down below. "What was I supposed to say? You think these people are going to pussyfoot around with us on the money? It's like we gotta throw a Hail Mary pass."

"Who are you? Joe Montana?"

"Have you got a better idea?"

Tony, "We've gotta kill them. That's the only answer."

"You're crazy. Who's going to do that?"

"I'll do it. I'd be happy to do it. We get 'em out here for another late night meeting. I shoot 'em. We take the bodies out past the mile buoy and drop 'em down. Done."

"We kill them, you think Vincent won't send more people just like them down here?"

"We kill them too."

"How many people are you gonna have to kill to make it all go away? Look, we've got no good choices here, but maybe I bought us a couple extra days to figure it out. And to tell the truth, I think we've gotta take a closer look at what the Pelican's got. If there's something

227

to it, if we could pull it off, we buy these people off and they go away. I'll talk to the Pelican. And then I'm going to talk to Chuy."

Tony gave him his "OK-have-it-your-way" stare. Then he angled his head toward the walk-in freezer. "So what are we going to do with him?"

"What we always do, I guess."

"Maybe you didn't notice, but I'm on crutches. I can't be dragging a body around the way I've gotta do."

Nico sighed. It was getting to be too much for him to handle. "I don't want to think about it right now. He'll keep."

****

At seven in the morning, Nico got little Nicky up so he could get ready for school. Nico looked like hell and felt like it too. He almost yelled at his son, who didn't want a cheese sandwich packed for his lunch. Nico almost snapped, "You'll get what I give you!" But he didn't. He set the cheese sandwich aside for himself, and made Nicky what he wanted—what he always wanted—a peanut butter and jelly sandwich. After he dropped little Nicky off at school, Nico headed down to the wharf to get things set up so he could leave for an hour before the market opened. He brought Schnitzel with him, tying up the little dog outside, looping her leash over a fence railing. Everyone, especially Bianca—who he could barely stand to look at—was taken with the cute little dachshund, sneaking it food in spite of his warnings not to. Please don't do that, he told them, she's got a delicate stomach. But of course no one listened.

A little after 10:00, he untied the dog's leash and started walking her down the wharf. He was going to talk to the Pelican first, then Chuy.

Even with her short legs, Schnitzel could really motor. She tugged at the leash that Nico held, setting what for him was a blistering pace as they turned down Beach Street, heading them toward the purple and gold Moorish spires of the Bay-View. She seemed to know the way.

With all of the extra weight he was carrying, jiggling in more than ten different directions, exhausted by lack of sleep and stress, Nico was quickly out of breath. When Schnitzel stopped to poop, Nico took a moment to bend over and grab his knees, gasping. His heart was pounding. It felt like he might be on the verge of a heart attack, and that would be OK with him, as long as he just keeled over and died quickly. It might be the only way he'd be able to get out of the mess he was in. The more he thought about it, the bleaker it seemed. He'd gotten home from the market around 4:00AM, and hadn't even bothered to go back to bed; instead he sat in his living room, looking out the sliding glass doors at dawn breaking over his gopher-ridden back yard, eating Doritos and thinking, wondering how he and his brother had gotten into this mess.

Maybe he and Tony should have just been upfront with the Maladagos after Big Nicky died, let them know that they wouldn't be carrying on the business. Maybe he could have gone up to San Francisco, to the offices of Argiento Linens, and talked to Vincent,

229

man to man, just cut the cord. Maybe Vincent would have understood and everyone could have just moved on. Shoulda, coulda, woulda. It was a waste of time trying to ask yourself what you could have done differently. As Big Nicky used to say, What's the fucking point? Don't think about the hands you could have played, make the most out of the cards you're holding now. So that's what he was going to do. He was going to channel the spirit of his old man, Big Nicky, and get on with it.

"You need to clean up after your dog."

Still catching his breath, Nico lifted his head to see an older woman in a jogging suit facing him down sternly.

"Huh?"

"Your dog made a mess on the sidewalk and you're responsible for cleaning it up. If you don't have a bag, there are some in that dispenser over there."

Nico looked down the sidewalk and saw the toxic pool of poop that Schnitzel had deposited. How was he supposed to clean *that* up? It was like a puddle of chocolate pudding—chocolate pudding with a stink that would singe your nose hairs.

"She's not my dog," he explained. "I'm just walking her."

"It doesn't matter *whose* dog it is. You're in control of her. Or supposed to be. She's your responsibility."

"The thing is I'm feeling kinda ill," Nico said. He wiped away the sweat that had gathered in the corners of his eyes. "And I'm kinda in a hurry."

Another woman briskly walked up and joined the inquisition. She held out a plastic bag. "That's what these are for," she said. Several other women, all serious power walkers from the looks of them, had gathered around him like a group of crows surrounding a pigeon. Nico straightened up, composed himself.

"You're so worried about it, you clean it up," he said. "I gotta get going."

That didn't exactly shut them up, but he turned his back on their cawing and moved on.

A sign at the entrance to the Bay-View said No Pets. Nico ignored it and walked through. The security guard on duty was looking intently at his smart phone and took no notice.

You wouldn't think it would be that hard to find a six-and-a-half-foot pelican, but Nico walked up and down the main midway for almost ten minutes before he spotted Pete, sitting in costume at the Skeeball booth. When Nico approached Pete had just managed to sink a fifty pointer and was pumping his fist, which shook the fabric feathers of his wing.

"That's how you do it!" he cried through his pelican beak. "That's how you make this bitch cough up tickets!"

He had jumped up from his seat and had was taking the first steps of what Nico guessed was a victory dance when he spotted Schnitzel, who he almost stepped on with his big flapping pelican feet.

"*Schnitzel!*" the Pelican exclaimed, and then he slumped to his knees and gathered up the little wiener dog, whose tail was wagging furiously. "Did you miss Daddy? Did you? Yes, you did! Yes, you did!" After this first spasm of joy, the Pelican saw that Schnitzel was attached to a leash; and that the leash was being held by Nico.

"How's her tummy?"

231

Nico saw a pair of worried eyes through the holes in the big black pupils of the Pelican mask. "Her tummy? If you're asking does she still have the squirts, the answer is yes. I wouldn't hold her too tight or squeeze her or anything."

"Poor baby," the Pelican said, gently stroking her ears. "You're bringing her back?" he asked hopefully.

"That depends." Nico tugged on Schnitzel's leash just hard enough to yank her out of the Pelican's arms.

"Don't pull like that. You'll hurt her."

"Tony said you wanted to work out a deal. Trade some information to pay off your debt, get your little dog back." Because he couldn't see the Pelican's real face behind the mask, he wasn't sure if what he was saying was registering. "He said maybe you had a plan."

The Pelican looked left and right, making sure no one else was within earshot. "Maybe I do."

"Look, I don't have time to play games. You've got five minutes to give me what you got or I'm giving the dog back to Tony. He's itching to put this little guy in a crab pot."

"It's not a guy. It's a girl."

"Guy, girl . . . whatever."

"I told Tony I want some of the take. I mean above and beyond what I owe you guys. Did he tell you that? I need a stake to get out of this damn Pelican suit and get the hell away from here."

"Before we talk about anything like that you've got to tell me what you've got."

The Pelican was looking down at the dachshund. "OK. Let me show you."

The Pelican led them down the midway past game booths, food concessions and the lines to two kiddie rides, the Crazy Copters and the Lady Buggies. They stopped at the mouth of a shadowy alcove between the carrousel and the line to the Giant Anaconda. The alcove was about twenty feet deep, fifteen feet across. There were three closed doors in the dimly lit space; on the left was a Men's room; at the rear of the alcove the second door read "Authorized Personnel Only", which the Pelican explained provided access to a stairwell that descended to the amusement park's lower level. The third door, the one on the right, didn't have a sign on it. A security guard stood to the side of it, obviously bored, watching the crowd walk past the mouth of the alcove. Nico saw that the guard was wearing a service weapon and that the door had a sensor for a lock that required a key card.

"Behind that door, that's where they count the cash," the Pelican explained, whispering out of the side of his beak. The loud calliope music playing from the speakers around the carrousel forced Nico to put his ear next to the Pelican's beak so he could hear. The Pelican said that twice a day two guards made the rounds of the concessions and ticket kiosks, bringing the cash into the counting room. Inside, they had a couple old gals who fed the bills into these machines that count, bundle and band it. The last round of cash pickups started around 8:30 PM, a half hour before park closing and took fifteen, twenty minutes. "Whatever the ticket booths and concessions take in after that they use for starter cash the next day."

The guard at the counting room door spotted Schnitzel. "Hey—you can't have that dog in here. No dogs in the park."

The Pelican said, "I was just telling him that, Randy." He took Nico by the shoulder and led him away, walking him toward one of the exits on the Beach St. side of the park. On the way, he shared more details about the counting room and the cash pickups.

"They've got this little cart they push. The money cart. It looks a little like one of those popsicle carts you see Mexican guys pushing around. Conrad had the park's machine shop fabricate it."

"Who's Conrad?"

"Conrad Ferl. He's Chief of Security. A big fat douche bag."

Nico was sensitive to disparaging remarks about fat people—he thought of himself as "fat-ish"—but he let it pass.

"One of the guards is armed, the guy that was guarding the door back there, Randy Martin, another douche. It's only him and Conrad and one other guy who is usually at the other end of the park that are authorized to carry weapons in the park, so Randy leaves his post to guard the cart when they collect the money. One of the temporary guards they hire for the summer season takes his place. But that guard is unarmed. On the evening run they also bring back a couple of deep-fried Twinkies for Conrad, and a thirty-two-ounce Dr. Pepper."

"They have deep-fried Twinkies here?"

"Right across from the Tilt-a-Whirl."

Nico made a mental note, then asked, "So we take out the cart?"

"You could, but that's not the big score. The big score would be all the money in the counting room. I'm only telling you about the cart to give you a little background."

They reached the tall arched Beach Street gate, and not a second too soon. Schnitzel was clearly feeling the urge. It was all that crap they'd fed her down at the market. Nico pulled her toward a little patch of dead grass at the edge of the sidewalk and turned away while she did her business. The thought of it made him feel sick again.

"You're feeding her the kibble?" the Pelican asked. "I told Tony about her special diet."

"Sure, that's what we're feeding her," Nico said, just to get the conversation moving back in the right direction. "So what about the big score?"

The Pelican reached into his beak and from deep in its pouch he pulled out a slim 6-inch black e-cigarette, which he examined, then stuck further into dark recesses of the beak.

"They won't let me do this in the park," he said, blowing out a plume of vapor. "Teddy and Blaine and the rest of the cousins. But they don't get it. It's not really a cigarette, I told them. It's more like a medical device. The technology that goes into these things is really interesting—"

"I'm not interested in that. What about the big score?" Nico asked again. "The counting room . . .?"

"Yeah, OK, so when they come back with the cash they use a key card to open the door and roll the cart into the counting room. All the receipts are held there in this big old safe that looks like something out of the Wild West days, which they keep more or less open until everyone leaves at the end of the day. See, they don't want to have to keep screwing around with the combination, opening and closing the door on the safe, which must weigh like 200 pounds. Just the door, I mean, not the safe. That's got to weigh half a ton. These are a couple of little old ladies doing all the cash counting and sorting, the Carlson twins, they've been around forever, and they both have arthritis, so they just kind of leave the door of the safe open a crack until they leave at night. I told you about Conrad, the head of security. His office is through a door in the back of the counting room. It's like his man cave. All of the surveillance camera feeds come into a bank of monitors in front of him. He's supposed to be checking them all out, but in the summer he's usually got a Giants game going on one of the monitors, and he's more interested in that."

"How do you know about all this?"

"I've been here almost twenty years. You learn things. You see all that money going in and out you start thinking." He pushed his hand inside his beak and sucked on his e-cigarette. "Anyway, like I said, they let the money pile up in there over the weekend. The Brinks truck comes at midnight on Sunday unless it's a three-day weekend. Then they come for the pickup at midnight on Monday."

"So we wait till the Brinks truck comes and then hit them?" Nico shook his head. "Robbing a Brinks truck—I don't know. That's pretty heavy. Those guys are pros."

"Who said anything about robbing a Brinks truck?"

"So we rob the counting room? What about the guard? And it looked like there was a security camera pointing at the door."

"Before I give you any more, we need to make a better deal."

"How big do you think the score could be?"

"At the end of a three-day weekend? Just the cash? I'm guessing that they could stash at least fifty grand a day in there, so they'd have around a hundred and fifty grand, maybe more, piled up."

236

Nico was running the numbers in his head. "Let's say we give you five grand on top of forgiving your debt. And you get your dog back."

"I think you're going to have to do a little better than that."

"Like how much better?"

"We wipe the slate clean on what I owe you guys, and you cut me in for twenty grand out of the take."

It wasn't hard to agree to give the Pelican a cut of money they didn't yet have, especially if what he was saying about the size of the payoff was true. "OK . . . keep talking."

"So yeah, you don't wait for the Brinks truck; you hit the counting room. And here's how you do it. . ." The Pelican laid out the plan he'd formulated over the long nights he'd spent peering resentfully out of his big mascot head. It sounded doable, but Nico wasn't sure. One thing was for sure—Gina Quattro was right. Nico and Tony couldn't pull off anything like this by themselves. But if she was going to make them bring Hat and Benjie into the deal, they needed a least one guy on their side who could handle himself and stay cool. They needed Chuy.

But before he left the park to look for him, Nico made one more stop, circling back through the entrance to the shooting gallery, where he'd noticed super-sized stuffed animals arrayed on the back wall, apparently the grand prize for hitting five bulls-eyes, which probably happened as often as a rainstorm in the Mojave Desert. The kid running the booth was a little reluctant to sell him one for $20, but upping the offer to $25 did the trick. It was a big, fluorescent dolphin that was almost three feet tall. This might work, he thought. Lugging the big toy under one arm, holding Schnitzel's leash in the other, he headed for Gallo's.

****

Schnitzel made two pit stops on the short walk to Gallo's. Nico was ready to pay the Pelican to take her back. He went around to the back of the taqueria, to the service entrance, a battered door next to the dumpsters. It was open, and Nico walked through it into a hallway with boxes stacked along the side that opened into the work area and the kitchen. From a radio/CD player stuck on a shelf between plastic tubs of lard, Mexican music was playing, a jumpy accordion-backed number that sounded to Nico like a polka being played by a speed freak. A younger woman in an apron who he didn't recognize was holding a mop. Gallo's wife—or girlfriend or whatever she was— looked up from the hotel pan of enchiladas she was prepping. She wasn't happy to see him.

"Gallo's not here," she said. She recognized Nico from when he used to come by on a regular basis, asking for payments on the loan that Gallo never made. And she recognized the dog. For some reason, the big pink dolphin didn't brighten her mood.

Nico put on a friendly face, giving her a little smile, which she wasn't buying. "I'm looking for Chuy today." She didn't say anything, holding her dark gaze. "Is he here?"

She nodded to her left, in the direction of the dish area.

Nico walked around a prep table, stopping at the edge of a puddle of water that apparently was spreading from beneath the dishwasher. He saw Chuy in the classic plumber's pose, kneeling, bent over, working under the dishwasher. On the floor next to him were channel locks, a pipe wrench, a can of pipe dope, a couple of pipe fittings and a roll of duct tape.

"You having problems with the dishwasher?" Nico said.

Chuy flashed a look over his shoulder. A smudge of rusty grease streaked his cheek, and he looked more than a little pissed off. "Not really. I just thought I'd take this sonofabitch apart right before we opened today." Then he really looked at Nico. "What's with the big dolphin?"

"I thought I'd surprise little Nicky," Nico lied.

"How old is he now? Must be around six, right?"

"Just turned seven."

Nico knew a little something about dishwashers from the fish market, where he handled equipment purchases. He read the model name on the plate soldered to the dishwasher door. "That's a Bates-Stuckey Tornado, model 527. It's kind of an antique."

Chuy picked up the channel locks and stuck them into the guts of the dishwasher. He started twisting the channel locks, then paused. "Gallo traded a lawn mower for it twenty years ago," he muttered. "It was in pretty good shape back then; like it only broke down once every couple of months. Now it's more like once a week."

"Can you still get parts for it?"

"Sometimes. If not," Chuy held up the roll of duct tape, "I just apply a little Mexican chrome."

"I heard you were back from Tony."

Chuy rubbed his chin, thinking. He tried another turn of the channel locks and sat back on his heels. "Yeah, we talked yesterday."

"He's gonna have to be on crutches for a few days."

"I don't know what he was thinking, coming in here busting up things and threatening people."

"You know how he gets."

"He was swinging a bat, Nico."

"That's Tony, right?" Nico said. "What are you going to do?" He meant it as a rhetorical question, but Chuy had an answer.

"Me? I'm going to what I did, put him on crutches. And the next time he pulls something like that, I'm going to put him in a wheelchair."

Gallo wandered in from the rear apartment, wearing his big sombrero and baggy grey cotton sweats, a towel around his neck like he'd been training, doing road work. He looked at Nico, but didn't seem to recognize him.

"Who's this guy?" he asked Chuy.

"That's the Health Inspector," Chuy said.

"Health Inspector?" Gallo asked indignantly. He took a few steps closer to Nico, balling his fists. "I don't like Health Inspectors." He threw a quick combination, punching the air inches in front of Nico's face. Nico stepped back.

"He saw a few cockroaches, Dad."

"*Cockroaches*! We don't got no cockroaches here!"

"He saw them in the storeroom. Better check it out."

"There's no cucarachas here," Gallo insisted, then stormed off, disappearing into the storeroom, which was off the back hallway. They could hear him cursing as he searched for cockroaches behind the cans and boxes.

Chuy returned his attention to the dishwasher. Nico didn't say anything for a minute; then he said, "So, you're back for a while, huh?"

"You saw how Gallo is. He needs a little help." Chuy flipped a switch and waited, listening to the sound of a cranky pump filling the wash reservoir. He ran his hand under the fill hose, checking for leaks, more or less ignoring Nico, who was getting nervous about Schnitzel, who had scooted under one of the work tables.

Nico got to the point of his visit. "I could use a little help too," he said. "I got a thing you could help with."

"I've got my hands full." With a loud popping noise, the dishwasher kicked into the wash cycle.

"This thing, we pull it off, you could take care of the money Gallo owes. Wipe the slate clean."

Chuy turned to face Nico. "Didn't Tony tell you what I told him? You guys should have never loaned money to Gallo. It was a bad business decision. He can't be responsible."

"If it was just us, I don't know, maybe we could let it slide. But it's not just us. The Maladago's—they got me and Tony in a bind.

"What's that got to do with me and Gallo?"

"They want money from us. A lot of money. And in their minds they own a piece of our business, the loans and all."

"Sucks to be you."

"They got my ledger, the one where I recorded all the loans and who was paying us and who wasn't." Nico lied, needing Chuy to take him seriously. "If we don't come up with the money, it won't just be me and Tony who'll be in trouble. The Maladagos will come after your dad. And it won't be just with a baseball bat. I'm serious. I could show you a dead guy in our walk-in freezer down at the market, a guy who tried to stiff them."

"You and Tony still doing that? Dumping bodies for them?"

Nico looked around, and saw that Filomena and the girl with the mop were watching and listening. He tugged at the leash to pull Schnitzel out from under the table.

"Can we talk somewhere else?"

Silently, Chuy got up and led them out the back, stopping next to the dumpster. Schnitzel pulled the leash taut, exploring the space between the dumpster and the battered stucco back wall of the building. She was looking for just the right spot.

"What's up with the dog?" Chuy asked. Then his nostrils went wide. "Jesus—is that the dog?"

"I'm kind of dog-sitting for a while. She's got a little stomach problem."

They moved away from the dumpster. Nico thumbed the button on the retractable lead to lengthen it and give them more distance from the dachshund.

Nico said, "Anyway, like I was saying, I got this thing you could help with. You could wipe away Gallo's debt, square everything up."

"What kind of thing?"

"Like a score."

Chuy laughed, like Nico had to be kidding. "A score? Like a rip-off?" Nico shrugged. Chuy said, "I'm not doing that kind of thing anymore."

"I didn't even tell you what it is."

Filomena appeared at the back door. "Chuy, the dishwashing machine is leaking again."

Chuy cursed and kicked the dumpster. He seemed to get some satisfaction from the clanging hollow booming noise, and he kicked it again. "OK," he said to Filomena, calmer now. "I'm coming."

Nico saw another angle he could use to press his case. "If you come in with us you could wipe away the debt, and we could cut you in for another $5,000, something like that. Enough so you could get a new dishwasher. We're getting together tonight, kind of like a planning session."

"Who's we?"

"Me and Tony and these other guys."

"What other guys?"

"Look, before I give you anything else, I just need to know if you're interested."

It looked like Chuy was considering kicking the dumpster again, but he checked himself. He started walking back into the restaurant.

"Sure. I'm interested," he said with the enthusiasm of a guy agreeing to a colonoscopy. "But you've got to do better than $5,000."

"You don't even know what it is yet."

"Then why don't you tell me."

"Look, we're going to meet tonight around 8:30. In front of the merry-go-round at the Bay-View."

Chuy stopped and looked back. "You planning to rob some little kids of their ride money?"

"Are you gonna be there?"

Inside the building, Gallo had emerged from the storeroom. "Cockroaches!" he shouted.

"Sure," Chuy answered wearily, and then continued on into the kitchen. "I'll be there."

****

Grab, lock, pivot, pull. Grab, lock, pivot, pull. Grab, lock, pivot, pull.

Since his training session with Chuy the previous morning, Andrew been repeating that refrain, sometimes out loud, sometimes in a whisper, and sometimes just inside his head, over and over again, like a mantra or a magical incantation.

Grab, lock, pivot, pull.

It seemed so simple, so fluid when Chuy had shown him, but so complicated when Andrew had tried. He was determined to show Chuy that he'd mastered the move at their next training session, but just repeating the word sequence wouldn't get him there, even when he imagined a shadowy assailant coming at him with bad intent—he'd never get it down if he couldn't practice it with someone playing the role of the bad guy.

Carrying a wrinkled paper bag nearly filled with the green skittles that he'd promised Mr. Jefferson, he approached the Pelican first, asking him to grab him. The Pelican, in full costume, had just strolled into the park from the main gate. Andrew wasn't exactly keeping track, but it seemed like the Pelican was always going in and out of the park.

The Pelican just stared at him. It looked like smoke was coming out of the nostrils in his beak. Maybe he hadn't understood Andrew's request.

"Reach for me like you want to take me down," Andrew said.

"Beat it," the Pelican said.

Andrew found Ricky Wakefield flirting with his girlfriend at the counter of the arcade snack bar.

"Go ahead, attack me," he said to Ricky.

Ricky wouldn't cooperate. All he wanted to do was show off to his girlfriend, doing this thing where he waved his hands around quickly in front of Andrew, darting in little tap-slaps to his face, crying "*Hee-yah!*" each time he tapped him.

Andrew backed away. "That's not what I meant. You're supposed to grab me."

Ricky looked at his girlfriend who was wearing her little elf's cap turned sideways—not the way a real elf would wear it, Andrew wanted to tell her—and smirking.

"Why should I grab you when I can smack you so easily?" Ricky asked.

"So I can disable you."

"*Hee-yah!*" He thwapped his fingertips on Andrew's nose.

"Hey—that hurts!"

"*Hee-yah!*" Ricky grinned.

Frustrated, fighting back the urge to go off on Ricky and show him what a ninja could do if he really got angry and wasn't just practicing, Andrew left the arcade. He had thirty minutes before his shift started, and he wanted drop off the Skittles he'd promised Mr. Jefferson. On his way to the door to the basement level, he saw the young blond guard who was with Lieutenant Martin the day before when they'd chased him and Chuy off the beach. She was standing by the Giant Anaconda. As Andrew came closer, he saw that she was having what looked like a confrontation with a man next to the sign at the ticket taker's booth, the one with the horizontal line drawn 48 inches from the ground, and the admonition, "You must be taller than this line to ride the Giant Anaconda".

The man's face was red, except for a fluorescent green spot of hot dog relish on his chin. He was wearing a T-Shirt that said, "I'd Rather Be A Conservative Nut Job Than A Liberal With No Nuts And No Job." He was a shade shorter than the blond guard. His daughter, a chubby girl of around eight wearing pink leggings that bagged at the knees and a pink top with ponies on it, looked to be more focused on trying to work open her jaws—which had gotten locked tight by a huge wad of salt water taffy—than the Giant Anaconda.

"I'm the parent," he was saying. "I'm the one who should decide if it's safe enough for my daughter, not some jackbooted armed guard."

"I'm not armed," the guard pointed out. "And what's a jackboot?"

"She's short for her age. It's not her fault. I was short for my age too. James Madison was short. Do you know who James Madison was?"

"I'm not saying it's her fault," the guard explained. Andrew thought she was the prettiest security guard he'd ever seen, if not the prettiest girl period. "The rule is there because she could get hurt."

"Hurt how?

The guard, still miraculously patient, explained that the Giant Anaconda plunges at a high rate of speed, so the seat bar is important. But it was designed to restrain bigger people; someone his daughter's size could slip through and be thrown out.

"How would you like to see your little girl go flying out of her seat at 100 miles per hour?"

"I'd rather see her die free than enslaved by your petty laws."

"It's not really a law. Just a rule the park has."

His daughter had finally managed to work her jaws open. Tugging at her father's hand, she said. "We can we ride the merry-go-round, Daddy. It's right over there."

"I suppose they'll want to lash us to the ponies," the man said. He'd given up arguing, but he still wanted to take a parting shot. "Or chain us. Chains might be better. Just in case one of the ponies gets spooked and tries to throw us."

"Please, Daddy?" Still muttering, he allowed his little girl to pull him toward the carrousel.

The guard watched them walk away. Andrew edged closer to her. "Hi," he said.

She looked at him with a smile that made him forget what he wanted to say.

"Yes . . .?"

"My name is Andrew. And you're Corporal Cartwright. It's on your nameplate."

She was being patient, she was being kind, but the conversation with this slightly strange guy was getting just a little awkward for her—not that Andrew was aware of it. He explained that he was a co-worker, the Smiles Ambassador.

"My shift doesn't start until noon. These are my civilian clothes," he explained, looking down at his T-shirt, cargo shorts and basketball shoes.

Her eyes lit up. "That's you? The Smiles Ambassador is so cute. I love that little hat he wears. I mean that *you* wear."

"It's called a boater." He shared some research he'd done on the Internet. "Boaters were popular as casual summer headgear in the late 19th century and early 20th century, especially for boating or sailing. That's why they call them that. Boaters."

Then he couldn't think of anything else to say. He stood silently, smiling serenely, marveling at the blueness of Corporal Cartwright's eyes. Andrew also saw that she had tiny dimples just beyond the corners of her smile. He thought they were amazing.

Then he thought of something.

"Can I ask you a favor?"

"A favor?"

"Can you attack me?" She looked confused. Her cute little dimples disappeared. "Not really attack me, but just grab at me."

"I don't think so."

"Not for real. I was learning a karate move on the beach yesterday when you told us to leave."

"That was you?"

"Me and Chuy. He's a friend of mine, a martial arts expert. He was showing me how to defend myself when someone comes at me and tries to grab me. Grab, lock, pivot, pull. I can show you."

"I can't." He was relieved to see the dimples reappear. "Sorry. I appreciate you're asking me, though."

Andrew didn't know how to respond. Corporal Cartwright was still smiling, but somehow he knew it was time to walk away. He looked at his watch. It was 11:28, and he still had to get dressed in his Smiles Ambassador outfit before his shift. But if he hurried, he thought he'd have time first to drop in on A.E. Jefferson to give him the green skittles he'd promised.

"OK, thanks anyway. Later, gator."

There was no response to Andrew's first tentative knocks on the door to A.E. Jefferson's workshop. He rapped a little harder; this time he got an answer—an irritated voice shouting, "Read the sign! No one's allowed in here unless I invite them, and I don't recall inviting anyone!"

"It's me. Andrew. I brought the Skittles."

"Skittles?"

"The green Skittles."

Andrew took the silence from within as permission to open the door, which wasn't locked. Like the first time he'd ventured in to A.E. Jefferson's inner sanctum, the interior was dimly lit—the only source of illumination coming from two lights on hinged arms, one with a magnifier, clamped on to the main workbench. Andrew entered carefully, casting a wary eye over his shoulder to see if Frankie might be coming up from behind him, but the big animatronic monster stood still in his shadowy corner, staring silently ahead. Mr. Jefferson had trained one of the work lights on the larger of the two praying mantises—this one jade green and close to six feet tall— that he had set up next to the workbench. He was tinkering with one of the insect's formidable arms. "Re-thinking this attraction," he muttered by way of greeting. "The boss wasn't happy with my original concept, which in my humble opinion was not only scary but educational. Small minds run this park—Mr. Teddy Wakefield only wants scary. So, all right. He'll get scary." Squinting through a pair of half-lens reading glasses perched on the end of his nose, he was concentrating on a thin cable running through the exposed inner workings of one of the mantis' arms. "I think I've just about got down a new arm movement. I want to achieve a rapid, almost explosive extension, so I had to insert a more powerful spring at the joint." He finally looked at Andrew. "You said you brought green Skittles? They're in that bag?"

Andrew nodded. "892 of them. I counted them last night."

"Go ahead and set it down on the table there, next to that spool of fiber."

Peering again at the exposed mechanicals of the mantis' arm, he plucked the cable, testing its tension, which apparently wasn't quite satisfactory. He had a little tool in his hand which he used to turn a screw that tightened the spring. "The praying mantis is the apex predator of the insect world," he continued, testing the cable again, then adjusting the screw slightly. "They can lash out at an unsuspecting prey with these long arms—see the nasty hooks on them?—grabbing them faster than you can blink your eye."

Andrew was fascinated by insects and in fact had been obsessed by them for six months when he was ten. He still remembered verbatim some of the research he'd done then.

"The Goliath Bird Eating Tarantula can reach up to one foot in length and has one inch fangs. Could a praying mantis beat it in a fight?"

A.E. Jefferson looked up over his reading glasses and for the first time favored Andrew with a smile.

"This one could," he said. He laid the little tool down on the table and picked up a controller. "OK, let's see what we've got."

Working the controller, he first caused the mantis' alien-looking head to sway back and forth. It looked like it was studying Andrew with its big compound eyes, its mandibles opening and closing. Then, suddenly, it reached for him, its hooked arms extending so quickly, and coming so close to Andrew, that he fell backwards.

"Excellent! Looks like we've got it," A.E. Jefferson said, returning the mantis back to a benign, prayerful pose. Then, to Andrew, who was still sitting the floor, he said, "Are you all right? Did you hit your head?" Andrew nodded in response to the first question and shook his head to the second.

"Sorry I didn't warn you, but the thrill-seekers riding in that little train through the Creepy Cavern won't be warned either. The surprise is what makes it so scary."

Pleased, A.E. Jefferson made the mantis repeat the lightning-fast reaching motion several times as Andrew picked himself up.

Out of nowhere, he heard something that sounded like a doorbell.

"Lunch is here," Mr. Jefferson said happily, putting down the controller.

The doorbell rang again; Andrew tried to figure out where it was coming from.

"Keep your pants on, Chao Li!" Mr. Jefferson shouted. He headed for the back of the workshop, past a couple rows of shelving units, and Andrew followed. The doorbell rang again, exasperating Mr. Jefferson. With his short legs and his limp, he was making slow progress.

"I'm coming!"

He stopped in front of a door that was almost completely hidden behind a stack of boxes. After turning a deadbolt, he opened it, and Andrew saw a Chinese man in a spattered white cook's jacket holding a plastic take-out bag. Mr. Jefferson produced some bills from one his pockets to pay him, took the take-out bag and thanked the man, who counted the bills and left. Mr. Jefferson closed the door behind him and turned the deadbolt.

Mr. Jefferson saw that a question was forming on Andrew's lips.

"Egg rolls, Andrew," he said, happily hoisting the bag. "The perfect geek fuel." He started limping back to his work area with Andrew following.

"Where'd he come from, that Chinese man?" Andrew asked.

"Originally? Wuhan, China, I think."

"Where did he come from just now?"

"The Golden Buddha, that little Chinese restaurant across the street." A.E. Jefferson opened the plastic bag, popped open the wide

Styrofoam take-out container that was inside, and stared lovingly at its contents—twelve egg rolls laid out in two rows of six, along with packets of hot mustard. "Way back when, maybe a hundred years ago or so, they ran the utilities to the park under Beach Street through a tunnel. I think it must have flooded once, so they closed it up. I like to snoop around, and when I found that door in the back of the workshop, I got it open and found the tunnel. It was dark, and smelled like an old sewer. I could see a light at the other end, and I was curious, so I got a flashlight and headed toward the light. When I got to there, I found stuff like brooms and mops, cleaning supplies, cases of soy sauce, frying oil, that sort of thing." He picked up an egg roll and blew on it. "The family that owns the Golden Buddha was using their end of the tunnel as a storage closet. Long story short, I opened the door at the other end and scared the hell out of two cooks chopping up chickens. They were so shocked when they saw me that they threw their cleavers down and ran."

Satisfied that the egg roll he was holding had cooled enough to eat, he spread hot mustard on one end and took a bite. As he ate the first egg roll, he finished his story.

"I'd been getting take-out from the place, but going back and forth across Beach Street is not so easy for me. As you may have noticed, I've got a little ambulation problem. So I talked to Mrs. Jong—she's the owner—and arranged to have her send her nephew over down the tunnel with the egg rolls—or sometimes a little chow mein, or those dumpling things—when I call. I rigged up the doorbell so if I was working on something here, I'd know when he was at the door."

He wiped his fingertips on a paper napkin, then gestured toward the Styrofoam take-out container.

"Don't be shy—help yourself."

Andrew was getting nervous about the time. He didn't want to be late for his shift. He looked at his watch. He had less than ten minutes to transform himself into the Smiles Ambassador.

"I have to get ready for work," he said. "I just wanted to bring the Skittles to you."

"I appreciate it. I'll get into those after I finish off these deep-fried beauties." Mr. Jefferson turned his attention to his second egg roll as Andrew backed out of the workshop.

"Later, gator," he said, but Mr. Jefferson was too focused on his lunch to respond.

****

After his meetings with the Pelican and Chuy, Nico put Schnitzel and the big plush dolphin into the market van, and dropped both off at home. He hid the stuffed toy in a closet and put Schnitzel into the backyard, which was starting to look like a battlefield after a mortar barrage, cratered by gopher holes which the dog had made even worse with her frantic digging. Screw it, he decided—he had bigger things to worry about.

Like how he was going to rob the Bay-View.

And a little personnel problem at the fish market.

254

"You can't fire Hilario!" Bianca said after she'd stormed into Nico's office to confront him. Nico was at his desk, his meaty forearms resting on stacks of invoices. Even with everything else going on he still had a business to run. Bianca came right up to the edge of the desk, staring down at him, her nostrils flaring. Hilario, AKA Freebie, her Latin lover boy, was standing behind her, just outside the doorway. The first thing the little weasel had done after Nico gave him a final paycheck and asked for his apron was run to Bianca, like a kid running to his mommy. He was hanging back, not willing to meet Nico's eyes, probably thinking that Bianca was going to fix things. That she was the real boss. Think again, you slimy fuck.

"He's not productive. Every time I see him, if he's doing anything, he's doing it in slow motion. Except the one thing. He does that pretty fast."

Bianca acted like she wasn't really hearing him. "Nico, he's my right arm man," she insisted. Left arm too, Nico wanted to say. And it doesn't stop there. "I taught him how to make my chowder."

"I've seen him stir your chowder. That he can do."

"He does more than just stir it. He can make it from start to finish."

Nico leaned back a little in his chair. "You like the way he makes your chowder? Well, I don't. I don't want him messing with your chowder at all. I want him outta here."

A flash of anxiety crossed Bianca's eyes, as if she were suddenly wondering what Nico really knew, not that she could ask him directly. She softened her tone.

"Nico . . . just give him another chance."

Nico thought about it. Then he nodded and said, "OK, but he needs to step up and show me something. He's gotta be more than just your chowder boy. He's gotta be willing to really pitch in." He locked onto Bianca's hopeful gaze. "With Tony banged up we need help tomorrow with his crab line. Freebie can show me that he's serious about keeping his job by helping out. We'll need him down at the harbor early, around 4:30 in the morning."

Bianca turned to look at Freebie, who had been listening intently. A fretful look pulled at his cheeks. His little mustache turned down at the corners. He said something to her, so softly that Nico couldn't make it out.

"What's he saying?"

"He's saying he can't swim."

"I'm not asking him to swim. I just need him on the boat to help pull up and empty the traps, bait them, and throw 'em back in."

"But if he can't swim—"

"Ma, your old man couldn't swim, and he went out on a fishing boat almost every day of his life. None of those guys from the old country could swim. They were a little more careful for exactly that reason. The last thing they wanted was to go into the water."

Bianca tried another angle. "Maybe you could get one of the kids who work out front to help . . ."

"Would you trust any of those knuckleheads to show up at that hour of the morning? They can barely make it here by 9:00, most of them. Look, I'm trying to give the guy another chance. Does he want to help or not? Hey, Freebie," he called, and Freebie stepped forward, sidling in to share the doorway with Bianca, blinking deferentially. He looked like a guy standing before a judge, waiting to be sentenced. "You gonna help me and Tony out tomorrow morning or not?"

Freebie almost said something, but the words wouldn't come out. It looked like he might have nodded; close enough anyway.

"Meet us down at the Giovanna, you know, down at the harbor. You gotta be there by 4:30, 'cause we need to get an early start.

Bianca again came to his defense. "You can't make him do something he's not comfortable doing."

"Quatro y media, en la mañana, right?" Nico said to Freebie, ignoring her.

"OK," Freebie nodded.

"Now get back to work and put a little more into it. Start showing me something."

After Freebie had hurried off, Bianca stayed behind, standing silently in the doorway looking at Nico.

"What else do you want, Ma?"

"When did you become a bully, Nico? It's not like you."

He looked down at the invoices he'd been working on, letting her know he didn't have time for this soul-searching bullshit. "I'm just tired of people taking advantage of us. That's all. Nobody would pull the shit they're pulling if Big Nicky was around . . ." He paused, almost not going to say the next thing, forcing himself to look up from the paperwork and meet her eyes. "And you know exactly what I'm talking about."

Did she? Nico searched her face, but he couldn't tell. She decided not to say anything more, though. He returned his gaze to his invoices and she silently backed out of his office.

****

Chuy got to the Bay-View a few minutes before 8:30, but didn't show himself, wanting to get the lay of the land first. Knots of people, mostly teenagers, roamed the midway, which was bathed in an electric twilight. Approaching carefully, he saw Nico and Tony and another guy he didn't recognize standing in front of the carrousel. Tony was on crutches. Nico was pushing a hot dog into his mouth with one hand, holding a plastic Target bag in the other. The third guy was a wiry restless little dude, bobbing his head, balling his hands into fists, relaxing them, clenching them again, checking everything out. He was wearing wraparound shades and one of those stupid little hats with the short brim, a hipster hat. Only this guy didn't look like a hipster. Hipsters were cool, laid back. There was nothing laid back about this guy. Even when he was standing still he looked tightly coiled. Chuy hung back, out of their line of sight, mixing into the press of parents watching their little ones and waving as the kiddies came around on their bright wooden ponies, clutching the grab poles for dear life. A recording of calliope music played scratchily over speakers. Then a big goofy-looking kid of around twenty or so swung by, so big you could barely see the painted pony he was riding. Nico, Tony and the skinny guy waved at him, like they were messing with him. The big kid, who was wearing a flat-brimmed skater cap turned sideways, didn't look like he was enjoying the joke. He flipped them off as he rode past on his little pony.

Just walk away, Chuy told himself, whatever these clowns have in mind is gonna end in some kind of cluster fuck. But he had decided earlier that he should at least check it out, see what Nico's plan was, and that's what he was going to do. It was all about the taqueria and Gallo. He never thought it would matter to him if Gallo's business failed and Gallo ended up in some dementia warehouse walking the corridors in a hospital gown with his ass open in the back, his mind slipping away. But when it came down to it, it did. So he had to see if Nico was on to something. They needed cash.

He walked into Nico's line of sight, caught his eye and said hey. Nico was happy to see him. He shook Chuy's hand, grabbing onto it the way a guy who's fallen out of a boat grabs the hand of his rescuer. *"All right, Chuy! All right!"* He had mustard in the corner of his mouth.

The rest of the welcoming committee wasn't as enthusiastic. Tony stared at him, silently mouthing "Fuck you", letting him know they had unfinished business. His nose wasn't as swollen as the day before but he still had those two black eyes. The little wiry guy in the hipster hat just looked at him, something between a smirk and a sneer playing across his thin lips.

"This is the guy I was telling you about," Nico said to hipster hat. "My guy Chuy. Chuy was an MMA fighter. Mixed martial arts. You know, fighting in the cage and everything."

Hipster hat wasn't impressed. "You ever been in prison?" Chuy just looked at him. "You want to fight in a cage, that's where you do it."

"Hat is like a consultant. With the Maladagos."

"Hat?" Chuy said, like maybe he hadn't heard it right.

Hat wasn't interested in shaking hands, which was OK with Chuy. Chuy looked at Nico, then at the carrousel as the big doofus kid swung by again.

"Who's that? Another consultant?"

"That's Benjie," Nico explained. "More like an associate of Hat's. Hat asked him to get on the merry-go-round so it would look like we're watching him instead of casing out a heist."

"Every time you say that word I feel like slapping you," Hat said.

"You got mustard all over your mouth, Nico," Tony said.

Nico dabbed at the corners of his mouth with a wadded up napkin. "Did I get it?"

"Good enough," Tony said.

"So I'm here," Chuy said. "What have you got?"

Nico inclined his head toward the alcove in front of them. "Behind that door there, with the guard in front, that's where they count the money. Every stinking dollar they take in for every stinking ride and every stinking hot dog. Piles of cash."

"Some guard. She's just a girl," Hat said, checking out the security guard. "With a cute little can of mace, but no gun."

"Yeah, security isn't exactly airtight," Nico said. "What I heard from the Pelican is that most of the guards around the park are part-timers, either retired guys or kids just out of school."

"The Pelican?" Chuy asked. "Pete Wakefield?" Chuy remembered him as a gloomy older guy who used to buy beer for them when they were kids. Some kind of cousin of the Wakefields, owners of the Bay-View, kind of a loser that they used to make fun of.

"Sure. He knows this place inside and out. He tipped me off to this thing. Anyway, mostly what security around here is worried about is stuff like high school kids drinking beer and doing stupid stuff to show off for their girlfriends, like maybe a guy dumps his soda out at the top of the Ferris wheel." In fact, Nico said, sharing what the Pelican had told him, only three members of the security force were authorized to carry guns—the head of Security, Conrad Ferl, and his two lieutenants, Randy Martin and Travis Stuckey. Ferl was usually sequestered in his office at the rear of the counting room, chewing on a toothpick, scanning a bank of monitors that gave him views provided by security cameras located at fifteen park hotspots, though more likely watching a Giants game. He always had one of his armed guards patrolling the far end of the park, the other guarding the counting room door. Stuckey and Martin took turns. Twice a day, the armed guard assigned to the counting room broke away, joining one of the lower ranking members of the security staff to make the round of cash pickups from the concessions and ticket kiosks. In his place, a non-armed guard temporarily stood watch at the counting room door, like the blond who was stationed there now. As Hat had observed, her only weapon was a can of Mace secured to her utility belt.

"OK, so the guard with the gun left with the other guard and the cart to make the last cash pickups about ten minutes ago. If the Pelican gave it to me right, they should be coming back with it in about five to ten minutes."

Hat said, "How could it be the last run? The park's still open . . ."

"The two ladies in the counting room don't like to stay up late. They're like aunts of the Wakefield family or something, kind of old

261

and they get a little cranky if they have to stay much past 9 PM. So they try to get most of the day's cash counted and put away in the safe by then. Whatever's left in the registers is used for start-up cash the next day. The armored truck guys won't come around till early the next morning on weekday, or Monday after a weekend."

"Unfuckingbelievable," Hat said. "This place is a joke."

Nico's backgrounder was interrupted by a six-foot tall turtle wearing a headband and sunglasses who had decided to perform a hip-hop dance in front of them, blocking their view of the alcove.

Hat was not amused, especially when the turtle mascot tried to playfully grab his hat. He grabbed the mascot's arm, snarling, "If you don't get the fuck out of my face, I'll pull you out of that shell and kick your ass."

"That's not cool, dude," the mascot said, edging away to spread his brand of wacky joy somewhere else.

"So the deal is," Nico continued, waving again at the big unhappy kid on the merry-go-round as he came around, "that they got all this money in the counting room at the end of each weekend, even more after a three-day weekend. It's in a safe, but the safe is open all day because it's like this ancient safe and it's too much trouble for the old gals who have arthritis in their fingers or something to keep locking and unlocking it. Once we get inside the door we take over the counting room and grab the cash, then get out."

Chuy was thinking over what Nico had just told them, trying weigh the pros and cons, when all of his thoughts dissolved like cotton candy at the sight of a beautiful dark-haired woman walking toward them. Like straight at them, as though she wanted to talk to them. He couldn't take his eyes off her as she approached, looking as out of place as a slumming goddess in the scruffy tank-top-and-shorts crowd clogging the midway. Tall—about 5'8"—she wore a black sleeveless top that hugged the contours of what was clearly a gym-sculpted figure. She wore white shorts, showing off most of her long, tan legs. Her feet and ankles, right up to her firm calves, were crisscrossed by lace-up sandals with sharply tapered four-inch heels. As she came closer, he saw that she was subtly made-up, except for her full lips—there was nothing subtle about her glossy, blood-red lipstick. Her eyes were hidden behind a pair of designer sunglasses, which she lifted and set on top of her head when she stopped in front of them.

"This place is fucking disgusting. It's filthy. I must have stepped in at least five wads of salt water taffy." Frowning, she showed the bottom of one of her sandals. None of the men knew what to say. Then she looked at Chuy.

"Are you Nico's boy?" she asked.

"This is Chuy," Nico said.

"Gina Quattro. Welcome aboard, Chuy," she said, seriously checking out the way he filled his T-shirt. She extended her hand for a handshake, just the fingers, which Chuy grasped a little awkwardly. Then to Nico and Hat she said, "You boys got your heist figured out?"

Hat shrugged. "It's a work in progress. Whatta you got?"

"OK, so first I tailed the cash cart, trying to see what was actually going on with it. They went down the right side of the midway; I guess they come back down the left side. At each one of the games and concessions they picked up a zippered cash bag. All the bags seemed pretty full, but I couldn't see what was inside. So then I just watched a couple of the concessions, trying to get a sense of how much cash they were taking in versus credit and debit card payments, and it looks like it's mostly cash." She made a face. "Grubby kids with their grubby hands shoving money at other grubby kids who are also preparing the food. Disgusting. Bottom line, though, this park takes in a significant percentage of their revenue in good old-fashioned cash, that's pretty clear."

"They're coming back now," Nico said, and they all turned to look at the two security guards, one tall, with a service weapon holstered at his side, one short, the short one pushing a cart that looked like a sheet metal box on wheels. They were coming down the left side of the midway, trying to hold a straight line through the milling crowd. Chuy recognized the taller guard as the prick who kicked him and Andrew off the beach the day before.

Nico said, "Wave to Benjie so they don't think we're watching them."

But Benjie was now standing next to them. "The ride was over," he said, still resentful over having to be the decoy. "They made everybody get off. Can I go get a corn dog now?" he asked Hat.

Hat gave him an acid look. "Bend over. I'll give you a corn dog."

The guards had turned the corner into the alcove and were stopped in front of the counting room door. The young girl guard stretched a key card attached to lanyard on her belt and pressed it against a sensor next to the door. The light on the sensor went from red to green. Then she opened the door and let the two guards roll the cart inside.

"That's when we hit them?" Hat asked. "See how all of them got their backs turned, no one looking at what's behind them? We're waiting here like we're part of the crowd, maybe we're just coming out of the Men's room, then we rush them. Get inside, tie them up and grab the cash."

Nico shook his head. "No, the better play is to just go after the cash that's already in the counting room, like right after they go off to pick up the cash. Let the guard with the gun get out of the picture. We give him ten minutes or so to make it down toward the far end of the park. Then all we have to deal with is that little girl who's out front now, the two old ladies inside and the guy who's watching the baseball game."

Chuy said, "But he's got a gun right? The guy watching the baseball game?"

Hat said, "Is Mr. Cage Fighter afraid of guns?"

"We take his gun away," Nico said. It looked to Chuy like he was making it all up on the fly. "Threaten the girl or something. We'll have guns too."

"You want me to get a gun? Do you and Tony have guns?" Chuy was thinking about the Glock he'd taken from the pimp.

"Sure." He looked to Tony, who nodded. Apparently Tony kept the guns. Then Nico looked to Hat for an expert's opinion. "What do you think? Is that how you'd do it?"

"How would I do it? Shock and awe, baby. Rush in there yelling, waving our guns, get everyone face down on the floor, grab the cash and get the hell out. In and out in a coupla minutes. Planning is for pussies. You think about something like this too long and you end up not doing it."

"You thinking about tying up the girl and whoever's inside the counting room," Chuy asked, "or is that too much planning?"

"Takes too long," Hat said. "Tell them you'll have someone watching the door from the outside and that you'll shoot 'em one by one if they come out after you're gone, right here." He pointed to his forehead. "Right between the eyes. You got to get in and out as fast as you can, like a smash and grab on a jewelry store."

"I was thinking we should tie up their hands at least, so they can't get on the radio or use a phone," Nico said. He fished an item out of his Target bag. "Like with these cable ties."

"You've been watching too many movies," Hat said.

"I already bought a whole bag of them."

"Then you can be the cable tie guy. I'm gonna be grabbing cash."

"But no shooting," Nico said. "That's gotta be rule number one. No shooting."

Hat sneered again. Chuy pictured him sneering in his baby pictures. "From what I've seen of this clown outfit, you show them a gun they'll lay down right away. The other thing you do is grab that girl by the door and tell anyone who is thinking about being a hero that you'll blow her brains out if they make the wrong move."

"Listen to what Nico's saying, Hat," Gina said.

"What's that supposed to mean?"

"You've got to keep your cool. No loose cannon stuff like last night."

"What about last night?" Hat snapped.

"You know what I mean." She'd put him on notice and Hat wasn't going for it, but he held his tongue.

The young guard at the counting room door was now looking straight at them. Nico got nervous and herded everyone a few yards further down the midway. They ended up in front a gaudy food concession where Benjie purchased a corn dog.

Chuy was trying to convince himself that it could work. "So, we're running away with these bags of money, there are security cameras everywhere, probably an alarm that has been tripped, how are we not going to get caught? What's the getaway plan?"

Nico had answers for both questions. "First of all, we're going to be in disguise."

"Like masks?"

"Not exactly. You didn't hear about this zombie invasion thing?" Nico filled them in on the promotion slated for Memorial Day. "Everyone in the park is going be made up like a zombie. So *we're* going to be made up like zombies. Even if they catch us on the security cameras, how are they going to positively ID us?"

"Zombies?" Gina said. "Seriously?"

"Yeah, seriously. It's getting a lot of play. The young guys at the market have been talking about it all week."

Chuy remembered what Jana had said about the promotion she was working on.

"It's like they thought it up for us—the perfect cover. There's going to be around two thousand zombies walking around everywhere around the Bay-View. How are they going to pick us out?"

"Interesting," Gina said.

The big kid, Benjie, staggered toward Hat, his arms stretched out. "I'm coming to get you, Hat," he said in a fake-eerie voice.

"Cut that shit out," Hat snapped.

"OK, there'll be zombies everywhere, but we'll be the only zombies carry bags of money," Chuy said. "That could kinda make us stand out."

"I thought of that," Nico said, his chins swelling with pride. He reached into the Target bag that he'd been carrying and pulled out what looked like the limp pelt of a pink animal. Chuy saw that it had a face with two button eyes.

"What'd you do, skin a teddy bear?" Hat asked.

"It's a dolphin. One of the prizes you can win at the shooting gallery."

"*You* won it?" Tony asked, finally chiming in. He'd been mostly leaning on his crutches and glowering at Chuy up till then.

Nico ignored his brother's question. "I just opened it up along the seam and took out the stuffing," he told the others. He pulled it open to show them. "We stick the cash inside and then look—we put a zipper here" meaning along the open seam, "and you close it up that way. It'll look like we won these big stuffed animals. We just walk out of the park."

"You didn't win that," Tony insisted. "You never won a prize in your life."

No one else said anything, thinking over Nico's plan. Then Hat burst out laughing. "I like it! Fucking zombies hauling away fucking stuffed animals stuffed with cash! It's insane, but I like it!"

Everyone looked at Gina. "You're saying we go with this, Hat?"

"Why not?"

Nico was so surprised and relieved by Hat's endorsement that he could barely contain his excitement. He looked at his brother first. "Tony, you in?"

Tony shrugged. "I'm in, but I can't do the robbery part. Not on one leg."

"Chuy, what do you think?"

"How much do you think could be in that counting room? Like $150K?"

"At least. Maybe more. Are you in?"

Chuy looked around at his potential criminal associates, Nico, who was almost pleading with his eyes; Tony sullenly staring out of his black and blue raccoon mask of bruises; Gina Quattro, who had taken off her sunglasses and was slowly inserting one its wide stems into her slightly parted lips, her eyes fixed on Chuy's T-shirt; Hat, bobbing his head and cackling like a loon; and Benjie, who was puzzling out how to eat the last part of the corn dog without poking himself in the eye with the sharp end of the stick. Chuy thought about the layout of the alcove, and the door in the back, the one that said "Authorized Personnel Only", wondering where it led.

"Sure. Why not?"

****

The amber LED's on the digital clock display of the cable box above the TV read 9:17, and in his silent lair the Shadow Warrior sat hunched over his laptop, his face inches from the screen. He was wearing his black ninja mask, black shirt and cargo pants. "How can you catch a shadow?" he typed onto his Facebook page. "The answer is you can't. The shadow is there and it's not there. And a shadow completely disappears in the dark."

After posting his update, Andrew paused to think about the mysterious-sounding observations he'd just made. He suspected—even hoped—that they had a deep meaning, which was true of a lot of stuff related to being a ninja. Laying open next to the laptop, beside the last of the three Hot Pockets he'd microwaved for dinner, was his go-to source for ninjitsu lore, *Secrets of the Ninja (Abridged),* by Masaaki Nishikori. The book's pages were swollen and rippled along the edges. Andrew often read it in the bathtub; although he was careful not to let it fall in, he sometimes turned the pages without remembering to dry his hands. After his first meticulous reading of the book, he'd gotten into the habit of randomly dipping into it for nuggets of wisdom. Tonight he'd opened the book to the chapter on stealth and concealment.

"Perhaps more important than acquiring the supreme fighting skills for which they are known," the chapter opened, *"the Ninja must first master the art of stealth, for the element of surprise is more powerful than any weapon.*

"Legend has it that the Ninja of long ago was able to vanish in a puff of smoke or change into a wild animal form in order to escape a foe. In actuality, it is the Ninja's understanding of invisibility that gives them the advantage. Were Ninjas really able to make themselves invisible? Or was the reality that, through years of

training and disciplined practice, ninja warriors developed the ability to fool their enemies' senses in order to remain undetected, much like a magician misdirects in order to mystify and confuse?"

"Like a puff of smoke," Andrew typed into a new update box, "if you reach for the Shadow Warrior, he's gone."

He read further:

"Two natural senses are susceptible to deception. The first is the sense of Hearing. Noises attract attention, and if the mind fails to identify a sound, it becomes curious. This is where the Ninja employs the art of 'Himitsu iri,'the ever-elusive method of 'Silent Movement' and 'Kage aruki,'or 'Shadow Steps.'"

Master Nishikori provided a detailed description of the exaggerated freeze-frame sequence of heel-toe strides that the warrior seeking to become proficient in Shadow Stepping must practice over and over. He recommended an exercise: Choose a person that you would seek to approach. Slowly advance toward that person, maintaining such complete silence that your approach goes unnoticed until the moment that you reach out to touch your prey.

It is advisable, the master cautioned, to first practice on a person who is known to you and friendly.

With no one else in the apartment to practice on, Andrew targeted Spunky, who was dozing on top of the back of the sofa, one of her favorite lie-down spots. He started in the kitchen, creeping forward with exquisite deliberateness, stepping with his heel first, carefully rocking onto the ball of his foot, then swinging his other leg forward to repeat the sequence. It took him nearly four minutes to cover the twelve feet he had to travel before he was standing within reach of his quarry. Spunky's eyes were closed contentedly, her paws tucked beneath her. Slowly, he reached out his hand. Spunky shifted slightly and he froze, barely breathing, waiting until he was sure that he was still undetected. Then, so slowly that his muscles almost started quivering, he stretched his hand across the last five inches of space to touch one of Spunky's whiskers.

Startled, she jumped straight up. Complaining bitterly as she landed on the floor, she ran to the front door, her tail raised straight up. *Let me out!* she demanded in cat-speak, tossing in a few cat swear words that Andrew couldn't exactly translate but understood clearly.

After opening the door for Spunky to slip into the night, Andrew returned to his study of stealth. In addition to deceiving an opponent's sense of hearing, he read, the ninja must also be adept at fooling his sense of sight by means of camouflage or the cover of darkness. Master Nishikori also advised novice warriors to commit themselves to countless hours of practicing and perfecting *Hayagakejutsu* (Running Skills); *Hofukojutsu* (Crawling Skills) and *Gionjutsu* (Making False Sounds).

"In the application of this method, the Ninja creates noises that might deter attention from his presence. Therefore, if an enemy sentry was patrolling the land surrounding their lord's castle and he heard a strange noise, he would most certainly investigate. This is where the Ninja can employ false sounds because, often times, it is a simple sound that will calm the sentry's suspicion. The Ninja could mimic the sound of a cricket to deter attention from his specific location. This is because crickets stop chirping when they are approached, and if the sentry hears this sound he may not

investigate that particular area because he thinks if there was someone there, the cricket would cease his song. Or perhaps the Ninja would imitate the sound of a cat, making the sentry believe a feline was responsible for whatever noise occurred, and since the sentry does not fear cats, he may feel somewhat foolish for searching."

Andrew paused to try chirping like a cricket, but wasn't happy with the result, which sounded like a creaking door, not an insect. Cat sounds were easier. He practiced meowing until he was satisfied that even a cat would be fooled.

"What was that noise in the dark?" he typed onto the Shadow Warrior's Facebook page. "Don't worry. It was only a cat. Or was it?????"

As usual, his post elicited no "Likes" or comments, not even from Ricky Wakefield, who had not chimed in for a couple of days. Andrew consoled himself with the knowledge that someday everyone would want to follow the exploits of the Shadow Warrior. Until then, he could always show what he'd written to Jana when she got home.

He ate the last no-longer-Hot Pocket and stared off into space for a while, absentmindedly popping Skittles into his mouth as he imagined legendary combat with faceless, evil foes . . . *The setting is the approach to the gloomy castle of an evil lord. Twin torches flank the entrance, blazing in the darkness, the reflection of their flames glinting off the armor of the castle guards. Suddenly one torch goes out, then the other. The guards are confused, murmuring among themselves, then completely surprised as the Shadow Warrior materializes, seemingly out of thin air, to confront them. They try surrounding him, but he vaults over them, turning a flip in mid-air. Landing on his feet, he slashes at them with his blade-like hands. They back off; then the gang of cowards regroups, edging forward. As they close in, he whirls like a top, throwing kick after kick to back them off. But this mission isn't about saving his own skin. A princess is being held captive, a beautiful shy princess with long blond hair and soft blue eyes. Running like the wind, he flies to the wall of the castle. It's almost like he has wings on his feet, the way he seems to run straight up the rough stone face, springing from the slim ledge of a window sill to a protruding stone gutter spout, from there to the bulbous nose of a grinning granite gargoyle, higher and higher he goes until he dives through an open window, lands with a somersault— and there she is, the captive princess. And then . . . and then . . .*

What?

He reached for another Skittle to fuel his inspiration. The bag was empty. How could he let that happen? A tiny bit panicked, he flattened the bag, smoothing it with the flat of his hand, and found one Skittle stuck in the back corner. But his relief turned to disappointment when he fished out a green Skittle, for Andrew as appetizing as a poison pill.

This was serious. He looked at the time: 9:46. La Tiendita closed at 10:00. Jana wouldn't be home till 10:20 at the earliest. He had time to make a Skittles run and get home before her, but just barely.

This time he would make sure to avoid trouble; in fact, this little sortie would give him an excellent opportunity to practice the stealth techniques that Master Nishikori recommended, roaming the streets completely unseen. After making sure he had a few dollars to make his purchase stuffed into his cargo pants, and that the eyeholes of his ninja mask were lined up correctly behind his goggles, he set out, carefully closing and locking the front door behind him.

Keeping close to the sides of buildings, he moved deliberately, making sure he was taking Shadow Steps, which made him look like he was tiptoeing through field of trip wires, where any wrong step would trigger a shrieking alarm. Every five paces or so he stopped to practice vigilance the way Chuy had advised. All he could hear was his own breathing, until he stumbled over a pile of concrete rubble. He pitched forward, caught himself, and held completely still until he was sure that no enemy had been alerted before advancing.

The thing about Shadow Walking, he was finding out, was that it took a long time to get anywhere. He looked at his watch and saw that it was 9:55; he only had five minutes to achieve his objective, and he still hadn't gotten to where the alley intersected with Barson St., and the little market was two blocks down from there. Now he had to hurry. He broke into a clumsy trot, emerging onto the twilight of Barson St., all attempts at stealth completely forgotten, his feet slapping the sidewalk.

But he never made it to La Tiendita. A little over a block ahead he saw them—his enemies, the three bullies that had beaten him up three nights before, the big guy in the flannel shirt flanked by the two hoodies. They were walking shoulder to shoulder in his direction, commanding the width of the sidewalk. They caught sight of Andrew at the same time. Andrew quickly reversed course—tonight all he wanted was a bag of Skittles, not a fight—hurrying back into the dark alley. Knowing he'd never outrun them, he looked for a place to hide.

He didn't have many options. There was a line of heavy plastic trash and recycling bins arrayed against the side of the building to his left, but not enough space behind them for concealment. To his right, a clump of thimbleberry canes looked like his safest bet. He plunged into the springy tangle of canes and wormed his way through them until he could worm no further, stopping against the wall of a garage.

He waited, listening, his breath shallow and fast, his heart thumping. Now that he was in it, the clump of thimbleberry suddenly didn't seem very substantial. He could easily see through the open lacework of canes. He felt exposed and had the urge to bolt. But it was too late. They'd be coming up to the mouth of the alley by now.

All he could hope for was that it was dark enough, even as close as he was to the lights of Barson St., that they wouldn't see him. He had to remain silent, which was almost impossible. Every move he made snapped a dead cane. And the sharp ends of the broken canes poked him, no matter how he shifted his body, so it was almost impossible to hold still. Fearful that even if he wasn't seen he'd be heard, he remembered what Master Nishikori had written about *Gionjutsu* and the tactic of making false sounds. Tentatively, he meowed, rehearsing for the moment he'd need to fool his enemies if they got too close.

****

When Chuy's cell phone buzzed in his jeans pocket, he was just starting another game of dominoes with Gallo and Filomena, sitting at the dinette table just off the apartment's kitchen. Filomena had shuffled the tiles, which were face down in a loose scatter in the center of the table. They were each supposed to draw a tile; whoever drew the highest double would start play. Gallo always openly cheated, peeking at the tiles until he found a double six, crowing happily when he showed them his winning tile. They let it go; it wasn't worth arguing with him, and the point of the game was to keep Gallo calm and occupied. And anyway, Gallo, by virtue of his own magical arithmetic, always won. Filomena had one eye on the game, and one eye on the high drama of a telenovela playing on the television in the corner. And Chuy was just bored. When he felt the buzz of his phone in his pocket, he was grateful to have a chance to leave the table. He saw that it was Jana. He walked off down the hallway before he answered, hopeful, but playing it cool.

"Hey."

She sounded breathless, like she was walking, walking fast. "Andrew's gone! He wasn't in the apartment when I got home and it's after 10:00." Panic edged her voice. "I'm going up and down the streets and I can't find him."

"OK. I'll go out and look. Where are you now?"

"Catalpa and Barson."

"I'll head that way and we'll meet up."

Chuy told Filomena about the call, and went out, heading toward Jana's. He was alert, a little on edge. He wasn't out the door more than a couple of minutes when he saw two blocks ahead the figure of a guy in a flannel shirt, his back toward him, moving in and out of the pools of light and shadow created by the streetlights. *Motherfucker! You again*! Chuy didn't have to think about what he'd do next. The flannel shirt was like a red flag, and Chuy was the bull. Instantly he knew that this dirtball was behind whatever might have happened to Andrew. He charged, aiming himself at the flannel shirt like it was a target. The guy wearing it wasn't aware of the brutal collision that was about to overwhelm him until Chuy was about twenty feet away and he could hear his pounding footsteps. He didn't even have time to fully look around to see what kind of bad thing was coming before Chuy was on top of him, hitting him like a defensive end sacking a quarterback.

The guy didn't say a word as he went down.

Chuy was roaring. "*You sonofabitch!* Where is he? Where's the kid, you worthless piece of shit—"

He didn't stop yelling at the guy until he'd roughly turned him around, pinning his shoulders with his knees, and had cocked his fist just above his face.

Then he looked more closely and saw that badass he'd taken down was actually Lupe, the clerk at La Tiendita. They'd known each other for years, but Lupe was looking at Chuy like he was a crazy stranger.

It took a moment for Chuy to shift gears and calm down. He lowered his fist. "Aw, shit. Lupe, I didn't know it was you. I thought you were someone else. I thought—"

Lupe was trying to figure it all out; you could see it in his pouchy eyes. For some reason, Chuy had gone completely berserk, and the last thing he wanted to do was set him off again. As calmly as he could, but in a strained whisper because most of Chuy's weight was on his chest, he said, "Can you get off me?"

"Of course. Sure . . ." Chuy said, grabbing Lupe by the shoulders to help him up.

Then he heard Jana. "What happened?" She'd come up behind him. Andrew was with her, wearing his mask and goggles. Chuy smiled weakly. Jana said, "We saw you tackle . . . is that the guy from the market? Oh my god, Chuy!"

"I thought he was somebody else. One of those guys that beat Andrew up."

"That's Lupe," Andrew said. He pulled his goggles away from his eyes. "Lupe, it's me, Andrew."

"Is he OK?" Jana asked as Chuy helped Lupe up. "He's bleeding. On his forehead."

Chuy looked more closely at Lupe, turning him by the shoulders to get a better angle from the streetlight. It looked like he might have hit his head on the sidewalk. "He's got a little bump and a scrape. But you're OK, right Lupe? Not woozy or anything?"

"Ninjas can summon healing powers to their hands," Andrew offered.

"I'm OK," Lupe said, pulling himself up. "Can I go home now? It's just down the street." He made his appeal to Jana. He didn't want anything more to do with Chuy.

Chuy said, "I'm really sorry, dude. Come by Gallo's tomorrow, I'll take care of you. You can have anything on the menu." He offered Lupe a bro handshake, which Lupe accepted warily, almost like he was afraid that Chuy was going to take him down again. "I mean it.

Anything you want. You like that goat stew, that *birria*? Filomena made a big pot of it tonight."

Lupe edged away. He threw one last perplexed look at Chuy and resumed his trudge home. Chuy watched him for a moment, then turned back to Jana and Andrew. "Where'd you find the Shadow Warrior?"

"He was hiding in some bushes in an alley near the bus stop down the street. He's OK." From the tone of her voice, Chuy wasn't the only one in hot water.

"A gang was chasing me, Chuy, but I vanished right in front of their eyes. Like a puff of smoke."

Chuy said to Jana, still trying to explain himself, "I thought Lupe was one of the guys who beat Andrew up the other night. I kinda went after him. It was the flannel shirt. One of the guys who attacked Andrew the other night was wearing a flannel shirt."

"So now you're going to attack anyone who's wearing a flannel shirt?"

"I just reacted. What can I say?"

"OK Andrew. Let's go home," she said. They started walking back to the apartment.

"I'll walk you back," Chuy said. "It's not safe this time of night."

"That's probably what Lupe's thinking right now."

"I told him I was sorry."

"Did you ever hear about *Gionjutsu*?" Andrew asked him. "You can fool your enemy into thinking you're a cricket. Or a cat." As they walked the two blocks back to their apartment, he demonstrated how he could meow like a cat—an angry cat, a startled cat, a hungry cat, a cat that wanted you to open the door for her. Chuy and Andrew trailed behind Jana, who obviously thought of herself as the only adult in their little troop. Chuy wanted to engage her in conversation, but every time he tried, she responded tersely, so he gave up on it.

When they got to the door of the apartment, he stood behind her on the first step, awkwardly trying to think of what he was going to say—because he'd decided he had to say something—as she fitted the keys into the three deadbolt locks and opened them one by one, a process that took a couple of minutes and several swear words. He noticed for the first time that she had an Ace bandage wrapped around her wrist and palm. He asked her about it after she pushed the warped door open and ushered Andrew inside.

"Grab, lock, pivot, and pull," she said. "Sound familiar?"

It took him a moment to make the connection. "Sure. It's like a jiu jitsu move."

"—that you showed Andrew, and Andrew got it stuck in his head and had to show me. He kept after me to come at him like I was going to grab him, and for some stupid reason I finally gave in and reached for him . . . I think he sprained my wrist; I just hope it isn't broken. I don't have the money to see a doctor. I can barely afford this Ace bandage."

"That's like a defensive move I was showing him. He's got to learn to protect himself."

She turned back to him, looking down, holding the door handle.

"OK, well, good night. Thanks for coming out to help," she said, but there wasn't a lot of gratitude in her voice.

"You don't have to thank me for anything." As she was closing the door, he said, "Hang on a minute, Jana. Can we talk?"

She looked at him blankly, not a yes, but not a no.

He mounted the remaining two steps to the landing in front of the door and stood close to her. From within, he could hear the sound of rushing water; Andrew was filling a bath.

"I feel like I'm always saying the wrong thing to you, or doing the wrong thing. I really was trying to help tonight, and now I feel like a dick."

"I don't think you're a dick. I just think you are who you are."

He tried to sound like Popeye. "I yam what I yam, Olive."

Jana didn't even smile. "I'm just tired, Chuy. I had a long day and then I came home to find Andrew gone. I get so worried about him. And then when I saw you tackle Lupe and I thought you were going to punch him in the face and I literally got a knot in my stomach. It's still there."

"Lupe's going to be OK. He'll be down at Gallo's tomorrow wolfing down free tacos."

"I can't deal with the violence."

"What can I say? I thought he was one of the bad guys."

"Sure." What was the look in her eyes? Pity, sadness? Maybe just weariness. She backed into the apartment another step and was closing the door. "Anyway, good night," she said.

After she set the deadbolts one by one, he stood by himself for a couple of minutes staring at the closed door. He wanted badly to kick it, but stopped himself. Then he kicked it anyway, hard enough to make it shudder, but not hard enough to make any headway against

282

the three deadbolts, which would have required a battering ram carried by five strong men.

Jana's worried voice came from within. *"Chuy—what are you doing?"*

"Expressing myself."

"Are you finished?"

"Kind of."

"Can you leave now?"

He was already heading down the short flight of steps, walking away, heading back to Gallo's. He would have loved to stumble on the opportunity to slug someone—almost anyone who looked at him a little cross-eyed would do—but the streets were quiet. He came in through the back and went into the apartment where he found Gallo and Filomena still sort of playing dominoes. He stood in front of them, his hands jammed in his jeans, shifting uneasily from foot to foot, responding tersely to Filomena's questions about his mission to find Andrew. He left out the part about Lupe.

"Bueno," she said. "A happy ending." She nodded toward the chair he'd been sitting in earlier. "Now *ven*, sit and play with me and Gallo. I promised him one more game, and then it's time for bed."

"I'm not going to bed. I'm going out for ice cream," Gallo informed them. It took Filomena a minute to gently steer him away from that idea, the way she always did, by promising they'd get ice cream tomorrow.

She looked at Chuy for a little help. "One more game with Chuy."

Chuy had something else on his mind. "Look, he blurted. "Something's come up. I've got to get back to Bakersfield. I'll be leaving Monday night."

"For how long?"

"I'm going back, that's all."

Gallo didn't seem to be paying attention. He was concentrating on erecting a mini-Stonehenge with his tiles. Chuy's news rocked Filomena. She quickly got control of her face, the way guys in the ring would do when they'd been hit hard but didn't want to show it, even if their knees were buckling.

"Why?" she asked evenly. "Why now?"

Chuy didn't want to go into it. He'd made up his mind, and that was it. "I just gotta go, that's all."

Her face sagged a little; he could see fear in her deep brown eyes. "Chuy, I need your help with the taqueria. With him." She was trying to keep all emotion out of her voice. At some point during her dirt poor childhood, or first marriage to a guy who regularly used his fists on her, she must have made a vow that she would never beg or plead for anything. That she would just accept whatever fate dealt her and carry on. Which made Chuy feel even guiltier. The stupid telenovela was still playing on the TV in the corner; the camera has zoomed in to the face of a sobbing actress. Tears were filling and spilling from her eyes and running down her cheeks, streaked with mascara.

Christ, Chuy thought.

"Look," he said, "Gallo's a veteran. They owe him something for getting his ass shot at in Nam. They've got places vets can go. They take care of them."

"Gallo would die if he went into a place like that."

"What place?" Gallo said.

"You could sell the taqueria. Get out from under all of this. Have a life."

"I have a life. This is my life."

Gallo said, "I don't like pink ice cream. Or green ice cream."

"Look," Chuy said, "I'll get you some money to pay off all the bills. Let you get a fresh start."

Filomena's face had composed itself into an emotionless mask. She turned her attention to the dominoes, arranging them neatly. "Gallo, it's your move," she said. "Pick a domino to see who starts."

"I like brown ice cream," Gallo said.

Z-Day Minus 2

By 4:30 the next morning they were ready to head out to Tony's trap line. Nico had helped Tony dismember the Vietnamese guy's frozen body, bagging up the parts and bringing them down to the harbor in Tony's truck. It wasn't as bad as he thought it would be. In the end it was only meat, bone and blood, not too different than butchering a big tuna, except for the arms and legs. And the face. That was the hardest part, seeing the face. The eyes were open and they seemed to be staring at him with contempt every time he made the mistake of looking at them. You shouldn't have tried to be a hero, he felt like saying to the dead guy; it was only squid. Using the hand truck from the fish market, with Tony crutch-walking alongside of him, Nico had brought the bags down the dock and up the ramp to the Giovanna and had them stowed away before Freebie showed up, right on time.

Tony, at the helm in the enclosed cockpit, had the engine idling. A burbling sound came from the back of the boat and diesel fumes mingled with the fog. Nico had freed the last of the lines from the dock and was holding it to keep the boat in place.

The fog was thick over the harbor, and it was cold, a damp cold. Freebie, his hair carefully oiled and combed even at this hour, wearing a thin nylon jacket, stood uncertainly at the side of the Giovanna, his shoulders hunched, hands jammed into his pockets, trying to stay warm.

"What are you waiting for?" Nico barked. "Get your ass on up here so we can shove off."

Clumsily, without any help from Nico, Freebie clambered into the boat. Tony looked over his shoulder. Nico yelled, "Let's go," tossed the line onto the dock and Tony carefully motored them out of the harbor.

After a glance around the deck to take it all in—the stacked spare crab traps, the live well, the trap puller—Freebie looked to Nico for instruction.

"It'll take us about thirty minutes to get out to the trap line. You can just hang out till then. Once we start hauling the traps up, you'll be humping your ass, don't worry. Just sit in the back here, out of the way for now."

A steady swell rolled rhythmically beneath the boat—not a particularly heavy swell, but powerful enough that Nico had to plant his feet widely as he negotiated the deck of the Giovanna as it plowed through the thickening fog. The fog horn attached to the mile buoy sounded periodically, a sad, lonely sound. Nico stationed himself next to Tony in the cockpit, making small talk, listening to Tony's playlist. They had a couple of tall cups of 7-11 coffee and a bag of Little Debbie sugar donuts that they dipped into. As far as Tony knew, the only reason that Nico had brought Freebie along was to lend a hand with the heavy work. Nico hadn't told him what he had planned, mainly because he wasn't sure if he could actually do it when the time came— pull the gun out of his duffle and level it at Freebie. But all he had to do to keep his resolve was look at the greasy little weasel, and remember what he'd seen through the louvers of Bianca's closet door. He had to fix the situation. He was the head of the family. It was his duty to restore the family's honor.

Tony presented another challenge. On the way out, he shared a conclusion he'd come to—he didn't want any part of the counting room robbery. He'd been thinking about it, and it was just too dicey.

"You got a better idea?" Nico asked him.

"Salmon season's starting up in Oregon," Tony said. The bruises on his face had faded, but he still had blackened blood between the bridge of his nose and the corners of his eyes. "I've been thinking I'd take the Giovanna up there for a few months. Get away from all this shit for a while."

"And leave me with this situation?"

"Nico, at this point in my life I could give a fuck about the market and all that. It's getting too heavy. This is where I'm happy. Out here on my boat. I don't want to deal with all the other crap."

"Look—you're going to have to deal with it for a few more days. You're not dumping it all on me."

Tony didn't say anything. They were getting close to the trap line. Nico left the cockpit and saw that Freebie was bent over the back of the boat, puking. He was still a little green when they started hauling in the traps, but he was trying, Nico had to give him that. Tony only had a couple of pairs of work gloves on the boat. Nico took the pair that was in the best shape. The gloves he tossed to Freebie were worn through in spots, and didn't offer much protection, especially to the fingers of his right hand, which were soon cut up by the rough rebar frames of the traps. But Freebie didn't complain. After hauling out the first few traps and figuring out the process, he and Nico worked silently, while Tony maneuvered the Giovanna down the trap line from yellow buoy to yellow buoy. The fog was so thick that Tony had to navigate by intuition.

Once they got into a rhythm, the work went smoothly. Nico made sure that Freebie was doing most of the heavy lifting. It took them a little over two hours to run the length of the line. After they emptied the last trap's wriggling cargo into the live well, they baited it and sent it back down.

"That's it," Tony said, standing at the opening of the cockpit, steadying himself by grabbing on to the door frame as the boat pitched. "Now let's get rid of that other stuff."

The other stuff was the three bulging burlap bags in the stern that Nico had loaded onto the Giovanna before Freebie had arrived. They lay in lumpy pile, each one cinched at the top with nylon rope attached to a trawl weight.

"Give me a hand here, Freebie," Nico said. Freebie seemed to know better than to ask what was in the bags, but he was hesitant. He approached them reluctantly, like they were bags of snakes.

"Recycling," Nico explained. "We'll each take an end and just slide 'em over." Freebie's eyes widened when he saw blood dripping from the bags, but he did as he was asked. Each bag sank quickly after it entered the water.

"Now, one more thing," Nico said. He retrieved the small nylon duffle he'd brought on board from where it was stowed on top of the life jackets. Freebie looked at him as Nico pulled Big Nicky's Ruger

SR9 out of the duffle. He didn't say anything, but Tony did. He had turned to look at them from the cockpit.

"The fuck are you doing?"

Nico waved the gun barrel in the direction of the stack of spare traps. "Freebie, open up that top trap there and get inside." It'd be a tight fit, but Nico couldn't see why one of the big circular traps couldn't accommodate a skinny 5'5" dishwasher if he squeezed in. Easier to toss him over that way, and make sure he plummeted down to the bottom of the bay.

"Nico, what the fuck?" Tony said.

Freebie's eyes darted back and forth between Nico and Tony.

Nico took a step toward Freebie. "Get in the trap, you sonofabitch."

"*Nico!*" Tony shouted.

Nico shot his brother a look. "He was doin' Ma."

"What do you mean, *doin'* Ma?"

"I mean *doin'* her. Like a frickin' horny dog. Like a Chihuahua with his little Chihuahua dick. I saw it. When I went to get the raffle money, they came in and I had to hide in Ma's closet."

"He was humping Ma?" Tony exploded. He lurched out of the cockpit, taking handholds on the live well to take the weight off his bad leg. Freebie backed away until he came up against the waist-high gunwale.

"It made me sick to my stomach," Nico said as a swell— unexpectedly bigger than the gentler swells that had been rolling underneath them—lifted the boat up sharply, throwing Tony off-balance and pitching him to the deck. Nico was able to steady himself by grabbing onto the trap puller. And Freebie, who had been running series of calculations on his odds of survival given the few options available, took the opportunity to launch himself off the side of the Giovanna. Another sharp swell swung the boat around just as Tony was getting to his feet, putting him on the deck again. Nico had to hang on to the trap puller. They were both swearing. It was like a swearing contest, which Tony won, hands down. Nico fired the Ruger into the fog. When he recovered his balance he staggered across the deck to look for Freebie, but within the tight perimeter of visibility around the boat he was nowhere to be seen. Nico peered out into the thick mist and again fired the Ruger blindly four times.

"Did you get him?" Tony asked.

"Maybe. I don't hear anything. . ."

"Don't waste any more bullets. We're over a mile out. He's not going to make it in from here, not in this soup."

Freebie wasn't lying when he told Bianca he couldn't swim. He'd never really tried it. Where he grew up in Mexico the only body of water was a knee-high stream where his mother and sisters washed the family's clothes. But as soon as he surfaced from his desperate dive into the chilly waters of the bay he suddenly figured it out. Maybe it wasn't swimming so much as thrashing, but the wild windmilling of his arms somehow kept him afloat and propelled him away from the Giovanna. The gunshots ringing out behind him in the fog gave him a second wind just when he thought he couldn't keep going. And then he saw a yellow buoy, about the size of a basketball. He grabbed it and unclipped it from the line running down to the crab trap below. It didn't provide much extra buoyancy—just enough to keep him on the surface if he held it straight out in front of him and kicked. He could hear the Giovanna circling, even saw it once about ten yards away, materializing out of the mist briefly before it was swallowed up again. Another five minutes of kicking brought him close to another yellow buoy, which he also unclipped. He stuffed both buoys into the front of his jacket and zipped up over them. With a ballooned chest that would be the envy of any surgically-enhanced porn star, he was able to float with little effort. The sound of the Giovanna's engine receded. He caught his breath and tried to guess which direction he'd have to point himself to get back to Mexico.

****

Later that morning, around 10:30, Gina Quattro had packed her Louis Vuitton Pégase 65 suitcase, wheeled it out to the foyer of the suite and stood for a moment looking at Hat and Benjie. Benjie was sprawled on the sofa, staring at the suite's big screen. Hat was out on the little balcony off the sitting room smoking a cigarette, with the sliding glass door closed tightly, because Gina hated cigarette smoke. He'd been sitting there for over an hour, smoking and staring off into space, drumming his fingers on the arm of his chair. He used a nearly-empty coke can for an ash tray, carefully tapping the spent ash into it, followed eventually by each butt. He liked the brief sizzling sound they made as they went out. Hat could tell Gina wanted him to come into the suite so she could say something to him, but he just looked at her and lit another cigarette off the butt end of the one he'd been smoking, squinting at her through the smoke curling up around his eyes.

Then she started crooking her finger, that thing the nuns used to do in grade school when they wanted you to come up to their desk in the front of the classroom, usually so they could smack you. He pretended not to notice, shifting his gaze off toward the water and the point break off to the right, where surfers were carving a wave.

Then he heard her tapping on the glass.

"Yeah?" he mouthed. She could open the sliding door if she wanted to talk to him; he wasn't getting up. Which is what she did, opening it about a foot with that sucking sound that heavy glass doors make when they're pulled out of the tight rubber gasket of the jamb.

"I'm leaving now," she said.

"OK." Like it was no big deal to him.

"I'll be back tomorrow morning." An hour or so earlier Gina told them that she gotten a call from San Francisco. They wanted her up there for some big meeting that evening, which could run late. It only made sense, she said, to spend the night.

He took a drag off his cigarette, letting the smoke drift in her direction and squinting at her. "You told us that."

But she wanted to say something else, because she was a control freak, and she wanted to say it badly enough that she was willing to face his cigarette smoke just a little longer. "I want you to stay out of trouble."

He didn't even know what to say to that. So he just gave her a little dismissive salute, tapping his index finger on his forehead and then pointing it at her.

"I'm serious," she said.

"I got it, boss." Now just leave, he thought.

"All right. Then I'm going. Call me if anything comes up."

"Nothing's going to come up," Hat said. He turned away and looked back at the surfers. He heard the glass door sliding closed. He waited a few minutes before he turned to look back into the suite, just to make sure she was gone.

He'd just about had it with her, especially in the last couple of days, wondering what the fuck he'd gotten himself into. It had come to a head after she'd reamed him about the truckload of squid he'd hijacked and the guy he'd whacked. You said we had to show the gooks we meant business, he said. That's how you do it.

"You didn't run it by me first," she said. This was after he called her that night, after he'd shot the guy. He and Benjie had gone off on their own, taking the Mercedes while Gina was sleeping. Hat couldn't stand just sitting around doing nothing, so he got the idea to pay a visit to Happy Squid, not sure what he was going to do, maybe just trash the outside of the building, break a few windows. But when they got there the freezer truck was running unattended, parked by the loading dock around the back, so he decided to jack it. Then the Vietnamese guy came out as Hat was pulling the truck out, running up to the truck yelling and yanking the driver's door open, waving a gun. Well, Hat had a gun too. The difference was that Hat didn't hesitate to use his. One shot. Bang. You could tell he was dead right away, the way he fell back onto the gritty asphalt. But no use crying over it. They were in the rear of the building, nothing behind it but a chain link fence and behind that a scrubby hill. There were three stacks of pallets up against the building covered in heavy plastic. He got Benjie to help pull a sheet a plastic off one of the stacks and wrap the dead guy up in it. Then they opened the heavy insulated door of the truck and stuck him in there with the boxes of frozen squid. After they'd gotten a mile or so down the road he called Gina.

She was pissed. Really pissed. She called him a skinny wop dumbfuck, shit-for-brains. The words didn't sting—he'd heard them all before plenty of times. What got under his skin was that they were coming out her mouth. Like she knew it all. Shit, Hat had been a criminal since he was twelve—over thirty-five years. Longer than she'd been fucking alive. And sure, maybe her family was in the organization, but she wasn't part of it, or hadn't been until about a year ago. Supposedly, she was a college girl, a banker or something like that. All he knew is what she told him. His guess was that she came out to San Francisco and the first thing she did was start kissing up to Vincent, who was susceptible, having had the stroke and all. And she had those tits and that nice ass. Now it was like she'd decided to take over the whole operation, when guys like Hat—guys who'd made their bones—still had to suck around the bottom of the pond. Like carp.

But she wasn't so smart. She'd see.

He finished his cigarette and went inside.

"Ding Dong the witch is gone," he said, but Benjie didn't get the reference. What was the crap he was watching? On the TV screen, giant animated robots were battling.

"How can you watch that shit?" Hat asked, but Benjie didn't know. In fact, he wasn't watching it, not really. He was mostly looking at his phone.

Since he'd briefly captured Benjie's attention, Hat said, "It's almost 11:00." Benjie looked at him blankly. "Time to call your mom."

Benjie's mom was Kathee. Kathee was more or less Hat's girlfriend. She thought that Hat was a salesman for Argiento Linens and had pestered him into find a spot for her son in the business. Benjie had managed to graduate from an alternative high school, even started a couple of classes at the community college. But he hadn't been able to find himself, is the way Kathee put it, and it was time he got serious about his life and started a career. As a condition of keeping his monthly allowance, Benjie had agreed. He'd been tagging along with Hat for a couple weeks now. He was mostly worthless, Hat had decided; but he was big and strong and, while he wasn't naturally mean, he didn't shy away from violence either. If you told him what to do—like push someone around or carry a stiff rolled up in plastic—he'd do it, and that was a start.

When they were on a business trip like this, Benjie had to get on Skype for a video call with his mom once a day, even though the two of them were also texting back and forth all the time. Kathee was needy, and she didn't get that she was probably the main reason her kid was such a spoiled loser. Hat didn't indulge her. She was his girlfriend, not his mother, and she didn't need to know what he was thinking or doing every second of the day.

"I'm going out for a while," he told Benjie. "You make your call."

"What are we going to do today?"

"Something. I don't know what. We'll figure it out. Say hi to your mom for me. Tell her we're nailing down some big accounts."

It was good to get out and get some fresh air, he thought as he lit a cigarette outside the hotel.

He walked away from the water, toward Santa Carmela's downtown, which was three blocks in from the beach. What he liked to do for fun was walk around commercial districts, checking out the shops, not from a shopper's point of view, but through a criminal's eyes. He especially liked to walk into jewelry stores and check out the goods, ask himself how easy or hard it would be to smash and grab a handful of necklaces or high-end watches. The store employees were always so polite, especially the women when he told them he was looking for something special for his girlfriend. They'd pull out the diamond necklaces—because he was a diamond guy and nothing else would do— arranging them on the black velvet cloth they'd lay out on top of the glass case and let him pick up the necklaces to examine them, the delicate gold chains flowing over his fingers. Sometimes he'd ask them to try one on so he could see how the necklace might look on his girlfriend, which they'd always do, leaning in toward him across the counter so he could check it out. And it was as exciting, having them lean in toward him like that, the sparkling diamonds lying across the delicate skin of their necks, maybe offering a glimpse of cleavage. He'd think about how easy it would be just to tear the necklace off and run like hell. But that wasn't the thrill he was after. It was more exciting to hold himself back, to reach out almost timidly to touch the necklace and maybe brush their throat, just brush it with his fingertips, and say something admiring. Trying to see if he could spot the pulse beating right there in that little tender hollow spot at the base of their fragile necks.

He walked into three jewelers on the tree-lined main drag, playing his little game, having fun with it. He decided he didn't like Santa Carmela, too many bums and hippies hanging out, a lot of them tweakers, you could tell. Up to no good. He bought a hot dog at one of the food kiosks that dotted the wide sidewalk. After he'd paid, and gathered up his change, he turned to continue up the street, thinking he'd eat and stroll for a while, and almost walked right into a scruffy young guy wearing a stocking cap. Over eighty degrees out and the fool is wearing a stocking cap like it's the middle of winter.

"Spare some of that change, man?" the young guy asked.

"Get the fuck out of my way," Hat said.

The stupid kid didn't move. Smiling like he thought he was cute or something. "Just a dollar. I'm hungry too." It looked like maybe he was reaching toward him, a grimy hand with grimy fingernails. Smiling cockily, showing his scummy teeth.

Hat let him have it, a quick shot right in the teeth. That got the kid's attention. His hands flew to his mouth and he backed off. He mumbled something in a pained voice. Hat was tempted to say something, about how if he wanted to keep his teeth he shouldn't get into people's faces, but why bother? He had a hot dog to eat.

He wandered back toward the beach, and sat on a retaining wall that separated the sidewalk from the sand to finish off his hot dog. It was hot and sunny; the narrow brim of his hat didn't shelter his face and big nose as he checked out the beach through his wraparound shades. He wasn't a beach guy—too much sand—but he could stare at young girls in bikinis for hours.

After a while he walked down the sidewalk the quarter-mile or so to the Bay-View Boardwalk. He walked down the midway to the carrousel, and stood in front at the spot where they'd all stood the night before as Nico laid out his idea for the job. He must have gotten there at the time when they went off for the first cash collection run of the day. There was a girl in a blue security uniform standing by the counting room door, it looked like the same girl from the night before, and he saw the counting room door open and two other guards—one with a holstered handgun—came out rolling the cash cart. Everything matter-of-fact. Making a joke between themselves as they pushed the cart out into the midway.

I could get in there right now, Hat thought. Show the guard the little .25 automatic he had in his pocket and she'd let him in. Or wait till they brought the loaded cash cart back and rush up behind them when the girl opened the door for them. Push them all in with his Raven .25 pointed at them, tell them to lay down on the floor, grab as much cash as he could, then get the hell out. It'd all be over in two or three minutes.

But he wasn't ready. He didn't have a getaway car, for one thing. And if he waited, he could help himself to a really big score. So he'd wait. It'd only be another day.

He walked back toward the Sunset Inn, stopping at a liquor store to buy a fifth of Southern Comfort and a six pack of 7-Up. He stole a pair of sunglasses from a display rack on the counter just to see if he could. When he got back to the suite Benjie was gone. To kill time, he watched the NASCAR channel with the volume as high as he could get it, sipping Southern-and-Seven.

By the time Benjie got back around 5:00, Hat was getting restless. Benjie had been watching the surfers, trying to pick up girls, with nothing to show for it but a fiery red sunburned face.

Hat had decided he was going to show the kid how to have some fun.

"You ever steal a car?" he asked. Benjie shook his head. "Well, we're going to steal a car. We're going to steal a car, rob a liquor store, eat dinner at some fancy restaurant and screw some girls. How's that sound?"

Benjie guessed that it sounded pretty good.

"You'd think it would be hard to steal a car, but it isn't," Hat said after they'd walked a couple of blocks toward town. He was feeling particularly good, cockier than usual after five Southern-and-Sevens. "You just need a couple items from the hardware store. And a pair of balls."

There were no hardware stores to be found along the main street. There were stores where you could buy ninety-nine flavors of taffy, specialty socks, gift cards, kitchenware, books and shoes, but nothing as practical as a hammer and screwdriver. He stopped a couple of people to ask if they could direct him, but each time drew a blank. One guy suggested they try the Rite-Aid, which was a couple blocks removed from the shopping district, on a grittier street with fewer trees. Inside, the Rite-Aid was as big as a couple of football fields, and had just about everything, including an aisle with a limited hardware selection where Hat picked up a cheap hammer and a flathead screwdriver.

After paying, they walked out. From a pants pocket, Hat pulled out a Milky Way that he'd filched while the cashier was ringing them up. He was pretty happy with himself, eating his candy bar, waiting for Benjie to ask what they were going to do with the hammer and screwdriver. But Benjie was looking at his phone.

He finally had to ask. "What the fuck is so fucking interesting on that phone?"

"I don't know," Benjie said.

"Put it away for now. It's a distraction. You've got to pay attention if you're going to learn anything." A few minutes later, Hat said, "That's what we're looking for—right there." He pointed them at a big four-story parking structure down the street.

"What you want," he said when they entered one of the parking structures stairwells, "is to find like a public parking garage because they usually don't have security. And you want the free garages, like this one, if you can find one. They don't have those fucking gates at the exits. If it's not free, look to see if they left their ticket on the seat, or between the seats, which is what most people do." He threw the crumpled Milky Way wrapper on the sidewalk as they entered a side door into a stairwell that smelled of urine. "Start at one of the higher levels, and look around to see that no one else is around. You're going to need three or four minutes." They walked up the stairs. Hat led them out on the fourth level, where he spent a few minutes walking and looking.

"That's the one," he said finally, "That Honda." It was an Accord, at least twenty years old.

"Why can't we steal a newer car, something nicer?"

"Why are you always whining? Look, you're not going to get into anything new with these," he said, holding up the hammer and screw driver. "When I was your age, it was all we needed. But then they went and started making steering wheel and transmission locks standard even on crap cars. But that Accord we can do." He walked briskly up to the Honda, positioned screwdriver into the door lock, and looked around. Satisfied that no one would see him, he said, "Now watch." With one sharp whack of the hammer he punched in the lock cylinder and opened the door. He got in and hammered and pried out the ignition cylinder. That took about a minute. Then he stuck the screwdriver into the exposed lock mechanism and turned it. The Accord started just like he was using a key. Pleased with himself because it had been over ten years since he'd stolen a car this way, he smiled at Benjie.

"I still got it," he said. Benjie was sneaking a glance at his phone. "Were you even watching? How the fuck are you going to learn anything if all you do is look at your stupid phone? I should take this hammer and smash it to bits."

"My mom was texting me."

Hat was beyond disgusted. "Come on, get in. Let's get the hell out of here."

Then they just drove around for a while, did a little sightseeing. Eventually they headed up the coast, leaving the strip malls, fast food outlets and gas stations behind. The scenery changed abruptly as the highway took them north. On their left were fields of Brussel sprouts and artichokes and then the Pacific. To the right was rolling pasture land, gentle hills rising toward a low coastal range. Cattle grazed on the slopes. Hawks sat on telephone poles. It was getting a little dull until they came to a beach where kite surfers were flying across waves and launching themselves high into the air. They got out of the car and sat on the hood for a while watching, the strong wind in their faces. Hat lost his hat and had to run after it. When he got back to the car, Benjie asked, "When are we going to rob a liquor store? This is getting kind of boring."

Hat had to agree. After you watched for a couple of minutes you got it, it was just guys showing off. And when the wind gusted in from the ocean it picked up sand, driving it into their faces. There were no girls in bikinis on the beach, probably because of the wind.

"It's a little early to rip off a liquor store. You want to wait till it's dark. Makes it easier to get away." That said, Hat felt obliged to show Benjie something. He looked down the rows of cars parked in the lot facing the beach. "We can rip off one of these cars for now." The parking area was narrow; a single line of around twenty cars. A jumble of rip-rap protected it from high waves. Then there was a wide beach—about twenty yards to the water and the shore break. Hat grabbed his hammer and walked down the line of cars. Many of them were nicer than you'd expect—newer trucks and BMW's—like these kite surfers were pretty well-off. Peering inside a steel-gray Audi5 he saw what he was looking for, a neatly folded shirt and pants on the passenger seat. Nice car, nice clothes, wallet and phone probably "hidden" underneath. Stupid rich guy—maybe the guy who was showing off the most, soaring above the waves beneath a bright orange kite, filled with wind and curved like a comma, taking big air off the wave faces, twisting and spinning and gracefully landing on another wave. Flying through the air like an angel screwing around on his day off. The last thing he's thinking about is some lowlife breaking into his car. Oh well, Hat said to himself as he bashed in the passenger side window with his hammer. Shit happens, Mr. Angel. You'll see.

The car alarm went off, but it was easy enough to kill it by pulling out a couple wires beneath the steering wheel. Anyway, the only person on the wide windy beach was a guy who was just getting ready to go out, and the way the wind was blowing in, he didn't hear anything. Just as Hat expected, there was a wallet and a phone beneath the neatly folded clothes. He didn't have any use for the phone, so he left it, but he grabbed the wallet and walked back to the Honda. He got in and handed the wallet to Benjie. "Easy, huh? Like picking an apple off a tree."

The wallet held a bit of cash—after a few false starts, Benjie counted $63 in bills—the real prize was the gold American Express card.

"So now we're going to have some fun," Hat said as he pulled the Accord back out onto the coastal highway, pointing them back toward town.

They ended up in the upstairs bar above a redwood and glass restaurant by the harbor, the kind of place that describes itself as "upscale casual". Feeling pretty good about the way the day had gone, Hat started drinking. He regaled Benjie with tales of his criminal exploits, a few of which were actually true. After three Southern-and-

Sevens, he looked out over the water as the sun was going down, the sky streaked with red, and anything seemed possible, which led him to approach a pair of California girls with long blond hair and ask if he could buy them a drink. Exchanging a smirk between themselves, they declined. Hat didn't get it. He stood in front of their table with a frozen smile on his face that gradually twisted into something uglier, his hipster hat a little cockeyed, the girls purposefully ignoring him. He finally said, "All right. Fuck you very much," and went back to the bar to collect Benjie. They were going to find a place where everyone wasn't so stuck up, and drinks weren't nine frickin' dollars a pop.

That place was the 7001 Club, a small dark bar whose gloomy interior was illuminated by beer signs and a cone of light over a pool table. It was good to be in a place with normal people, Hat thought, meaning a few old drunks hunched over their drinks, four construction workers playing pool and arguing over sports and a couple of thirty-something women sitting at the bar who were happy to have him buy them drinks. One was Francie, one was Barb, and they weren't super-models by any stretch, but as the night wore on it didn't matter. Hat told them that he was a hit man for the mob, which they thought was a crackup, and Hat played along, like he was just goofing. Benjie was being an idiot, looking at his phone all the time. Hat told them he was in town on mob business; that he had a fancy suite at the Sunset Inn. Why don't we go back there and party, he said. Oh sure, a penthouse suite at the Sunset Inn, Barb, who was the heavier one said, throwing her head back and laughing. But she was game, and talked Francie into coming along.

Hat had a good feeling about Barb; she looked like she'd be up for just about anything. When it turned out that Hat and Benjie really were staying in a fancy suite at the Sunset Inn, which might have also made her think there was something to Hat's claim to mob connections, she didn't get hung up on it. She didn't get hung up on much of anything, in fact. After they all smoked some weed that Benjie brought out, she followed Hat into the master suite where they fell on the king bed and went at it like they were the first people to ever have sex.

****

By 3:07 AM, when Gina Quattro unexpectedly opened the door to the bedroom, rolling her Louis Vuitton bag behind her, Hat was riding Barb for the third time. They'd never bothered to turn off the lights. The room was a mess, the bedding torn off the bed, their clothes strewn on the carpet. An empty Southern Comfort bottle lay tipped over on the credenza surrounded by 7-Up cans. At some point during their romp, Hat had talked the front desk into sending up every dessert on the room service menu. The room service tray was on the floor; chocolate and custard-smeared dishes scattered around it. A porno was playing on the bedroom's big screen.

Strapped tight around his pale, narrow chest, Hat was wearing one of Gina's lacy black brassieres; he couldn't remember why.

Gina sounded strangely calm, but there was steel in her voice. "What are you doing?"

Barb had pushed him off and was reaching for the sheets to cover herself.

"Playing hide the salami," Hat said. He sat on the edge of the bed, his erection bobbing in front of him. "You want to jump in?"

"Get her out of here!"

"OK—just give me a couple more minutes. I got this situation here."

"*Now!*"

Hat looked down at this penis, which remained standing at attention, like a private waiting a command from a general.

"What am I supposed to do with this?"

"Bring it here, I'll slam it in the door."

From beneath the sheet that Barb had pulled over her head came her muffled voice. "Can I leave?"

Hat grabbed his smokes and walked out to the bedroom's balcony and lit one up, just to piss Gina off—as if she needed another reason. He stared out into the night, his back to the bedroom where apparently Barb was scrambling back into her clothes. He imagined her embarrassed exit, hurrying past Gina, trying to avoid looking at her as she grabbed her purse and headed out the door. He was done anyway. The only way he could get it up again now is if Gina stripped and spread herself out on the bed like a $1,000 hooker. Then maybe.

When he finished his cigarette Barb was gone and Gina was pulling some things out of her dresser drawer, packing the second suitcase she'd brought when they first checked in.

"You want this?" he asked, meaning the bra he was still wearing.

"You're a disgusting animal," she spat, unwilling to look at him. He was still naked. He couldn't remember where he'd left his pants.

"Welcome to the world of criminals. This is the kind of shit we do." She probably wasn't listening, pulling out and slamming drawers, grabbing stuff from the closet, but he went on anyway. "We don't give a shit about what people think or what's gonna happen if we get caught. That's why we can rob and cheat and shoot people. You got your business degree and all, but most of the rest of us are just kind of psychos." It looked like she had removed all of her things and gotten them into her suitcases.

"You going somewhere?" he asked.

"I'm leaving. I'm going back to the city. Something big has come up." She still wouldn't look at him. Bent over her suitcase, the back of her hair falling away from her neck. He'd never seen the back of her neck before. It was surprisingly pale and delicate. He considered putting his hands around it and strangling her, just for the satisfaction it would bring.

"Tonight?"

"I can't stand being in the same room with you. You're a disgusting piece of dirt."

"I got your point already. But what about the job? The Bay-View?"

She went into the bathroom to gather all of her hair and skin products, which by themselves would fill another special case.

"Forget the job. It's not going to happen."

"I was casing it out again earlier. It's gonna be a piece of cake."

"I said forget it."

The better way, he decided, would be to pop her, and do it quickly. So he walked out, got his Raven .25, then quickly walked back into the master suite. Gina was still in the bathroom, facing the mirror. She saw him reflected behind her as he came up, surprised as hell when she realized what he was going to do, but what did she expect?

He quickly raised the gun and gave her one in the back of the head. She fell right down, her eyes still open.

Z-Day Minus 1

Chuy didn't really have a plan, but he had an idea for a plan. He started with what he knew: there would be a boatload of money in the counting room of the Bay-View at the end of the Memorial Day weekend; he was part of a gang Nico had thrown together to go after it; and he knew that if he was going to risk his neck, he wanted to come out of it with a lot more than the chump change Nico was offering. All he had to figure out was how he was going to peel away a bigger piece of the loot for himself and give the other bozos the slip.

Getting the money was one thing; there was bound to be a lot of confusion during the robbery; he could create a little more. Maybe just cold-cock the amped-up little jerk Hat after they grabbed the cash—no need to worry about the big doofus Benjie or Nico—grab the lion's share of the loot and take off.

But how was he going to get away?

He didn't sleep much, thinking about it. He got up early and started going through his old things, stuff he'd left behind when he left home at eighteen. That summer Gallo had gotten him a job on his roofing crew. Chuy stuck with it for a month, walking away because Gallo was always busting his balls. The heavy, tarred-up boots he wore for the job were still in his old closet; so was a beat-up straw cowboy hat that he wore. A pair of faded jeans and a white T-shirt completed his outfit. From the storage shed behind the taqueria, he grabbed a roofing spade and carried it over his shoulder as he walked to the Bay-View. The long street front of the amusement park was relatively quiet at this hour—just past 8:00. The park wouldn't open for paying customers for another couple hours. There was activity though. A crew was cleaning up litter along the sidewalk; other workers were driving up and down an asphalt maintenance path in utility carts; a delivery truck was backed up to a narrow loading dock next to the arcade. Chuy idled along the maintenance path, checking things out. With the shovel slung over his shoulder, no one paid him much heed; he was all but invisible, just another Mexican tidying up around the Bay-View, no one to worry about or even pay attention to.

He paused to get his bearings. The park was about five hundred yards from end to end, and much of what faced the street was nondescript—putty-colored cinderblock walls filling the spaces between the backsides of the single-story food concessions and carnival games. A long stretch was taken up by a graffiti-scribbled wooden fence behind which rose the complicated geometry of the Giant Anaconda's century-old wooden support structure. He was looking for a narrow ramp he remembered—just wide enough to accommodate a delivery van—that led down to the sublevel. When he was a kid living nearby, Chuy and his buddies hung out a lot at the park, even though they rarely had money for the rides; they'd race up and down the midway, playing hide and seek or ditch, trying to evade security. Once he managed to sneak into the Bay-View's lower level by darting down a ramp—the one he was looking for now—but had promptly been cornered, collared and marched out.

He figured that there must be a way to get from the ramp through the basement and up the stairs to the door he'd taken note of the night before, the one just beyond the counting room. If he could map that route, he could run it in reverse to make his getaway after he got his hands on as much of the Bay-View's cash as he could carry, leaving the others behind.

He found the ramp around 100 feet to the left of one of the sidewalk entrances to the park—the entrance, in fact, that was closest to the carrousel, only yards away from the counting room. He wandered up to the ramp's mouth and looked down. At the end of the ramp, a serious-looking steel gate prevented entry. Diligently turning over clumps of dirt around a scraggly bush—actually the same clump, again and again—he waited ten minutes before someone within activated the gate which slowly opened, accompanied by the low hum of a motor, to let in a maintenance worker driving a utility cart carrying paint and a stepladder.

After the cart passed him, Chuy had about twenty seconds to slip through the open gate before the humming motor—on a timer, he guessed—activated again and closed the gate behind him. Once he was through, he saw that inside there was also a manual gate opener—a big red button—that he could press to let himself out.

Beyond the gate, the ramp fed into a larger passageway. From his single short foray into the bowels of the Bay-View when he was a squirt, he dimly remembered some of what he saw as he looked left and right down the main corridor—polished concrete floors and low ceilings with pipes and electrical conduits strapped to them.

Guessing at his position relative to the counting room, he went off to explore the corridor to his left first. About thirty feet in he came upon a closed door with a handwritten sign advising the curious to keep out, followed by some bullshit about horrible consequences and grotesque monsters. Chuy had never seen a closed door that didn't intrigue him. He tried the knob and carefully opened it, just far enough to look inside.

Silhouetted against the dim light from within, a shadowy giant— some kind of robot—lumbered toward him. A shrill cackling voice coming from somewhere deeper in the room yelled, "Get 'im, Frankie! Get 'im!"

Chuy quickly shut the door and stepped back. If he had more time, he might have tried to figure out what the hell he'd just run into; for now, it was enough to know that he didn't want any part of it.

Fifteen feet further on, he came upon another door. It looked beefy enough to be the kind of heavy, fireproof door that would close off a stairwell or an exit. But it required a key card to open. He paused to re-orient himself. He had the nagging suspicion that access to the stairs he was looking for would be closer to the ramp, and that he must be wandering in the wrong direction. He went a little further, stopping just short of a noisy machine shop before turning around and backtracking toward the ramp entrance.

Not far beyond the ramp he found it—a side passageway heading in what he was sure must be the right direction. It ran toward the beach side of the Bay-View, past a door that opened into what looked like a locker room, the passageway ending twenty feet later at a heavy metal fire door with a thick glass window. Through the window he could see a stairwell. He went quickly up the stairs, getting a hint of fresh air as he ascended, and pushed open the door at the top. Squinting in the sunlight of a sweet Santa Carmela morning, he saw in the distance a bit of the sky and the sun glinting on the bay. But the more immediate view was even sweeter—four feet to his left was the counting room door. Next to it stood a security guard, practicing his cop stare, which he trained on Chuy.

"Buenos días," Chuy said, grinning like he'd won the lottery. With his shovel on his shoulder, he walked past the guard and out onto the empty midway.

****

208 over 120.

Nico stared at the digital display of the home blood pressure monitor cuff that he'd wrapped around his fat wrist and heaved a distressed sigh. He was sitting on the side of his bed in his pajamas, strands of hair standing every which way on his scalp, an anxious frown pulling down his unshaven jowls. Jesus Christ, he thought, no wonder my head feels like it's going to explode. He was totally stressed; he hadn't gotten more than a couple hours of sleep in any of the past four nights. All he could do was worry. Lying awake in the dark he went over his list of what-ifs: what if the heist goes wrong?

What if the heist succeeded but Vincent Maladago still wasn't happy? What if Gina, Hat and Benjie snatched little Nicky and tortured him?

What if his overstressed heart burst like a distended water balloon?

Hoping that maybe the previous reading had just reflected a passing spike in his blood pressure, he tried to calm himself, taking ten deep breaths and exhaling slowly. He took another reading. This one was a little better—189 over 118. Not good, not where it should be, but better. Going in the right direction anyway. He told himself to do the deep breathing thing when he could throughout his day. Get a grip. Take control of this thing.

Even though he'd been miserably awake for five hours, he'd put off getting out of bed for as long as he could. It was after 8:30. Little Nicky was up; he could hear the television in the living room. Saturday morning cartoons. He had to have him at the Little League field by 9:30. Nico pulled apart the Velcro cuff, put the blood pressure monitor aside. He willed himself to stand up and get on with his day.

Little Nicky had brought his pillows into the living room, and, along with every cushion off the living room chairs and sofa, he'd used them to construct a fort. His head, chin propped up on his elbows, stuck out the front. The dachshund's narrow little muzzle also peeked out of the fort. They both seemed mesmerized by the animated action on the big screen television that dominated one wall of the living room. Giant robots, taller than skyscrapers, were destroying a metropolis.

"Nicky, you got Little League today."

"I don't want to go to Little League."

315

"Your gramma's going to take you. You gotta get ready." Usually he was able to take some time off for Nicky's baseball games. But Memorial Day weekend was one of the busiest of the year at the fish market—plus he had this other thing that he was dealing with—so he'd arranged for Bianca to take him.

"Little League sucks."

"Don't say sucks."

Nicky was a chubby little kid, just like Nico had been at his age. Not very good, or very interested in sports. Nico could relate. But still.

"Come on. You gotta eat breakfast." Nico grabbed the dog's leash. "Was Schnitzel good last night? Did she crap in the house?" Little Nicky didn't answer—making a point of ignoring his dad. The dog seemed calmer when she was with Little Nicky. She was reluctant to leave his side, but allowed Nico to coax her out the back door.

Nico could only shake his head as he surveyed his back yard. Four months ago, when he was planning to redo the lawn, he had this vision of it, of bright green grass, a thick emerald carpet. After he'd first laid the sod down it was beautiful, like a lawn in heaven where angels would play croquet. Now he could barely stand to look at it.

Schnitzel did her business and then started digging furiously at a fresh gopher hole. Nico didn't even yell at her. He went back into the house. Nicky was still in his pillow fort.

"Come on, Nicky—get your ass in gear."

"I don't wanna go."

"You gotta go."

"Why?"

Nico stormed over to the pillow fort and started roughly dismantling it. "*Why*? You don't have to worry about why. Because I'm telling you that's what you gotta do, that's why. Now just do it!" Little Nicky, his face fearful, lay on the floor hugging one of his pillows, the last piece of the fort that Nico hadn't yanked away. Nico grabbed one end of the pillow and started tugging on it, but little Nicky held tight. He was crying now.

Nico caught himself. What the hell was he doing? He was like a crazy man, terrorizing his kid. He'd never even yelled at him before. He released his hold on the pillow and knelt down next to his son. He stroked his soft hair. Nicky wouldn't look at him.

"I'm sorry. I've got a lot on my mind. I didn't mean to go off on you like that," he said gently. "But you gotta get ready for Little League." He picked up the remote and turned off the TV. "Go get some cereal now."

It took Nicky another forty-five minutes to get ready. He examined every spoonful of Cocoa Puffs before he put it into his mouth. He couldn't find his left baseball shoe; that took ten minutes. Then he had to say good-bye to Schnitzel. Then he had to go to the bathroom. Then he had to say good-bye to Schnitzel again on their way through the backyard toward the gate to Bianca's house.

They went in to his mother's house through the door on the back patio. Nico expected Bianca to be waiting for them. But the house was quiet. The kitchen was dark. He called for her, and she answered in a thin, distraught voice from her bedroom. He walked down the hallway and stood in front of the closed door.

"Ma, you gotta take Nicky to his Little League game, remember?"

She said something, but it was muffled and he couldn't make it out. "What? What are you saying, Ma?" She said it again, but he still couldn't make out the words. It sounded like she was sick.

"Something wrong? Are you sick?" He tried the door and opened it. "I'm coming in, Ma."

She was sitting on the side of her bed. She was in her robe, hanging her head, looking at her hands in her lap. She barely glanced at him. Her room was turned over. Drawers hung out of her dresser, her underwear hanging over the sides. The louvered doors of her closet were open; clothes and shoe boxes were strewn on the carpet.

"It's gone, Nicky. The raffle money we've been collecting for Father Mikey. I looked everywhere."

For a moment, Nico felt like a rat. But he remembered what he'd seen, her disgusting little romp with Freebie, and the feeling passed. "You sure you just didn't hide it somewhere and forgot where?"

No, she said. She was sure she put it in the cookie tin, which was always in her underwear drawer. She had some more money to put away last night and couldn't find it. She tore the room apart, thinking maybe she had stuck the cookie tin somewhere else, even though that didn't make sense, unless she was getting Alzheimer's like poor Anna Maria Battistini. But it was gone; the money was gone and she hadn't been able to sleep a wink worrying about it.

"I need your help, Nico." She was looking at him now. She looked really old, even haggard. He hardly recognized her. "First I was thinking I would just burn the house down. Then people would feel sorry for me, and no one would question me about the raffle money, because it would be lost with everything else. They might even hold a raffle for me, to cover what the insurance didn't pay for. But this house . . . is my life. But I got another idea." Her voice brightened a little. "You hit me a few times, tie me up, you know, gag me. Take a few more things, like the silver service. Mess the place up. Maybe like jimmy the back door. Then you call the police. Tell them you came here this morning and found me, like I was tied up all night and you found me this morning."

"Ma, Nicky's got to get to his game."

"You should also take my jewelry box. We've got a rider on the insurance. It's all itemized—"

Nico realized that Little Nicky, who had lagged behind him, was now in the doorway of the bedroom. His eyes were wide.

"Nicky, your Gramma's gotta get ready. You go watch TV. *I said go.*"

After Nicky left, Nico said, "Ma, I think you know you stole the money."

It was like he'd slapped her. What was he saying?

"When you sin, when you commit a mortal sin in the eyes of God and the Virgin Mary, you have to expect a punishment. You think you can have a little fling and there won't be any payback? Guess what, there's always a payback. And these Latin lover types, with their greasy hair and little mustaches, they're as low as you can get. You think you can trust them but they're figuring out how they can rip you off even while they're humping you. You think it's a coincidence that Freebie didn't show up for work yesterday? I'll bet you a hundred dollars he doesn't show up today either. Why? Because he's gone, probably already down in Michoacán, or wherever the fuck he comes from, drinking tequila and partying with a bunch of whores."

He let it all sink in. Then he said, "Come on, now get dressed. Nicky's game starts in twenty minutes."

"Nico, you've got to help me," she implored. "I need $11,000. The raffle is next week."

"You didn't hear what I was just saying? About punishment?"

"Nico . . ." The anguish and fear in her eyes was getting to him. It was like she was in a boat that was sinking, and he could see her face through a porthole, looking out at him, her eyes saying, *"Save me! Save me!"*

He let out a defeated breath. "Look, you don't have to fake a rip-off. You *were* ripped off. The way it happened was I sent Freebie out here on Friday. You and me were busy at the fish market so I sent him to get a couple boxes of paper napkins that were stored in your garage. We trusted him. He must have broken into the house and went through your things. The sick fuck went into your underwear drawer. Found the money. You only discovered this today—you sold some raffle tickets at Nicky's Little League game and when you went to put it in with the rest of it, you saw that it was all gone. We put two and two together."

"What if he comes back? Freebie?"

"He's not coming back, Ma." Nico said with heavy conviction. "He's gone forever." He let her think about it for a moment. "Come on now. Get dressed and take Nico to his game. When you get back, you go to put the money for the raffle tickets away and you find that the money's gone. You call me and I call the cops."

320

"What about Father Mikey?"

"Maybe he's going to have to wait on getting the rectory fixed up, I don't know. What I do know is Father Mikey's the least of our worries."

****

The day before Memorial Day and the big Zombie Invasion didn't start off very well for the Smiles Ambassador either. Thirty minutes or so into his shift a little kid, maybe four or five, came up behind him and started whipping the backs of his legs with a rubber snake he'd won. The kid's parents thought it was pretty cute, maybe the cutest thing they'd seen since Junior pulled the cat's tail. They encouraged their little darling to keep it up as they snapped photos with their phones, even as Andrew started jogging away, still smiling, which took all of his self-control. To his horror, he caught himself fantasizing about wheeling around and whip a side kick, *yoko giri*, at the little monster, which would have been a serious breach of the Code of Conduct he'd been given the day he was hired, which, among other no-nos, strictly prohibited touching guests. About an hour later, a nacho bomb exploded at Andrew's feet, dropped from above by a pimply-faced bombardier riding in one of the Sky Train gondolas that traversed the length of the park. When a basket of tortilla chips covered by four generous squirts of goopy yellow cheese hits the ground after falling twenty-five feet, the impact radius is ugly, especially if you're standing within inches of the detonation. Gooey gouts of the cheese, dotted with jalapeño rounds, splashed all over his shoes. By the time he had found a paper napkin to wipe it off, the cheese had cooled; it had the consistency of melted plastic. He was able to smear it around a little, but he couldn't remove it. His efforts only seemed to make the situation worse, adding bits of the paper napkin to the mess.

He felt a large presence looming over him. "You're lucky they only got your shoes." He looked up and saw Pete the Pelican. It sounded like he might be chuckling inside his pelican head. "Last month one of those damn things hit me smack on my beak. It looked like snot just kind of hanging there, a lot of snot."

Even though a shadow had fallen across his day, Andrew resolved to maintain a sunny front. He was, after all, the Smiles Ambassador, and it was his duty to dispense smiles and good cheer. But a final humiliation pushed him even closer to the edge. He was standing near the Ride of Death when a couple of teenage boys started messing with him, calling him names like 'tard and loser. He tried to ignore them, which only seemed to incite them more. One of them snatched his hat, the straw skimmer. He waved it at Andrew, daring him to grab it back, snatching it away as Andrew flailed for it. Then the two bullies got the notion to use the hat like a Frisbee, tossing it back and forth between them in a game of keep-away as Andrew ran slap-footed between them.

Andrew quickly grew exhausted. It seemed like everyone around him was laughing at him, like he was caught inside a kaleidoscope of mocking faces. He felt like he was going to burst into tears and blindly lash out. Then an angel appeared—a pretty blond angel in a blue security guard uniform. Corporal Cartwright. Andrew's two tormentors stopped their horseplay as she marched up to the one holding Andrew's hat.

"Give him his hat back," she said. "You're being mean." Her voice was girlish, lacking any steely ring of authority. But her scrubbed blonde prettiness exerted its own calming power over the two delinquents. Andrew could see in their faces that they would be happy comply with any direction she gave.

"We were just goofing around," the one holding Andrew's hat said as he walked it over to Andrew.

"We didn't mean anything," his partner assured her. He was wearing a T-shirt that said "Porn Star in Training".

"If I see either of you acting up again I'll have you marched out of the park."

"We'll be good."

"Honest."

The one in the Porn Star T-shirt said, "You want to go to a party tonight?"

She ignored them and approached Andrew. He was examining his straw skimmer. The brim was a little bent.

"Are you OK?"

He nodded, transfixed by her kind blue eyes. He wished the situation was reversed, that he had rescued her from some dangerous situation. She took the hat out of his hands and placed it on his head. "There you go, Mr. Ambassador."

"My real name is Andrew," he reminded her.

"All right, Andrew. You let me know if these two or anyone else gives you any more trouble. I'm usually over there, either around the line to the Giant Anaconda or near the doorway to the lower level."

"I know."

"I've got to get back to my post now." As she walked away, Andrew watched her, marveling at the effect she had on him. Something about being near Corporal Cartwright, or even thinking about her, made him happy and calm.

Checking his watch, he realized his shift was almost over. Trying hard to smile and wave with a refreshed attitude at what the employee handbook called "our valued guests", Andrew wandered toward the arcade. Entering the big noisy space, Andrew saw Ricky Wakefield walking toward him. It looked like Ricky was happy to see him, which felt like trouble.

"Andrew, my man. My main man. My old buddy. I've been looking for you."

"You have?"

"I have," he nodded emphatically. "I've got a favor to ask you. But it's not like a favor-favor. More like I'd be offering you a very cool opportunity that would also help me out. But you're really going to like it."

"Like what?"

Ricky looked around, then pulled Andrew aside, off to a quiet corner of the arcade where a couple of old shuffleboard tables were gathering dust, artifacts of a bygone time before digital circuitry ruled the world.

"First, this is between you and me. No one else can know about it."

"About what?"

"Hold on. I need you to swear to secrecy." He put his face close to Andrew's. Andrew could see three little bruises on the side of Ricky's neck. He couldn't stop looking at them.

Andrew hesitated. "Will I get into trouble?"

Ricky grinned. "Only if you get caught. But you won't get caught," he quickly assured him. "Anyway, no guts no glory."

Andrew was too intrigued to back away now. "OK. I swear."

"I'm serious, dude. No one can know about this except you and me."

"I won't tell."

"So, here's the deal. You know Laura right? My girlfriend?"

"From the snack bar?"

Ricky nodded. "OK, you know this Z-Day thing that's happening tomorrow?" Andrew nodded. "Laura and all of her friends are going together. They're getting all made up like zombies, and they're all really stoked about it. It's this huge deal for Laura. She wants me to go with all of them, like our own zombie crew. She's going as a zombie ballerina. She wants me to be like a zombie computer nerd, with this skinny black tie and nerd glasses, with my clothes all messed up and a fake axe sticking in my head. It's going to be totally cool. But my Mom and them won't let me take off work. I asked her like twenty different times, but she says Memorial Day is the most important day of the year for the park, and this big family responsibility because all of the Wakefield's will be here working. Blah, blah, blah. No excuses, no argument. But then I got an idea. Can you guess?"

Ricky didn't wait for him to answer.

"You can be me."

Andrew tried to process what Ricky had just said.

"I mean you can be Toby. All you do is after your shift, after you change, you go into one of the toilet stalls and put on my Toby costume. I'll give you the combination to my locker and it'll be in there. Just wait till no one else is in the locker room. Once you're wearing the Toby costume, no one's going to know if it's you or me. How about it? Can you help me out?"

Andrew hadn't had much practice handling moral dilemmas. The code of honor that he'd created for the Shadow Warrior didn't allow for dishonesty or sneakiness, but at this moment he was only Andrew. And Andrew, especially after the day he'd had, was over being the dopey Smiles Ambassador; he was ready to jump at the chance to be a real mascot, a costumed character with a zany personality who made everyone smile, and never got whipped by rubber snakes.

Still, he hesitated.

Ricky could sense he was close to sealing the deal. "All you have to do is what I do—run around, high-five the kids, shadow box, act silly. Do a little dance every now and then. You'd be good at it."

"You don't think anyone will find out?" Jana had told Andrew that she'd be at the Bay-View that night, so she wouldn't know if he wasn't at home in the apartment.

"Who's going to tell them?" Ricky raised his hand, holding it palm-out at eye level. "Come on, high-five to seal the deal!"

Caught up in the spirit of the moment, Andrew tried to slap Ricky's hand. He didn't hit it dead on, but close enough.

326

****

"Where's Gina?" Nico asked when Hat and Benjie arrived for the final planning meeting, which Nico was holding in the fish market's prep area. He had set the meeting for 11:00 PM, a couple hours after closing, when all the market staff would be gone. Hat and Benjie didn't saunter in until around 11:15, Hat wearing his short-brimmed hipster hat, Benjie his flat-brimmed skater cap, twisted almost sideways. Chuy was already there, leaning against the sink, arms folded across his chest. He never wore a hat.

"Gina's not going to be here," Hat said.

"How do you mean?"

"She's not coming," Hat said, like he didn't think he had to explain. "She had a meeting with the big boss and he wanted her to stay up in the city."

"Why didn't she tell me?"

"Why should she tell you? She doesn't have to tell you. I'm telling you."

"I'm surprised she didn't tell me, that's all."

"So now you know," Hat said. Subject closed.

"Is she gonna be here tomorrow?"

"Depends on what the boss wants. For now, she left me in charge down here. Is your brother coming to this meeting?"

"He's got something else going on."

"Something else?"

"I'll fill him in."

"You and your brother . . . I don't get you guys," Hat said. Then he said to Benjie, "Quit fucking around with the seal."

Benjie had stuck his head down the hole framed into the floor where they dumped the fish cutting scraps. He was holding a conversation with Sammy the sea lion. He'd bark, and Sammy, expecting a treat, would bark back. The sea lion's barking echoed loudly under the wharf's wooden structure.

"You got to give him something," Nico said. "You just can't tease him. You'll make him crazy and he'll never shut up."

"Why don't you piss down that hole?" Hat said. "See if that shuts him up."

Nico bustled into the walk-in freezer and came out with a tray of mackerel that hadn't been selling well out front. It had been sitting in the display case for almost a week, now destined to be chopped up and put into the little Seal Snacks they sold out front. "Here, give him a couple of these. Just toss them all down there. It'll keep him quiet for a while." He handed the tray to Benjie, who started dropping the mackerel down the hole one by one.

Hat looked at Nico impatiently. "OK, mastermind, what'cha got?"

Nico went into his office and came out with four oversized stuffed animals, which he set on the stainless steel prep table. There was the dolphin he had modified as his prototype, a penguin, a shark and a big yellow banana.

"This is that idea I was telling you about. These are just like the ones you can win at some of the games there. It's how we're gonna carry the cash out." Proud of his inventiveness, Nico demonstrated on the dolphin how one of his loan customers, a guy with an upholstery business, had put a zipper on the back seam. From the same guy, Nico had also gotten big chunks of foam stuffing which he'd used to replace the original cotton batting.

"Like I was telling you last night, when we get in there, we take out the foam stuffing and that's where we'll stuff the cash," he said, showing them. "Then, you zip up the back again. So when we walk out of the counting room, we're just another bunch of zombies carrying the prizes we've won."

"Dibs on the penguin," Benjie said. Hat looked like he wanted to slap him. Chuy gave Nico a sideways glance.

"Sure," Nico said, putting the stuffing back into the dolphin, and zipping up the back. He handed Benjie the penguin.

"I'm not going to carry around a big fucking banana," Hat said.

"I got the shark for you," Nico said, handing it to him. "The dolphin's for me, and Chuy gets the banana. You're cool with the banana, Chuy?"

"Yeah, why not."

"The other thing is that, whatever stuffed animal you've got, that's going to be your name during the job. Like Benjie, you're Penguin. Hat, you're Shark. Chuy's Banana. No real names."

After he passed out stuffed toys he had them try the zippers, pull out some of the stuffing and put it back in for practice. While they were doing that, Nico went back into his office and came out with three plastic shopping bags. Printed on one of the bags was the logo for a costume shop, Maskerade. He dumped its contents on the table next to the stuffed animals—four Deluxe Zombie Makeup Kits.

"OK . . . everyone gets a makeup kit." Nico handed them out. Each kit included zombie teeth, a tray with green, grey and blood-red makeup, and a bloody scab that you could stick on. "Remember, this is about disguising yourself, so you want to put the makeup on thick. The instructions say put the scab on first, since it won't stick to the makeup."

Hat tore open his kit and stuck his pair of rotting veneers over his own teeth and puckered his lips around them. "Hey Benjie, you want a kiss?"

"Come on, this is serious," Nico said. Hat leaned into Benjie, who pulled his face back, cringing. "Everyone clear on the makeup?" Nico asked. "Banana?"

It took Chuy a couple seconds to get that Nico was talking to him.

"Can we drop the fake names for now? It's confusing."

"I thought it would be good to practice."

"Yeah, I get it."

Nico picked up a smaller bag from Home Depot and reached into it. "Now these are the zip ties. Penguin, you can be the zip tie guy."

Benjie seemed OK with the assignment. But he had a question. "What's a zip tie?" Again, Chuy shot a sideways glance at Nico.

Nico opened the bag of zip ties and took one out to show him. "Stick your hands out." Nico fastened the zip tie around Benjie's wrists and cinched it tight. "We're going to put 'em around the hands and ankles of everyone in the counting room. I'll give you a few to take with you tonight so you can practice."

Benjie looked at his hands. He strained against the zip tie. "How do you undo them?"

"Here." From the Home Depot bag, Nico produced a pair of heavy duty wire snips and cut the zip ties. "These," he said, handing them to Chuy, "are what we're going to use to cut all the wires coming out of their communications consoles and any land lines. Banana, that'll be your job. We also got to get all their cell phones."

Nico looked around at his gang. "Everybody clear on all this so far?" Chuy had a blank look on his face, like he was waiting at a long stoplight. Benjie had returned to the scrap hole; he had a few more mackerel to drop. Hat was reading the copy on the cardboard backing of his makeup kit. "'Looking dead has never looked so good.' That's pretty damn funny."

"I also got us latex gloves to wear too. So we won't leave prints."

"You're a criminal genius," Hat said.

"And one more thing." Nico went back into his office, and from one of his desk drawers he pulled out a couple of firecrackers. Big Nicky kept them around to scare off the sea lions if they got too aggressive. He walked them out into the prep area in the palm of his hand.

"This is what we're going to use for a diversion."

"M-80's. Cool!" Benjie said. "Let me see one." Nico handed one to him.

Hat had a lighter in his hand. "Let's light that sucker and throw it down the hole."

"Would you guys quit screwing around? Give it back." Nico held his hand out and Benjie gave back the big firecracker. "So what we're going to do," he continued, "when we see the cash cart leave, we give them like ten minutes to get down the midway. Then Benjie, I mean

Penguin, goes into Men's room with the M-80. He lights it and puts it in the metal trash can next to the door. We'll bring a couple in case the first one's a dud. When the M-80 goes off it's going to make one hell of a noise, like a bomb. Then Penguin comes come staggering out like he's hurt. Are you guys seeing it?"

He wanted them to nod their heads, which no one did. But at least they were looking at him.

"So Penguin, you come staggering out and collapse in front of the girl guard. She's going to crouch down to help you, and that's when the rest of us rush her. We get her to open the door of the counting room, and then we push inside. We got our guns out, waving them. Get everyone's attention. There will be two old ladies and the head of security inside. They're probably already a little panicked because of the explosion. First thing we do is get their hands and ankles cinched up with the zip ties. That's you, right Penguin? Remember, practice tonight. Banana, you cut all the wires for communication. Shark, you make sure you get all their cell phones. The safe should still be open. We grab the money and stuff it into our animals. I'll be checking the time. We want to be in and out in five minutes tops.

"Remember—no one gets hurt. We don't want that. All we want is the money. Once we get it, we get the hell out. Then everyone spreads out. We'll meet back at the fish market van, which is going to be parked up on Catalpa St."

"Where's that?" Hat asked.

"It's close to the main Bay-View parking lot. You'll see when we park there. I'll have towels and stuff in the van so we can get the zombie crap off our faces. Then we drive back to the wharf and split the money. You guys get the $100,000 for Vincent and then we're done."

He let it all sink in, studying their faces. "Any questions?"

Only Benjie spoke up. "You got any more fish I can drop down the hole?"

"I meant questions about the plan. No? OK then— I'll pick everyone up in the van. I'll come by the Sunset Inn for you two around 7:45. Chuy, I'll swing by for you a little before that. You guys take those make-up kits with you so you can have your zombie faces on when I come to get you. All the other stuff will be in the van. This is going to work, guys. Everyone just stick with the plan, and it's going to work good. We'll come out of there with a shit pile of money."

After Hat and Benjie left in Gina's Mercedes, Nico walked up to Chuy who was firing up his Harley in front of the market.

"Are you OK with the plan?"

"I'm OK." Chuy was revving the engine.

"It's just you seemed, I don't know, like you weren't very excited about it. I put a lot of thought into it. A lot of work. Hat wants to make fun of me and call me mastermind, OK. But not everyone could come up with a plan like this."

Chuy shrugged. "I'm good with it." He was ready to ride off.

"I need you in this all the way, Chuy. I don't trust these guys, so you need to be watching them."

"Watching them?"

"I mean we're gonna come out of there with a hundred, maybe a hundred and fifty thousand in cash. This guy Hat . . ." he shook his head. ". . . you know what I mean? I just want to pay them off and get them out of my life. So that's gonna be your number one job, OK? I want you behind him when we come out of there. Stay behind him. Be ready."

Chuy cut the bike's engine. "You want to rip these guys off?"

"I just don't want them to rip me off. Just keep your eye on them. On Hat especially. If he looks like he's going to make a wrong move, back him off. Once we get back to the van, Tony will be there too."

"On his crutches?"

"He's gonna be hiding in the back of the van with a big Smith and Wesson that used to be Dad's. I want us to outnumber them when we count out their money and give it to them. Then we're done."

"Done," Chuy repeated the word like he was thinking of everything it could mean. He started the bike again. "I'll see you tomorrow."

"I'll swing by a little after 7:30. Be ready."

"I'll be ready."

Z-Day

"What do you think?" Teddy Wakefield asked. "Give me your honest opinion."

Jana studied his face. "I think you hit the right notes. I especially like the oozing wound above your eye. The way the red blood pops against the green skin."

He and Jana were the first ones in the conference room, arriving ten minutes prior to the start of the 8:00 AM meeting. It was highly unusual to convene an executive staff meeting on a Monday, which they usually took off after working through the weekend, but today was no ordinary day. Today was Z-Day, and Teddy wanted to make sure that his staff was absolutely primed and ready. He sat at his customary place at the head of the conference table, his short hair neatly combed with its straight white side part, his bow tie, patterned with red and blue balloons, knotted jauntily at his neck. But between the bow tie and his hairline it was anything but business as usual. The skin of his face had a deathly green pallor. Dark shadows pooled around his eyes and in the hollows of his cheeks. A streak of what looked like bright red blood slashed across his forehead and on the left side of his nose was a crusty scab.

"It's not too much?"

Like most junior employees, Jana knew that the best answer to a boss's question was the one he wanted to hear. He'd applied the zombie makeup without Jana's help this time and was clearly pleased with the results. "It looks . . . great. Your nose looks like you stuck it into a meat grinder."

Teddy smiled, basking in the compliment. "That scab alone took fifteen minutes. Getting the right texture was a little tricky."

Making himself up for the meeting was a little gambit he hoped would inspire his siblings to get into the spirit of the Zombie Invasion. None of the other Wakefields had exactly embraced his idea; the general consensus was that Teddy had gone off his nut. They'd gone along with it, grudgingly, the way they always went along with his schemes, because between all of them they had the imagination of a doorknob and even if Teddy's inspirations—particularly his latest one— were a little crazy, they all acknowledged that the aging hulk of the Bay-View needed an injection of *something* to keep it off life support.

Still, the Bay-View's executive staff was a cynical bunch. Arletta, Stanhope and Conrad Ferl pretended not to notice anything different about Teddy's face as they filed in and took their places around the table. The exception was Glenda, who lived to give her brother a hard time.

"Looks like maybe you ate a bad egg, Teddy," she said. "Are you feeling all right?"

"I've never felt better!" Teddy assured her. "I may look dead, but I've never felt so alive!"

Glenda refused to crack a smile. "Oh, OK, I get it. You're supposed to be a zombie, with your creepy-looking makeup. I was just a little confused, because zombies don't wear bow ties. Or starched shirts."

"Since when did you become an expert on zombies?"

"I've seen the movies, that TV show," Glenda replied. "Zombies wear nasty old tattered clothes. They don't look like they're dressed to sell you whole life insurance."

"For your information there is no zombie dress code."

Since Teddy seemed to be looking to Jana to back him up, she offered, "I think they pretty much wear whatever they were wearing when they became infected."

Conrad, whittling what was either an elephant without a trunk or an obese cocker spaniel, said over the secret frequency he pretended only he and Jana shared, "The last infection I got, I was wearing a tiger-stripe thong and a Lone Ranger mask."

"Can we get on with the meeting?" Arletta asked. "What's the agenda, Teddy?"

"Jana's just provided me with an updated report on the metrics from her social media campaign, and based on the numbers, today's going to be big—and I mean really big! I want to make sure we're ready." Teddy looked down at the printout that Jana had given him. "Jana's been tracking Twitter, Facebook, YouTube and Instagram. Yesterday she posted eight times on our Facebook page, which drew over 700 comments. Her twelve Tweets were re-Tweeted 847 times." He looked up, pausing to let the numbers sink in. "And today interest is still mushrooming. There's a buzz out there that makes me think this Zombie Invasion is going to be the most successful promotion we've ever done!"

"It better be," Blaine said. He had his own report laid out in front of him, and his numbers weren't so positive. "So far Memorial Day weekend has been soft. Receipts are down 14.7% from last year. And last year wasn't a great year."

Teddy wasn't about to stand for any negativity. "We're going to come roaring back today, starting with the ribbon cutting ceremony for the Creepy Cavern. Stanhope, are we ready on that front?"

Stanhope responded in his Mission Control voice. "All systems are go. I took another run-through last night. The mantises are behaving themselves. Spider Number Five had a gimpy leg, but Mr. Jefferson sprayed a little WD-40 on it, and it's all good now." Stanhope had brought in a pair of sheet metal scissors that were at least three feet long. "And I made these for the mayor." The giant scissors were on the table in front of him. He picked them up to show them off, but as he attempted a pretend ribbon cutting, the scissors came apart, the pivot screw dropping onto the table.

"I can fix that," he muttered. Frowning, he retrieved the screw and tried to put the scissors back together.

Teddy had another question for his Facilities Manager. "I heard that people were getting shocked when they got into the bumper cars yesterday. Did you get that fixed?

Still grappling with the scissors, Stanhope said, "Almost."

"*Almost?*"

"We're tracking down the short in the circuitry. Something gnawed through the insulation on one of the wires."

Arletta said, "It's those mice. They're everywhere."

Stanhope paused in his struggle with the two scissor blades to reassure Teddy. "It's only like a little tingle anyway. And you can barely feel it unless you grab the power pole on the back of the bumper car. I put a sign up yesterday that warned people not to touch them. They're supposed to keep their hands inside the cars anyway."

"I don't want a sign. I want the problem fixed before we open."

"We're on it, Teddy," Stanhope said. He'd managed to get the big scissors back together. His face brightened as he held them up to demonstrate. The pivot screw fell out again, bouncing on the conference table.

Teddy was moving on. He asked for Arletta's report on the readiness of the food concessions. He was particularly interested in the corn dog situation; something in his gut told him today would be a huge corn dog day. "The good news," Arletta said, "is that since it was slow yesterday, we didn't burn out the oil in the fryers. The bad news is that it looks like mice got into all those bags of corn meal that Blaine bought in January." Blaine had gotten a special deal on a truckload of fifty pound sacks of corn meal, enough to coat 753,591 corn dogs by his calculations, or five years' consumption. The bags were stored in teetering stacks behind the motor oil barrels in the machine shop in the basement.

"We don't know that the mice got into *all* of the bags," Blaine insisted.

"That's true. Just the ones we've opened so far."

Teddy said, "They couldn't have eaten that much."

Arletta was happy to clarify the situation. "It's the poop that's the problem."

"Mouse poop?"

"In the corn meal."

"A lot?"

"I don't know how much is a lot, or how much is a little. If you think about it, even a little is a lot. It's kind of mixed in."

Teddy wasn't going to be stymied by any obstacles, especially today. "We'll have to make a thorough assessment later. For today, let's screen about twenty bags." He instructed Stanhope to knock together a wooden frame. Two feet square ought to do it, he said. "Tack a screen across the bottom. Blaine, you own this. Get the screen from Stanhope and get right on it." Blaine started to protest, insisting that they should get one of the minimum wage employees for the task, but Teddy cut him off. "This has to be a top secret operation. No one outside this room should know about it. I'm confident that the frying oil will kill any germs, so there'll be no real health problem, but if our guests catch wind of it they may react negatively."

"They're a persnickety bunch," Conrad said.

"They expect a lot from us," Teddy said without a trace of irony. "When they enter the park, they're counting on us to entertain them with thrilling rides, challenge them with clever games of chance, and provide fun foods at reasonable prices—all in a safe, family-friendly environment. Conrad, how do we look on that score?"

"You mean on the safe part? I guess we're as ready as we can be, given the staffing we've got." He cast a sideways glance at Blaine to let him know—just in case there was any lingering confusion on the point—that he thought he was an idiot. "Would have been nice to have a few more uniforms on hand, but I've been told the budget won't allow it."

Blaine was quick to defend his position. "That's why we installed the additional security cameras. The cameras cost almost nothing once you get them in place. Each guard, on the other hand, costs over $150 a day." Blaine called this "Virtual Security", borrowing the term from the brochure the security system salesman had given him.

"You could go blind looking at all those monitors at the same time," Conrad said. "You should try it. After about five minutes your eyes start bouncing around your head like BB's. And, like I told you yesterday, nine of the cameras are on the fritz."

"The technician is coming out tomorrow. They charge an arm and a leg to come out on weekends and holidays. Besides, even a non-working camera is a deterrent. That's been documented."

"Well, let's just hope all these zombies that are invading are well-behaved. Otherwise it could get ugly."

Stanhope finally got his big scissors back together. He raised them in triumph. "Anyone need a haircut?" he asked, forcing a chuckle as he opened and closed the blades.

Teddy raised an open hand. "All right everyone. Let's get serious for a moment. We all know what's at stake today, how important it is that each of us, and all of us together, execute at the highest level." Jana noticed that one edge of the big scab that Teddy had affixed to his nose had worked loose. The scab trembled as he spoke. "The glory days of the Bay-View are not behind us. No, our best days are in front of us. And when this day is done, when the carrousel has spun for the last time and the last guest has left, I want to see a smile on every one of your tired faces, a smile that says we rose to every challenge—and that this was the Bay-View's finest hour!"

The scab peeled off entirely and fell onto Jana's report. Teddy looked at it for a moment, then picked it up without a word and stuck it back on his nose.

"Let's make the magic happen, folks!"

✳✳✳✳

"Look at that little girl—she's got a cleaver sticking out of her head! How cute is that?" Teddy said to Mayor Wilma Swump as they made their way to the Creepy Cavern ribbon-cutting ceremony, wading through the day's first wave of zombies, the little kids and their parents. Jana trailed behind them. Teddy had pulled her out of her cube where she was still busy tweeting and posting on social media to keep the buzz going, though it was already apparent by now—it was a little after 10:30 AM—that Z-Day had truly gone viral and had its own quickening momentum. Teddy's makeup was not holding up well. His face was prone to perspiring and, on this unusually warm morning, rivulets of sweat had clotted the thick layer of grey-green foundation he'd applied earlier. The nose scab just wouldn't stick, and he'd finally given up on it. Because Teddy expected it, Jana had darkened her eyes and nostrils and put on the dark blue lipstick she used to wear as an everyday thing. When she saw her reflection in the mirror, she could see the Goth she used to be when she was a freshman in high school, and it made her smile.

Mayor Swump, who was clueless on the whole zombie thing, but determined to show that she was a good sport, was wearing a neon green fright wig. "This was a fantastic idea, Teddy!" she said. The Mayor and Teddy were good buddies from Rotary. "What a hoot!"

Smiling proudly, Teddy stuck out his smart phone and took a photo of the little cleaver-struck cutie. He handed his phone to Jana. "Post that to Instagram," he said. "And get a shot of that zombie mom over there pushing her two zombie toddlers in the tandem stroller. Caption it 'Zombabies'." Everywhere he looked, Teddy saw another photo opp that he wanted Jana to share with the world. The kids were kind of cute, Jana had to admit. There were already hundreds of them in the park and scores more streaming through the gates, tugging their parents' hands, amped up by the promise of cotton candy, cheap prizes and the indescribable thrill of going 'round and 'round on one of the kiddie rides. It looked like many of them were wearing re-purposed trick-or-treat costumes. There were zombie fairies, zombie mermaids and little zombie cowboys, even a tiny zombie lady bug.

Following Teddy and the Mayor as they resumed their slow progress toward the Creepy Cavern, Jana looked for Andrew, finally spotting the Smiles Ambassador in a quiet area between the Tea Cups and the Tilt-a-Whirl. He was surveying the stream of tiny zombies warily. Jana told Teddy that she'd catch up to him and the Mayor at the ribbon cutting, and went over to check in with her brother. When she got up close to him, she could see fear in his eyes.

"The little kids keep trying to bite me," he said. "A zombie princess just tried to sink her teeth into my leg."

"That's because you're not a zombie. They're trying to make you one of them." Jana tried a gentle laugh, but Andrew didn't think any of it was funny.

"It's stupid. Their parents should have better control over them."

"We'll have to make you a zombie too." Andrew looked at her questioningly. "After the ribbon cutting ceremony I'll come get you and I'll put some makeup on you."

"I don't think the Smiles Ambassador should be a zombie. Zombies don't smile."

"Maybe just for today," Jana said, leaving Andrew to think about it.

She made it to the ribbon cutting ceremony just as Teddy was calling for attention from a knot of people gathered around the Creepy Cavern ticket booth, a group that included a photographer from the Santa Carmela Bugle and a dwarfish black man with wild white hair, who she guessed was the animatronic wizard, A.E. Jefferson. A wide paper ribbon stretched in front of the turnstile. Teddy began his windy remarks by invoking the memory of the Wakefield innovators who had come before him, starting with his great grandfather, Hiram Wakefield, who had come to Santa Carmela in 1902 with $3.00 in his pocket and a recipe for taffy, which he sold from a cart on the beach. The cart became a stand; the stand became an arcade with coin-operated musical instruments and a mechanical gypsy fortune teller. "In 1908, Hiram installed the first ride, a carrousel with hand-carved horses, the same carrousel that takes youngsters on a magical gallop to this day. How surprised would Hiram be," Teddy asked, "if he could see the enchanted realm that has sprung up around that first arcade and carrousel?" Teddy then touched on the contributions of Hiram's son, Sterling, who oversaw the construction of the Giant Anaconda, the longest surviving wooden roller coaster on the West Coast. Teddy skipped over Sterling's other claim to fame, his brainchild, the ill-fated Paul Bunyan's Slingshot, a thick rubber band anchored at either end to two wooden posts that catapulted thrill seekers in the general direction of a sawdust pit, except when it didn't. Sterling's son, Carleton—Teddy's father—took the helm after World War II, and expanded the park to its present dimensions, adding innovative rides and attractions like the Fearful Flume, the Ride of Death and the Ant Hill, which Teddy was proud to say had now been re-imagined as the Creepy Cavern.

Teddy nodded toward the line of empty cars on the track at the entrance of the Creepy Cavern. "What awaits you is an amazing journey through a subterranean world featuring encounters with some of the scariest members of the insect world enlarged to a terrifying size. Trust me when I tell you that this could be the scariest journey you'll ever take!"

On that dramatic note, Teddy nodded to Stanhope, who was standing by with his big scissors, which he handed to Teddy.

"Mayor Swump, can I ask you to help me do the honors?"

Jana watched through the camera lens of her phone, waiting to capture the historic moment as Teddy grabbed one of the scissor handles and the Mayor the other. Wearing frozen smiles, they faced the photographer from the Bugle. But, in spite of a heroic struggle, the big scissors wouldn't open. Apparently, Stanhope—determined that the scissors blades shouldn't come apart again—had overtightened the pivot screw. Jana, who had learned during her brief tenure at the Bay-View that almost nothing was going to happen as planned, had thought to bring along a real pair of scissors. As discreetly as she could, she handed them to Teddy. With a happy flourish, he cut the ribbon and turned his makeup-encrusted face to the small crowd.

"Welcome to the Creepy Cavern!"

****

The crowds continued to swell as the day progressed. The older kids started streaming into the park by mid-afternoon, many of them fresh from the beach, sunburns glowing beneath their zombie makeup. Bands of zombie boys in board shorts and tank tops surged up the midway, their arms circling the waists of zombie girls in bikinis tops, bringing with them a different energy, raw and hormonal, that seemed to throb in sync with the bass lines of the rock music blaring from the park's loudspeakers. They crowded the games of chance, queued up in snaking lines to brave the scarier rides; they necked in the darkness of the Creepy Cavern, oblivious to the dripping jaws of the giant spiders and the raking arms of the mantises, and they consumed heroic quantities of slushees and sodas, deep-fried Twinkies, gyros, soft swirl ice cream and funnel cakes—and of course more corn dogs than you could shake a stick at. All of this fun was purchased with wadded currency pulled from their tight pockets—

singles, fives, tens and twenties—all of it eventually conveyed to the counting room, where the bills were carefully, even lovingly, straightened out and fed into the humming counting machines.

Even the most jaded of the Wakefield siblings had to admit that Z-Day had the makings a huge success. It wasn't just the money that was flowing in; even more heart-gladdening was an air of celebration and contagious joy in the old park that hadn't been felt in for years. Arletta and Stanhope looked for excuses to leave their offices to survey the scene and exchange wondering glances at the size of the zombie horde that had taken over the Bay-View. Even Glenda Wakefield seemed to get a little caught up in the excitement; once or twice she almost smiled. Blaine couldn't stop himself from scurrying down to the counting room at least once an hour to watch the currency being fed into the counting machines, his eyes big at the sight of the stacks of cash piling up like bricks within the cavernous antique safe. More than once he had to fight an uncharacteristic urge to whoop like a lunatic, tear apart a stack of twenties and toss the bills up in the air like confetti.

Teddy was in his glory. Unable to stay in his office, he was constantly in motion. He circulated around the park, offering words of encouragement and praise to even the lowliest seasonal employee. He jumped in to help with the kind of everyday problems that usually never crossed his radar—running for paper napkins for the soft serve stand, taking a little lost zombie by the hand to the security office behind the counting room, working with Stanhope to fix the slushee machine that had suddenly started jetting a stream of cherry slushee randomly into the crowd. Once he saw that the squirting blood-red slush was attracting teenagers eager to get a splash of it on their shirts, he called off the repair effort. He ran off and returned ten minutes later with a hand-printed sign that read "Zombie Juice!"

Teddy was especially lavish in his praise of Jana, who continued tweeting and posting to Facebook and Instagram from her phone as she too roamed the park, amazed at what she'd been able to pull off with only her imagination, her smart phone and her quick tapping fingers. In a particularly effusive moment, his eyes wild with triumph, Teddy even offered her a permanent salaried position. But before she could get too excited about the offer, he caught himself, saying he'd have to check with Blaine on what they could fit into the budget.

Others weren't so thrilled with the Bay-View's big day. Conrad Ferl was particularly cranky. It wasn't that the teenagers were acting up any more than usual, it was just that there were more of them. His security staff was stretched, breaking up scuffles, collaring line jumpers, shoplifters, graffiti scribblers, and pot smokers. A couple of times Conrad himself had to wander out of the calm confines of his security nerve center and into the seething throng of zombies—once to help give the heave-ho to a big kid who had somehow sneaked a super soaker into the park, a second time to ID a young miscreant who was caught on camera mooning the cars behind him in the Creepy Cavern.

Pete the Pelican, who didn't like crowds, especially crowds of young people, chose to hide out, like an old dog shying away from the commotion of a loud party. He was also having serious second thoughts about his role in the planned robbery, and didn't want to be anywhere near the action when it went down. So he sequestered himself in one of the two toilet stalls in the downstairs locker room, which is where he was—his big pelican feet sticking out— sipping a pint of Old Overholt, when Andrew came downstairs after his big digital watch blinked 4 PM.

Andrew slowly changed out of his Smiles Ambassador get-up. Stripped down to his BVD's, he paused to ask himself if he was really going to go through with Ricky Wakefield's ruse. He looked at his watch again. Now it was 4:05, which made him anxious; Toby the Turtle was supposed to be topside by now. He downed a handful of Skittles; the burst of sugar gave him energy and a surge of courage. He looked at the scrap of paper with the combination to Ricky's lock and, with the concentration of a safecracker, opened Ricky's locker.

The locker stunk like a jock hamper. The body of Toby's costume was piled at the bottom, like the shed skin of a purple animal. Toby's turtle head was set on the top shelf, wearing an expression of frozen glee. Andrew grabbed both and went into the open toilet stall.

It didn't take more than a couple of minutes to don the body of the costume—the difficult part was pulling the legs over his sneakers— which he stepped into and pulled up over his tightie-whities and T-shirt. In the next stall, he could hear Pete the Pelican murmuring something about stupid people with stupid ideas and stupid, stupid, stupid . . . but it didn't sound like Pete was actually seeking a response, so Andrew ignored him. After strapping his watch around his wrist, he settled Toby's head over his own, lining up the eye holes. He took a deep breath, opened the door and stepped out of the stall.

At first, he didn't feel anything special. He looked down at his legs, then held up his arms and looked at them, and it wasn't much different than wearing a pair of rumpled purple pajamas. But when he stepped up to the mirrors above the sinks and got the full effect—the face, the shades, the shell—he was electrified. He was Toby! He was totally, awesomely cool! He threw a few shadow punches, spun on his heels. Then, with a bounce in his step, he mounted the stairs, telling himself, *"I can do this!"*

Emerging onto the midway, he jogged into a Bay-View that seemed changed completely from the one he'd left just minutes before. Typically, no one ever noticed Andrew; even in the role of the Smiles Ambassador he was next-to-invisible. But now he was suddenly the focal point of the crowd, drawing smiles and waves and shouts of "Yo, Toby!" "Over here, Toby!" from the zombie horde. Without thinking about it, he just *knew* how to respond. He ran into the throng, high-fiving, throwing air-karate combinations, pumping his fist, stopping only to put his arm around pretty girls so they could take a selfie. When a tune with a particularly catchy beat blared over the overhead speakers, he started to dance a goofy dance. He pulled girls from the circle of zombies that gathered around him, held their hands and got them to join him for a few silly steps. Andrew had never even tried to dance before—but in the Toby costume he was amazingly light on his feet. Time flew by, the bright afternoon gradually becoming a soft evening on the midway. Zombies continued to stream into the park, and Toby was their manic cheerleader. Andrew could barely contain his happiness.

****

Just after 7:30, the sun was slowly descending toward the waters of the bay, tinting a few thin clouds pink and red, and the lights above the Bay-View were coming on. Jana and Teddy leaned on a railing outside the administrative offices on the upper deck, marveling at the crowded midway below. Jana snuck a peak at her phone, trying to think up another Tweet. Beneath his clumpy zombie makeup, a look of sweet exhaustion had settled over Teddy's face.

"I think you can stop now," he said to Jana. "Tweeting and all that. We close in an hour and a half, and we couldn't hold any more people anyway. And we just ran out of cotton candy. We've never run out of cotton candy . . ."

Blaine staggered up to them, reeling like a happy drunk. "I just checked the counting room. We've taken in over $70,000 in cash receipts alone today, over $147,454 since Saturday. That's just the cash—and we're not done yet!" He looked at Teddy with what Jana suspected was warm affection, though she'd never seen him express tender feelings for anything that didn't have a dollar sign in front of it. "You know I had my doubts, Teddy. About this zombie thing. But you were right."

He was apologizing without actually saying he was sorry, but that was enough for Teddy. He embraced his younger brother, who, even in his semi-euphoric state, was clearly uncomfortable with the gesture. "Thanks, Blaine. The Bay-View may be getting a little long in the tooth, but I think we proved tonight that the old girl's got some life in her yet."

****

351

They'd had a busy day at the fish market too, but business had tailed off sharply by 7:00 and Nico told the staff they could close in fifteen minutes. After the last check had been settled, he took the day's take into his office. Maybe because he was anxious, he'd been eating more than usual all day. Bianca had made a pan of lasagna and another of eggplant parmesan for the staff to share; he'd eaten nearly a third of it, and now he was nibbling on a Drumstick as he organized and tallied the receipts, glancing up every few minutes at the wall clock. He kept asking himself if he was really going to go through with it, the heist. He'd been so consumed with all of the planning that up until now it kind of seemed like a game, a mental exercise. But it was all going to be real in less than a half hour. Show time. He almost wanted to throw up, but steadied himself and downed the pointy end of the Drumstick cone, where the last little bonus, the dense chocolate filling, was hidden.

At 7:30, he told Bonnie, the lead waitress, that he was leaving, asked her to close things up. Walking across the parking area to the fish market van, where he'd already hidden the stuffed animals and the rest of it under a tarp in the back cargo area, he had a direct view of the Bay-View, about four hundred yards away across the glimmering water. All of the Bay-View's lights were on now. He could see them reflected in the rippled water and he could hear the faint screams of the roller coaster riders as they plummeted down the first big drop of the Giant Anaconda. His heart was hammering, but he told himself if he ever needed a pair of balls, it was now. He drove into River Flats, pulling into a narrow alley near Gallo's, where he got out and affixed a couple of magnetic signs over the fish market logo. He had the signs made up a few days earlier to disguise the van. The signs said "Acme Cleaners." Then he got back in and, looking at his reflection in the rearview mirror, applied his zombie makeup. He thought he got the skin color of his face right, but he wasn't happy with the way his shiny pale scalp showed through his thin hair. It was going to have to do, because he didn't have time to mess with it any more. It was 7:40. Chuy would be waiting.

He drove the short distance to Gallos' and pulled into the back. Chuy came right out, not in a hurry, but carrying himself like he was ready, which made Nico feel good. Chuy's zombie makeup had been applied to make his face look like a skull. When he got in the van he told Nico that his dad's girlfriend had helped him with it. He said she kind of got into it, creating what looked like a Day of the Dead mask— *Dia de los Meurtos*, some Mexican thing.

"What'd you tell her you were doing?" Nico was worried that maybe Chuy had said something he shouldn't have.

"I told her me and you and some other guys were going to rip off the Bay-View."

"No, really. What'd you tell her?"

"Just that I was going to check out the Zombie Invasion. She'd heard about it. It's no big deal."

They headed toward the Sunset Inn to pick up Hat and Benjie. It was less than a half mile away.

Nico waited for Chuy to say something, but he just sat there, looking straight ahead through the windshield. So Nico said, "You got the Glock?"

Chuy nodded. Nico's gun, the Ruger, was in the glove box. Nico was wearing a loose, untucked shirt and he planned to stick the Ruger in his waistband, hang the shirt over it. It was uncomfortable carrying it that way, the hard metal digging into his soft fat, but how else were you going to do it?

"You feeling good about this?" he asked Chuy, looking for reassurance.

"I'm OK."

"I've been going over the plan, looking at it from different angles. It's not perfect, but I think we can pull it off. We gotta be quick, though. In and out." He glanced at Chuy, who didn't seem to be listening very closely, thinking his own thoughts. They were coming up to the Sunset Inn already. "And these guys," Nico said as they pulled up in front of the hotel, just beyond the entrance, meaning Hat and Benjie, who had been waiting in the in the reception area and now were walking out. "Keep your eye on them. Especially the little hard-ass. I think he could be playing his own game. In fact, I'm almost sure of it. Know what I mean?"

Nico was watching them approach in the side mirror. Chuy was still looking straight ahead.

"I won't let him get away with anything."

"Well, remember—shove your gun up his ass if he even looks like he's acting funny."

When they opened the sliding side door the van to get in, Nico turned to look at them. Benjie had done a good job with his makeup. He looked like he'd been dead for a few days. Hat had done the bare minimum. He didn't look dead at all, just a little sick. He was wearing his little hipster hat. Benjie had on his skater cap.

"You guys gonna wear those hats?" Nico asked.

"Why not? Zombies can't wear hats?" Hat said as he climbed in. "This van stinks. It smells like a big sardine can."

"It's the market van. We use it to deliver fish."

"It says Acme Cleaners on the sign. Like the Road Runner cartoons. Everything thing is Acme. Acme Rockets, Acme Anvils."

"I thought it would be a good idea to disguise it."

"Good thinking, mastermind," Hat said. Benjie was in now too, pulling the sliding door closed behind him. He was wearing earbuds.

"Where are we supposed to sit?"

"Anywhere. On that tarp there."

"I'm gonna puke it smells so bad in here."

"It's only a couple minutes from here."

"It's like someone threw a pile of fish guts back here a couple weeks ago and just forgot about it. I'm serious. This smell is actually going to make me puke."

That's how it went for the five minutes it took to get to the parking spot on Catalpa, a side street in River Flats. Hat slid open the door before they were even stopped and jumped out of the van, pulling in deep breaths of air through his flared nostrils. Everyone else got out and stood on the sidewalk. Nico pulled out the stuffed animals and distributed them. He gave the zip ties to Benjie who stuffed them into one of his big cargo shorts pockets, and the wire snips to Chuy. Before sticking them in his back pocket, Chuy used them to cut the white wires of Benjie's earbuds.

"Time to pay attention."

Benjie looked at him like he wanted to say something, but Chuy had his game face on, set hard as stone, and stared him down.

Nico wanted to go over the plan once again. Hat cut him off. "Save it," he said. "We know the plan. Let's just go do it."

They started walking the two blocks to the Bay-View—four men in zombie makeup carrying oversized stuffed animals. "OK, but remember what I said about the guns—we don't want anyone to get hurt." Nico was already a little breathless. "We're only carrying them so everyone in the counting room knows they better do what we say."

Hat said, "They're like props, is that what you're saying?"

"Not like props . . ."

Hat smirked. "Does yours say Acme on it?"

Chuy jumped in, giving Hat a look. "He's saying don't shoot anybody."

"Why would I want to shoot anybody?"

✳✳✳✳

What does a turtle mascot do when he has to pee? You can't just waltz into one of the park's public Men's rooms and stand spread-legged in front of a urinal. It wouldn't look right. The Bay-View's mascot handbook was specific on that point. If a mascot had to obey the call of nature, he had to use the facilities in the downstairs locker room.

356

Luckily, Andrew really hadn't felt the urge until about three hours into his shift, and he'd been holding it for the hour since then, because this had been his best night ever and he didn't want risk breaking the spell by leaving the excitement of the midway.

But now his bladder felt like it was going to burst, and even if he didn't want to take a pee break, he really had to. In fact, he *really, really* had to, he thought, as he danced and high-fived his way to the door to the basement, a little voice inside his head singing "Gotta go, gotta go, gotta go-go-go". On his way he passed Corporal Cartwright, standing in front of the counting room door. In spite of herself, because she was clearly a young woman who took her responsibility seriously, she smiled at him. Andrew couldn't resist stopping and giving her a little dance. She responded gamely with a few goofy steps of her own, getting into the spirit of it. Then Toby did something Andrew never would have done—he took her hand and gently twirled her around. She was pleased, but also embarrassed. "It's me, Andrew." He said, his voice muffled. She didn't seem to understand what he was saying, and then seemed to catch herself and disengage, like she wanted to reassume the serious demeanor that her official capacity required. Feeling a little awkward now, Andrew let her go and backed up to the door to the stairwell, heading for the locker room, hoping to make it to the toilet before his bladder burst.

****

Nico looked at his watch and then at the counting room door. He was standing around ten yards away, flanked by Chuy and Hat, aka Banana and Shark. All three men held big stuffed animals. Nico held two—his and Benjie's. Benjie had disappeared into the Men's Room a couple of minutes earlier, shortly after they had watched the counting room door open, and the tall guard with the gun had emerged, rolling the cash cart, leaving the young blond guard on her own, just the way it was supposed to happen.

In less than two minutes, Benjie was supposed to set off the M-80 and it would all start. But now something Nico couldn't have planned for happened. The Bay-View's stupid Turtle mascot came waltzing up into the alcove. He stopped in front of the blond guard, dancing and showing off. He even took her hand and spun her around a few times, shuffling a little dorky dance.

"Christ!" Nico said to Chuy, who was staring ahead impassively. He didn't want to look at Hat. "This screwball is gonna mess everything up. Leave, you freakin' idiot," he muttered under his breath. And, almost miraculously, he did, disappearing down a door at the back of the alcove.

"That's all we would have needed," Nico said. "A freakin' dancing turtle."

He took a deep breath. Go-time came and went.

They waited. Nico's heart was pounding. He stared at his watch. Thirty seconds passed, then thirty more. No explosion.

"What do you think he's doing?" Nico asked Hat.

"Fuck if I know."

358

"He was supposed to blow off that firecracker over a minute ago. We synchronized watches."

"Maybe you shoulda asked him if he knew how to tell time."

Some joke. Did he really think this was funny? Nico hurried toward the restroom. The blond guard smiled at him as he waddled by with the two stuffed animals, one in each arm.

"Looks like you've been lucky tonight!" she said.

He looked at her like he hadn't heard her right and ducked into the Men's.

He didn't see Benjie right away. Then he bent over to get a floor-level angle and saw his size thirteen Nikes in the far stall.

"What are you *doing*?" he asked in an urgent whisper.

The voice that came back from inside the stall could have been a five-year-old's. "I got diarrhea. . . I'm nervous."

Nico wanted to go off on the kid, but he told himself that wouldn't help. "OK—it's OK to be a little nervous. But you gotta wrap it up. We're losing time."

"Can you get me some t.p.?" Benjie asked timidly. "I can't pull any off the roll in here."

Cursing to himself, Nico set the stuffed animals down and bustled into the next stall. Fumbling—his hands were trembling a little—he managed to pull a few sheets off that stall's roll. He slid the sheets under the door of Benjie's stall.

"That's *all*?" Benjie asked.

"Make it work. And hurry up!"

Nico rejoined the others, trying to hide the panic that was welling up inside him. Chuy had that look on his face that was difficult to read, especially with the Dia de los Muertos mask painted on it. Hat wore that little trace of a smirk that never seemed to leave his face.

"You get him back on track, boss?"

Nico could only shake his head and look at his watch. The window of opportunity was closing.

A minute or so later, Benjie walked out with a sheepish look on his face.

"Were you supposed to give me matches?" he asked Nico.

Nico looked at his watch. They were now six minutes behind schedule. A voice in his brain screamed, *"Abort Abort, Abort!"* His heart was no longer pounding. It seemed like it had stopped altogether.

"We've got to call it off," he said to Chuy and Hat. "We're running out of time. Chuy, what do you think?"

"Hell, I don't know," Chuy said. "I mean we're here and everything."

Hat didn't have to think about it. "We're not calling it off." He had a throwaway lighter in his hand which he shoved at Benjie. "Here— now get your ass in there and do it."

The explosion, when it finally went off a minute later, startled Nico. It was really *loud*, like a bomb blast. Then Benjie staggered out of the restroom and it all started unfolding just the way Nico had planned it. Benjie collapsed, falling to the ground about two feet away from the blond guard. When she went to him, kneeling next to the big dope and bending over him to check him for injuries, Hat, Chuy and Nico rushed her. Hat grabbed her blond hair and stuck his gun in her neck, ordering her to open the counting room door. The blond guard was really scared, almost frozen.

Chuy grabbed Hat's shoulder. "Not so rough," he said. "She gets it. You get it, right?"

She nodded, her eyes wide.

Chuy spoke to her calmly. "We need to open that door. I'm going to take your key card, and we're all going to get up and go open it. OK?" She nodded again. They pulled her up and pushed her to the counting room door. Chuy pulled off the key card attached to the retractable lanyard clipped to her utility belt. He pressed it against the sensor next to the door; the LED went from red to green, and they were in.

****

When the M-80 went off, Conrad Ferl was settled in nicely in the Bay-View's Security Command Center, slouched in his bonded leather home theatre recliner in front of the bank of security monitors. He'd set aside his latest whittling project—clearly destined, like all the others, to result in a toothpick—and removed his gun belt to accommodate the two smoked turkey legs and double order of deep-fried onion rings that he'd eaten for dinner an hour earlier. His gut rested happily on his lap like a thirty-pound medicine ball. He'd also pulled off his tooled cowboy boots in favor of a pair of carpet slippers that were easier on his bunions. His attention was divided between the Giants-Dodgers game on Monitor # 7 and what he called his Perv

Cam, which fed into Monitor # 3. The Perv Cam was positioned above the calm waters just beyond the climactic plunge and big splash at the end of the Fearful Flume, a ride that hurtled thrill-seekers huddled in simulated redwood logs down a steep water slide into a pond at the bottom of the drop. The latest contestant in this night's wet T-shirt contest was a buxom zombie in a tight white top seated in the front of the log, screaming as she got drenched at splashdown. He always wanted this part to last longer, the part where the log boat bobbed gently as it floated toward the disembarkation point and the drenched shirt clung to the contours of the contestant. It always broke his heart a little when the sopping lovelies disappeared from the Perv Cam's view. But he was philosophical about it—enjoy life's fleeting magical moments while you can, and wait for the next log, the next splash, the next clinging T-shirt.

So he was a little distracted when he heard the muffled blast, which to Conrad, deep in his inner sanctum, sounded like someone had banged a metal drum with a full swing of a sledge hammer. He tore his attention away from the Perv Cam and scanned the other monitors. At first, he saw nothing out of the ordinary—then, in the feed from the camera in the alcove outside the counting room door, he saw a big guy staggering out of the bathroom, collapsing, and Corporal Cartwright going to his aid. In seconds she was obscured by three more people, who looked like they had also rushed to help. No doubt about—they had a situation here. He kicked off his slippers, pulled on his cowboy boots, and, while he didn't exactly hurry out of his office— he hadn't hurried for anything except the last donut in the box in over twenty years and was out of practice—once he had successfully

362

struggled into his boots, he strode purposefully into the counting room, where the two Carlson twins were cringing under their desks. Blaine Wakefield, who had been in and out of the counting room all day, was standing next to the open safe, a profoundly uncertain look on his face. When he saw Conrad, he asked, "What was that?"

And then the outer door of the counting room flew open and four zombies burst in, pushing young Cartwright in front of them. They were waving handguns and yelling that they were sticking the place up and everyone had to get on the floor and shut up. Conrad didn't have a taste for gunplay, and cared for his own skin far more than he cared about the Wakefield's money. As he complied with the robbers' barked commands, he said a brief prayer of thanks that he had left his gun belt in his office, since if he had a weapon he might have to pull it out. A person could get shot that way.

✳✳✳✳

Once they had gained entrance to the counting room Nico and the gang saw two terrified gray-haired women in their seventies cowering under 1950's-era steel desks, arms covering their heads in the posture of a Cold War "duck and cover" drill. On top of each desk was a bill-counting machine and stacks of currency. Blaine Wakefield was also in the room, by the open safe, which Nico hadn't counted on. Then a big, shambling guy wearing a blue uniform shirt with epaulets shambled in. Nico guessed this was the head of security, coming in from his back office. He stopped in his tracks when he saw them, his face saying he wasn't going to give them any trouble. Which wasn't the case with the Blaine Wakefield. Challenging them with every bit of pipsqueak authority he could muster, he said, "You can't be in here. This area is for authorized personnel only . . ." and then he saw the guns.

In a panic he went to slam the safe shut but Hat had him in a headlock before he could fully close the heavy door.

"We're only here for the money," Nico told them, trying to sound calm. "We'll be out of here in a few minutes. These are real guns, so don't try any monkey business. Penguin, secure their hands and feet."

For the next few minutes things went just the way Nico had planned. Benjie cinched the cable ties around their captives' wrists and ankles. Hat put a length of duct tape across their mouths. Chuy quickly cut the phone cords and computer cables; then they all opened their stuffed animals, pulled out the foam stuffing, and started jamming in the tightly strapped bundles of bills that were stacked on the desks and in the safe. Soon enough, it got to be a frenzy. Nico, Hat and Chuy quickly figured out that the different colored straps denoted different denominations: blue for singles; red for fives; yellow for tens, violet straps for twenties. There were only a few stacks banded in brown, which were the fifties. Hat pawed through the stacks, spilling them out of the safe, trying to find the brown bands while Nico and Chuy more quickly stuffed their plush toys with stacks of tens and twenties. Benjie was left with the blue banded stacks of ones and the red banded stacks of fives, which he seemed happy with. Nico checked his watch. It had taken them less than three minutes to get the safe cleared out.

"All right—zip 'em up and let's go," he told the others. As he worked closed the zipper of his now over-stuffed dolphin, Nico's attention was diverted by Blaine Wakefield, writhing hog-tied on the floor like a worm on a hot skillet, veins popping on his reddened forehead, his eyes bulging behind his glasses.

"Don't have a heart attack, buddy. It's only money."

Nico's advice didn't calm Blaine. If anything, it sent him into more powerful paroxysms of despair.

"The zipper on my penguin's stuck," Benjie said.

"Just hold it closed then," Nico snapped. "We gotta get out of here." Nico, Chuy and Hat were now bunched at the door, waiting for Benjie to join them.

Then the outer door opened and the tall guard who had left earlier with the money cart stuck his head in. Nico immediately tried to slam the door shut, momentarily wedging the tall guard's head between the door and the jamb. It looked like it was about to pop like a pimple. With help from a push from Nico, the tall guard managed to extricate himself. Nico pulled the door shut. He braced the door closed with all his weight. Outside, the tall guard and who-knew-how-many others were pounding on the door.

What now? Nico tried to think, but the only output he received from his brain was this summary of the situation: *We're screwed! We are so totally screwed!* For his part, Hat had already decided on his response. So quickly Nico didn't even see it, he had pulled out a switchblade and cut the cable tie around the blond guard's ankles, hauling her up roughly, his gun stuck in her neck.

"Back off," he yelled at the door. "We got hostages in here and if you don't back off we'll start shooting them. Tell them I've got a gun," he ordered the blond guard.

"He's got a gun," she said in a barely audible voice.

"And I'll blow her head off if you don't back away from the door."

"Try the door now," he said to Nico. "Slowly."

****

Andrew hadn't taken any notice of the explosion. When the M-80 went off, he was standing in front of the toilet in one of the locker room's toilet stalls, the Toby costume puddled at his feet, concentrating on the sweet sensation of finally being able to relieve his swollen bladder. The sound of the blast had been muffled, reduced to a dull thud by the heavy steel door at the top of the stairs, the tons of poured concrete overhead and, more immediately, by the loud, seemingly endless stream of his pee jetting into the toilet bowl.

Pete the Pelican was still in the second stall. "You must have a bladder the size of a basketball, Ricky," he said admiringly. "Wait'll you get to be my age. You can't take a swallow of your own spit without having to piss ten seconds later." His words were slurred. "Are all the zombies still running around topside?" Andrew ignored him, not wanting to tip the Pelican off that tonight it wasn't Ricky Wakefield in the Toby costume. Pete the Pelican didn't seem to require a response anyway. He had moved on to a description of his prostate, about how it was the size of a Fuji apple.

After finishing up at the toilet, Andrew put his costume back in order in front of the locker room mirror. He threw a few air punches, checked his watch—exactly thirty-eight minutes and twenty-six seconds left on his shift—and trotted toward the stairwell. As he ascended the steep stairs, a feeling that had been building inside of him since he'd first donned the Toby costume suddenly became a revelation: *making other people happy made him happy. That* should be his mission! It didn't mean that the world didn't need a Shadow Warrior to right wrongs and clear the streets of human scum, but it should probably be someone else, not Andrew. It was kind of fun to fight imaginary foes in the safety of the apartment, but outside, on the streets and alleys of River Flats, it got a little scary. Making people laugh and smile—that was way cooler. And safer. Maybe what he could do, he decided as he grabbed the handle of the door to the main level to return to the midway, was talk to Ricky Wakefield, see if he'd be interested in being the Shadow Warrior, letting Andrew take his place as Toby on permanent basis. To sweeten the deal, he'd throw in his ninja mask and goggles. And maybe the *bokken*. But he'd have to think about that. The wooden practice sword was one of his prized possessions.

He opened the door onto a chaotic scene. The alcove was crowded; people were yelling, tense voices echoing in the narrow space. Something was really wrong. He saw Corporal Cartwright in the middle of the commotion, four zombies were behind her. The zombies were carrying big stuffed animals. Then he saw that one of the zombies, a guy wearing a little hat, was pushing a gun into the pretty guard's neck. Andrew caught the flash of her frightened eyes.

367

Lieutenant Martin was facing them, holding his own gun.

"Back off!" the zombie in the hat barked at Lieutenant Martin.

"Let her go!"

"Back off or I swear to God I'll put a bullet in her neck."

The Shadow Warrior had one more fight to finish. Without hesitating, Andrew targeted the zombie in the hat, the one threatening Corporal Cartwright. He threw a side kick, *yoko giri,* a move he'd practiced over and over again in the apartment, whipping his leg around with so much wild force that he lost his balance and went over backwards, but not before he'd connected with something—so hard it felt like he broke his foot. As he fell to the ground he heard a gunshot, really loud in the tight, echoing space. He rolled and saw that the bad guy in the little hat had also gone down. His hat had fallen off and his eyes had a funny look. Next to him was a big stuffed shark. Andrew grabbed the wrist of his gun hand and held on for dear life, but he didn't get any resistance. Everyone else seemed to be shouting. He heard the door to the basement slam.

Lieutenant Martin jumped on top of Andrew's zombie, who was clearly out cold.

"Nobody move!" Lieutenant Martin yelled. His eyes swept the scene, but the other zombies had disappeared. Corporal Cartwright was safe, standing off to the side, hugging herself.

"Where'd they go?" Lieutenant Martin asked her.

Since Lieutenant Mart seemed to have the unconscious zombie under control, Andrew released his grip on his wrist. He adjusted Toby's head, which had gotten a little cockeyed, so he could see better. He was relieved to see that Corporal Cartwright seemed to be OK.

"I'm not sure," she said. "Maybe one, the biggest one, ran out onto the midway. I think the other two ran downstairs. . ."

She came over to Andrew, who was slowly picking himself up. His foot really hurt. Toby's sunglasses had fallen off. He picked them up but didn't put them back on. "Ricky, are you all right?" she asked. Her caring blue eyes sought out his eyes behind the turtle mask.

"It's me. Andrew," he said.

✳✳✳✳

As he raced down the stairs, Chuy heard someone coming behind him. He didn't turn to see who it was—he just hoped he could reach the door to the street with enough of a lead to get away cleanly. A breathless voice called out, "Banana, wait up," It was Nico—*Shit!* No way was he going to wait up for that lard-ass. He took the last four stairs in a single jump and hit the ground sprinting. Behind him Nico must have lost his footing; it sounded like a wheelbarrow load of potatoes cascading down the narrow stairwell.

Chuy wasn't feeling lucky, not yet. But he was feeling a lot better about his chances than he had a few minutes earlier, after they'd emerged from the counting room. Things had gotten crazy right away. Hat was shouting, digging the barrel of his Desert Eagle hard into the neck of the blond security guard, pushing her forward, trying to back up the other   guards waiting outside. They were shouting back, the tall guard pointing his gun at them, not moving. It was a standoff; Chuy sensed that it could get ugly any second. The tall guard held his weapon with two hands, the way cops did on TV, screaming like a TV cop, *"Put your weapons down!"* Hat had a psycho look in his eyes, like he was itching to shoot someone. Chuy had decided that he had to take Hat out quickly just as the door to their right, the one to the basement, flew open. Out came the guy in the goofy turtle costume, launching himself at them, throwing a wild side kick that landed on Hat's bony ass at the same instant that Chuy was also nailing Hat with a short powerful chop to the back of his neck. A gunshot rang out. Hat and the turtle guy both went down, but Chuy didn't stay to see how it was all going to turn out. He was already moving, clutching his big yellow banana full of cash. He slapped the key card he'd taken from the blond guard against the sensor next to the basement door, yanked the door open and headed down the stairs.

Chuy followed the route he'd mapped out the day before, racing toward his goal, the exit to the Beach Street ramp. Once he got there, he quickly realized that he was screwed.

The way out wasn't blocked only by the gate he'd seen yesterday, the one he could open with the big red button. A second barrier to the outside—a corrugated metal rollup door that he hadn't noticed earlier that apparently was only lowered at night as an additional security measure—had been pulled down just outside the gate. The gate retracted when he hit the red button on the side; the metal rollup door didn't budge. Trying to stay calm, he looked for another way to open it and saw a lighted key pad, one that required a code.

Which he didn't have.

He slammed the flat of his hand against the door in frustration. Telling himself to stay cool, he took off down the hallway, looking for another way out. Somewhere behind him, he heard Nico calling, "Banana! Banana. . ."

Thinking back to his reconnaissance mission two days earlier, Chuy remembered what might be another way out, the door he'd come upon that required a key card—which had stopped him then, but maybe not today, thanks to the guard's key card that he still held in his hand.

He ran toward it, past the door with the hand-lettered "Keep Out" sign with the weird robotic giant inside, not stopping until he came to the door he was looking for. The locked fire door.

Breathless, he pressed the key card against the rectangular plastic sensor to the right of the door. A tiny red LED turned green. He pushed the door open ducked inside.

In the faint illumination provided by an Emergency Exit light above the door, he saw that he was peering down a tunnel, hewn out of what looked like raw rock. When he touched it, the rock didn't feel like rock at all—more like molded fiberglass. Running down the center of the tunnel's floor was a narrow-gauge train track. Trying to puzzle out what he'd just stumbled into, he'd taken a few steps in when suddenly all hell broke loose. Garish lights flashed from a recess in the wall to his right, revealing a giant spider in a giant web. It was obviously mechanical, but still, it startled him with the suddenness of its appearance. The spider scrambled down its web, mandibles clashing, intent upon making a meal out of an animatronic fly the size of a rat terrier that was struggling in a corner of its web. Strangest of all, the fly had a face; the face of a little worried man. The spider was almost on top of its prey, mandibles scissoring, when the lights blacked out and all Chuy could see were their after-images, weird floating blobs that gradually dissolved into the darkness.

Blinking to clear his vision, he became aware of a clattering noise, then a flashlight—no, a headlight—approaching from behind. He stepped off the tracks and onto a narrow ledge to get out of the way as a diminutive six-car train approached, carrying five to six zombies in each car. The little train tripped the sensor, setting off the lights and the scrambling spider. All the passengers cringed. Girls shrieked; guys swore loudly. As the train passed by, Chuy jumped into the last car, cramming himself in next to a young couple from Fresno who had heard about Z-Day on Facebook, and were open to any wild fun the day might bring, including the surprise addition of the new passenger with a face painted like a skull, carrying a big yellow banana.

Five minutes later, after surviving attacks by a giant centipede, three enormous ants and two huge praying mantises, Chuy disembarked along with the rest of the passengers. He melted into the crowd, heading toward the exit, a plush banana stuffed with $68,400 in cash clutched tightly in the crook of his arm.

****

Nico had quickly become disoriented in the Bay-View's basement. He felt like a rat in a maze. Why didn't Chuy answer him? He thought he could hear him running up ahead. When Nico came to the T at the end of the first corridor, he tried going to his left first, and quickly ran into a dead-end—a storage area closed off by a floor-to-ceiling cage.

So he reversed direction, calling, "Banana!" as he ran, his man boobs bouncing, clutching his stuffed dolphin and the Ruger, which he'd never loaded. He was going to get caught; he knew it. He was going to get caught and thrown in jail and the fish market was going to go belly up and little Nicky would be put in an orphanage run by evil nuns and pedophile priests. . . But he ran on, waddle-jogging down the empty corridor, because he didn't know what else to do. A vehicle exit on his left provided a glimmer of hope, but its roll-up door was rolled down, closed tight, and there was no way to open it. Off he went again, muttering, *"I'm screwed, I am so screwed. . ."* A bit further down the corridor he saw a door on his right. A sign on the door said "Keep Out", and something else about monsters, but the door was slightly open, so he peered inside. An urgent voice spoke to him from somewhere within the darkened room. "Come on in! Quick! I'll show you a way out."

Nico didn't know what else to do. Willing to grasp any lifeline, he took a couple of tentative steps into the room.

"Come on—they're going to catch you! You've got to move faster. What the hell are you waiting for?" the voice asked.

"It's dark. I can't see anything," Nico replied weakly, taking a couple more tentative steps.

The door closed behind him and he felt two powerful hands grabbing his shoulders in a grip so strong that his arms felt paralyzed. Slumping to his knees, he tried to lift his gun, but couldn't raise his arm. His other arm went dead and he lost his grasp of his cash-stuffed dolphin. It fell to the floor.

"Hey," he cried out. "What the hell!"

"It's only Frankie. He's a big strong boy, but doesn't know his own strength."

"Frankie?" Nico croaked, crumpled on the floor.

An overhead light snapped on. Nico tried to twist around to look at the person or thing that held him, but he could only turn far enough to see a pair of huge, rubber-skinned hands, one on each shoulder. Swiveling his head, Nico took in his surroundings—a workshop populated by a strange collection of mechanical animals, humans, and near-humans, some clearly works-in-progress; a work bench cluttered with mechanical and electronic parts and test gear. He couldn't make any sense of it.

"Put that gun down," the seemingly disembodied voice said. He felt increased pressure and pain in his shoulder muscles. The gun fell from his loosened grip.

A dwarfish black man—a real man, not a mechanical animatron—emerged from the lineup of robotic creations. The man's long, nappy gray hair was teased out wildly, creating a cloud around his head. He had a pitying look on his face.

Walking with a slight limp, the dwarfish man approached Nico. He picked up Nico's gun and brought it over to his work table.

"I've been watching you and your gang," he said, turning a laptop around to show Nico thumbnails of video streams from the park's surveillance cameras. "I thought you might get away with it. You had a window of opportunity, but you let it close."

"It was the kid, Benjie. I mean Penguin. He took too long in the bathroom."

"Definitely a weak link. And that sweetheart in the little hat—he could have killed someone with that cannon he was waving around. Good thing that shot he took went wild."

"No one got hurt?"

"Only your trigger-happy friend. Knocked out cold." He pointed to a feed from the camera angled above the door to the counting room, then zoomed in. On the laptop screen, Nico saw Hat, groggy and hatless, being hauled up to a sitting position and being cuffed.

"Who are you?" Nico asked.

"Just someone who can save your bacon."

"You said you could show me a way out. . ."

"It'll cost you."

Nico looked down at the dolphin.

"That's right," the little man said. "I mean to gut your fish. Small price to pay for freedom."

He wasn't asking if Nico agreed to the proposition. They both knew that Nico wasn't in a position to dicker.

"Frankie's going to let you get up, then I'm going to walk you to the back of the workshop. There's a door back there, and a way get out that no one's going to be watching. After I get Frankie to let you go, you're going to get up and do what I say. You got that?

"There's probably $25,000 in that dolphin, maybe more. We could split it."

The little man's tone grew more insistent. "You're wasting time." He angled his glance to his laptop screen. "Looks liked the police have arrived topside. They'll probably be down in here in a minute or two.

"Now like I said," the little man continued, "I'm going to have Frankie let go of you. Then, if you want to save your ass, you'll follow my instructions." Holding Big Nicky's Ruger in one hand, he worked the joystick and keys of Frankie's controller with the other. Frankie loosened his grip. Nico felt sensation flowing back into his arms.

"Now get up."

Nico rose to his feet. Waving the gun, the little man directed him to walk to the back of the workshop. Nico hesitated, looking longingly at the cash-stuffed dolphin at his feet.

"Forget about that fish. Just think of it as the one that got away. You want to get out of this mess, you'll do what I tell you. Now start walking to the back of the workshop."

Pointing the way with his gun, the little man directed him past the work area and shelving units toward the workshop's back wall, stopping him in front of a door.

"Behind that door is a tunnel. The tunnel goes all the way under Beach St. At the end of the tunnel you'll see mops and brooms and that kind of thing. And there'll be another door. When you open it, you'll be in the basement of a Chinese restaurant. The Golden Buddha, you know it?" Nico nodded. He knew the place and had a particular fondness for their pot stickers. "Just walk through like you know what you're doing. You'll end up in the kitchen prep area, and they'll probably chase you out, maybe yell at you. If someone throws a cleaver at you, duck."

The little man inclined his head toward the door, and Nico opened it. Before he entered the dank tunnel, he paused. All of that, he was thinking, for this. All of the planning and worrying and risk for nothing. Then he started walking and didn't look back.

****

When the four uniformed Santa Carmela policemen arrived, Teddy ushered them into the counting room, which was already crowded. Conrad's home theatre chair had been pushed in from his office and Corporal Cartwright was sitting in it. Jana and Andrew, who'd removed Toby's head, hovered over her solicitously. The Carlson twins had emerged from under the desks and were sitting quietly, hands folded, waiting to be told what to do. Blaine clutched a big stuffed shark, staring disconsolately at the open, nearly empty safe. Hat, now conscious and sullenly defiant, sat on the floor, his cuffed hands pulled behind his back. Lieutenant Martin was holding a gun on him. Conrad Ferl, freed of the zip ties that had bound his hands and feet, and the strip of duct tape that had covered his mouth, his gun belt now strapped on low beneath his gut, had recovered his man-in-charge demeanor. Teddy asked him to fill in the steely-eyed men in blue.

Rolling an exquisitely hand-crafted toothpick around in his mouth, Conrad provided a quick summary. "There were four of them with guns, obviously professionals. They created a diversion, stuck a gun in this young lady's face," he nodded toward Corporal Cartwright, "and pushed their way in here to rob the safe. Kinda got the jump on us. I probably could have taken a couple of them out, but I didn't want any of these ladies to get hurt by starting any gunplay, so I cooperated."

"They were armed?" one of the cops asked. He was clearly the senior member of the group. His badge read, "Sergeant Lewis."

"I thought I just said that." Conrad nodded toward Hat, who looked back at them with contempt. "This bird was waving around a Desert Eagle, that one on the desk there, looks like the .50 caliber. Took a shot at us with it."

"Anyone hurt?"

Conrad shook his head. "The turtle must have deflected his arm."

Sergeant Lewis lifted his eyebrows. "The turtle?"

"That boy there in the turtle costume. He's like a park mascot. Well, he isn't, but he's filling in for the guy who is. He threw a karate kick at our friend there and we got him on the ground." Andrew realized that Conrad was talking about him and beamed. Jana caught the smile with her phone's camera and in less than ten seconds had tweeted it and posted it on Instagram. "The other three ran off."

"They got away? Did you seal the exits?"

Conrad studied the cop like he might be a little dim. "There's no way to seal the exits to the park. Hell, it runs practically unenclosed along the beach for five hundred yards with nothing but a railing between the park and the sand. One of the gang, the one with the penguin, ran off in that direction."

"Penguin?"

"A big stuffed penguin, like you'd win at the bottle toss. What they did was, they hollowed out these big stuffed animals to carry away the cash. This guy" he nodded again at Hat, "had a shark. That one there that Blaine's holding. Looks like the other two got through the door to the basement and went down below, down the stairs into the park's underground level. They're probably still down there. We lock up the street-side exits at 6 PM and you need a code to get out."

"Anyone else down there?"

"We usually have a maintenance guy on call. And our animatronics developer could be in his workshop."

"Have you sent anyone down there after them?"

Conrad was trying to be patient, but Sergeant Lewis just didn't get it. "Well, we've been kind of busy up here. And it seemed prudent to wait for backup. Like I said, they're armed, and we're short-staffed here."

With a terse admonition not to get their asses shot, Sergeant Lewis sent three of his men down the stairs, while he attempted to extract information out of Hat, who made it clear that he wouldn't be cooperating.

The search of the lower level turned up only Fred Rickard, the maintenance man, who had to be wakened from a deep sleep; Pete the Penguin Wakefield, who was still in the toilet stall and had just gotten to the seventy-third level of Angry Birds; and A.E. Jefferson, who said he'd been busy fine-tuning the individual finger movements of the right hand of a large robotic Frankenstein monster and hadn't noticed anything unusual. While he was being questioned, he was testing the adjustments he'd just added to Frankie's grip. The cops lingered, fascinated. Working the monster's controller, A.E. Jefferson first had Frankie stretch out his right hand toward them. Then he directed the monster to slowly close his fist; finally, he transmitted the wireless command that he'd been working on and—slowly but surely—Frankie extended his middle finger.

"Any more questions, gentlemen?"

****

As he walked away from the Bay-View, Benjie couldn't believe his luck. With all the shouting and confusion and the takedown of Hat after the gunshot, no one seemed to be paying attention to him, so he simply strolled away, out onto the crowded midway, past the carrousel and the arcade entrance and right on through the Bay-View's main Beach Street portal. Not only was he getting away, but he was making off with a 36" plush penguin.

Stuffed with CASH!

Probably enough to cash to buy a new truck, like a Dodge Ram 1500, with leather interior and a killer sound system. Enough to get the truck, a diamond stud for each ear, and a ginormous tattoo to commemorate this legendary score, like maybe a grinning zombie face stretching from his shoulder blades to the small of his back.

Fuck yeah!

The further he walked away from the Bay-View—the clattering sound of the Giant Anaconda and the screams of its riders becoming fainter behind him—the better he felt. But he had to figure out how he was going to get out of town, back home to San Francisco. He thought about calling his mom, but he didn't want to have to explain anything to her, not yet. She was going to be freaked out when she heard about the robbery. She'd also be freaked out about Hat. Benjie had seen him go down and saw the turtle and the guards pile on top of him. And that gunshot—maybe Hat shot someone. Hat was screwed. He was a total dick anyway. His mom would be better off without him.

Benjie remembered seeing a Greyhound Bus station in town; maybe there would still be a bus going up to San Francisco tonight. He guessed he was headed in the right direction, but he'd wandered into a neighborhood that looked kind of sketchy, like some kind of barrio or something, with crappy little houses and storefronts with Mexican signs. Menudo. Frutas y Verduras. Frenos. The streets were shadowy, and guys were hanging out in doorways, checking him out. He started walking faster, but not too fast, not like someone in a hurry to get away from something.

He told himself not to look over his shoulder, but he got this weird feeling, and he had to turn to look. Three guys were behind him, about twenty yards back, two in hoodies, one in a flannel shirt. Were they following him? He quickened his pace. A minute later, he turned to see where they were and they had cut the distance between them to ten yards. He started running and they started running, and he couldn't outrun them. They were on him in less than a minute, taking him down like a pack of hyenas taking down a clumsy wildebeest. One of them tripped him from behind; as he fell another one hit him with something. The blow glanced off his head and landed hard on his shoulder. Then he was on the ground and they were all hitting him and kicking him. "*Qué traes, zombi?*" they were saying to him. "*Un pinguino! Qué chido!*"

Benjie was a big strong kid, but not much of a fighter. He tried to hang onto the penguin, but let go when he was kicked in the stomach, the wind knocked out of him. Then he took a blow to the head and blacked out for a few seconds.

He was only dimly aware that one his attackers was going through his pockets, coming away with his wallet and his phone. Another one took his skater cap.

They kicked him a few more times, having a good time with it, and then they were gone.

Their names were Jaime, Mono and Freddy.

Jaime was the alpha dog in the flannel shirt. Mono was his second-in-command and Freddy was the fat kid they let tag along. When they split the loot, Jaime kept Benjie's Samsung Galaxy phone and $23 of the $43 they found in his wallet. Mono kept the rest of the money and Benjie's cap; and Freddy got the stuffed penguin, which he gave to Lourdes García, a fifteen-year-old girl he was sweet on.

She accepted the gift, but didn't think much of it, because it was lumpy and dirty, and she didn't think much of Freddy anyway.

She tossed the penguin on top of her collection of stuffed animals, which she kept in a jumbled pile in a corner of her closet, and promptly forgot about it.

****

Saying good-bye to Gallo and Filomena had been tough, and the memory of it ate at Chuy as he drove south on Highway One, behind the wheel of Gallo's Impala. *His* Impala now, purchased at a more-than-fair price an hour earlier with two banded stacks of $100 bills that he shoved across the kitchen table to Filomena while Gallo sat in his Barcalounger, focused on his flat-screen TV. Chuy had been driving for half an hour. On either side of the road, hidden in the darkness, cultivated fields with rows of lettuce stretched to the hills; he could smell the rich soil of the Salinas Valley through his open window. Traffic was sparse on the highway; Chuy was tempted to push it; the growling V-8 under the Impala's broad hood seemed to be asking him to put a heavier foot on the gas, to let it show him what it could do on the open road. He was anxious to put as much distance as he could between himself and Santa Carmela, but the last thing he needed now was a speeding ticket.

A little over an hour earlier, after he'd walked away from the Bay-View—casually, not in any hurry, the big banana under his arm—he went straight to Gallo's. He'd already decided what he was going to do and he was hoping the money would make it all a little easier. Filomena had just closed the taqueria, and she was cleaning up with Clarita. He came in the back and asked her to meet him in the back apartment. Gallo was back there, watching *Cops*, of all things, rooting for the bad guys. "Run! You gotta run faster!" he yelled at the television. Chuy went into the bathroom and wiped off his face makeup. When he came out, Filomena was standing by the little kitchen table. She knew something was up. He asked her to sit down and took a seat himself, putting the plush banana on the table between them.

"You won a prize," Filomena said. She pronounced it "price". She didn't look very happy for him.

"I did," Chuy said. He pulled down the zipper that ran the length of the banana and started pulling out tightly banded stacks of bills.

"They give away prices like that?"

"Not exactly."

"Sonofabitch!" Gallo yelled. Apparently the miscreant he was rooting for had just gotten caught. "I told you to run!"

"I'm buying Gallo's car," he said, pushing the two stacks of hundreds toward Filomena. "And I'm throwing in some extra." He added two more stacks of hundreds and four stacks of fifties. "You can use it get the taqueria out of hock."

Filomena had a good head for numbers, especially when the numbers were printed on currency. "That's $60,000. You stole it?"

Chuy didn't respond, because Filomena knew the answer to her question before she asked it. She shook her head, and lifted her eyes from the table. She was still wearing her apron. It was spotted with enchilada sauce and mole. She kept her eyes on Chuy. "We don't want it."

"You need it. Get a few things fixed. Hire someone to help. You can make this place work, I know it. Remember we talked about raising the prices? If you charge half a buck more for each taco, you'll clear another $150 a day easy. That's like another $4,000 a month, pure profit."

"What about Gallo?"

"You've got to check with the VA. They must have some program, a place he can go to maybe, where they can take care of him. He was in the army. Got his ass shot at in Viet Nam. They owe him."

"I don't know how to do that."

"You've got to figure it out. This money will buy some time for you to do that."

"We need you to help. He's your father."

Chuy shook his head. "I've got to get outta here."

"When will you come back?"

He hated it when she stared at him the way she was doing now. "I don't know. . ."

His duffle was already packed. He went into the back bedroom and grabbed it. He'd already pocketed the car keys. He was going to leave his Harley in the garage. Maybe he'd come back for it sometime, maybe not. What he wanted right now was to drive away in the Impala.

"Where are you going?"

"Back to Bakersfield, I think. Anyway, I'll be in touch." He walked over to Gallo and put his hand on his father's shoulder. There wasn't much meat on it, but what muscle he had was still hard and ropy.

"Dad, I'll see you around."

"Don't let the cops catch you. They come after you, you've got to run like a sonofabitch. Not like these losers." He nodded toward the television. "Every damn one of them gets caught."

"Sure."

And then he left.

The Impala didn't have much gas when he started out, but enough to get him out of town, which was the first order of business. He was reminded now, thirty miles down the road, to check the gauge by a couple of tall gas station signs looming over the highway in the distance. Seeing that he had just over a quarter tank, he got off the freeway and pulled into a Chevron. Filling the Impala's gas tank, he was close enough to the highway to see cars pulling onto the on-ramps—the southbound ramp heading them toward Salinas, Paso Robles, L.A. or maybe Bakersfield; the northbound ramp toward Santa Carmela and, further down the road, to San Jose and San Francisco. Everyone had a destination, everyone except Chuy. He only said he was going to Bakersfield because had had to say something, but it was almost the last place in the world he wanted to go. He didn't know where he was going to go, or what he was going to do. After he filled the tank he paid for the gas, breaking out a fifty from the stack of bills he'd kept for a stake, he got back in behind the wheel. He started the car and sat for a moment, his foot on the clutch, his hand on the shifter. He heard his phone buzz. He almost didn't check it, expecting that it was Nico again. Somehow Nico must have gotten away. He'd sent Chuy at least ten texts in the past forty minutes, which he'd ignored.

But it wasn't Nico this time. It was Jana. Along with a text she'd sent a photo.

"Hey-did u hear about Andrew? He's a hero!!! Can u come by to help us celebrate? We're still up. Andrew asked."

In the glow of the instrument lights of the car's dash he looked closely at the photo and was able to make out Andrew, Jana, and the young guard from the Bay-View, all smiling. It took Chuy a moment to see that Andrew was wearing the turtle mascot costume, except for the head, which he held under one arm.

Chuy laughed out loud. *Sonofabitch!*

He stared at his phone. He wasn't thinking so much as waiting for his heart to tell him what to do.

A minute later he texted back, "Sorry. Tonite's not a good nite."

Tossing his phone on the passenger seat, he eased his foot off the clutch and pulled out of the gas station. He steered the Impala toward the on-ramp that fed traffic south, away from Santa Carmela.

****

The next morning, after yet another sleepless night—the most miserable night of his life—Nico sat at the breakfast nook off his kitchen, facing the sliding glass doors that opened on to the little patio and his back yard. He was in his pajamas, the ones with the sailboats. Traces of zombie makeup scored the creases around his bleary eyes and darkened the deep fold in the flesh between his chin and neck. Salt and pepper stubble shadowed his cheeks and his thin hair stood at all angles from his head, like he'd been hit by an electrostatic charge. A bowl of little Nicky's Cocoa Puffs was on the table in front of him, which he was distractedly spooning into his mouth. Next to it was his cell phone. Nicky was at Bianca's, where he'd spent the night. Nico had put Schnitzel outside to do her business. He was aware of her wandering around the wreckage of his once-pristine sod lawn, looking for just the right place to squat, but he wasn't really watching her. He had too much on his mind.

The heist had been a cluster-fuck. He'd been lucky to get away, even without any of the cash. The weird little black dwarf's tunnel to the Chinese restaurant was a lifesaver. Even still, he spent the night fully expecting an army of cops to show up at his house. The arrival of daylight made him slightly more hopeful; he was starting to let himself believe that Hat wouldn't rat on him, that he'd abide by *omerta*, the code of silence. On the early morning news, the spokesperson for the Santa Carmela Police Department said that they were reviewing the surveillance video of the suspects, but their zombie disguises would make it difficult to ID them. The suspect they had in custody—whose real name, it turned out, was Clarence Pasquale—was not being cooperative.

But Chuy wasn't answering his phone or responding to texts, and who knew what had happened to Benjie. If either of them got nabbed, and the DA offered them a deal, why wouldn't they squeal on Nico? If it was him, he'd start singing the second they offered to shave some time off his sentence.

And there was another problem—probably a bigger problem—Gina Quattro and the hundred grand the Maladago family was demanding. The deadline had passed, of course. Obviously, there was a good reason for missing it, but they weren't the kind of people who gave a shit about good reasons. He'd left a number of messages on Gina's phone, but hadn't gotten an answer. All the uncertainty was killing him. He couldn't just sit there, worrying. If Gina wasn't going to answer him, maybe he could work something out directly with the man, Vincent himself. It was risky, but he had to get in front of it—not wait for them to come after him or his family. And pressure was building inside of him—he had to do *something*. If he could talk man-to-man to Vincent, tell him how things had gotten to where they were, maybe he'd give him another chance to work something out. It was a long shot, but what else did he have?

Vincent kept an office at Argiento Linens. Nico had never had occasion to call there, so he didn't have the number in his phone. He got to the receptionist after getting connected through 411.

The woman who answered the phone had a nice voice, which gave Nico hope. "Argiento Linens, how can I help you?" she asked.

Nico gave his name and asked to speak to Vincent Maladago.

The nice woman at the other end of the line paused.

"I'm afraid Mr. Maladago is not available." She paused again. "Actually, Mr. Maladago passed away. Can I put you through to someone else?"

"Vincent died? Oh my God. . . when?"

"It's been almost a month now."

"A month?"

"He'd been sick for a while. He had a stroke last year and just never recovered."

"But I talked to him . . ." Nico started to say. "How about his niece, Gina, can I speak with her?"

"Gina?"

"Gina Quattro, Vincent's niece."

"Gina's not Vincent's niece. She was our bookkeeper."

"I thought she was the CFO"

"The what?" The nice lady was getting a little impatient. "Do you have a question about a bill?"

"Not exactly." He was off-balance, floundering. "Maybe. Is Gina available?"

"Ms. Quattro isn't in. Actually, she no longer works for Argiento Linens. Can someone else help you?"

What the fuck? Nico thought. Then he started to get it. He couldn't connect all the dots, but he had enough to see that he'd been scammed. Big time.

"No. Thanks."

He didn't say good-bye. He simply ended the call, put down his phone and shoveled in the last spoonful of Cocoa Puffs. Then he drank off the chocolate-flavored milk at the bottom of the bowl, the best part.

Later

If you opened the Santa Carmela Bugle the morning after the robbery, you would have been greeted by the screaming headline: "Armed Gang Robs Bay-View. One Robber Caught. Three At-Large. Mascot Hero."

The story, which took up most of the front page, was accompanied by a photo showing Andrew in the Toby costume, sans the turtle head, which he held under an arm. He was standing next to Corporal Karlie Cartwright of the Bay-View Security force. Both look a little dazed. Andrew's hair plastered on his sweaty forehead. He was, of course, smiling.

The lead article detailed the facts. Four armed robbers wearing zombie disguises overwhelmed security personnel and stormed the cash control room of the Bay-View Boardwalk amusement park shortly before closing on Monday night. Using a young security guard as a shield, they attempted to flee with what was estimated to be over $100,000 in cash. Andrew Bagley, the young employee playing the role of the Bay-View's popular sea turtle mascot, Toby, surprised the gang before they could get away, throwing a martial-arts kick at the lead gunman, subduing him and deflecting a gunshot. The captured gang member has been identified as Clarence Pasquale, 45. He has a lengthy criminal record. His three associates managed to flee with an unspecified amount of currency hidden in oversized stuffed animals.

They are still at-large. Police are continuing their investigation. The FBI is being called in.

The article went on to explain that Bagley, 20, was actually filling in for a co-worker who usually plays the role of the mischievous turtle. Describing his heroics, Bagley said that his training in the ninja arts took over when he saw the robbers. "That's why you practice for hours, because someday you could be a hero."

The article ended with a quote from Bay-View CEO, Teddy Wakefield.

"I'm confident that the police will apprehend the other gang members and bring them to justice. More importantly, speaking for the entire Bay-View family, we are all so grateful that no one was seriously injured. Young Andrew showed us all something about real bravery tonight."

The next morning Jana 333really got to work. She knew she really had something, a news story with just the right elements to go viral: a quirky crime, an unlikely hero, and a happy ending for everyone, even the Wakefields, for whom the publicity would be priceless. She posted the grainy surveillance footage of Andrew the flying sea turtle taking down the zombie gunman on YouTube, then unleashed a storm of tweets with links to the video and the *Bugle* article on the robbery. Before noon the tale of Andrew's derring-do started showing up everywhere on the Internet. Producers for several major network news programs saw it, and by some magic three different anchors mentioned Andrew's exploits at the end of that day's evening news, in that brief segment just before sign-off when they get a chance to wax warm and fuzzy as a counterweight to their grim recital of the horrors of the day.

Then the jackpot—a producer from The Today Show called to see if Andrew and Jana would fly out to New York for an interview with Matt Lauer. *Matt Lauer!* Everyone at the Bay-View was thrilled, with two exceptions: Teddy's sister Glenda, who had never been known to express a positive opinion about anything except the death penalty, and Andrew.

He refused to consider a trip to New York. He didn't want any more photos taken, any more interviews. The more Jana pressed, the more he dug in his heels, finally pitching one of his little fits. The whole experience had over-stimulated him as it was. He wanted only to shelter in the comfort of his routine—the purring of his cat, the warmth of his bath, his books, the chewy, fruity flavor of his Skittles, and the anonymity provided by the turtle costume that he wore for his new job as the fun-loving Toby.

That was enough.

About the Author

Kevin Kearney lives in Santa Cruz, California. He is the author of two previous novels, *River Rising*, a dark thriller, and *Herky Jerky*, a comic thriller. Both books can be purchased on Amazon.

56056025R10224

Made in the USA
San Bernardino, CA
10 November 2017